Heartbreaker

KAREN ROBARDS

Heartbreaker

Delacorte  Press

Published by
Delacorte Press
Bantam Doubleday Dell Publishing Group, Inc.
1540 Broadway
New York, New York 10036

Library of Congress Cataloging in Publication Data
Robards, Karen.
Heartbreaker / by Karen Robards.
p.   cm.
ISBN 0-385-31038-2
1. Man-woman relationships—Utah—Fiction.   2. Mothers
and daughters—Utah—Fiction.   3. Wilderness areas—
Utah—Fiction.   4. Outdoor life—Utah—Fiction.   I. Title.
PS3568.0196H4   1997
813′.54—dc20   96-8247
CIP

Manufactured in the United States of America
Published simultaneously in Canada

January 1997

10 9 8 7 6 5 4 3 2 1
BVG

This book is dedicated to my newest son, John Hamilton Robards, born November 16, 1995. It is also dedicated, with much love, to Doug, Peter, and Christopher.

Heartbreaker

PROLOGUE

June 19, 1996
3:00 P.M.

"ARE YOU READY to die?"

Jess Feldman exchanged glances with his brother, Owen, and tried to sidestep the wild-eyed man who suddenly blocked their path.

"I said, are you ready to die?" The man stayed with them, his voice rising an octave. One of a group of sign-carrying marchers in front of Salt Lake City's airport, he was fortyish, balding, wearing a cheap gray polyester suit, a yellowing white shirt, and an ancient-looking black tie.

"Bug off," Jess said, not gently, as Owen caught the sleeve of his plaid flannel shirt and dragged him past.

"Repent!" the man screamed after them. "The end of the world is at hand!"

"Oh, yeah?" Jess tossed back over his shoulder. Owen towed him forward implacably. "When?"

"June twenty-third, nineteen ninety-six, sinner! At nine A.M.!"

A police car with flashing lights pulled up to the curb. The doomsayer turned away.

"Talk about specific," Jess said to his brother. "I wonder what happens to these guys when they make a prediction like that and the world doesn't end on schedule?''

Owen shrugged. "Predict again, I guess. Come on, we don't want to be late for the guests. This group's from a swanky girls' school in Chicago, remember."

"That's my kind of group," Jess said with a grin.

As Owen pulled him through the double doors Jess glanced back. A pair of uniformed cops talked to the marchers. One of their signs drooped his way. Jess read it.

REPENT!
THE END OF
THE WORLD
IS
AT HAND!

Beneath the warning was a bloodred heart, broken in two, with one half toppled over on its side. Under the heart were the words LOVE HEALS.

"Bunch of nuts," Jess muttered, shaking his head. Then the big glass doors closed behind him and he forgot all about them.

1

"SOMEONE'S OUT THERE."

Sixteen-year-old Theresa Stewart dropped the edge of the faded yellow gingham curtain and backed away from the window. Her voice was hushed, fearful. Outside, the vast, mountainous wilderness that surrounded the trio of ramshackle cabins had been swallowed up by night. Hidden deep in the folds of Utah's Uinta National Forest, the abandoned mining camp had felt like a sanctuary. More than once Theresa had overheard her father reassure her mother that they were unfindable.

Now, for the first time since the Stewarts had moved into the structure eight months ago, there were strangers outside. Moonlight had silhouetted them briefly as they had stepped from the forest into the clearing surrounding the camp. Theresa had seen three of them, possibly more.

"Probably a bear." Theresa's mother, Sally, looked up from the rocking chair where she was nursing Elijah, the youngest of the seven Stewart children. Elijah was six months old, a plump, happy baby, and Sally was in the process of weaning him. But she still liked to nurse him just before putting him down for the night. He slept better that way, she said.

"Mother, it isn't a bear. I saw men coming out of the woods."

"Probably just some campers then. It's summer, you know. We don't have the forest totally to ourselves like we did during the cold weather."

Sally sat in front of the fire that was the cabin's only source of warmth as well as illumination. Despite her reassuring words there was an underlying tension in her voice. She, Theresa, and the four youngest children were alone in the cabin. Michael, her husband, had taken the two older boys and gone to Provo to conduct some business and pick up supplies. He would not be back until the following day.

"I don't think they're campers." Theresa's voice was hushed as she moved to stand beside her mother. The cabin was small, two rooms on the ground floor with a sleeping loft above. She stood almost in the center of the large front room, which suddenly seemed alive with shadows, her hands clenching into fists at her sides. Terror, raw and primitive, rose like bile in her throat.

Theresa didn't know how she knew who was out there. She just *knew.*

"Kyle then. Or maybe Alice, or Marybeth. Or one of the kids, needing to use the necessary." Marybeth and Alice were Michael's sisters. Kyle was Alice's husband. They and their eleven children, who ranged in age from eight to eighteen, occupied the other two cabins. Since the camp had been constructed and abandoned in the late 1800s, there was no indoor plumbing. Anyone needing to answer nature's call used a shack near the entrance to the old silver mine that had been converted for just that purpose. Or hied himself off to the woods.

"It looked like a man. Men. More than one. They came out of the forest." Theresa's voice cracked.

"Are you sure?"

Theresa nodded.

Sally detached the sleeping baby from her breast and stood up, pulling her blouse closed. "Theresa, honey, it can't be *them.* It can't be."

"Mother—"

A knock on the door interrupted. Theresa and her mother

drew closer together instinctively, both staring at the rough-hewn wood panel. The baby whimpered, as if sensing their fear. Sally pressed him closer to her breast.

Sally knew as well as Theresa did that none of their relatives would ever knock like that. It was a soft knock, so soft it was sinister.

"Hush, now," Sally whispered to the baby. Then, handing him to Theresa, she added, "Take him into the back room."

The instruction scared Theresa. She realized that her mother, too, felt the evil on the other side of the door. She accepted the baby, clutching him to her bosom, vaguely comforted by his milky smell, the warm weight of him, the feel of his little head brushing against the underside of her chin as he rooted in search of a comfortable position.

"Go on," Sally said, giving Theresa a push. "It's probably just some lost campers, but still . . ."

A few steps took Theresa into the tiny dark room that served as their kitchen-cum-storage-room. Turning, she forgot what she was going to say as she watched Sally pick up the double-headed ax that stood in a corner of the front room.

Clutching Elijah, Theresa backed deep into the shadows as her mother faced the door, hefting the ax.

There was a thud, a crash, the shriek of splintered wood and broken hinges as the door was kicked in.

Scrambling for cover, holding Elijah close, Theresa heard the sounds of a struggle, her mother's scream.

Then she heard a voice, a voice she recognized, a voice straight out of the nightmare she had tried and tried to forget but never could.

It was Death's voice, whispering: "It's time."

2

HER BUTT HURT.

Lynn Nelson stifled a groan and rubbed the offending body part with both hands. Not that the impromptu massage did much good. The ache did not abate.

Realizing how peculiar her actions must look, Lynn dropped her hands and cast an embarrassed glance around to see if any-one was watching. Her fellow vacationers—a group of twenty fourteen- and fifteen-year-old girls, two teachers, and two other parent chaperons like herself—all seemed to be going merrily about the business of setting up camp for the night. Nary a watcher in sight. Nor a fellow butt-rubber, either.

Did they all have buns of steel?

Apparently. No one else seemed to be walking around as if she had a corncob shoved up where the sun don't shine. No one else even limped.

"Did you find what was bothering him yet?" The speaker was a wiry, twenty-something pony wrangler whose name, Lynn thought, was Tim. Dressed in jeans and boots, with a cowboy hat shoved down over his short blond curls, Tim looked every inch at home on the range. Which, Lynn had already guessed, was the idea.

"Not yet." Lynn cast a look of loathing at the cause of her misery—a shaggy mountain pony named Hero—and retrieved the metal pick from the ground where she had stuck it moments before while she attended to more pressing needs. Grabbing the beast around the foreleg as Tim had shown her earlier, Lynn tried to pry a muddy hoof off the ground.

What must have been a thousand pounds of sweaty, stinky horse leaned companionably against her. Its rotten-grass breath whooshed past her cheek.

Pee-yew. Lynn remembered why she hated horses.

"Get off, you," she muttered, shoving the animal with her shoulder, and was rewarded by a soft nicker and even more of its weight.

Though she pulled with all her strength, the hoof didn't budge.

"Here." Grinning, Tim moved to help her, picking up the hoof with no trouble at all and handing it to her.

"Thanks." If her tone was sour, Lynn couldn't help it. She felt sour. And sore.

Bent almost double, straddling a hairy, muddy animal leg, Lynn once again stabbed her pick into the mud-packed hoof that was clamped between her knees.

Hero leaned against her. Lynn contemplated horse-icide.

"Dig in there a little deeper and I bet you'll find a rock," Tim said.

You'll learn to take care of your own horse, the brochure advertising the trip had promised.

Remembering, Lynn thought, whoopee.

Another dig, and the mess in the hoof popped free. A rock, just as predicted, packed in with a dark substance too malodorous to be mud. Yuck.

"Good job." Tim gave her an approving pat (or maybe whack was a better word) on the shoulder. Losing her balance, Lynn staggered backward, dropping both hoof and pick. The pony stomped its foot, snorted loudly, and turned its head to look at her. If the animal had been human Lynn would have sworn it snickered.

"Oh, sorry," Tim said, *his* amusement obvious as he retrieved the pick. "We'll make a horsewoman out of you yet. You'll see."

"I can't wait."

"Here, give him this and he'll love you forever."

"Lucky me." Under Tim's supervision Lynn clumsily fastened a feed bag around Hero's head. The pony twitched its ears at her and began to eat.

"Now pat him," Tim directed. Patting was not Lynn's first choice of things to do to the mangy beast, but she swallowed her less civilized impulses and complied. Hero's hairy hide felt rough as she bestowed a perfunctory pat. Turning her hand palm up, she looked down in distaste at the dirt and reddish-brown hairs left clinging to her fingers.

"Good job." With a nod Tim moved on down the line of the tied string of ponies.

Dismissed at last, Lynn pushed her fist hard against the aching small of her back and tried not to dwell on the fact that this was only the second day of a ten-day-long wilderness "vacation." And she tried not to rub her butt again either.

What had possessed her to come?

Rory, Lynn acknowledged, tottering toward one of the small campfires that was supposed to provide protection—hah!—from the no-see-ums. Her fourteen-year-old daughter had not asked her to be part of this freshman-class trip. On the contrary Rory had groaned when Lynn told her she had volunteered. But Lynn felt Rory needed her. And she needed time with her daughter, to shore up a relationship that lately felt like it was coming apart at the seams.

Anyway, the promotional literature advertising the trip had made it seem educational, fun, and the experience of a lifetime, all rolled up in one all-inclusive package deal.

So she had taken two weeks off from the daily grind of television broadcasting—her first real vacation in three years, and here she was, on the side of some godforsaken mountain in the High Wilderness area of Utah's Uinta Range, tagging along on a teenage girl's horseback-riding fantasy trip.

The question was, was she having fun yet?

The answer was an emphatic *no!*

Lynn collapsed on a bale of hay placed near the campfire for just that purpose and tried to look on the bright side of things. Indulging Rory's love of the outdoors was at least preferable to dealing with her escalating boy-craziness. This trip—her daughter's reward for sticking out a whole year at Collegiate, an exclusive girls-only academy—had cost the earth, but it was thankfully male-free.

Except for the guides. Six of them, all male. All attractive. Of course. That was the way life worked. She should have expected it.

Just as she should have expected her new riding boots to pinch, her butt to ache, her nose to be sunburned despite lashings of sunscreen and the wide-brimmed hat she had worn all day, and her skin—even where it didn't show—to feel like it needed a once-over with a Dustbuster to remove the grit.

She hated horseback riding.

Lynn shifted position, winced, and rubbed the knuckles of her clenched fists hard against her thighs. She felt like she was getting charley horses in every muscle below the waist.

"This might help." The man hunkering down beside her—yes, hunkering was the right word; men in Utah really did hunker down—held out a flattish gold can.

Doc Grandview's Horse Liniment was scrawled in black letters across the top. Yeah, right, Lynn thought. When even the salve she was offered looked like it could have belonged to Wyatt Earp, Lynn's skepticism was aroused. Everything about this trip, from the outfitters themselves to the flies that buzzed around the horses' ears, would have been right at home in the Old West. Lynn's verdict was, too touristy for words.

"Was I that obvious?" Lynn managed a smile nonetheless, accepting the can and turning it over in her hand. Owen Feldman was part owner, with his younger brother, of Adventure, Inc., the outfit that had arranged and was guiding the trip. Owen was tall, broad-shouldered, and lean-hipped, with close-cropped tobacco brown hair, a craggy, square-jawed face, and baby blues to die for. Maybe a couple of years older than her own age of thirty-five, he was allegedly a born-and-bred Utahn, who knew the Uinta wilderness like few others. According to the brochure he was honest, competent, and utterly reliable—and a real cowboy.

Two days into the trip Lynn had already figured out that she hated cowboys. Especially phony ones. Every time the Feldmans and their crew swung into the saddle, she half expected to hear a hidden orchestra strike up the theme song from *Bonanza.*

Rory, though, was eating it up. She had already pointed Owen out as a potential playmate for her mom. As for herself, Rory said, she preferred the younger brother, Jess.

The memory made Lynn frown. Where *was* Rory? And where was Jess?

"Lots of people get saddle sore the first day out," Owen said, apparently attributing her grim expression to chagrin at being such a wimp. "Just rub this on your . . . uh, the affected part, and you'll feel lots better by morning."

"Thanks, I will." Lynn slid the shoe-polish-size can into the pocket of her blazing orange windbreaker—new for the trip, the color chosen to prevent some gung-ho hunter from mistaking her for a moose—and stood up. The insides of her knees screamed in protest. The backs of her thighs throbbed. Her butt still ached. Trying not to whimper at the pain, Lynn glanced around the camp. "Have you seen Rory? Or your brother?"

Owen smiled, the tanned skin around his eyes crinkling just the way the tanned skin around a cowboy's eyes was supposed to crinkle. He stood up too, topping her five foot two by almost a foot. Central casting couldn't have chosen better, Lynn reflected dryly.

"Rory's your daughter, right? The little blonde? She and a couple of the other girls wanted to learn how to cast. Jess volunteered to demonstrate before chow."

"Oh, great." Lynn couldn't help the tartness of her tone. While Owen obviously had no problem with his brother taking a gaggle of impressionable young girls off somewhere alone, Lynn did. Jess Feldman was not cut from the same leather as his older brother. *Utterly reliable* didn't even begin to apply. "Which way did they go?"

She was trying for a humorous tone, but didn't quite make it. Owen's gaze sharpened.

"Come on. I'll show you," he said.

"I don't want to take you away from anything you need to be doing." Though there was a grain of truth in her reply, the larger reality was that Lynn was simply not comfortable accepting even small favors from anyone. She had been alone for so long, battling her way through the world so that she and Rory could have something better than the nothing with which they had started, that she had grown to like it that way. *Never depend on anyone* was her motto.

Especially fake cowboys.

"Bob and Ernst are on chow detail. Tim is seeing to the horses. There's nothing I need to be doing at the moment." Owen smiled at her. "Come on."

Lynn returned his smile reluctantly and fell into step beside him. They headed through the campsite toward the thick lodgepole forest that climbed the steep slope on the other side of the clearing. Towering pines had shed enough needles over the decades to make the ground soft underfoot. Lynn felt as if she were walking on an inches-thick carpet.

Most of the girls sat together in a semicircle, singing, on burlap sacks thrown on the ground. Pat Greer and Debbie Stapleton, the other mother-chaperons, glanced up from their self-appointed task of leading the impromptu sing-along to watch as Lynn passed by with Owen.

". . . and if another bottle should fall, there'll be eighty-seven bottles of milk on the wall. . . ."

Milk.

It was all Lynn could do not to gag. The determinedly cheerful and even more determinedly G-rated warble made her want to barf. Pat and Debbie were Tipper Gore clones: They would never permit their young charges to sing about something as age-inappropriate as bottles of beer.

Lynn *liked* beer. If there had been one available she would have chugalugged it on the spot just to annoy her fellow mothers.

Because they were annoying *her* with their cheerfulness, their nosiness, their perfect-motherness.

Lynn could feel the weight of their combined gazes stabbing her in the back as she walked past. Stylish suburban matrons comfortably married to successful men, Pat and Debbie seemed to harbor an instinctive distrust of her. As a single working mother who lived on coffee and cigarettes and had a high-profile, demanding job, Lynn supposed they considered her a different species.

And, she supposed with some reluctance, maybe they were right.

"You have any other children?" Owen asked as he stopped to hold a branch aside so that she could enter the woods ahead of him.

"Rory's it." Lynn strove to lighten her mood as well as her tone as she stepped past him onto a well-worn trail. It was dark and gloomy under the trees, and ten degrees cooler. Moss covered everything, from the rocks to the tree trunks to the path. The smell was damp, like somebody's basement. "My one chick."

"She looks like you. I would have known her for your daughter anywhere."

Lynn walked smack into a nearly invisible spider web suspended across the path. Shuddering, she wiped the clammy threads from her face and kept going.

"She does, doesn't she?" Lynn concentrated on responding intelligently to Owen and tried not to think about the spider that went with the web. She hated spiders. In fact, she and Rory did look alike. Both of them had blond hair—though Lynn admittedly gave nature a hand in keeping her chin-length shag bright—fair complexions, and large, innocent-looking blue eyes. Both were less than tall (she despised the word *short*), their lack of stature compensated for by slim builds. The difference was that for the last several years Lynn had had to work hard to keep her weight down, while for Rory such slenderness was still effortless. "Poor kid," she said to Owen.

"I wouldn't say that." He was behind her. Lynn couldn't see his expression, but his tone told her that he admired her looks.

Lynn made a face. She hoped he wasn't going to hit on her. Ruggedly handsome or not, he was going to be disappointed if he did. She had no interest in a vacation fling and no fantasies about bedding a faux cowboy.

"Do you have any children?" Lynn asked, for something to say. The path sloped upward, away from the rocky plateau where they would spend the night. Roots and the protruding edges of buried stones made it necessary to watch where she put her feet. Ahead, Lynn could hear the splash of tumbling water. Cracklings and rustlings and chirpings from living things that she preferred not to speculate about were nearer at hand.

"Nope." There was a smile in Owen's voice. "No wife either. My brother says I'm not a keeper. Once they get to know me, women end up throwing me back."

Lynn was surprised into glancing around. "Surely you're not as bad as all that."

Owen's eyes twinkled at her. "That's what *I* think. But Jess was pretty positive."

Lynn walked on. There was something about that rueful smile that made her wary. It was too charming, almost practiced. Part of the shtick. He might very well be lying to her. For all she knew, the rat could be married with a dozen kids.

Not that she cared whether Owen Feldman was married or not. But it was irritating to think that he might think she was dumb enough to succumb to a smile, blue eyes, and a cowboy hat. She had her faults, but stupid wasn't one of them.

A sudden bright shimmer of light ahead drew Lynn's attention. Through a frame of swaying branches, sunlight bounced off the surface of silvery water. As she walked toward the light her view broadened to take in a wide stream, a slash of sunny sky, and the brown and green wall of the forest climbing the mountain just beyond the opposite bank. A well-fed muskrat sat up on a smooth-surfaced gray rock rising from the middle of the current, whiskers quivering as it stared at something the humans could not see. As Lynn watched, it dove beneath the surface with scarcely a ripple, its sleek brown body disappearing from view.

Enchanted by the display, Lynn stepped from beneath the overhanging foliage into a scene of breath-stealing beauty. A wide creek, its water a deep green, flowed over smooth stones toward a rocky staircase some fifty yards away. There it tumbled for nearly twelve feet into a noisy, misty froth of white before continuing its quiet journey down the mountain.

Perched on boulders overlooking the waterfall were two slender, jeans-clad teenage girls. A third, blond and petite and laughing, was thigh-deep in the center of the stream just above the waterfall, legs braced apart, blue T-shirted back resting securely against the white T-shirted chest of a tawny-maned, bronzed-skinned pretty boy.

Rory and Jess Feldman. Lynn's eyes narrowed. Despite all appearances to the contrary—she was a hair taller than Lynn now, and her childish wiriness had recently been augmented by budding curves—Rory was still a child at fourteen. A boy-crazy child.

Jess Feldman, on the other hand, was no boy. He had to be at least thirty. And, unbelievably, the no-good so-and-so had his arms around her daughter.

3

FOR A MOMENT Lynn did nothing, just watched in silence as
her fingers curled into fists at her sides.

Jess Feldman's big, tanned hands covered Rory's smaller ones.
He guided her in slowly arcing overhead and then snapping a
thin bamboo fishing pole. The neon-green line looped and sang
as it spun out. With a splash the sinker struck the water about
twenty feet from the pair and promptly sank.

The girls on the rock applauded. Laughing, Rory turned in
Jess's arms to say something to him, saw her mother on the
bank, and froze. Following her arrested gaze, Jess glanced
around, discovered Lynn and his brother, and waved.

Nonchalantly. Friendly-casual. Like there was nothing in the
scene to upset the mother of the innocent child in his embrace.

"Jess is good with kids," Owen said comfortably in her ear.

Lynn registered that remark with disbelief, never taking her
eyes off the pair in the water. "Good with kids" was not how she
would have described Jess Feldman's demeanor.

"Rory—and the other girls—are not kids. They're teenagers.
Young women," Lynn said sharply, and beckoned to her daughter.

Rory scowled. Lynn steeled herself for an embarrassing scene if she insisted Rory come out of the water. She wondered, as she so often did these days, just when this hell-bent on self-destruction nymphette had replaced her sweet child.

The change had happened overnight, it seemed. When Lynn thought about it she sometimes conjured up visions from the movie *Invasion of the Body Snatchers.* Maybe an alien had taken up residence in Rory's body while the child lay sleeping.

The idea was almost comforting. At least it would absolve Lynn of any blame.

The noisy clang of metal on metal reverberated in the distance: the dinner triangle. Lynn had seen one of the men unpack it earlier.

"Chow!" Owen cupped his mouth to bellow at his brother, who grinned, gave him a thumbs-up, said something to Rory, and deftly reeled in his line. Shouldering the pole, Jess held Rory's arm above the elbow as the pair clambered from the water. Lynn moved toward them. Owen followed.

"Thanks, Jess," Rory said with an adoring glance upward when they reached the bank. The other girls—Rory's best friend, Jenny Patoski, and her second-best friend, Melody James—slid down from their perch to crowd around the two. Jenny was taller than Rory, with curly black shoulder-length hair, big chocolate eyes, and fine features. She was a pretty girl, prettier than Melody, whose light-brown hair was as long and straight as Rory's but who was unfortunately afflicted with a largish nose and smallish eyes. But even Jenny was not, Lynn thought loyally, as pretty as Rory—especially when Rory was beaming, as she was now.

"You're welcome." Jess gave Rory a heartbreaker's practiced smile, then turned his attention to the other girls as they vied for his notice. He held up a hand for silence. "I'll catch you ladies later. Right now, let's go eat."

Identical bedazzled expressions crossed three young faces as the girls watched him lay aside his fishing pole and reach for a flannel shirt draped over a nearby rock.

As he pulled it on with deliberate slowness, muscles rippling, they practically drooled.

It was all Lynn could do not to let loose with a sarcastic wolf whistle.

Not that she didn't know where the girls were coming from. On the contrary, she understood only too well. At fourteen she might have been dazzled by Jess Feldman herself. He was sexy, she had to admit, but too deliberately so, though the girls were a little young to make a fine distinction like that. He sported a shoulder-length tangle of gold-shot brown hair (she wouldn't have been surprised to learn that his blond streaks were as artificially enhanced as hers were), broad shoulders, a leanly muscled torso, and enough tanned hide to reupholster a couch. Add the appeal of narrow hips and long legs in tight, wet-to-the-thigh jeans, the same to-die-for baby blues he shared with his brother, and a crooked, roguish smile, and he was the physical embodiment of a young girl's fantasy man. It took an adult woman to discern the phoniness behind the package. Everything from his shoulder-length locks to his tight jeans seemed calculated to give females a thrill.

Lynn wondered if the brothers' last-cowboy shtick helped bring in the tourists. She guessed that it probably did.

The women tourists, anyway.

Though Jess appeared oblivious to the teenagers' rapt attention as he buttoned his shirt, there was no way he could be unaware of the havoc he was wreaking on their vulnerable libidos: Their hearts (or whatever) were in their eyes. Lynn didn't doubt that he was tantalizing them deliberately.

He probably got off on giving them a thrill. He was that kind of megalomaniac, Lynn was sure. She'd met the type before, too often. He probably considered himself a stud and proved it as often as possible. The thought made her eyes narrow.

Not with her little girl, he wouldn't!

"Where's your jacket?" she asked Rory, tight-lipped. The blue T-shirt with its snarling-bulldog emblem clung too closely to Rory's budding breasts. Some combination of the cooling air and her wet jeans had chilled Rory to the point where her nipples had hardened and were nudging at the thin knit, plainly visible.

At least, Lynn hoped the reaction was caused by the cold.

The child wasn't wearing a bra.

"I left my jacket back at the camp. It's warm. I don't need one, anyway." Lynn eyed her child. Rory returned the look with interest.

"Along with your bra?" Lynn asked the question pseudo-sweetly, in a voice too soft for the others to overhear.

"Get a *life,* Mother." Both Rory's voice and demeanor bristled with dislike. "And get off my back."

"Listen here, young lady—" Lynn heard her own voice rising and bit her lip, cutting herself off. Engaging in a shouting match with Rory would result only in her own embarrassment, she knew from experience. The debacle would end with Rory bursting into noisy tears and Lynn feeling as if someone had punched her in the stomach.

There had to be another way to deal with her daughter. But Lynn was at a loss as to what it could be.

There was another clang of metal. Rory's gaze shifted from her mother to Jess and instantly grew adoring. Lynn gritted her teeth.

"If we don't get back we're going to miss out," Owen said to his brother. Jess grinned.

"Bob'll save enough for us. We're the bosses, after all. Now, these ladies . . . sad to say, they're a different story."

They were moving toward camp now, with Owen ushering them along. The girls chorused a protest at the prospect of missing a meal, while Owen gallantly soothed the waters his brother's teasing had stirred up.

Lynn tuned the ensuing conversation out. Having fallen into step just in front of Owen, who brought up the rear of their little procession, she silently contemplated the pros and cons of giving Rory a lecture on the dangers of predatory older men as soon as she could get her alone. Worthless, was her verdict as she eyed her daughter's squared shoulders and swinging backside. Rory was already well aware of her mother's feelings. Lynn could tell that from the very way the child walked.

And she was defiantly determined to do as she pleased. Lynn could tell that too.

She sighed. When Rory was a baby Lynn had thought that

motherhood was bound to get easier as the child grew older. Little had she known!

By the time they reached camp the paean to milk bottles was, thankfully, over. Those who had remained behind were washing up and then standing in line for chow, tin plates in hand. With a cheery word to her friends, Rory scampered off to change her wet jeans.

Lynn and the other two girls walked over to wash their hands in the bucket provided for that purpose. The Feldman brothers headed off together to who-knew-where.

Good riddance, Lynn thought.

"Isn't Jess a babe?" Jenny said to Melody, who stood behind her in line. Lynn, behind Melody, barely managed not to roll her eyes.

"Bodacious," Melody agreed. Glancing around at Lynn, she added, "Don't you think so, Mrs. Nelson?"

"Oh, absolutely," Lynn said dryly, relieved to see Rory, clad now in dry jeans and a zip-up gray sweatshirt, crossing the clearing toward them. The half-dozen or so bright yellow geodesic tents were clustered together, and it seemed fair to speculate that Jess Feldman had gone inside one to change his wet jeans too. The idea of her hormone-jazzed daughter in close proximity to the object of her latest crush while both changed clothes was not conducive to motherly calm, to say the least.

"What are you guys talking about?" Rory asked her friends as she joined them.

"Jess Feldman," Melody said. "Your mother thinks he's an absolute babe."

"She does?" Rory turned wide eyes on her parent as Jenny reached the bucket and began washing her hands.

Lynn couldn't help it. This time she did roll her eyes. "Oh, a hunk."

"Well, *I* think so," Rory said, lifting her chin. Lynn could tell that Rory thought her mother was hopelessly old, hopelessly dull, and just hopeless, period. The other girls sent Rory commiserating looks.

"Don't you think he's kind of too mature for us?" Melody asked her friends as she took a turn washing her hands. That piece of good sense would have impressed Lynn had not the three girls exchanged glances, said, "Nah!" in the same breath, and burst into giggles.

"You girls better hurry if you want to eat!" called Pat Greer from the head of the chow line. The food and other necessities had been brought in by four-wheel drive—a red Jeep Grand Cherokee, to be precise. The vehicle, which had taken a different, presumably more accessible route to the campsite, had been waiting when they arrived. Now tantalizing smells of barbecue and baked beans emanated from kettles suspended over the largest of the fires.

"We're coming!"

Melody handed Lynn the soap, and she and Jenny dashed off. Lynn passed the soap to Rory, electing to wait to wash her hands until after her daughter had finished.

Left alone with her mother, Rory soaped her fingers and cast Lynn a hooded glance. Lynn returned her look without speaking.

"*Yes*, Mother?" Rory said, her voice dripping sarcasm.

Until this last year Rory had called her Mom, or Mommy, in a warmly loving tone that Lynn had never imagined would change, world without end. When it did Lynn had been caught by surprise. The way Rory said *Mother* sounded both cold and calculated to wound. Lynn hated to acknowledge that it hurt, but it did.

"You know, it would be really easy for you girls to give Jess Feldman the wrong impression," Lynn said gently. By referring to "girls" rather than just "you" Lynn hoped to defuse some of the animosity that was bound to result.

"I doubt it." Rory set the soap down and plunged her hands in the bucket to rinse them. "I already told him I want to have his baby."

"You told him *what*?" Lynn knew that revealing maternal consternation to Rory was as fatal as showing fear to a snarling dog, but she couldn't help it. It just came out.

"I told him I want to have his baby," Rory repeated with malicious enjoyment.

"Rory Elizabeth," Lynn said, all but gasping as she fought to recover from this body blow. "You didn't."

"You are so *lame,* Mother." Rory began to dry her hands. The blue eyes that were so like Lynn's own glittered with hostility. "Owen's the one you think is a babe, isn't he? You really ought to try getting it on with him while we're here. After all, you only live once, Mother, and you haven't done it in a long time."

"Rory!" Shock stole Lynn's breath. Rory grinned, clearly pleased at the result of her bombshell. Tossing away her paper towel, she snatched up a plate from the stack near the bucket and scampered off to join her friends in the chow line. Left reeling, Lynn watched as Rory, in a characteristic gesture she'd been prone to ever since she was tiny, twisted her long blond hair into a rope over one shoulder while she said something in Jenny's ear. Melody joined in, and the three girls whispered back and forth, leaving Lynn to wonder what they were talking so animatedly about.

Lynn decided she didn't want to know.

Recovering enough to plunge her hands into the bucket, Lynn found herself praying that Rory was lying to her. Surely she hadn't said any such thing to Jess Feldman. Surely she knew better.

"So just how long *has* it been?" prodded a man's voice behind her as she dried her hands on a paper towel.

Startled out of her reverie, Lynn glanced over her shoulder to find Jess Feldman, of all unwelcome people. Flannel shirtsleeves rolled up to his brawny elbows, he plunged his hands into the soapy water in the bucket. He was wearing dry jeans now and a different, predominantly blue shirt, but he still looked like Brad Pitt auditioning for the Marlboro Man.

Horrific visions of Rory telling him she wanted to have his baby unspooled across Lynn's mind.

"How long has what been?" she asked evenly, trying to keep from overreacting before she sorted the mess out in her mind.

"Since you've done it," he said, and grinned.

4

"THAT'S NOT REALLY any of your business, is it?"

If Lynn sounded hostile it was because hostile was exactly how she felt. He'd picked the wrong time to try a come-on with her. She wanted to pound him over the head with the nearest blunt object. Wadding up the paper towel, she aimed it at a nearby bucket earmarked for trash, wishing the paper towel were a rock and the bucket were his head.

The paper wad hit its target with commendable accuracy. Three years as star pitcher on her high school softball team had left a permanent mark: She nearly always hit what she aimed at.

"Hey, I just want you to know, if you're looking for volunteers I could probably be persuaded." Jess was still grinning at her as he soaped his hands. Apparently her hostility had not yet made an impression. Lynn wondered if he was too stupid to recognize dislike when it hit him in the face.

Probably. Pretty boys usually were.

"I just bet you could." She looked him up and down, her gaze cold. "Keep your pants zipped, Romeo, you're not my type." Her voice dropped, and her expression turned deadly as he rinsed his hands and reached for a paper towel. "And while we're on the subject, you're not my daughter's type either. She's only fourteen years old, in case you didn't know. Jailbait. I'd remember that if I were you."

"She's a cute little kid." Amusement lit his eyes.

Lynn felt her temper ignite. With an effort she held on to a precarious surface cool. "Keep your hands off her. I warn you."

"If you're so concerned, you could distract me." He wadded up his paper towel and tossed it toward the trash bucket. The missile fell short, and Lynn smiled nastily. *He* had never been a star pitcher, it was clear. He smiled back at her, seeming unperturbed by either her hostility or his missed shot. "Your kid's cute. You, on the other hand, are hot."

"And you're obnoxious."

"Think so?" Jess walked over to pick up the paper towel and drop it into the bucket, then turned to look at her again, hands sliding into the front pockets of his jeans. "You ought to know that Owen's just getting over a real bad marriage. He's vulnerable right now, and the last thing he needs is some sex-starved tourist using him for a vacation fling. I, on the other hand, am heart-whole, fancy-free, and available to satisfy your every desire. Obnoxious or not, if I were you I'd choose me."

"Sex-starved . . ." Lynn couldn't believe her ears. "Are you *serious*?"

"Serious as a grave. Rory says she thinks you haven't gotten laid since you broke up with her dad when she was a baby. She thinks that's why you're so crabby all the time."

"She never said that!"

"Didn't she?" He grinned tantalizingly.

"No!" Lynn was afraid Rory *had* said it and the bit about wanting to have his baby too. Lately, sex talk seemed to be a staple of Rory's conversations.

"Lynn! You better come on if you want to eat! You too, Jess!" Pat Greer called. An outdoorsy, rah-rah type, Pat, with her curly dark hair and round, apple-cheeked face, had already assumed the persona of the expedition's den mother. Clad in jeans that were a tad too tight across her ample rear and a tied-at-the-waist denim shirt, Pat looked like the kind of mother who was president of the PTA, made home-cooked meals every night, and never exchanged a cross word with her children. The kind of mother, in fact, that Rory wanted Lynn to be.

The kind of mother Lynn felt she should be, and wasn't.

"Stay away from my daughter," she said warningly to Jess Feldman. Turning her back on him, she walked toward the main campfire and supper.

Despite all the fresh air, hard physical work, and abundant food, Lynn found she didn't have much of an appetite. She nibbled at too-spicy barbecue and gummy baked beans, scratched bumps on her neck where the no-see-ums had penetrated the layers of insect repellent slathered on her skin, blinked smoke from her eyes, and in general had the kind of down-home good time promised in Adventure, Inc.'s glossy promotional literature.

Seated around a roaring campfire, you will dine on authentic Western cuisine while you commune with nature.

She couldn't claim she'd been lied to, Lynn had to admit. She was doing everything the brochure had promised—but it sure had sounded like a lot more fun when she was reading about it in the comfort of her living room.

Caveat emptor. Let the buyer beware. She knew that. What had she expected? A horsey, mobile Ritz-Carlton in the wilderness?

Lynn finally gave up on the "authentic Western cuisine" and threw her plate into a dishpan with most of the food uneaten. She looked around for her daughter. If she could just spend some quality time with Rory, the trip—despite all its attendant misery—would be worthwhile. Maybe if they talked enough they could find a bridge across the huge chasm that seemed to be widening between them.

Lynn hoped so. She wanted her little girl back.

Rory, her half-eaten plate of food on her lap, was in a huddle with a group of her friends. Lynn headed toward her.

"Feel like going for a walk after you've finished?" Lynn put a conciliatory hand on Rory's shoulder from behind. Rory glanced up at her.

"Sure," Rory said, then spoiled it with a gesture encompassing the circle of girls. "With them. We're going to explore the woods. Jess says it's perfectly safe as long as we make lots of noise, so the bears or whatever hear us coming. And as long as we don't go too far.''

"Bears?" Lynn asked, forcing a smile. *I meant go for a walk with me,* she thought *just us two, alone, and you know it.* But Rory's eyes were bright with defiance, and it was clear that she had no intention of changing her plans to accommodate her mother.

Lynn wasn't going to insist. To do so, she felt, would be counterproductive. But it hurt that Rory preferred the company of her friends to that of her mother.

"They're out there, Mrs. Nelson. They're probably watching us right now. That's why we have to be careful to put the food up at night," Melody said earnestly.

"Have a good time, then. Be careful," Lynn said, smoothing a hand over Rory's hair. It was an automatic gesture, one she had been making for years. Rory jerked her head away, casting an impatient look at her mother.

"Sorry," Lynn mouthed, knowing how much Rory hated being made to look like a baby in front of her friends. Lynn had learned the hard way that any affectionate gesture from a mother had that effect.

"Leave," Rory hissed with a brief flash of white teeth (whose straightening had cost the earth) that was apparently supposed to pass for a smile. Before Lynn could respond, Rory was already turning back to her friends.

A reprimand for rudeness sprang to Lynn's lips, but she swallowed it. Whatever was going on with Rory—whether it was the teenage thing, as Lynn's mother put it, or something more serious—staging a battle in front of her friends was not going to help.

Lynn accepted her dismissal with a wry quirk of her lips. It was ironic, in a way: in every other aspect of her life she was, by every inner and outward measure, herself a success. How could she be such a failure as a mother?

Knowing that Rory would not appreciate her hovering, Lynn moved away. She saw that Debbie Stapleton was talking to ruddy-faced, stocky Irene Holtman, one of the teachers. Lucy Johnson, the other teacher, a sixtyish woman with stylishly short silver hair, was heading for the tents with a ponytailed brunette in tow. The teenager looked on the verge of tears, and Lynn guessed she'd been stricken by homesickness. Last night, the first of their trip, two other girls had been similarly afflicted. Since the night had been spent at the barrackslike dorm on the Feldmans' ranch, the entire group had overheard the girls' misery.

Rory wouldn't have suffered from homesickness had her mother not come with her, Lynn felt sure. Lately, Rory seemed most pleased to be wherever home wasn't.

A quartet of girls assigned to KP for the night was washing dishes in a pair of rubber dishpans. Pat Greer was tidying up the campsite, picking up trash, rescuing a forgotten sweatshirt from a tree limb, helping the outfitters Bob and Ernst who'd been in charge of supper pack uneaten food into the back of the Jeep. Pat's daughter, Katie, stayed close by her mother's side, helping her—cheerfully. Of course, since Pat was the perfect mother, she would have no problems with *her* daughter.

Lynn glanced at Rory again and felt now-familiar twinges of helplessness and inadequacy. She loved her child desperately and had tried her best to be a good mother, but somehow their relationship had gone awry. She had hoped this trip would help put things right between them. But far from improving, their relationship just seemed to be going from bad to worse.

What she craved was a cigarette, a vice that Rory deplored and that Lynn was quite unable to give up. A habit of twenty-some years' duration was not easily kicked, Lynn had found. Besides, smoking helped her stay slim.

Every time she thought about the twenty pounds she would almost certainly gain if she succeeded in quitting, she lit another cigarette. In her line of work smoking was pure self-defense.

She skirted the edges of the clearing, afraid that if Pat saw her she would be drafted for some project or other and not feeling up to putting on a show of cheerful industry at the moment. Lynn found a lonely hay bale and sank down upon it. Sitting brought pain with it—but so did not sitting. It just hurt in different places.

Wriggling around to find the most comfortable position, Lynn finally ended up perched on the edge of the bale with her legs crossed at the knees. Not that that position didn't hurt. It merely hurt less than any other she tried.

Extracting her lighter and cigarettes from the pocket of her windbreaker, Lynn lit a cigarette and inhaled.

"How're the sore muscles?"

Lynn looked up to find Owen standing over her. It was full night now, and the air had cooled dramatically, even though this was the third week of June. She took another drag on her cigarette, started to stub it out, then thought better of it and defiantly inhaled again. Why should she feel guilty about smoking, especially out here in the open air? The only creatures at risk from her secondhand smoke were the no-see-ums, and she could only pray they choked.

"Sore," she said, and smiled. As if her smile were an invitation he sat down beside her. What Lynn really wanted, needed, was to be alone. But Owen seemed like a nice enough guy, even if he did have a prick for a brother. Politeness wouldn't kill her, she decided.

"You tried that liniment yet?" Owen's denim-jacketed elbows rested on his blue-jeaned knees as he glanced at her. The orange light cast by the fire ended some yards away; shifting shadows made it hard to read his expression. Somewhere in the darkness a pony whickered and stomped its feet, echoed by its fellows, one after the other. The forest rustled endlessly. The smell of smoke and barbecued ribs drifted in the air.

"Not yet. I thought I'd use it before I went to sleep." Lynn patted the too-quaint can in her pocket.

"Good idea. The stuff works better than any insect repellent to help ward off the creepy-crawlies."

"What kind of creepy-crawlies?" The idea of things scuttling around in the dark while she lay sleeping made Lynn uneasy.

"You name it, and it's probably out here." Owen grinned. "What's a camping trip without bugs and spiders and snakes and—"

Lynn held up a hand to shut him up. "I'd love to find out." She took another drag on her cigarette.

"Can I bum a cigarette off you?"

"You smoke?" Lynn glanced at him in surprise.

"Yeah." He accepted the cigarette and lighter she held out to him and lit up. "I quit for years. After—a few months ago I started up again. It helps me to relax."

"Me too." He passed her lighter back. Lynn dropped it in her pocket with her cigarettes.

"You enjoying the trip so far?"

"Oh, I'm loving every minute of it."

Owen laughed. "Why do I get the impression that the great outdoors is not your thing?"

"Maybe because it's not."

"Jess said you're on TV. He said you've got some kind of real glamorous job."

Lynn's eyes narrowed as she slowly exhaled smoke. "I don't know how Jess would know—oh, Rory, I guess—but I'm an anchorwoman for WMAQ in Chicago. Believe me, it's not particularly glamorous."

"You been doing it long?"

"Four years."

"Oh, yeah? How'd you get a job like that?"

"I majored in communications at Indiana University. While I was still in school I started working as a gopher for a station in Indianapolis. When I graduated I got a job as a reporter for a station in Evansville. From there I went to Peoria as a weekend anchor, and from there I went to Chicago to work for WMAQ. Voilà." It was an oft-asked question. Lynn's bare-bones response had been whittled down over years of answering.

"Impressive."

"Yeah." Lynn took another drag on her cigarette. To outsiders, being an anchorwoman sounded like a dream job. Only someone in the business knew how stressful and uncertain a career it was. Gain ten pounds, develop a few crow's-feet, and it was over.

Then what?

That was the fear that nibbled constantly at the edges of her mind. She was thirty-five—and she feared it was starting to show. How much longer did she have?

"Owen, Tim needs to see you. Something about tomorrow's

schedule." The voice behind them that materialized out of the darkness belonged to Jess. Lynn tensed.

"Can't you handle it?" Owen swiveled around to look at his brother.

"Nope."

Concentrating on her cigarette, Lynn didn't look at either man. But she was conscious of something—a small shimmer of wordless communication—in the air between them. It dissolved as Owen turned back around with a disgusted grunt.

"I guess I'd better go, then," he said to Lynn as he stubbed his cigarette out on the heel of his boot and stuck the butt in his jacket pocket. "Don't forget to use that liniment."

"I won't. Thanks." Lynn smiled at him. He smiled back at her, stood up, and strode off into the night.

"What liniment?" Jess walked around the bale and sat down in Owen's place. Pushing his cowboy hat to the back of his head, he leaned his flannel-clad elbows on his knees just as Owen had, and looked sideways at her. His profile was etched in orange against the distant glow of the fire. The ridge of his nose had a bump on it, as if it might have been broken once. His lips were a shade too thin, his chin and forehead a hair too prominent. He was not *quite* as good-looking as Brad Pitt, Lynn was pleased to decide. And for her, at least, he was totally resistible.

"None of your business," Lynn said, glancing away and blowing a cloud of smoke into the cold night air. "Go away."

"You seemed ready enough to talk to my brother."

"I like him. I don't like you."

"Now why is that, I wonder? Most people like me fine."

Lynn slanted him a glance of disdain. "People? Or women?"

"Either. Both."

"In that case maybe you should start a fan club."

"Maybe I will. Wanna join?"

"In your dreams."

Jess laughed. "I guess that means you don't want me to rub that liniment on for you."

"I guess you're right."

"You'll be sorry in the morning. The second day is a whole lot worse than the first when it comes to being saddle sore."

"I'll live."

"You're wasting time, you know." The words were soft, provocative.

Lynn took a final drag on her cigarette, dropped it, and ground it out with the toe of her boot as she exhaled.

"You lost me. I don't have the slightest idea what you're talking about," she said.

"We've only got eight days left for that vacation fling." He grinned at her as she stiffened with outrage, then warded off any reply she might have made by bending to retrieve the butt she had discarded. "By the way, you don't want to leave that cigarette on the ground. It might spark up again, start a fire."

Lynn's lips tightened as she watched him stash the butt in the pocket of his denim jacket. He was right, she knew; she should have remembered how careful Owen had been.

"I'll remember that." The words were abrupt. She stood up, wincing as her sore muscles shrieked a protest. "I think I'll go check on Rory." It was all she could do not to rub her thighs, her knees, her butt. God, she ached.

"Give the kid some space, why don't you?" Jess stood too, looking down at her. Like his brother, he was tall. Lynn felt more vertically challenged than usual in her flat riding boots. At work, and nearly everywhere else as well, she always wore three-inch heels.

"I don't need your advice about my daughter. All I want you to do is stay away from her."

"You've got a dirty mind, you know that?" His voice was almost a drawl.

"Only when it's warranted."

"And you think it's warranted with me?"

"Lynn, there you are!" Pat materialized out of the darkness before Lynn could reply. She looked from one to the other of them, beaming, completely oblivious to the atmosphere. "And Jess too! That's perfect! We're dividing into groups to sing in rounds. Come on, we need you!"

"Count me out," Jess said with a shake of his head, his expression relaxing into an easy smile. "I've got the singing voice of a frog. And I've got chores to do too, if you ladies want to make it to Mount Lovenia tomorrow."

"Oh, I can't wait! I've got my camera in my saddlebag, in case we see an eagle!" Pat sounded ecstatic at the prospect.

"Believe me, we will, sooner or later. Excuse me." With a smile and a nod for Pat and an unreadable glance for Lynn, Jess took off. Lynn found herself being dragged toward the campfire by Pat.

"I have to tell you, I watch you on the news every night. You are so good at what you do! And Katie is so envious of Rory for having a mother who's on TV," Pat said, her hand curled around Lynn's arm so that there was no evading her.

"Is she?" Lynn gave up on trying to get away. Obviously, if Pat wanted her to join the group, she was going to join the group. Without resorting to outright rudeness there was no hope of escape. "Believe me, Rory is envious of Katie for having a mom who stays home all the time."

"Kids." Pat shook her head, her smile rueful. "Isn't that the way of it? With them the grass is always greener."

It was a moment of connection, mother to mother. Lynn found herself liking Pat, and she smiled back at her even as she was pushed down on a hay bale in the midst of the assembled group. It was nice to know that Katie didn't think her mother was so perfect either.

It was almost an hour later when Lynn finally managed to creep away. The strains of "This Old Man," sung in rounds, followed her as she fled.

You'll enjoy sing-alongs by the campfire. . . .

Remembering the wording in the brochure was starting to drive Lynn nuts. How could anything sound so much better in print than it was in reality?

A high-domed tent, positioned a short distance from the others, had been set up as the women's shower. Extracting her towel and the sweat suit she meant to sleep in from the rest of her gear, Lynn emerged from her tent and headed toward the shower, careful to skirt the firelight. They had moved on to telling ghost stories now, and she had no wish to be roped in.

Rory, though, looked rapt, probably because she had taken

advantage of her mother's absence to move. Whereas before she, Jenny, and Melody had perched together on a burlap sack, she now leaned against a tree at the edge of the crowd, talking to Jess Feldman as he hoisted something high into its branches.

Lynn took a deep breath, fighting the urge to march over there and drag her daughter away. It would be useless anyway. Rory in her growing truculence would in all likelihood refuse to come with her, and Lynn didn't think she could physically force her daughter, even if she wanted to. Which she didn't. Violence had never been part of their relationship. She had never even spanked the child. Maybe, Lynn reflected, that was precisely the problem. Maybe she should have.

Motherhood, Lynn decided with a sigh, was not a job for sissies.

At least she had warned Jess Feldman. Unless and until matters escalated, that would have to do.

Even as she watched, he finished his task and, with a hand on Rory's elbow, strolled with her back to the group. They sat down side by side on a burlap sack.

Lynn had just decided that, counterproductive or not, she was going to have to dump rain on her daughter's parade, when Jess stood up. The assembly was looking at him, clapping. With a grin and a bow he headed toward the front of the group and seated himself on a bale of hay. Once there, he waited for the clapping to die down and then started to talk.

Lynn presumed he was telling a ghost story, though she was too far away to be sure.

At least he was no longer alone with Rory.

Uprooting herself, Lynn resumed her pilgrimage to the shower tent, her thoughts grim. The question ran through her mind again, unbidden: Was she having fun yet?

Not!

Fortunately she and Rory slept in the same tent, so she'd be able to monitor her daughter's whereabouts at night. Each woman had been placed with four girls. Lynn's group included Rory, Jenny, Melody, and Lisa Hind, a newcomer to the school.

Of course the other three girls, fast friends, excluded Lisa. Lynn had already had a chat with them about that.

Not that talking seemed to do much good. To any of them. About anything.

Lynn sighed. *This* was a vacation? Give her work any day.

Ducking inside the shower tent, Lynn was grateful for her lack of height for one of the few times in her life. She could stand upright with several inches to spare. Something brushed the top of her head. Lynn reached up to discover a lantern flashlight hooked over a tent pole, obviously put there to provide illumination. Turning it on, Lynn eyed the facilities. Primitive, but adequate. A showerhead attached to a hose dangled through a hole in the roof. Lynn presumed it was connected to a water tank set up outside.

With a quick glance around to make sure her shadow wouldn't be thrown on a nylon wall for the world to view, Lynn stripped out of her clothes and fumbled, shivering, with the valve that controlled the flow of water.

A hot shower was just what she needed to soothe her aches and pains and wash away the grit, horse smell, and insect repellent, which, combined, made for a pungent eau de trail.

The valve proved resistant. Lynn took hold of the hose to steady it, grasped the cold metal handle in her other hand, gritted her teeth, and twisted. Success! She could hear the water coming, creaking and gurgling as it rushed through the narrow channel.

Releasing the valve, she stepped back and turned up her face in anticipation.

Water gushed forth, cascading with surprising power over her face and hair and down her body.

Ice water.

Gasping, Lynn jumped back out of the stream. For a moment she stared, naked and shivering, at the pouring water as realization slowly dawned: Arctic was as warm as it was going to get. There was no hot water.

Even as you experience the wilderness you will be provided with every amenity, including showers.

The word *hot* had not been mentioned.

When she got back to civilization, Lynn vowed, whoever had written that freaking brochure was going to get sued.

5

MICHAEL STEWART WAS HOME. Her brothers Thomas and James would be with him. From her hiding place in the root cellar Theresa heard the braying of the burros they used to haul gear from the camp to where the truck was kept, out near the gravel road some five miles away. For the first time since the nightmare had begun, she felt a glimmer of hope.

Daddy would save them. He would work a miracle, as he always did.

A miracle was what it would take to defeat the demons in the cabin, Theresa knew.

But miracles were what Daddy was all about.

Elijah whimpered, squirming in his nest of old clothes that were being stored until they could be turned into rugs or quilts or something useful.

"Don't cry, baby. Please don't cry."

Theresa found him by touch and picked him up with a hand over his mouth, thrusting her little finger between his lips to pacify him as she felt around for the nurser she had jury-rigged out of a plastic water bottle and a rubber glove.

The root cellar was so dark that she could see next to nothing.

It was small and cramped, hardly more than a crawl space, gouged out of the dirt and rock under a portion of the cabin more than a century before. The storage-room floor was its ceiling. The only entry was a trapdoor behind the washtub.

So far the demons hadn't found the trapdoor. They had entered the storage room only once, for what seemed like a cursory look around, and left again.

Hearing their footsteps directly overhead, Theresa thought her heart would stop.

"Shh, sweetheart," she whispered to Elijah.

Sitting cross-legged on the dirt floor, Theresa unzipped his fuzzy blue sleeper to check his diaper—a ragged shirt she had reclaimed from the clothes pile and tucked inside his plastic pants. She nudged his mouth with the makeshift nipple, which he accepted greedily.

Crooning meaningless words in his ear, Theresa rocked him back and forth. His warm, solid little body nestled against her, and one tiny hand curled around her finger as he sucked.

The root cellar was cold and musty-smelling. The Stewarts used it to store canned goods and other staples. Earlier residents of the camp had used it to hold everything from potatoes to mining gear.

Elijah gave small grunts signifying baby contentment as he gulped down the mixture of reconstituted milk and blackberry wine Theresa had concocted for him. He had done nothing in the root cellar but eat and sleep, and for that Theresa blessed the intoxicating effects of the wine. Poor baby, she hoped it wouldn't do him any harm. But even if it did, it couldn't be as bad as what would happen to him if they were discovered.

They would die.

At first Theresa had been scared, so scared, that Elijah would cry and give their hiding place away. She remembered a story she had read once about a mother in the Old West who had been hiding with her children from marauding Indians. When the baby started to cry, the mother had suffocated him with her own hands rather than have him reveal their whereabouts and risk death for her and the other children.

One life sacrificed for many. It had undoubtedly been the right thing to do.

But Theresa knew she would never be able to sacrifice Elijah to save herself.

Knew it, that is, until she heard her little sisters being herded into the front room with her mother. The girls were crying. Sally said something, her voice pleading. There was the sound of a blow.

A few minutes later the screams began.

In that instant Theresa faced a terrible truth: To save her own life she would sacrifice Elijah.

Please, dear Lord, she prayed again as she had prayed every time she thought of her baby brother since confronting her own capacity for evil, please keep him quiet.

Please don't let either of us have to die.

6

*B*OUNCE, *THUD. Bounce, thud. Bounce, thud.*

The pony—Hero—trotted dutifully after his mates. On his back Lynn bounced into the air and smacked down against the saddle with a hideous repetition that made Chinese water torture seem kind by comparison.

Bounce, thud. Bounce, thud.

Oh, God, her butt hurt. The discomfort she had experienced yesterday was nothing compared to the pain she was feeling today.

If the two extra-strength Tylenol tablets she had taken that morning were dulling anything, she didn't even want to imagine what she would feel like without painkillers in her system.

Doc Grandview's Horse Liniment had proved useless too—except maybe as an insect repellent. If she were a bug the odor would certainly repel her. Twelve hours after she had massaged it into her aching muscles, the smell was still strong enough to make her wrinkle her nose when the wind blew a certain way.

Worse, the slimy stuff was nearly impossible to wash off. Despite all her efforts with soap, a washcloth, and cold water, the skin of her thighs and butt still felt greasy and adhered to her jeans in a most unpleasant way.

Would somebody please wake her up and tell her this was all just a hideous, horrible, very bad dream?

"Mother, you're not keeping up." Rory dropped back to ride beside her. Collegiate had offered riding lessons, for which Lynn had been paying through the nose all year. Obviously, they had taken. One glance told Lynn that Rory was experiencing none of the difficulties that plagued her mother. In fact, except for her obvious fear of being embarrassed by her parent, the child looked to be having the time of her life. Her eyes shone beneath the wide brim of the pink cowboy hat she had insisted on buying. A rosy flush colored her cheeks. Her long blond ponytail bounced rhythmically in time to her movements. She looked happy, healthy, and at home on the same kind of merciless animal that was meting out such punishment to Lynn.

"I'm trying my best," Lynn said, gritting her teeth against another jarring landing and summoning up every bit of her self-control to keep from snapping at her daughter. For Rory's sake, she would wrestle alligators. She would twist a tiger's tail. She would sleep in a roomful of rats. She could certainly be a sport about getting a little saddle sore.

A lot saddle sore, she amended with an inner groan. Would this accursed day never end?

The most horrible thing was that it couldn't be much past ten o'clock in the morning. They hadn't even stopped for lunch yet, and the schedule had promised an all-day ride. The prospect made Lynn want to weep.

Bounce, thud.

They were crossing an open meadow now in a loose kind of double-line formation, having left the forest behind for the moment. Lynn was—at least before Rory joined her—alone at the tail end of the posse of vacationers, though she had a vague awareness of a couple of the outfitters, including Jess Feldman, even farther back, bringing up the rear. The sun was bright, the air was crisp, the sky was cerulean blue with fluffy little white clouds scudding across it. Snowcapped mountains formed a breathtaking horizon, stretching away into the distance like row upon row of shark's teeth for as far as the eye could see. There were even tiny purple wildflowers blooming in the stubby green grass through which they rode. How, Lynn asked herself, could she feel so miserable in such a beautiful setting?

The answer was, she just did.

"You're supposed to *post,* Mother," Rory offered, assessing Lynn's horsemanship, or lack of it, with a critical glance.

"Post," Lynn echoed, hanging on to her smile as her backside whacked the saddle.

"You know, like this." Rory demonstrated, rising and falling in her stirrups in time with her pony's movements. "You grip with your knees. Like Mrs. Greer. And Mrs. Stapleton."

Pat and Debbie were riding together about three horses ahead. The women seemed to have no trouble at all carrying on a conversation while avoiding being jounced to death. In fact, they looked as if they were enjoying themselves.

Pat Greer was too perfect to be believed. She could even ride a horse without suffering. But her rear was a little large—okay, a lot large. Lynn squeezed what comfort she could from that.

Maybe that was what she needed, Lynn thought—more padding on her backside to make the never-ending barrage of blows endurable.

Or horseback-riding lessons. For which it was too late now.

One of the trip requirements for the girls had been riding lessons. The adults had just been asked if they knew how to ride.

Lynn remembered checking the *yes* box on the form Rory had brought home. At the time she had thought it was just a little white lie that no one would ever uncover. After all, how hard could riding a horse be?

In the case of this pony, and this saddle, very hard.

Ouch!

"Don't worry, I'm getting the hang of it," she lied to Rory with as much jauntiness as she could muster, while every tooth in her head was being jolted loose. Doing her best to grip the accursed beast's hairy sides with her knees—the pain that went shooting up the insides of her thighs when she squeezed was unbelievable—Lynn managed to rise out of the saddle and lower herself again in rough approximation of the other riders' smooth styles. She did it twice, three times.

"That's better. How can you not know how to ride? I thought *everybody* did." Rory's impatient superiority annoyed Lynn.

"Not everybody. Only people who are fortunate enough to have someone pay for their lessons," Lynn answered tartly. This home truth made Rory scowl.

"And that's why you work so hard, and that's why you're gone so much, and that's why you never have time for me, so you can pay for things like my lessons, right?" Rory's reply dripped sarcasm.

"Rory—" Lynn was already regretting her words.

"I hate you!" Rory cast her a malicious look and kicked her mount on up the line.

Left alone again, Lynn sighed. Everything she said to Rory nowadays seemed to provoke a fight.

Of course, Rory didn't really hate her. Lynn knew that.

But, oh, how that *I hate you* hurt!

This trip wasn't working, Lynn decided wearily. She had hoped it would draw them together, but if anything it was just pushing them further apart. She should have taken her station manager's advice and spent her vacation on a cruise ship in the Caribbean being pampered.

Without her daughter.

But the only reason Lynn had even taken a vacation was to spend time with Rory. With all the changes going on in the newsroom, this had not been a good time to leave.

A thirty-five-year-old woman anchor was too easily replaced. *Smack!*

She had lost the rhythm again. Remembering the knifelike pain in her thighs when she gripped with her knees, Lynn couldn't summon up the strength of will to give posting another shot.

Bounce, thud. Bounce, thud.

Oh, God.

"Heigh-ho, Silver!"

Though Lynn wouldn't have believed it possible, bad suddenly got worse. Riding up beside her—grinning—came Jess Feldman.

"Bug off!" Lynn said through clenched teeth.

"Now, now." He rode as if he were born doing it, on a mount that was taller and sleeker than her own shaggy steed. A horse, in fact, not a chubby pony. His tan cowboy hat and suede vest over a flannel shirt were picture-perfect. His blue eyes twinkled. His tawny hair blew in the wind. He could have posed for one of those God's country ads that were always being used to sell Jeeps and jeans. Like his lying brochure he was all glossy superlatives—on the surface. But on the subject of men, at least she knew enough to read between the lines.

"That's not very friendly," he said.

"I don't feel very friendly." And that was an understatement if she had ever uttered one.

"You ever ridden a horse before?"

"Frequently. Can't you tell?"

"We don't generally encourage nonriders to come on one of these trips. I think we make that pretty clear in our literature."

"So I lied on the form. So shoot me. Please."

"That bad, huh?"

"Worse." The word emerged sounding embarrassingly like a groan.

He laughed. Lynn shot him a look that should have blasted him backward out of his saddle. Instead of falling, he cupped a hand around his mouth.

"Yo, Owen!" he bellowed to his brother, who was near the middle of the column talking to Lucy Johnson. Lynn suddenly remembered that Mrs. Johnson was the teacher who had recommended this particular experience as something that would be "good for the girls." The woman had to be a couple of cards short of a deck—or maybe, Lynn speculated with pain-filled venom, Adventure, Inc. paid her some sort of kickback for all the poor fools she helped rope in.

"Owen!"

Owen glanced around. Like Jess, he wore a wide-brimmed hat, vest, jeans, and boots, and rode a horse, not a pony. He looked one hundred percent at home on the range—but of course, he was a faux cowboy too. Lynn wasn't about to forget that.

"Speed it up!" Jess yelled.

"What?"

Jess repeated himself. Lynn just managed to swallow an appalled whimper and fixed Jess with a look of burning hatred. The fiend, to deliberately torture her even more by increasing the hell-born beast's speed, when he knew she was hurting already!

Owen's horse pulled away from the others, galloping to the head of the group. Without any further warning the animals all increased their pace, flying across the meadow at what seemed like breakneck speed. Hero bolted along with the rest. Lynn gasped and grabbed the pommel. It was all she could do not to close her eyes.

Mountains and sky and earth formed a weirdly beautiful kaleidoscope around her as she clung to the saddle, convinced that she would be flung from her mount and thus meet her Maker at any moment.

But it didn't happen.

And there was no bounce. No thud.

The pace was scary, but the ride was—sort of—smooth.

"Better?" Jess yelled, keeping pace alongside her.

Lynn glanced at him, found that the earth and sky and mountains were settling down again just where they should be, and nodded grudgingly.

"It's called a canter. Gentle as rocking in your own rocking chair."

He grinned, saluted, and left her, moving along the column until he caught up with Owen. After a few seconds of conversation with his brother, Jess dropped back to ride beside Debbie Stapleton.

Of course, schmoozing with the customers was part of the job. Lynn wondered if he was offering to rub liniment on Debbie. If he did, the tall, athletic mother of three would probably deck him. Lynn smiled at the thought.

Her smile vanished as Rory and Jenny rode up behind Jess. Watching Jess fall in beside her daughter made Lynn almost forget about the pain that, whether she was bouncing or not, seemed to have become a permanent part of her anatomy.

Almost.

By the time they stopped for the noonday meal, Lynn could barely slide out of the saddle. When her feet touched the ground her knees threatened to crumple. The hot throbbing in her thighs and rump was excruciating.

All around her, her fellow riders dismounted with apparent ease, laughing and chattering about such mundane matters as the weather and what they would be having for lunch. Nobody collapsed. Nobody complained. Nobody even groaned.

It was unbelievable.

To the remarks that came her way Lynn managed to reply with smiles and nods. If everyone else could hold up under this hellish torment, then by God so could she.

She hoped. No, she prayed.

"Need some help?"

Jess Feldman came up behind her as she clung to the edges of the saddle with both hands and rested her forehead for a moment against the cool leather. Lynn saw his hand first, long-fingered and brown, when he reached past her for the strap that held the saddle on the horse—the girth, she remembered. The riders were expected to unsaddle their mounts during the two-hour lunch break, tether them, and let them graze. Most of the others had done so and gone to eat. The way she felt, Lynn wasn't sure she could lift a cup of coffee, much less a heavy saddle. But she was not going to wimp out—and she was not going to accept favors from Jess Feldman either.

"I can do it," she said ungraciously, glancing at him over her shoulder. His hand dropped, and he stepped back, waiting. Lynn was forced to make good on her words. Gritting her teeth, she straightened and went at it. It took several minutes to work the knot in the leather strap loose, but she did it. With what felt like the last of her strength she grabbed the saddle with both hands and half pulled, half lifted it from Hero's back.

It was heavy, heavier even than she remembered from that morning or the day before. But Lynn managed to hang on and lower it to the ground—just.

"Good job." Jess had his hat pushed back on his head, his arms crossed over his chest, and a lurking smile in his eyes when she turned, task complete, to face him. "Don't forget the bridle."

"Don't you have something else to do?" Lynn said to him with loathing before turning back to her steed. Hero was already munching grass, head down. The reins rested loosely halfway down his neck, with the middle third of the leather straps trailing the ground. Lynn realized that she had forgotten to secure the animal before unsaddling him.

Good thing he was more interested in filling his belly than running off.

"You need to tie him up before you turn him loose. Or he just might not be here when we're ready to leave."

I couldn't get so lucky, Lynn thought. Then she reached down—an action that required a whole range of painful movements on her part—grabbed the reins, and yanked upward.

Hero kept on eating grass, shaking her efforts off with more indifference than he would have shown a buzzing fly.

Lynn swallowed the not-very-nice word that sprang to her lips and jerked on the reins again, hard.

This time Hero's head came up—for a second. Then he lowered it to the grass again, ignoring all Lynn's subsequent tugging as he grazed.

"Tcch!" Jess walked around her with a shake of his head, picked up the tether line that was attached to a long rope stretched between two stakes to which all the horses were secured, and fastened it to the metal loop on Hero's halter. Then he pulled the bridle over the pony's head and turned to lay it across the saddle, which rested on the grass.

"I could have managed," Lynn said as he straightened.

"I didn't want you to miss lunch." The barb was accompanied by that annoying lurking smile.

"Mother, do you need help— Oh, hi, Jess." Rory came around Hero's rump and stopped short in simulated surprise, barely glancing at her mother before focusing all her attention on her target. Jenny and Melody were right behind Rory. Rory's whole demeanor made it clear that the detour had been carefully planned. The girls were chasing Jess, and pretending to offer help to Rory's mother was simply the means to an end.

Lynn decided then and there that she was going to put her foot down where her daughter and Jess Feldman were concerned, and let the chips fall where they may.

"We were wondering . . ." Jenny began as the trio advanced on Jess, leaving Lynn alone and forgotten a few paces behind.

". . . if you could give us another casting lesson. Please," Rory finished with a beguiling smile.

Jess looked at the girls, then glanced over their heads at Lynn. With a frown and a shake of her head, she nixed that idea.

He grinned and refocused on the girls.

"Sure," he promised, chucking Rory under the chin in an exaggeratedly avuncular fashion that set Lynn's teeth on edge. "We'll be making camp near Lake Fork River tonight, and that's where you'll find some of the best trout in these mountains. If we get lucky we'll be having fresh trout for supper. If we don't get lucky it's leftover barbecue and refried baked beans."

"Euuw!" the girls said in unison.

Jess's grin was wicked as he glanced at Lynn again.

7

AFTER LUNCH IT STARTED to rain. Not just a gentle shower, but a deluge. An *icy* deluge. Mounted on Hero's back again, Lynn resigned herself to utter misery. She was wet, cold, saddle sore, grumpy—and to top it off she felt as if she might be coming down with a cold. Her throat tickled, her nose had started to run, and every five minutes or so she gave vent to a mighty sneeze.

Trying to make use of a tissue under such conditions was a waste of time. By the time she extracted one from the wad in her jeans pocket and brought it to her nose, the rain had soaked it through.

Finally she gave it up and—*yuck!*—resorted to swiping at her nose with her sleeve.

Not that that was much help either.

Bounce, thud. Slog, splash. Shiver, quake.

Would the day never end? Would the vacation never end?

Vacation, hah! Lynn thought. It wasn't a vacation, it was an endurance contest!

At last they took a break, crowding beneath a stone overhang around a small fire Owen lit. Snacks carried in saddlebags were eaten, instant coffee and hot chocolate were drunk. The outfitters, impervious to the rain in what looked like army-issue ponchos and cowboy hats, saw to the horses. The girls chattered animatedly among themselves, barely paying attention as Mrs. Johnson pointed out what she said might be Anasazi drawings on the layered rock. Pat Greer passed out packets of trail mix. Debbie Stapleton and Irene Holtman stood near the edge of the overhang, talking as they peered out into the silvery curtain of rain.

Resting wearily against the stone wall, Lynn savored the cessation of movement and enjoyed being alone. She pulled out a semidry tissue and blew her nose. She rolled her head and shoulders to stretch the cramped muscles of her neck. She eased off her boots and wiggled her pinched toes in their damp socks. Changing her socks—as well as the rest of her soggy clothes— would have been smart, but her gear was being transported along with everything else by four-wheel drive to the site of the evening stop. Besides, anything she put on would just get wet again anyway.

Her waterproof poncho (suggested gear in the to-bring list) was bright yellow, very sporty, very cute, manufactured by a trendy designer. Unfortunately, it ended at her thighs, leaving her legs and feet at the mercy of the elements, which were not very merciful. The poncho's loose cuffs allowed rain to soak the wrists of her white turtleneck. Dampness had wicked through the thin cotton until it didn't feel like there was an inch of her left dry above the waist. Hero's saddle had turned into one big puddle beneath her by the time they stopped, so her butt was soaked too, clear through to her underwear. Only the top of her head, which had been protected by both the hood of her poncho and her cowboy hat, felt dry.

"Oh, look, a rainbow!"

Lynn glanced up from her disgusted contemplation of her sorry condition to find that the downpour had at last slackened to a fine drizzle. The sun peeped out from behind the thick bank of gray clouds that had dogged them all afternoon—and an enormous, sparkling rainbow arched from somewhere on the mountaintop above to the horizon.

The sight was breathtaking, and it improved Lynn's mood instantly. Translucent bands of gold, pink, lavender, and orange melted into each other, their beauty rendered more spectacular by the knowledge that it was ephemeral.

We promise you sights you'll never forget.

For once the brochure was right on target. Standing, Lynn tugged on her boots, stomped once, twice to get her heels in place, then followed the group out to get a better view.

She emerged into a cleared area strewn with boulders. The overhang the group had sheltered under was an outcropping of a stony cliff that rose about thirty feet straight up on the north side of the clearing. A rocky, sparsely treed slope curled around the cliff and out of sight; that was the terrain over which they would ride after the break. The lush blue-green of the pine forest was below them. To the west the mountain fell away. It was there, over a breathtaking panorama of snowcapped peaks that stretched like an ocean of vertical rock to the horizon, that the rainbow shimmered, beckoning.

Lynn's gaze skimmed the ooh-ing and ah-ing girls as she searched for Rory. She found her, as she would have expected, standing with Jenny at the forefront of the group.

Rory's hot-pink poncho, bought to complement the paler pink of her had-to-have cowboy hat, made her impossible to miss even amid the sea of colorful rain gear covering the other girls.

Maybe, Lynn thought, what was happening between the two of them *was* just a product of "the teen thing." Maybe she was making too much of what were basically just hormone-influenced teenage moods.

Sidling up beside Rory, Lynn glanced at her daughter's fine-featured profile. The look of wonder on Rory's face as she admired the rainbow was unmistakable. Suddenly Lynn was fiercely glad to be standing right where she was.

This *was* a sight they would never forget—and a memory they would always share. Even the fine cold mist that hung on in the aftermath of the rain did not detract from the magic. Some four thousand feet above the rest of the world, dwarfed by the vastness of the wilderness surrounding them, Lynn felt that she and

Rory and the others were being given a private viewing of the symbol of the oldest promise of all time.

"Gorgeous, isn't it?" Lynn put a hand on her daughter's shoulder. The Day-Glo vinyl felt slick and wet to her touch.

"Awesome." Rory glanced at her—and smiled. To Lynn, the beauty of that smile—the first genuine one she had had from her daughter in some time—put the rainbow to shame.

"Like totally." Jenny, on Rory's other side, glanced at Lynn and smiled too.

The group stood together on the rim of the mountain, just above a drop-off that plunged perhaps two hundred feet straight down before gentling into pine-robed slopes that ended in a valley far below. Icy-white water twisted across the center of that valley, looking slender as the output of a garden hose as it rushed through a canyon formed by jagged gray cliffs that fit together like interlocking fingers.

Directly overhead, the rainbow soared.

They could have been standing on the edge of the world.

Rory stepped forward, presumably to get a better view.

Behind them a male voice shouted something, the tone urgent. The words were unintelligible.

Lynn frowned, glancing around inquiringly.

The ground heaved beneath her feet. Distracted, Lynn looked down. Hair-thin cracks were shooting at lightning speed across the granite ledge on which she stood.

Cracks in granite?

In front of her, Rory seemed to teeter. Lynn's heart missed a beat as she realized that Rory was too close to the edge.

"Rory!"

The rock shelf her daughter stood on was shifting, buckling. In the split second after Lynn grasped what was happening, she grabbed at Rory's poncho and missed. Rory lurched out of reach.

"Mommy!"

Rory's cry was high-pitched, filled with fear. Her arms windmilled, and her boots scrabbled audibly for purchase on the rock as she seemed to topple sideways. Lynn grabbed for her again. Her fingers closed around Rory's. Her hand was damp; Rory's hand was damp. She couldn't hold on.

Lynn lost her grip just as the ground gave way. Rory screamed. Lynn cried out as her daughter slid straight down through collapsing layers of rock and mud as though she were on an amusement-park slide, arms flailing wildly as she tried to regain her balance.

In less than an instant she was gone.

It happened so fast that Lynn's foremost emotion was disbelief rather than terror. Her mouth was open, Rory's name on her lips. Her eyes were wide. Her stomach felt as though she were in an elevator, descending fast.

"Rory!" Lynn cried even as the ground fell out from under *her*. She was sliding down too, along with Jenny, who was shrieking, and God knew who else. Lynn knew that she was in trouble, but never, not ever, by any stretch of the possible did she understand that she was falling off a two-hundred-foot cliff—until her feet shot out into space and her sliding back and desperately grasping hands lost their last contact with anything solid, and her horrified eyes encountered the vast whirling grayness of endless cloudy sky and granite mountains and the rainbow shining like an epitaph overhead.

As she plunged downward, Lynn screamed.

8

BEING ALIVE HURT. That was Lynn's first conscious thought as she opened her eyes. Her body ached from head to toe. She was staring straight up into a broody sky. Fine droplets of water soaked her face, her hair, her eyes, making her blink. Remembrance came in a blinding flash. The fall. Rory.

Rory!

The rainbow was gone, vanished as thoroughly as if it had never been.

Lynn was afraid to move, afraid to put to the test how badly she might be injured. Surely she could not have fallen so far—she remembered how far away the ground had looked from the top of the cliff—without causing herself severe harm.

Maybe she *was* dead.

Maybe Rory was dead. The thought was so painful that Lynn couldn't even entertain it. If her daughter were dead . . . she would want to die too.

The recent turbulence in their relationship was suddenly meaningless. All that mattered was that Rory was her beloved child.

"Ohhh!"

The moan, if indeed it was a moan and not some cruel trick played by the wind, was enough to galvanize Lynn into movement. Her head swung around, her gaze searching.

At first she saw nothing but gray: gray sky, gray mountains, the sheer vertical rise of the gray rock cliff in front of her face. The summit, where they had been standing not long before, was snapped in two like a broken cookie. The outermost part hung straight down, parallel with and resting against the bulk of the mountain.

A pair of curious goshawks circled, surfing the wind currents, eyeing the damage.

A girl crouched on a ledge just beneath the crumpled granite shelf, about thirty feet above Lynn's head. Her torso was twisted to press tight against the mountain. Her arms were spread wide as though to embrace it.

Not Rory. Jenny. Lynn recognized the lime-green poncho, the black hair, and was glad the child was alive. But her heart and soul were focused on another girl: her daughter.

Where was she?

"Rory!" Lynn's cry was hoarse with fear.

There was no answer. Lynn tried again, screaming her daughter's name until her throat ached and her voice weakened to no more than a croak. Still no reply.

Lynn forced herself to stop, to lie still, to take deep, calming breaths. Panicking would not help Rory. Panicking would not help either of them.

As she absorbed more details of her surroundings, Lynn grew cold all over. The skin at the back of her neck prickled as the tiny hairs there jerked to petrified attention. Her own situation was impossible; Jenny's wasn't much better. She couldn't even bring herself to contemplate what might have happened to Rory.

Was her daughter sprawled lifeless in the canyon below?

Lynn refused to even consider the possibility. Instead, she focused on her own situation.

Growing awareness was accompanied by deepening horror. Lynn discovered that she had landed in the outermost branches of a stunted fir that grew out in gymnastic convolutions from the rocky face of the cliff. She was lying faceup, spread-eagled, her splayed limbs at least a foot higher than her torso. Her position was gravity-defying. Only a delicate-feeling web of slender brown branches and flat green needles stood between her and death. She was afraid—terrified—to move. Every time she breathed the branches swayed. If she dislodged herself or if her weight uprooted the small evergreen, she would plunge the remaining hundred and fifty or so feet to the hardscrabble ground below.

At the realization, her outstretched hands closed convulsively on the sturdiest limbs within reach. They were about the thickness of a gentleman's walking cane and felt terrifyingly supple as her fingers curled around them. The branches were soaking wet, icy cold, and not, Lynn feared, very strong.

From somewhere below and to her right came a low keening sound. As if someone whimpered, or cried.

Rory?

Holding tight, Lynn turned her head. Out of the corner of her eye—Lynn was afraid to move enough to get a clear view, because she had a sinking feeling that dislodging herself was a matter of shifting ounces rather than pounds—she caught just a glimpse of her daughter's hot-pink poncho. And there was movement.

Thank God!

Rory was below her, tangled like herself in a tree that grew at a near-ninety-degree angle from the vertical rock wall. There were several trees, in fact, a small, irregular copse of spindly firs, and they had saved her life and Rory's.

For now.

"Don't move, Rory!" Lynn cautioned, the words barely audible to her own ears. Then, putting as much force behind her voice as she could: "Rory, can you hear me?"

"Mommy!" Rather than an answer it was a faint, teary moan. It sounded as though, in extremis, a much younger Rory were calling for her mother.

Icy terror gripped Lynn. What if Rory was hurt? Lynn couldn't get to her; she couldn't move. No one could get to her, to them. They were no more than dust specks barely clinging to life on the side of a mountain, with a huge unknowing infinity stretching out below and above and all around.

What if Rory, only half-conscious, did not realize the precariousness of her position and flailed about? The child could fall so easily. Even if she didn't, her injuries might be such that she would die, alone, suspended in cold, wet space fifteen stories above the ground.

Despite the chill and the damp, Lynn felt herself begin to sweat.

One way or another, they both could die.

Oh, God, please, Lynn prayed. Protect my baby. Protect us both. And Jenny too.

"Rory!" Lynn tried again, sheer terror giving her voice volume. "Rory Elizabeth, do you hear me?"

The rustling of branches as the wind blew through them was the only reply.

"Rory Elizabeth, do you hear me?" The echo bounced back at her again and again. Mother-love overrode her sense of self-preservation. Lynn twisted, desperate to see her daughter better. As her weight shifted, the branches bearing it shifted too. Her stomach shot clear up into her throat as she dropped.

"For God's sake, *don't move!*"

The roar came from above, but Lynn was too busy holding on for dear life to note the source. Her butt and legs had fallen almost all the way through the fragile net. Only her death grip on the branches saved her—but the branches had bent now with her weight.

Lynn had a scary feeling that there was nothing but gray sky at her back.

One ankle was hooked over a branch approximately half as thick as the ones to which she clung. The other dangled in space.

Lynn was afraid to breathe, much less move.

"Just hang on!"

This time Lynn looked up, moving her eyes rather than her head. What she saw gave her a glimmer of hope.

Jess Feldman balanced like a tightrope walker on the ledge beside Jenny. A rope secured him to the top of the cliff. He had shed his poncho somewhere. Clad in a red flannel shirt and jeans, he was in the process of tying another rope around Jenny's waist.

Of course, there were plenty of hands topside to pull Jenny to safety. There were plenty of hands topside to pull herself and Rory up too—if Jess could get to them, and in time.

He was trying. Lynn clung to that thought.

From all indications Jenny had slid, rather than fallen, about twenty feet. The granite slab on which the group had been standing had apparently been an overhang. It had broken off even with the face of the cliff, then plowed a few feet down the mountain. Its underside was caught on a lip of granite much like the one on which Jenny had landed. Jenny was going to have to go up and over the flat slab of fallen rock to reach the safety of the summit.

The slab was about fifty feet long by twenty feet wide, and it must have weighed tons. Lynn, Rory, Jenny, and Jess were directly in its path if it should become dislodged. If it didn't crush them in passing, it would sweep them to their deaths. All except possibly Jess, who was tethered to the top of the cliff.

Lynn felt cold all over again.

Jess shouted something to someone on top. Owen, Lynn presumed, and the Adventure, Inc. crew. Moments later Lynn watched, transfixed, as Jenny came to her feet, drawn by the rope around her waist. Steadied by Jess, Jenny was pulled by inches up the vertical rock until she was just beyond the reach of Jess's outstretched arms. Jess stood alone on the ledge as Jenny, head flung back so that her black hair hung down the back of her lime-green poncho, clung to the rope for all she was worth and was hauled upward at what seemed from Lynn's perspective to be a snail's pace.

Jenny's shoulder caught on the edge of the slab as she was pulled over it. The slab protruded about ten feet from the face of the cliff, and getting past the ragged edge looked tricky. Jenny cried out in apparent pain, pushing herself out from the rock with one hand, and then was up past the trouble spot. Dangling at the end of the rope, she inched across the smooth granite face with agonizing slowness. Seen from below, her feet bicycled in what appeared to be a frantic dance to defy death. Lynn realized that Jenny was scrambling to find footholds.

The child was a third of the way to safety . . . halfway . . .

With a frightening roar and a shower of rubble, the slab slipped sideways.

Lynn cringed, ducking the debris that pelted her. A rock the size of a bowling ball bounced past her shoulder, causing her to cry out and almost lose her grip. A few inches to the left and it would have struck her. She would have been knocked from her perch; she would have been killed.

She could *still* be killed. Her gaze fixed on the slab itself. If it fell . . .

Time seemed to stop. Jenny froze in midair. Hanging motionless at the end of a rope that looked about as substantial as spider silk, she was as helpless in the face of disaster as Lynn or Rory below her.

Lynn's throat went dry. She realized that she was holding her breath.

Please, God. Please. God.

After what seemed like an eternity the slab stopped moving. It posed, precariously, its sharp nose caught on a narrow rock shelf.

It looked about as secure as a cow on a glacier.

Jenny was once again rising, swiftly now, being drawn up over the unstable shelf as if her life depended upon her unseen rescuers' speed—which perhaps it did. This time her feet did not move. She hung motionless from the rope, her hands gripping it for all she was worth, her face tilted back so that she might see where she was going rather than where she could still end up.

Where they could all end up.

In a matter of minutes hands were reaching down to grab her, and she was lifted up and out of sight.

Jenny was safe.

Now for Rory—and herself.

Lynn had been so caught up in watching Jenny's drama that she had all but forgotten about Jess. Now she realized that he was on the move, rappeling down the side of the cliff toward her and Rory. She would insist that he send Rory up first, and then she would go. The slab could shift again at any moment—but she wouldn't think about that.

"Rory!" she called urgently. "Rory, hang on, help's coming!"

There was no answer. Glancing sideways, Lynn found that she had no better view of Rory than before. She could catch the merest glimpse of the bright pink poncho tangled in branches about six feet below her and to her right. Thankfully, Rory seemed to be unmoving.

Thankfully, that is, unless she considered that perhaps Rory was not moving because she was badly hurt. Or unconscious. After all, they had fallen about fifty feet. Who knew what Rory might have hit before fetching up in the tree?

Oh, God. Please.

"Lynn! Lynn, are you hurt?"

Lynn glanced up to find that Jess Feldman was almost directly above her and only eight feet or so away. He had descended very fast, she thought, noting that he wore gloves to protect his hands from the blue-and-yellow braided rope that was his—their—lifeline. He appeared almost to be walking down the cliff, his booted feet braced against the gray-shingled rock, the rope passing around his waist and between his legs in a kind of jury-rigged climber's harness. More blue-and-yellow rope, maybe several hundred feet of it, was looped around his body from his shoulder across his chest to under the opposite armpit, much as a woman who feared being mugged might carry her shoulder bag.

Lynn was so certain of the color of the rope because a dangling loop snaked past her, just beyond her reach.

Lynn considered, and rejected, letting go of a branch to grab for the rope. Don't panic now, she told herself. Just wait.

"Damn it, woman, answer me: Are you hurt?" Jess was looking over his shoulder at her, his body twisted, his voice grim.

"N-no. I don't think so." Lynn stared up at the tight, blue-jeaned butt that Rory and the other girls so admired, at the hatless tawny hair that was blowing up toward the precipice, at the tanned, handsome face serious now with concentration, and felt despair.

He looked as if he belonged in an ad in a glossy magazine: the Marlboro Man as mountain climber.

She and Rory needed a real hero, not a phony one.

A sneeze exploded from her body out of nowhere, shaking her grip, shaking the tree, sending her plummeting another couple of inches closer to death. Lynn gasped, holding on for dear life.

"For God's sake, *stay still!*"

Jess shoved off from the side of the mountain. Riding the rope, he swooped down to land about a foot to the right of her tree.

Lynn decided that a phony hero was better than no hero at all. Much better.

"H-help," she said faintly.

"It's all right. I'll have you safe in a couple of minutes. Just don't move."

The caution was unnecessary. Lynn had no intention of moving, if she could help it. The misting had stopped at last, but the small fir was as soaked as she was and the branches she clung to were growing increasingly slippery beneath her death grip.

Her nose itched.

The thought of sneezing again filled her with terror. Grimly, she willed herself think of something else.

"Rory," she said, her voice stronger. "Get her first. Please."

"I'll get her, don't worry." He bunny-hopped across the rock toward her. The evergreen grew about fifteen feet out from the face of the cliff, and Lynn lay along its outermost branches. That put her some nine feet beyond his reach. Dangling as she was above a drop of approximately fifteen stories straight down, those nine feet might as well have been nine miles.

"I think . . . I think Rory might be hurt." The conversation was conducted at a near shout as Jess jockeyed for position at the base of the tree.

"She's alive; I saw her move." His noncommittal answer told Lynn that he, too, suspected Rory was hurt.

"I want you to rescue Rory first!"

"I don't give a damn what you want. You're higher up than she is, which means I got to you first, so you get rescued first. If you'll just shut up and do what I tell you, I'll soon have you both safe."

"Rory—"

"The longer you argue, the longer it is until I get to her."

That silenced Lynn.

"How sturdy does that tree feel to you? Do you think it'll support my weight as well as yours?"

Lynn realized what he was thinking: that he could walk out along the tree trunk to reach her.

"No!" she cried, clinging tighter as rising wind currents made the branches shake. Near though Jess was to her, if the fir uprooted now there was no way he could catch her before she plunged to the ground. For Lynn, who weighed about 110 pounds, the tree was a precarious perch. Add Jess's approximately 170 pounds to the equation, and Lynn feared the probable result.

"Okay, okay!" He seemed to reconsider. He looked down, looked up, and appeared to come to a decision. Lynn watched warily as he did something to the rope at his waist. The air was growing colder. Gusts were shooting up from the canyon floor, causing the tree to sway, sending her hair—and his—billowing skyward. Lynn realized that she was wet through, and freezing with it. The cold and the fear were making her shiver.

"Lynn." The way he said her name put her on red alert. "Lynn, listen to me. I've tied myself off so that I can't drop any lower. *I can't fall.* Do you understand that?"

"You can't fall," Lynn repeated, thinking, *bully for you.*

"I'm going to swing out and get you. When you feel me touch you I want you to let go of the tree and grab on to me for dear life."

"*What?*" Lynn's eyes widened as she absorbed the implications of that. She clung tighter to her branches.

"I'm going to swing out and get you. All you have to do is let go of the tree and grab on to me."

"That's *all*?" It was hard to pack the appropriate degree of sarcasm into a near-shout. "Have you looked down? We're about a hundred fifty feet up. What happens if you miss? What happens if the tree uproots? What happens if I can't hang on— or you can't? Maybe *you* can't fall, but *I* can."

"It's the only way."

"It can't be!"

"It is unless you can think of something better."

Lynn thought.

A gust of wind shooting up from the canyon floor made the tree bob. Lynn felt her body slipping lower as the net shifted beneath her, and she gripped the branches even harder.

Her gaze fixed on Jess.

She couldn't stay where she was forever, that was clear. She wasn't even sure she could stay put much longer. Already her fingers were starting to cramp from holding on so tight. Her legs were going to sleep. Her feet felt cold and wet and dead.

Just like she would be if he grabbed for her, missed, and she fell.

Lynn shuddered at the thought.

But what were the alternatives? *Was* there an alternative?

He couldn't climb out along the delicate fir. It might break beneath his weight; it might uproot. She couldn't climb down the tree to him; she could barely turn her head without putting herself in mortal jeopardy.

If he threw her a rope she couldn't let go to catch it, much less tie it around herself.

He couldn't leap out into space and tie the rope around her waist for her.

Lynn stared up at the lowering sky. She thought of Rory, of her mother, of her job. She thought of how much she didn't want to die.

And she came to a reluctant realization: If there was another way, she couldn't discover it.

Which left his way.

"Lynn?"

"Okay," she said.

"Okay?"

"Yes!" Her voice was panicky. If he gave her too much time to think, she was afraid she would tell him to forget it after all. She would just stay in the tree until she rotted—or fell.

"Okay. I'm going to jump out and grab you. Remember, I can't fall. Once you grab on to me, *you* can't fall. This is safer than it sounds, I promise. I'll grab you, you grab me, and you can't fall."

"Okay." If her voice was shaky it was nothing compared to

the way her skin felt. Fear, icy cold, raced up and down her spine. Her life depended on a stunt that she wouldn't wish on a professional trapeze artist.

She couldn't do it.

"Here I come!" With that warning, Jess leaped out from the sheer face of the rock.

9

LYNN SAW HIM COMING and braced herself for her leap to safety—or tried to. It was hard to brace oneself when enmeshed in a web of flimsy branches, she quickly discovered. Impossible, in fact.

"Now!" Jess shouted, crashing into the evergreen beside her and grabbing her wrist. His gloved hand was strong and warm—and the only thing that kept Lynn from plunging to the rocky ground below as she was knocked from her safety net.

She dropped like a stone. Terror shot through her body in an icy-cold rush.

Screaming, she plummeted through the fragile foliage, clawing at the air, kicking, doing everything she could to latch on to the one thing that might save her: Jess.

Her flailing arm hit his leg. Her pink-polished nails dug furrows in the surprising slickness of his jeans as she tried fruitlessly to hang on.

Her other arm was all but yanked from its socket as his grip on her wrist arrested her fall. Gulping air, stomach clenching, Lynn hung from Jess's hand and ankle like a rag doll and stared saucer-eyed at the white-capped backbone of mountains stretching away into the distance as she, Jess, and the rope arced back toward the cliff.

Below her, the pine forest was a blue-green blur. The icy-white river rushing through the gray canyon seemed to shimmy. Overhead, the clouds with their sky-riding goshawks were equally unstable.

Jess's grip on her wrist was so tight that the blood flow to her hand felt permanently cut off. Lynn tried to flex her fingers but found she could barely move them. She could only dangle in space, at the mercy of his strength—or lack of it.

Without warning she slammed backward into the rock wall. The breath was knocked out of her, and she saw a burst of multicolored stars. For a brief moment she didn't care if he dropped her or not, didn't care about anything except the pain in the back of her head, in her shoulder blades and left hip. His grip on her wrist seemed to slacken. . . .

Just like that, lightning-fast, she was falling. Her stomach shot into her throat.

And fall she did, but not far. Her arm was almost jerked out of its socket again as he grabbed her wrist once more. The fright of the near fall banished all consciousness of the pain in her head. She began to struggle, kicking and clawing at nothing as she tried to climb the air to safety.

"Hold still!" It was a roar, and it penetrated her panic. Lynn realized that she was making it difficult for Jess to keep his hold on her wrist. The mist had made her skin wet and slippery. What if he should lose his grip again?

She went as still as a rabbit with a dog nearby, deadweight as she hung from his hand.

Then his other hand joined the first around her wrist. Lynn reached up blindly as she felt herself being hauled upward. The pain in her shoulder was excruciating—but it was nothing next to her fear of falling.

His feet were braced against the rock wall so that his body formed a near forty-five-degree angle with the cliff, she realized as she touched his boot, gripped the sturdy denim of his jeans, and held on for all she was worth. Absurdly, a vivid picture of herself plummeting to earth clutching his jeans while he dangled from the rope in his shorts—briefs?—flashed through her mind.

His grip on her wrist shifted, seemed to slip. Her heart stopped. Then his gloved fingers were curling around her other wrist too.

Lynn let go of his leg as he began to pull her up the length of his body. She looked up at him, watching the effort in his face, fighting the urge to grab at him or move in any way that might undermine his attempt.

"Got ya," he said with satisfaction as he hauled her up and across his body. Panting, Lynn climbed atop him. Her feet found his left one where it was braced against the cliff, and she used it for leverage as if it were part of the mountain. With her feet beneath her she pushed herself up and hiked one leg over the rope that secured him to the clifftop. His hands released her wrists. One arm wrapped tightly around her waist. The other hand grabbed the rope, steadying them both.

Her whole body now sprawled on top of his. Her arms locked around his neck.

For a few moments she just lay against his body, trembling with exhaustion and the aftermath of fear.

He held her close as Lynn absorbed his warm, solid strength and realized that she was—relatively—safe.

"Good thing you're not fat," he grunted in her ear.

Lynn laughed. That she could surprised her. It felt good, life-affirming.

Glancing over his shoulder and down, she located her daughter. The bright pink poncho stood out like a beacon against the bleakness of the rock.

"Get Rory," she said.

"Yeah."

For a moment longer, though, they remained unmoving. Lynn realized that Jess was winded too. She also realized that she was not exactly rescued. True, she no longer hung in a tree fifteen stories above the ground. Instead, she clung to a man dangling from a rope the same fifteen stories up. If this was rescue, it was by a matter of degrees only.

"So where's the rope that hauls me up?" she asked. Her cheek lay against his shoulder. The rope coiled around his torso made hard little ridges beneath her breasts. She could feel the movement of his chest as he breathed. Considering their situation, she felt surprisingly secure—until she looked past him at the vastness of the pristine peaks rising all around them and calculated the distance to the ground.

"We're not going up. We're going down. That broken shelf is too unstable to take a chance on it shifting again."

Lynn saw the sense in that. She had witnessed what happened when Jenny was pulled over the slab.

"Can you get us down?" she asked.

"I got you out of the tree, didn't I?"

"Yes, you did."

"So trust me."

Lynn didn't answer.

"You ever done any mountain climbing?"

"No."

"Figures." He sounded resigned. "Okay. As long as we stay where we are I can hold on to you and you can hold on to me and you're not going to fall. Once we start moving down it's going to be a different story."

"It is?" Lynn felt a renewed rush of fear.

"I'm going to need my hands. I can't hang on to you and rappel at the same time. What I'm going to do is tie you to me."

"You have to get Rory."

"I'm going to get her, don't worry. First things first. We can't move unless you do what I tell you. When I say so, I want you to turn over so that your back is against my chest. I want you to put your feet on the cliff, your hands on the rope, and I want you to walk down the mountain with me."

Lynn shuddered at the thought of moving.

"Okay," she said.

"Right now I need you to let go of my neck and kind of lean to one side so I can get this rope off."

"Okay." Lynn released her stranglehold on his neck and leaned to the side—but not without first clamping on to fistfuls of the soft flannel at either side of his waist. The taut rope that was their lifeline brushed the inside of her thigh reassuringly.

"You're not gonna fall." Jess gave her a brief, crooked smile as he reached into his pocket for something—a folding knife, Lynn discovered—and then pulled the neat coils of rope over his head.

"How much weight will this rope support?" Lynn visually measured the meager thickness of the nylon braid.

"Plenty. Three hundred pounds, easy." Securing the loops over one arm, he opened the knife with his teeth. "Maybe a little more. Like I said, it's a good thing you're not fat."

"What would you have done if I was?"

A ghost of a laugh shook him. "Sent Owen."

The reply made Lynn smile.

"Okay." He finished sawing a length of rope and restored the knife to his pocket. The remaining loops were shrugged back over his head and arm. "Now I want you to turn around."

"Just . . . like . . . that . . . huh?" To her own ears, Lynn's voice sounded hollow.

"I won't let you fall, I promise." His left arm was solid around her waist.

"Oh, God."

"You can do it. Just let go of my shirt and swing your leg over the rope."

"Oh, God."

Trying not to even consider the possibility that she might fall, Lynn wriggled across him so that her right hipbone was positioned more or less on top of where his belly button should be, giving her plenty of room to roll over without losing contact with his body. She slid her left leg up and over the rope, let go of his shirt, and flipped onto her back with about as much grace as a landed fish flopping about on a riverbank.

"Jesus Christ!"

His feet lost their purchase on the cliff. He cursed as his legs slid straight down. Lynn screeched and grabbed for the rope. It seared her palms as she dropped.

His arm around her waist stopped her. For a frantic, twisting moment they dangled from the end of the rope. Somehow Jess managed to brace his feet against the cliff again and climb once more to form an angle with the mountain. Seconds later Lynn was lying atop him, facing up this time, holding on to the rope for dear life.

"Whew!" he said in her ear.

Lynn closed her eyes, said a silent prayer, and opened them again.

"You okay?"

She nodded. She was so shaken she didn't trust herself to speak.

"Good. Now shift your leg here over the rope—that's it. Carefully."

He nudged her right leg. Lynn straddled the rope. She felt his hands moving at her waist.

"You can't fall now. I've got us tied together. Ready to start down?"

Lynn nodded again.

"Just lay back against me and do what I tell you. All right?"

Lynn took a deep breath. That near fall had been terrifying—but it did no good to dwell on it. Let it go, she told herself, just let it go.

"Om," she chanted under her breath, trying for a state of Zenlike calm. Meditation was something she routinely did when under stress, and it never failed to strengthen her.

"What?"

"I'm ready."

"We're just going to walk down the mountain. All you have to do is lean against me and walk. Got it?"

Lynn nodded, trying not to *om* out loud.

"Here we go."

Jess began to move, and Lynn found herself moving with him. She abandoned her calming chant to concentrate. His legs were beneath hers. His back was behind hers. His arms reached around her waist to grasp the rope that rose between both their legs. His gloved hands slid down the thin braid just below hers.

They were backing down a vertical granite slope that felt as slick as a monument.

She couldn't fall unless he did, Lynn told herself.

"We're going to have to jump over a crevasse in the cliff face. Here, put these on."

With one hand he let go of the rope, drew his left glove off with his teeth, and held it while she thrust her hand inside. The buttery yellow leather was thin and warm from his hand. It was also a great deal too large.

"It's too big," she objected as he reversed his grip to draw off the other glove. "You keep them."

"We're going to slide down the rope. Without something to protect your hands you might not be able to hold on."

That silenced Lynn. Her palms already burned from the fall he had arrested, and it had lasted only a few seconds. The idea of falling so terrified her by now that she would have done anything to prevent it from happening—even taking his gloves while he suffered the rope bare-handed.

She rationalized it by telling herself that his skin was much tougher than hers.

Jess helped her with the other glove. Feet braced against chiseled layers of rock, newly gloved hands gripping the rope, Lynn waited, trying not to shiver.

Om ran through her mind in an endless loop. *Om, om.*

"When I say go I want you to push out from the cliff with your feet and let the rope slide through your hands. Just kind of rest against me and let yourself drop. It's not far, only about ten feet. Are you ready?"

Oh, God. Lynn nodded. Beneath her, she felt his muscles tense.

"Go!"

10

LYNN PUSHED OFF from the cliff at the same time Jess did, not
so much by choice but because his powerful thrust took her with
him. The rope slid through her hands. Again, this was more by
accident than design.

The sensation of falling made her stomach shoot into her
throat. If she ever got down off this mountain, Lynn vowed, she
would never so much as climb up on a kitchen stool again.

Jess swooped back in toward the cliff. Cradled by his body,
Lynn perforce had to do likewise. Her slippery-soled boots made
jarring contact with the rock wall. His chest thudded into her
back. Knocked off balance, Lynn's feet slipped. She tilted forward, her knees crashing into rock. Her fingers clenched the
rope. Her sliding feet hit the toes of Jess's boots and stopped.
His body, now solidly in place, steadied her. Regaining her balance, she climbed into a precarious position and tried to ignore
the quivering of her limbs.

Om.

"You're doing great," he spoke in her ear.

By glancing up and craning her neck, Lynn could see Rory.
They were below her now. The child hung in an almost upright

position, her poncho caught on what appeared to be a broken part of the trunk, her arms draped over green-needled branches, her legs straddling another branch. Her perch looked far more secure than the flimsy web that had saved Lynn. Realizing that, Lynn felt her terror for her daughter go down a notch.

But just a notch. Rory was emphatically not all right. Her eyes were closed. Her face was white as milk. To all appearances she was unconscious.

"Rory!" Lynn cried. Her daughter didn't answer, didn't so much as move a finger in response.

"She'll be okay."

"You've got to get her! Now! Please! Please!"

"I can't manage both of you at once. Let me get you down first. Then I'll come back for her." His tone was meant to be soothing, Lynn realized. Unfortunately, she was not soothed.

"She's unconscious!"

"At least the way she's situated she won't fall."

That was true, though the knowledge gave Lynn scant comfort.

"I can't do anything about her until you're on the ground," Jess insisted calmly. Then he started moving again. Bound together as they were, Lynn had no choice but to move with him. She scarcely took her eyes off her daughter for the rest of the descent. So worried was she about Rory that she wasn't even frightened any longer—except for her child.

It seemed to take eons to reach solid ground. When her feet at last touched down on the puddle-pocked hardscrabble, Lynn found to her surprise that her knees would not support her.

With a wordless murmur of dismay she started to crumple. Jess, behind her, caught her with an arm around her waist.

"Whoa," he said.

"I . . . can't stand up."

"You've had a big day." He kept one arm around her while he sawed through the rope that still bound them together, back to chest. When it was cut, Lynn sank to her knees. Only his arm around her kept her from keeling over onto her face.

"Please get Rory." Supporting her upper body with her hands,

Lynn turned her head to look up at her daughter, who at that distance was no more than a dot of vivid pink against the dark-green splash of evergreens punctuating the cliff.

"I'll get her, don't worry."

Jess, Lynn saw, was bent over, his hands resting on his knees as he breathed deeply in and out.

"Are you okay?" she asked.

"Never better." He straightened. "Better give me back my gloves."

"Oh. Sure." Lynn tugged the leather gloves from her hands and passed them to him. He pulled them on and turned back toward the sheer rock wall, adjusting his makeshift harness, tugging on the rope that was still connected to the top of the cliff to make certain it remained secure. Then, with an ease and grace that impressed Lynn, he started to climb the mountain, finding toeholds where she would have sworn there were none, clinging to impossibly small outcroppings of rock as he pulled himself up.

Watching his deft ascent, Lynn was surprised at how certain she felt that he would succeed in rescuing Rory.

And he did. Rory appeared unconscious when Jess reached the ground with her. As Jess traversed the last few yards Lynn got to her feet and reached for her daughter, steadying her as Jess cut through the rope that held them chest to chest. Lynn quickly pulled off her own poncho and spread it on the ground. Meanwhile, Jess lifted Rory's bound wrists over his head and lowered her onto the neon-yellow plastic. Taking in those bound wrists, Lynn realized that climbing down with Rory's deadweight tied to his body must have been even hairier than their own descent.

"Oh, her poor head!" Lynn crouched beside Rory's supine form. She smoothed back her daughter's bangs and the long tendrils of blond hair that had escaped from her ponytail, gazing in horror at the deep scrapes and bruising that marred the left side of her forehead from her brow to her hairline.

"She must have brushed a rock on the way down. Or maybe a falling one hit her." Sinking to one knee, Jess cut through the rope around Rory's wrists, then sat as he began freeing himself from his jury-rigged climbing harness. He was breathing hard, and sweat beaded his brow. For the moment, though, Lynn had no time or sympathy to spare.

"Rory!" Lynn's attention was all on her daughter. She chafed Rory's cold hands, laid a palm on her forehead, her cheek. The bright pink poncho was badly torn and stained. Ripping it the rest of the way off seemed the easiest way to remove it, so Lynn did.

"Let me check her." Without waiting for permission Jess knelt beside Rory and ran his hands along the teen's arms and legs, over her rib cage, down her spine, and finally used his fingers to mold her skull. He glanced at Lynn. "I don't think anything's broken. Probably she just caught a really good clout on the head."

Under the circumstances Lynn recognized that her earlier admonition to Jess to keep his hands off her daughter no longer applied. In fact, she welcomed any rudimentary medical knowledge he might have.

"She's so cold." Fear thinned Lynn's voice. Like herself, Rory was wearing a simple cotton turtleneck, jeans, and boots. Thanks to the torn poncho the outfit was wet through. "She needs dry clothes."

The temperature on the ground seemed warmer than had the air whooshing up and down the cliff, but still it couldn't have been more than sixty degrees. Too cold for an injured child to lie around wet.

Lynn felt her own turtleneck. It was damp in spots, particularly around the throat and cuffs, but not nearly as soggy as Rory's. The same could be said for her jeans.

"Turn your back," Lynn said to Jess.

He looked at her, started to say something, didn't, and obliged. After a momentary undignified struggle with her boots, Lynn managed to strip down to her undies. Then, shivering, she performed the same service for her daughter. Rory was trembling visibly, Lynn saw with distress as she lifted her child's head to put on the turtleneck. Goose bumps roughened every bit of Rory's flesh not covered by her pink cotton bra and panties.

"Mommy." Rory's lids fluttered up. The achingly familiar form of address stabbed Lynn through to the heart.

"It's all right, baby. You're safe. Mommy's here." Lynn bent over her daughter, temporarily abandoning the turtleneck as she crooned reassurance.

"My head hurts." Rory's eyes closed again. "And I'm cold."

"Rory!"

Rory didn't answer, but it seemed to Lynn that her daughter's shivering grew more pronounced. Frightened, she snatched up the turtleneck again. She had to get Rory warm and fast. It occurred to Lynn that her wet, cold, and injured daughter could go into shock.

"Put this on her. It's dry."

Jess dropped his flannel shirt on Rory's stomach. Glancing up, Lynn saw that he was wearing a short-sleeved white T-shirt that looked like it had originated with Hanes or Fruit of the Loom. Though his back was nominally turned it was obvious that he hadn't missed a thing.

"She needs a doctor," Lynn said.

"The first thing to do is get her warm."

Jess abandoned any pretense of keeping his back turned and dropped to one knee beside Rory.

"That goes for you too," he added, his gaze flicking over the amount of shivering skin left exposed by Lynn's ice-blue nylon-and-lace scanties. Though she was at least as well covered as she would have been if she were wearing a bikini—more so if one counted her brightly patterned trouser socks—Lynn felt acutely self-conscious under that look.

"Do you mind?" she demanded, bristling.

"For Christ's sake, don't you think I've seen women in their underwear before?" Jess asked, impatient, reaching for the shirt he had dropped. "I'll put this on her. You get dressed yourself. You're turning blue around the gills."

Lynn hesitated, then nodded reluctant agreement. She was freezing—and Rory looked even colder. The emergency in which they found themselves took precedence over all other concerns, including modesty and Jess's intentions toward her daughter. In any case the man's behavior had been above reproach since their fall, Lynn had to admit. He had saved their lives, at no little risk to his own. He had been resourceful, reassuring, a complete gentleman and a brave man. So he had ogled her in her underwear; at least he hadn't ogled Rory.

And now he had given up his shirt, which was made of thick brushed-cotton flannel. It was dry and warm from his body, and she was thankful to have it for her daughter.

Pulling on her own turtleneck again, Lynn watched as Jess eased Rory into the garment, then pulled it closed over her chest. As he began doing up the buttons, Lynn struggled into Rory's wet jeans. Fortunately, the kids all favored baggy clothes or Lynn would never have been able to get them on at all. Slim though Lynn was, her backside was two sizes larger than Rory's.

Jess had the flannel shirt buttoned almost up to Rory's neck when Lynn took over. She brushed his hands aside, finished the task, then turned up the shirt's collar for extra warmth and pulled the too-long sleeves down to cover the child's icy hands. The tails reached past her knees. Rory's socks were dry—her boots were apparently more effective than Lynn's at repelling water—so Lynn left them alone and wrestled her own jeans up her daughter's legs.

"All done?" A slightly ironic note underlay the question.

Lynn glanced up to encounter Jess's gaze again. He was standing, looking down at the pair of them, his hands thrust into the pocket of his jeans and his arms held close to his body as if he were attempting to ward off the cold.

"Thanks for the shirt," she said.

"No problem."

While Lynn covered Rory with the remains of the torn poncho to keep out the wind, Jess moved about twenty feet away from the cliff, then turned to face the vertical rock wall, looking toward the precipice as he waved his arms. Lynn realized that he was trying to signal the group on the top of the cliff.

"Do you think they can see you?"

Sitting beside Rory, she was pulling her boots back on over damp socks as she spoke.

"Yeah. At least, I'm pretty sure they can. Though Owen will be careful to keep everybody well back from the edge this time."

"Too bad he didn't think about that earlier." Lynn's rejoinder was more than a shade caustic.

"Yeah, well, I guess we made the mistake of putting too much faith in our guests' common sense. Live and learn. Ah, there's Owen."

The look Lynn sent his way was withering.

"You don't happen to have a pen on you, do you?" He was patting the pockets of his jeans as he spoke.

"A *pen*?"

"Or a pencil. Something to write with."

"Why?" Lynn was mystified.

"I want to send Owen a note." He indicated the rope that still snaked down from the top of the cliff.

"Oh." She patted her own pockets—Rory's, actually—and felt a lump. Digging, she came up with a slim blue-plastic lipstick case. "What about this?"

"That'll do," he said, accepting it.

Jess dropped to one knee, pulled out his knife, hacked off a piece of Rory's torn poncho, and used the lipstick to scribble something on the rough white lining.

"I assume you're telling Owen to come and get us?"

Jess paused and glanced at her. "You're kidding, right?"

"Not really."

"Look around you, babe." He went back to his writing.

"Don't call me babe." Lynn objected automatically—sensitized from years of battling sexism in the newsroom—while following Jess's advice to look around.

Though the area where they had fetched up was relatively flat, about thirty feet away the ground began sloping toward the pine forest, the edge of which was about a quarter of a mile distant. With the sheer rise of the cliff behind them, down was the only way to go. Climbing back up was not an option.

"Maybe the whole group can't get down here"—Lynn was willing to recognize the truth of that—"but the Jeep can, can't it? I mean, drive around or something? Rory needs to be seen by a doctor."

Jess gave her a wry smile. "There are some places even a Jeep can't go, and I'm afraid this is one of them. We're going to have to walk out. Luckily, I know where we are. There's a gravel road about a day's hike from here where the Jeep can pick us up. That's where I'm telling Owen to meet us."

"But Rory needs a doctor!"

"There's nothing I can do about it right now. Anyway, I don't think she's badly hurt. She was talking, and she looks to be getting a little of her color back. She'll be all right."

"And what if she's not?"

"Listen, you ought to be thanking your lucky stars you're both still alive."

Lynn ignored that to focus on her more immediate concern. "You mean you don't have some kind of contingency plan in case something like this happens? A helicopter or something that can reach inaccessible places to take injured people to the hospital?"

"Nope."

"*Nope?*" Annoyance at the nonchalance of his single-syllable reply lent a shrill note to Lynn's voice.

Jess met her look with a level gaze of his own. "We're in a federally designated High Wilderness Area, in case you hadn't noticed. The land is wild and primitive and largely inaccessible to any kind of machine. That's the attraction of it. Presumably that's one of the reasons your group decided to sign up for this trip. Or did you think this was some kind of Disneyland adventure, where everything's fake?"

That last bit of sarcasm on top of her fear for her daughter brought all her near-forgotten antipathy for this Marlboro Man wanna-be flooding back.

"Not everything, just the cowboys," she said nastily.

Jess stopped writing again to stare at her. "What?"

"You. And your brother. And the rest of your crew. Fakes, every one of you, with your stupid cowboy hats and your stupid cowboy boots and your stupid cowboy horses."

"I managed to save your ass, lady."

There was an edge to Jess's voice. That and the reminder that she and Rory owed him her life put the crowning touch on

Lynn's outrage. She hated to be beholden to anyone, especially a too-handsome fake cowboy.

"Well, you better figure out some way to get my daughter to a doctor, pronto, or I'll *sue* your ass, buddy. And you can bet your sweet life I won't do it halfway!"

11

So HE WAS a sucker for tough broads, Jess thought ruefully, staring at Lynn as she spat threats at him. In *Grease* he'd preferred Rizzo to saccharine-sweet Sandy. He liked Madonna. He liked Sharon Stone. Right from the start, when he and Owen had met this latest group of tourists at the airport, he'd zeroed in on that quality in Lynn.

Attitude, that was what she had, in spades. And it turned him on. To quote Owen: Little brother likes babes with balls.

Beautiful babes with balls. To be strictly accurate, his first thought upon setting eyes on Lynn when she had come striding down that airline ramp had been, *whoa,* Babe-raham Lincoln.

His appraisal had started with her feet in their sexy spike heels, swept up over a pair of breathtaking legs in sheer hose, approved a slim black skirt that ended at midthigh, and noted with interest the other assets imperfectly concealed by her businesslike blazer and silk blouse.

She'd had discreet gold hoops in her ears, a no-nonsense mouth rendered kissable by pale-pink lipstick, big blue eyes with thick brushes of lashes, and an elegant upswept hairdo the color of daffodils.

And a go-to-hell look on her face when he'd smiled at her.

As Owen had said out of the side of his mouth as they'd gathered up the group's luggage, that one was Jess's type of woman.

A bitch.

That bit of brotherly candor unfortunately had proved all too true.

Now the babe with balls was turning her bitchery on him. After he had just saved her life yet. And her daughter's too.

Talk about ingratitude!

He wasn't in the mood for it: He was bone-tired, he was freezing to death, he had rope burns on his hands, he had the mother of all cricks in his neck, and he still had to face the headache of getting her and her kid back to civilization in one piece.

And she was threatening to sue him? And Owen, and Adventure, Inc.? He should have left her hanging in that tree.

Too late now.

"I guess that's why we have liability insurance," Jess said mildly, and stood up, note in hand.

Heading toward the cliff, he could feel her fury rising behind him, silent but palpable. The muscles in his back tensed. In his experience babes with balls were inclined to throw things at the object of their ire.

Which in this case meant him. As it usually did.

But she didn't.

"By the way, you're welcome," Jess said over his shoulder as he sent his note snaking up the cliff. "I'd be glad to save your life again anytime. Babe."

12

SHE NEEDED A CIGARETTE. Trudging behind Jess, tromping through a primeval alpine forest along a barely discernible trail between stands of moss-covered undergrowth so thick and high it could have hidden a baker's dozen grizzlies, stumbling over rocks and roots and sliding on slippery things she preferred not to try to identify, that was the thought uppermost in Lynn's mind: She needed a cigarette.

She was marooned in this wilderness hell with a grumpy fake cowboy, an injured teenage daughter with the hots for said cowboy, a thirty-pound pack that felt ten times heavier, and no cigarettes.

Adventure, Inc.'s literature had promised: *You'll get in touch with your body in a whole new way.*

They were right: She'd never before experienced a nicotine fit the magnitude of the one she could feel coming on. By the time they got back to civilization she would not have smoked a cigarette in *two whole days*!

And that was the best-case scenario. Given the track record of the trip so far, there was about as much chance of things going

as planned as there was of spotting a hospital around the next
bend.

Scanning an old mountain-goat trail for discarded butts was
obviously a waste of time, but Lynn found herself doing it anyway on the off-chance that they were following in the footsteps
of a nanny goat with a tobacco habit. It was hopeless, of course,
just as discovering a stray cigarette on her person or those of her
companions was hopeless. She'd turned her own clothes inside
out, and Rory's too, out of pure desperation, though her daughter was an avid antismoker.

Jess had no cigarettes. She'd already broken her seething silence long enough to ask him. He'd given her a superior smirk as
he informed her that *he* didn't smoke.

Lynn hated that kind of smug nonsmoker.

There were no cigarettes in either of the packs Owen had sent
down the cliff. Lynn had already torn them apart, checking.

Her own cigarettes were tucked away in a saddlebag, left behind with that stupid horse. Of course, she couldn't really blame
herself for that. Though she was a planner by nature, it was a
little too much to ask to plan to fall off a cliff.

She needed a cigarette.

To distract herself Lynn dwelt on the growing discomfort at
the backs of her heels. The farther she walked, the worse the
pain grew. Obviously, the combination of damp socks and new
boots was giving her blisters.

Huge blisters.

If Adventure, Inc.'s to-bring list had not specified boots as the
only acceptable kind of footgear, she would be wearing comfortable sneakers right now, not shiny English riding boots that were
devilish to walk in. Everyone else had opted for cowboy boots,
including Rory, whose I-told-you-so had been the first words she
had said to her mother when the group all met up at the corral
for their initial ride.

And that was Adventure, Inc.'s fault too, for not being specific
enough. If they had been she'd have been spared embarrassment
and blisters, and the tight, tall leather shanks would not be chaf-
ing the area just below her knees with every step she now took.

Lynn dwelt on that too.

From there she dwelt on her tired knees, her sore back, the stinging in her palms.

She dwelt on her shoulder, which ached where it had slammed into the cliff.

She dwelt on her antipathy for the man she had—for the moment—no choice but to follow.

She dwelt on her anxiety about Rory. But that was so acute that it produced an even greater craving for a nicotine fix.

She needed a cigarette!

It was growing dark. Whether she disliked Jess or not was soon beside the point when there were *things* all around them in the shadows. Things that rustled. Things that slithered. Things that squeaked. She picked up her pace, trying to close the distance between herself and Jess's unyielding back, with little success.

Even with his pack, which had to weigh at least as much as hers, and Rory in his arms, he was moving faster than she thought she could ever move again.

She was so tired. What she needed was a rest—and a cigarette.

"Wait!" bubbled to her lips more than once as the distance between them gradually increased, but Lynn forced it back. She would ask for no quarter from Jess Feldman, ever.

"Whooo-ooo!" The sharp flutter of wings near at hand accompanied the cry and almost surprised a scream out of Lynn. It was an owl, of course, she told herself, as brilliant reflective eyes in a pale round face swooped past her to vanish again in the dark. Nothing but an owl.

Up ahead Jess stopped, waiting. With a feeling of relief Lynn tromped over roots and rocks and miscellaneous debris littering the path to his side.

"Get the flashlight out, will you?"

With a brusque jerk of his head he indicated his backpack. Get it yourself, Lynn almost said, but to be fair, with Rory in his arms he didn't have a hand free.

"How's Rory?" Gritting her teeth, Lynn unzipped his backpack and foraged for the flashlight.

"She's all right, I think. She was murmuring something a while back. She seems comfortable enough."

A glance at Rory confirmed that. Her head lay on Jess's shoulder, and her body was curled high against his chest. Zipped into a goose-down jacket—like the ones she and Jess wore, courtesy of the cliff rescue line—and wrapped in a silvery space blanket, she looked toasty warm and just a tad too cozy for her mother's peace of mind.

A suspicious glance at Jess's expression reassured her somewhat. At the moment he did not look like he had a sexual thought in his head. What he did look was very tired.

Lynn found herself wishing there was someone to carry *her.* She was tired too, so tired she could drop where she stood and sleep for a thousand years.

Jess had even more reason to be tired than she did. Rory weighed less than a hundred pounds, but even so, carrying her for so long must have required considerable strength. He was holding her in his arms too, like an infant, in deference to her injured state, instead of hauling her slung over his shoulder or in some other masculinely efficient way.

If Lynn hadn't been feeling so out of sorts, she might have felt a glimmer of gratitude toward him for his care of her daughter.

But she *was* feeling out of sorts. No, out of sorts was too mild a way to put it. What she was feeling was downright mean.

The smooth, cool plastic of a disposable lighter touched her probing fingertips. Lynn almost wept. What good was a lighter without cigarettes?

"Why would anybody pack a lighter and no cigarettes?" she demanded of no one in particular. It was a question she'd asked before, both out loud and silently, from the time she'd discovered the lighter in one of the packs when she had first searched them and concluded that cigarettes must be in there too, only to have her hopes dashed.

"Maybe to start a fire with, so we won't freeze." This was the first time Jess had answered a question he must have recognized as purely rhetorical, and Lynn would just as soon he hadn't bothered. His sarcasm did nothing to improve her mood.

"Oh, shut up," she said.

"Mom?" Rory's voice, thin though it was, was more welcome than even a cigarette would have been.

"Baby, are you awake? How do you feel?" Lynn abandoned her search of the backpack to come around to look at her daughter. Rory's forehead was shiny with salve from the first-aid kit in one of the packs. Lynn hoped that the shine magnified the degree of discoloration; half of Rory's forehead looked black. If not, the injury was growing worse—but then, bruising usually did get worse before it got better, she reminded herself.

Lynn prayed that bruising was all it was.

"My head hurts." Rory paused, looking as if she had to work to collect her thoughts. "What happened?"

"We fell off the cliff." Lynn smoothed her daughter's hair away from the greasy salve, touched her cheek, and smiled at her.

"I thought so. Jess saved us, didn't he? Or at least me. He brought me down the cliff. I thought it was a dream."

"It wasn't a dream," Lynn said sourly.

"Then he saved my life. That makes him a hero, doesn't it? Thanks, Jess."

Rory smiled up at him, her arms curling close around his neck, then planted a quick kiss on the underside of his jaw. The kittenish performance sent quivers of alarm through Lynn. Unable to do anything more constructive, she glared ferociously at Jess, who just happened to be looking right at her.

Did she read guilt in his expression? Or something more sinister?

"My pleasure." Dismissing Lynn with a glance, Jess smiled back at Rory. "*You* are very welcome."

His gaze moved back to Lynn's face. This time she had no trouble reading the silent mockery in his eyes. "Hey, Mom, do you think you could hurry with that flashlight?"

"I'm doing my best." Gritting her teeth against responding to that *Mom*—she knew perfectly well he had called her that just to irritate her—Lynn went back to fishing for the flashlight. Her fingers found the distinctive shape at last, and she pulled it out. Sized to fit in a palm, it was small and lightweight but powerful. Unfortunately, the net effect when Lynn turned on the light was to make the deepening shadows around them seem even darker in comparison. She glanced around uneasily.

"Do you think you can stand up?" Jess said to Rory. Before she could answer he was setting her on her feet.

Rory swayed and put a hand to her head. "I feel dizzy."

Jess's arm was still around her, supporting her, as she sat cross-legged on the path.

"Let's take a break," he said.

"Here?" Lynn asked.

The forest seemed to be coming alive as night fell. The flashlight was no help whatsoever. It was no more than a tiny pinprick of light doing battle against a looming, ever-deepening darkness. Red fir and ponderosa pines lent their distinctive scent to the rapidly cooling air. A mule deer, identifiable by its rabbit-like ears, was caught in the flashlight's beam. It turned to stare at the human intruders for a frozen instant before leaping out of sight. The crash of its passing alerted other nocturnal creatures. The light picked up a half-dozen pairs of eyes glowing at them from the ground and the trees and everywhere in between. At least, Lynn thought, shivering, they looked too small to belong to bears.

"No, at that Hilton over there." Jess's voice had an edge to it. He eased the pack off his back and crouched beside it and Rory as he spoke. "Could I have the flashlight?"

Lynn gave it to him, shed her own pack, and dropped down beside Rory, trying not to imagine exactly what kind of things were out there going bump in the night. Jess rummaged in his pack, coming up with green plastic bottles of spring water and packaged strips of beef jerky.

"I can't believe Adventure, Inc. doesn't have some kind of plan in place for when something like this happens!" she groused, accepting the water and jerky he passed her with a scowl. Anxiety and exhaustion—to say nothing of nicotine withdrawal—combined to make Lynn feel as if she wanted to jump out of her skin.

"Next time we will. Isn't there a famous saying to the effect that you can never go broke overestimating the stupidity of the American tourist?" Jess was still rummaging in his pack.

"No, there's not." Lynn twisted the cap from Rory's water bottle, passed it to her daughter, and with her teeth attacked the plastic wrap guarding the beef.

Jess glanced up. Their gazes clashed. "There should be."

"Go to hell." Lynn caught Rory's eye and wished the words unsaid. She forced what felt like an unconvincing smile as she passed the open packet of jerky to her daughter. Under the circumstances the last thing she wanted to do was upset her child.

"You don't have any cigarettes, do you, Mom?" Rory asked with an air of weary resignation.

"How can you tell?" Jess spoke before Lynn could reply.

"She gets really crabby when she's out of cigarettes. It's the only time she ever swears." Rory took a swallow of water.

"You mean she's not always crabby?" Jess asked, glancing at Lynn and feigning surprise as he started in on his own snack.

"Well, usually she is, kind of. Grandma says it's a mid-life thing. But she doesn't usually swear." Rory tore off a tiny piece of jerky and chewed it.

"What!" Lynn interrupted this unflattering two-way conversation, feeling as if she had been blindsided by her own mother's perfidy. A mid-life thing, indeed! Just like Rory was going through a teen thing? When she got home she was going to have to inform her mother that *she* had outgrown phases.

"Does she get hot flashes too?"

Jess was laughing at her. Lynn sent him a killing glare and took a big bite out of her own food. The spicy beef—not something that she would normally eat—felt dry and unpleasant in her mouth. She ate it anyway.

"Not that I know of." Rory's reply was serious. Her gaze shifted to Lynn. "Do you, Mom?"

"No!" Lynn stopped herself, then continued in a more even tone. "I'm only thirty-five, Rory. That's way too young for the symptoms you're talking about. I am *not* going through a mid-life thing. Grandma was mistaken."

"She says you're in a funk about your job."

"Grandma says too darned much." Lynn managed a smile to take some of the sting out of this—Rory adored her grandmother, and Lynn usually did too—but it was an effort. She felt—*admit it*—crabby. Mondo crabby.

"So," Lynn changed the subject brightly, addressing Jess, "are we going to spend the night in the woods? Or are we just going to keep walking until we drop?"

The questions had an acidic tone that Lynn regretted. She should have been more matter-of-fact. After all, sniping at Jess while they were wandering the wilderness together was probably not smart. He was the only one who knew how to get where they were going.

To compensate, she smiled reassuringly at her daughter. Rory's nose was wrinkled in distaste, but she was eating her jerky. The silver Mylar blanket was around her shoulders now, and it rustled every time she moved. It should be very effective, Lynn thought, in frightening away predators. Rory looked, and sounded, like something from outer space.

"There's a old mining camp a few miles farther up this trail," Jess said. "It's got a couple of cabins, kind of tumbledown but better than nothing. I thought we'd spend the night there. If we start walking from there pretty early in the morning, we should be on track to rendezvous with Tim about lunchtime tomorrow."

"That soon, huh?" Lynn couldn't help the caustic note in her voice. It was not something she was doing purposely. She was just so tired and aggravated at the whole situation that she couldn't control herself.

And she needed a cigarette!

"If we're lucky."

Jess's refusal to be riled had the effect of making Lynn feel crabbier than ever. He finished his water, screwed the lid back on the bottle, and stood up. "Ready to go?"

They were. Jess gathered up water bottles and trash, storing them in his pack. Lynn struggled into her own pack, resenting the ease with which he donned his.

He caught her gaze. Shifting so that his body blocked Rory's view, he whispered to Lynn, "What do you say, Mom? Do we let your hurt little girl walk, or does the big bad wolf carry her?"

Lynn cast a quick glance beyond him at Rory, who was still seated on the ground.

"Carry her," she muttered, tight-lipped.

"Sure?"

"Yes!"

"What are you two whispering about?" Rory sounded peevish. Stepping around Jess, who turned as she did so, Lynn smiled down at her daughter. Rory's glance up at her was bright with suspicion.

Uh-oh, Lynn thought, her sweet child was metamorphosing again; the alien was on its way back.

"Grown-up talk," Lynn said, reaching a hand down to Rory. Rory allowed herself to be pulled into a standing position, then swayed, clapping a hand to her head with a degree more drama than Lynn thought was called for.

Lynn steadied her, glancing around for Jess.

"Quit talking to me like I'm some kind of baby," Rory whispered to her mother, her arms sliding around Jess's neck as he picked her up. Then, louder, "I'm almost fifteen."

"Not quite grown up yet," Jess observed.

Lynn, tucking the space blanket snugly around Rory, was surprised at his response. She would have expected him to side with Rory.

"And you won't be fifteen for six months," she felt compelled to add. Not that fifteen was any better than fourteen where Rory's interest in a man like Jess Feldman was concerned. If the child had to be boy-crazy, why couldn't she at least fixate on specimens near her own age? Lynn wondered with exasperation. While Rory liked teenagers, every male she had had a serious crush on, from her physics teacher to her dentist, had been way too old for her. But at least the others had been lusted after from afar. Rory seemed determined to get up close and personal with Jess—and Jess didn't seem particularly intent on discouraging her.

Whoever had coined the phrase the *joy* of motherhood must not have had a pubescent daughter.

"*Four and a half* months," Rory corrected bitterly. "November nineteenth, remember?"

"Of course I remember," Lynn said. "I was there." Rory's hostility was returning by leaps and bounds, and Lynn was not up to dealing with it at the moment. In her present frame of mind she was not up to dealing with much. She just wanted to get out of the woods—and smoke a cigarette.

"Get the flashlight." Holding Rory, Jess nodded toward where it sat on the ground, tiny gray moths fluttering along the length of its beam.

Smack!

In a reflex reaction Lynn slapped the bare skin at the side of her neck even as she reached for the flashlight. Something had bitten her. A mosquito? A no-see-um! Of course, with the coming of night the little bloodsuckers were once again on the warpath, adding one more layer to her cocoon of misery.

Happy, happy, joy, joy.

Hunching her shoulders to give the vampires as small a target as possible, Lynn picked up the flashlight. Jess made a gesture that indicated she should precede him.

"Shine the light on the path, will you?"

This came as Lynn swept the forest with the beam.

"You want me to lead the way?" Lynn asked, with no small amount of concern.

"You've got the light."

Rats! Curses! He made the suggestion deliberately, she thought, to pay her back for all the things she had said to him earlier. He knew she felt intimidated—all right, scared—by what might be lurking in the woods at night. But she'd be hanged by her heels before she'd acknowledge that fear. Ninety percent of life, she had learned, was putting on a good front.

Lynn squared her shoulders and started walking, shining the light mostly on the path and only occasionally, when she just couldn't help it, into the *über*-blackness that was the forest. Something slithered out of the way at the edge of the light, too quick for Lynn to identify it, though she suspected it was a snake. More than once she crunched a beetle underfoot. They were the size of her thumb as they scurried across the path, their shells black and shiny. A brown hare hopped for safety as she touched it with the light.

All around them insects buzzed and whirred. Frogs sang. Rodents rustled and occasionally shrieked. A bird of prey screeched.

A sharp crack behind her made Lynn jump a foot straight up in the air.

"Ow! Shit! Damn it to hell!" Jess cried.

Lynn whirled, focusing the flashlight in time to catch Jess reeling backward, one hand clapped to his forehead.

"Jess! Oh, Jess!" Rory hung from his neck, legs dangling, as he staggered. Clearly, if it had not been for her grip on his neck, she would have been dropped.

"What on earth?" Lynn shone the light in Jess's face. He cursed again, baring his teeth, lifting his hand from his head to shield his eyes from the glare.

"What are you trying to do, blind me?"

"Sorry." Lynn lowered the beam.

"Why didn't you warn me?" It was a growl. He shook his head as though to clear it, then picked Rory up again.

"Oh, poor you!" Rory crooned, stroking his forehead. To Jess's credit he jerked his head away from her hand.

"About what?" Lynn was mystified.

"The branch!" From the way Jess was talking through his teeth, he must have thought she should know what he was referring to. She didn't.

"*This* branch," he elucidated, ducking under it as he stalked toward her, Rory in his arms.

All at once Lynn saw the light—or rather the branch. She grinned, then began to laugh.

"*Mother!*" Rory protested, siding completely with Jess. Jess just scowled.

It was a sturdy branch, about a foot in diameter, belonging to a gigantic pine and extending stiffly out over the path. Lynn had passed under it with a good eight inches to spare.

Jess had not.

"Sorry, I didn't realize," Lynn said, trying to sound contrite. A chortle spoiled the effect.

Jess's answering grunt was a masterpiece of inarticulate skepticism.

"Mother, it isn't funny!"

"*I* think it's hilarious," Lynn said sweetly. Turning, she began to walk again, the flashlight illuminating the path. She felt very much better in the aftermath of Jess's comeuppance. Her lips even turned up in an occasional tiny grin.

Except for a few murmurs to Jess from Rory, nothing more was said until at last the pitted, root-choked, now-you-see-it-now-you-don't path came to an end.

Lynn stopped as the woods opened into a clearing. Three small cabins and some rusty machinery were illuminated by the ghostly light of the half-moon.

"The mining camp," Jess said with satisfaction, walking up behind her. "We'll stay here for the night."

13

Theresa's slender body was curled into a tight little ball, her face contorting with fear as she fought to stay calm. Elijah, was whimpering in her arms. She clutched the bottle with the milk-and-wine concoction in it in one hand while she patted his back with the other and rocked frantically back and forth. He would not take the nipple, spitting it out every time she tried to get him to suck.

His whimpers were threatening to turn into a full-blown howl.

"You're such a good boy, such a good boy, 'Lije. Such a good little boy," Theresa crooned desperately in his ear. He *was* a good boy; in the real world he hardly ever cried, and down here in Hell he hadn't done more than whimper in two days. He couldn't betray them now. He couldn't. She couldn't let him.

The thought that went with that made her sick.

"Rockabye baby . . ."

The screaming from the rest of her family had stopped a long time ago. How long, Theresa couldn't say. It was pitch black in the cellar, just as it had been pitch black since she had taken shelter there with Elijah, and she had no real way to judge the time. The silence could have descended two hours ago—or two days.

Silence, that is, except for footsteps and the occasional sound of something being dragged across the floor.

The silence did not tempt her to emerge from her hiding place. Not even close. There was an evil to it, that silence, that was as real and substantial as a physical presence.

Theresa *knew* the evil was still upstairs, just as she had known it was outside the cabin door. She knew it in her gut.

She even knew who the evil was: Death himself, come to seek them out. Which was why she had dubbed this place of her torment Hell.

"His name was Death, and Hell followed with him." Her father quoted that verse from Revelations all the time.

Theresa shivered, from terror as much as from the very real chill. It was cold in this subterranean Hell, and it smelled of earth and rotten vegetables and the unmentionable things she had had to do in a corner. It smelled of dirty diapers and baby spit-up—and fear.

Elijah was quivering now, his knees pressing like hard, twin knots into her chest as he tried to draw his chubby little legs up to his body.

Theresa could tell what was coming: He was going to bawl.

"Lullaby, and good night . . ."

His stomach must hurt. He had already passed gas twice, three times. The concoction in the bottle must be hard for a six-month-old to digest.

"Hush, baby. Please don't cry," Theresa stopped singing to whisper despairingly to him, rocking with manic rhythm. "Please don't cry."

Abovestairs, the floor creaked. Death was walking again, accompanied by the dragging sound.

Elijah turned his wet little face into her neck, and howled.

The footsteps stopped.

14

JESS CROSSED THE CLEARING toward the cabins, moving quietly, cautiously. In his arms the kid was silent, except for the incessant rustling of that piece of aluminum foil she was wrapped up in. With a brief word in her ear Jess tugged it loose and dropped it. The space blanket, with the moonlight hitting it, was about as hard to miss as a neon sign and as quiet as a drumroll.

Why didn't they just shout that they were coming and be done with it?

An instinct honed and forgotten so long ago that he hadn't realized he still possessed it warned him to make as little noise as possible.

Something about the dark, silent clearing was giving him the willies.

Walking a few feet ahead, her slender body practically shapeless in the bulky jacket she wore, Lynn shone the flashlight over the knee-high weeds, lighting their way. The beam had already saved them from a close encounter with a long-abandoned pick. Its once-sharp blade was dark with rust; the wooden handle looked rotten.

The uneasy feeling grew stronger with every step he took. There was nothing to account for it. Except instinct.

Over the years he had learned to trust that shivery feeling at the nape of his neck. It had saved his life more than once.

The place seemed deserted, though, just as it should be. Nothing moved. The only sounds were the usual night sounds: the quiet murmur of the wind, the humming insects, the rustling animals.

Moonlight cast an eerie but functional light over a scene that could have come straight out of the previous century. The small mining camp with its ancient equipment had to be well over a hundred years old.

Jess had visited the place before, many times over the years, but always in broad daylight.

Maybe that was it: Maybe the moonlight was to blame for the sense of dread that seemed to hang over the clearing like a pall. Wisps of clouds glowed silver at the edges as they floated across the midnight-blue sky. Mist rose from the grass, stretching upward, insubstantial drifts of white that reminded Jess of ghosts ascending to heaven. A haunting, in fact, was what came to mind as he glanced around. He had the sudden, unsettling feeling that he was walking through a graveyard.

Which was stupid, he knew, but . . . he couldn't shake it.

There were enough ghosts in his past without conjuring up more, he told himself firmly.

Just then, right in front of him, Lynn stumbled, dropped the flashlight, crouched to retrieve it—and shrieked.

15

"**O**H, MY GOD! Oh, my God!"

Lynn was on her hands and knees, backpedaling frantically through the weeds. In front of her the body lay on its back, hands crossed between its breasts, eyes open and staring.

Lynn had never seen a sight so terrifying.

It was a woman, barefoot, clad in a pink flannel nightgown. Her hair—soft brown, and long—was braided. The braid trailed out to one side of her head like a snake twisting through the grass. A bit of pink yarn secured the braid at its end.

What appeared to be a ruby necklace adorned her throat. A wide ruby necklace, stretching like a smiling mouth from ear to ear. An oozing ruby necklace.

The woman's throat had been slit. Lynn thought she might faint.

"Mom, what?"

"What the hell's the matter with you?"

The two startled voices close behind her brought Lynn scrambling to her feet. She bumped into something solid—Jess, holding Rory.

Thank God for Jess. Atavistic or not, she was glad of his big, strong, solid presence. Her fight-or-flight response was suddenly working overtime, with the emphasis on flight. If necessary *he* could stand and fight. She and Rory would run for the hills.

"L-l-look!" she stuttered, pointing, plucking at the elbow of the goose-down jacket Jess wore.

The flashlight still lay where she had dropped it, almost on top of the body, its beam illuminating a swath from folded hands to slit throat to glassy dead eyes.

A cold chill ran up Lynn's spine at the sight.

"Oh, my God!" Rory echoed her mother's exclamation of horror with the same intonation. The child wasn't her daughter for nothing, Lynn thought grimly.

"Jesus Christ!" Jess's reaction was equally religious in nature, if a little more blasphemous.

Setting Rory on her feet, Jess moved forward to retrieve the flashlight. Lynn and Rory came together as naturally as metal shavings to a magnet, watching him. They huddled, arms around each other, Lynn taking comfort in her daughter's living, breathing, shivering warmth.

Jess shone the light over the woman, its beam moving from her feet to her head and back. He leaned down, touched the uppermost of her folded hands, then picked up her wrist and held it for a moment before letting it fall.

"She's dead," he said, turning to look at them.

Duh was Lynn's silent, idiotic response. Seconds later the gears of her brain, frozen by the shock of the discovery, began to regain some function.

"She was murdered." Shivering, Lynn acknowledged the obvious in a weak voice. A companion realization, equally intelligent, blinked to life in her mind: "That means there's got to be a murderer. Here."

"Mom!" Rory whimpered, shrinking in Lynn's embrace. Lynn's arms tightened around her daughter. Her gaze, wide and frightened, lifted from the corpse to fearfully scan the camp.

"Jesus *Christ*," Jess muttered again, shining the flashlight on something in the grass just a few feet away from the woman.

Another body, a teenage boy in jeans and a sweatshirt, lay end to end with the first. His black high-tops were less than a yard from her hair. Like the woman, he was neatly laid out, legs straight, hands folded on his chest. His eyes, mercifully, were closed.

Like the woman's, his throat had been slit.

"Oh, my God!" This time the gasp was Lynn's.

Jess moved, presumably to be sure this corpse was dead too. As he did, the beam picked up another shoe, another black high-top, to the side of rather than above this body's head. The shoe had a foot in it and was attached to a leg in jeans, which was attached to a torso in a sweatshirt that was dark wet red. Thin brown hands were crossed on top of each other in the midst of the gore.

Another teenage boy, Lynn was sure, although she shut her eyes, shuddering, before the beam confirmed her guess.

This had to be a nightmare. She and Rory couldn't really be standing in a dark field in the middle of the wilderness with three hideously murdered bodies.

Maybe she had fallen asleep. Maybe the whole unbelievable day was a nightmare, she hoped. Maybe—

A sharp intake of breath from Rory, accompanied by an expletive from Jess, popped her eyes open again.

What she saw stopped her breath, dropped her jaw, and held her momentarily paralyzed: A crude cross rising some ten feet tall had been erected about four car lengths from the bodies. The deep shadow cast by the forest's tall trees had concealed it from their view. Now it was caught in the flashlight's beam. A man was on it, naked and—crucified?

Blood ran in a gleaming red swath down his chest, over his genitals, down his legs. Lynn had no doubt that there was a pool of blood at the foot of the cross.

She blinked once, twice. The sight was too unspeakable to comprehend, but she had a sickening feeling that it was all too real.

"Mom, look!" Rory grabbed her arm, pointed. From the cabins emerged a trio—no, a quartet—of ghostly figures. Riveted to the spot, Lynn stared at the shimmering white shapes as they rushed toward her and Rory and Jess.

Their feet didn't seem to touch the ground.

If they even had feet.

Talk about your ultimate bad dream.

Lynn felt as if she had stumbled into one of those children's horror novels with the gimmicky titles that Rory and her friends were always mocking. Something along the line of *Night of the Living Dummy* meets *Horror at Camp Jellyjam.*

The only response she could summon was "Run!"

16

THE TRAPDOOR CREAKED in protest as it was yanked open. Crouched in the farthest corner of the cellar, huddled against the wall, Theresa kept her hand pressed hard over Elijah's mouth.

Oh, no, she prayed. Oh, no, please. Save us.

A faint orangey light filled the rectangle where the door had been. A shape, like a large, indistinct egg, was outlined by the glow.

Death was peering into her hiding place.

Theresa's fingers dug so hard into Elijah's face that she could feel his cheekbones and jawbones through his chubby flesh. His wet little mouth fought for breath against her palm. He squirmed urgently in her hold.

Despite her best efforts to silence him, she could hear his muffled cries. She pressed her hand even harder against his mouth and felt him struggle.

Death leaned closer, seeming to look toward where she hid.

Theresa felt a warm flood soak her cotton panties and trickle down her thighs to puddle beneath her. She smelled the harsh ammonia of her own urine.

Our Father, who art in Heaven . . . She was too scared to think of any other prayer.

Elijah went limp.

Death moved. Theresa's heart beat so desperately that it felt as if someone were hammering inside her chest. Her breathing grew erratic, frantic.

Death might hear it, she realized, and held her breath.

He vanished. For a long moment Theresa simply stared at the orange rectangle, empty now of all save air.

The baby lay against her chest, silent, unmoving. Theresa dropped her hand from his face, lifted him.

His eyes were closed. He hung motionless in her hold.

Elijah! 'Lije! She wailed inwardly, shaking him, trying to wake him up. He did not respond.

God forgive me, she prayed, the inertness of his still-warm little body a silent testimony to what she had done.

Anguished tears rolled down her face.

17

"**R**UN!" Jess yelled, echoing Lynn as he snatched up Rory, who he feared was too weak to make it under her own steam. Suiting the action to the word, he pelted toward the forest, Lynn behind him, while Rory hung down his back in a fireman's carry, screaming like a banshee.

Even after she shut up, the sound echoed and reechoed in his ears. God save him from hysteria-prone teenage girls.

And from other scary things as well.

What he had seen before taking to his heels had left him shaken to the core: There were bodies, lots of bodies, a dozen or more, laid out in some sort of weird pattern in the weeds.

Just what that pattern was he hadn't been able to make out.

But in its center was that guy on the cross.

What in God's name had they stumbled onto? A mass murder, at the very least. That much was clear.

And now the murderers were after them. That was clear too.

Talk about being in the wrong place at the wrong time! But then that was the story of his life.

This time it might cost him his life. And Lynn and Rory theirs as well.

Rory was lying still now, her fists clenched in his coat, pulling it so tight that he could feel the zipper threatening to give. A quick glance back revealed Lynn right behind him, running like the hounds of hell were on her heels.

Which, in an almost literal sense, seemed to be the truth. Jess had gotten a look at their pursuers as they rushed through mist and shadow into the cold light of the moon. And he was stumped.

They resembled nothing human. As far as he could tell they had no faces, no features. They were just amorphous white forms, seemingly flying through the night.

He might even have allowed himself to believe they were evil spirits incarnate, except for one thing: Even as his gang of three gained the relative safety of the woods, their pursuers were producing automatic weapons.

Ghosts with guns? Not in this life.

18

THE SILENCE WAS MORE FRIGHTENING than a scream. Theresa was scared to death. So scared she couldn't move—could she?

She tried. Terror became her ally, forcing her cramped limbs to propel her in a crablike crawl over the dirt floor toward the glowing orange light that promised escape. She had only three limbs, because she kept one arm clamped around Elijah. Whatever happened she was not leaving him behind.

She could not bear to think that he was dead. Or that she had killed him.

Please, God, she prayed over and over again. Please, God, let it not be so.

She had not meant to kill him; she had meant to save him.

She had only wanted not to be killed herself. She was just sixteen! Dear God, she wanted to live!

She was afraid to die.

Death had gone. Theresa felt his absence. He was not in the cabin any longer. And he had taken his demons with him.

She hoped. No, she prayed.

As she reached the trapdoor she hesitated. Her breath rasped painfully in her throat. Tears made scalding tracks down her face. Fear almost paralyzed her. For a long, agonizing moment she huddled beneath the opening, listening.

What if Death was waiting for her up there after all?

She had to take the chance. If she didn't, she knew that she would die here in this cold, clammy root cellar. She would die of thirst, or starvation—or Death would get her.

If he was gone one thing was certain: Sooner or later he would be back.

Looking in the cellar again.

Holding Elijah against her shoulder, Theresa gathered her courage.

"Into your hands, Lord," she whispered finally, and giving herself up to His protection she climbed up on the crate that stood almost directly under the door. Crouching, she stared one more time up into the orangey glow.

Shadows chased each other across the plank ceiling in the room overhead. Shelves of canned goods she and her mother had put by for the winter looked eerily normal. The top of the aperture one passed through to get to the main room was adorned with a cobweb in the upper right corner. All glowed in the reflected light of the fire.

Hell as a keeping room.

Theresa stood up, her head thrusting into the open. For an instant she waited, tense and quivering, like a hunting dog scenting the air.

An oppressive silence greeted her, along with warm air redolent of burning wood and cinnamon and pine. The smell reminded her sharply, painfully, of her family.

What had become of them all? So many! Mother and Daddy, and the little girls. And her brothers.

Surely they could not all be dead?

She couldn't think about them now. Or Elijah.

But she could not bring herself to let Elijah go.

Strain though she might, Theresa heard nothing besides the cheery popping of the fire.

Taking a deep breath, she scrambled through the opening. She got to her feet, weak and dizzy, but she had no time to dwell on these physical shortcomings. She had to go, she had to try to escape, even if her chance of survival was slim.

A fearful glance around told her that the main room was empty. The door to the outside stood wide open.

It beckoned her. Though it might be a trap.

Even as she considered the possibility Theresa was running, running for the door, bursting out of the cabin into the night, welcoming the cold fresh air that hit her in the face because it meant she was free, free—

There they were: Death and his henchmen. They were moving away from her, very fast, toward the tall black wall that was the forest. If any one of them even glanced behind, she would be spotted. Theresa had no illusions that she could outrun them. They would be upon her like a pack of wolves, tearing her to shreds.

She dropped like a combat soldier in the face of enemy fire, belly-crawling through the tall weeds, dragging Elijah's limp body with her. Rocks and sharp sticks and thistles tore through her nightgown and ripped at her skin, but Theresa barely felt the pain. Every atom of her being was focused on making it across the open ground to the shelter of the abandoned silver mine carved out of the mountain more than a century before.

In there she would be safe—if any place in the world was safe, now that Death was loose among them.

Theresa had only about a hundred yards to go when her reaching hand touched flesh—cold, inanimate flesh. She glanced up and froze. Just inches to her right her cousin Zach lay dead. She was touching his cheek.

His eyes, hazel like her own, were open and staring, sightless. His skin was utterly white. Discolored rings had formed around his eyes.

His mouth was open too. A tiny trickle of blood—dried now— ran from one corner.

He was wearing his prized Orlando Magic jacket and the Nike high-tops he'd cadged from Theresa's oldest brother James.

His throat had been slit.

The dampness permeating the ground was mixed with his blood. She had crawled through it.

Theresa felt the gorge rise in her throat. Stomach convulsing, she vomited until there was nothing left inside her. Then, blindly, forgetting everything in the face of this newest horror, she lurched to her feet. Clutching Elijah close, she ran stumbling toward the entrance to the mine.

That she made it was nothing short of a miracle. The black gulf of the mine swallowed her up; her running feet echoed wildly, bouncing off the chiseled walls. She ran until she could run no farther.

Finally she collapsed in a sobbing, shivering heap, cradling Elijah like a rag doll on her lap.

19

THEY WERE BEATING THE FOREST for them. Panting, heart pounding, Lynn could hear them coming, not too far away, being methodical now, spreading out. Whoever they were, they were human. And they had guns.

Bullets strafed the forest as she, Rory, and Jess darted through the trees. The sound of them smacking into the wood reminded Lynn of the sound a hand makes when it strikes flesh. The resulting rush of adrenaline gave her a speed she'd never suspected she possessed.

Jess too. Though he had to be hampered by carrying Rory, who was flung over his shoulder with scant regard for either her injured state or her comfort, he ran like a star quarterback, leaping and dodging while Lynn zigzagged desperately in his wake.

Despite the deadly rat-a-tat-tat of gunfire all around them, they were putting distance between themselves and their pursuers. Lynn started to think they just might be able to get away.

"Ugh!"

She watched, uncomprehending, as Jess went sprawling. He fell heavily to his knees, groaning, clutching at his right shoulder as he rolled onto his side, vines crashing down around him.

Rory, sent flying by Jess's fall, lay prone in the undergrowth a few feet away. To Lynn's relief she rolled over and sat up, blinking. After a glance at Rory, who appeared unhurt, Lynn rushed to Jess and dropped down beside him.

He was wriggling free of his backpack. Even through the shadows she could see that his face was a mask of pain.

"You're bleeding," she said, staring stupidly down at the stain blossoming on his right shoulder. A small black hole pierced the silky gray fabric of his jacket. Blood welled from it; the dark, wet circle on the front of his jacket grew larger even as she looked at it.

"No shit, Sherlock," he grunted, pressing his hand against the stain. Lynn forgave him the sarcasm: The circumstances were dire, after all, and he was obviously hurting.

He lay on his back, breathing hard, his knees raised and bent. Vines were wrapped around his legs; his head crushed a small, moss-covered bush.

Rory crawled over to kneel beside Lynn. After a quick exchange of glances they both focused on Jess.

Bullets sprayed through the air over their heads, smacking into trees both near and far. Lynn threw her arms around Rory, bearing her down, bending protectively over her. Dislodged droplets from the earlier downpour showered them like rain.

The gunfire stopped. In its place Lynn could hear voices, though she couldn't distinguish the words. Their pursuers were growing dangerously close, she realized as she straightened.

Fear threatened to close her throat. She struggled to draw breath. Rory, sitting cross-legged now, clutched her mother's arm, looking as scared as Lynn felt. Jess stared up at both of them, white-faced.

"You and Rory run," he said.

Lynn glanced at her daughter. Rory's lips were trembling. Her eyes were enormous with fear. The bruising on her head was dark and ugly. For her daughter's sake Lynn was prepared to take to her heels, to flee with Rory and leave Jess to his fate.

But she was deathly afraid that Rory couldn't run fast or far enough.

"They'll catch us," she said, licking her lips.

Bullets sang in a wide arc around them. Shredded foliage fell. Lynn and Rory cowered, covering their heads. As the shooting stopped, Rory whimpered.

The sound galvanized Lynn. Whatever it took, she meant to save her daughter.

"We have to hide." She spoke in a hoarse whisper as she scrambled into a crouching position, glancing around wildly. Their pursuers were crashing through the undergrowth toward them. It would not be long before they were upon them. Fleeing was not an option. Wounded as Jess was, he could not carry Rory and might not be able to run himself. Besides, the pursuers were too close. If they could not actually see the three of them take flight, they certainly would hear them.

Everywhere Lynn looked, moss, faintly shiny and phosphorescent in the gloom, lay in undulating waves over the undergrowth. To her left it formed a thick layer over a pyramid of deadwood.

Would the pursuers notice three more moss-covered logs among so many?

"There," she said, pointing, grabbing Rory's arm. "Get behind those logs and lie down."

Rory stared at her stupidly.

"Move!" Lynn shoved her daughter toward the hiding place, then reached down to lend a hand to Jess.

"Go!" He brushed her hand aside as he rolled into a crouching position. "I'm right behind you. Go on."

His voice sounded strained, but Lynn had no time to worry about him as she scrambled after Rory. A glance back showed that he was following at a crouching lope, his pack hooked over his uninjured shoulder.

Rory was kneeling, her face a pale oval in the gloom, digging at the moss like a dog burying a bone. Lynn shoved her down on the ground face-first and began to pull fistfuls of moss over her. To her surprise and relief, the moss came away in great intact sheets.

Bullets whined overhead. Time was running out.

Lynn shed her own pack and threw herself down beside Rory, wriggling close, squirming beneath the moss. It was cold and damp under there, and it smelled of earth. Reaching for her pack, knowing she had to hide it too, she pulled it in near her head.

More moss landed on her legs and feet. At about the same instant that she realized Jess was piling moss over her and Rory, he lay down and wriggled beneath the moss that covered them like a blanket. He rolled almost on top of them, shielding their bodies with his, crushing them between the outermost log and the ground as he pulled layers of moss over himself. Something silver clutched in his fist caught her eye. Lynn realized that he had armed himself with their one weapon: his knife.

Not that a knife would be much use against rifles. Unless he could catch one of their pursuers off guard and up close.

A trickle of fresh air past her nose told Lynn that there were gaps in the moss layers that concealed them. She suspected that parts of herself and Rory and Jess were still visible. If *she* were looking at the lump that was the three of them, she doubted that she would mistake them for mossy logs for so much as an instant.

Thank God for the darkness, Lynn thought. It was their best hope.

More bullets whistling overhead made Lynn cringe. She clung to Rory. Jess sprawled atop them both.

Closer and closer at hand, foliage rustled violently as their pursuers crashed through it.

Raw fear pushed out every other emotion. Rory trembled in Lynn's arms, her breathing shallow and frightened. Jess pushed them deeper into the thick mulch of rotting plants and pine needles. His weight made it hard for Lynn to breathe. Still, she welcomed the pressure of his body. He might provide only an illusion of protection, but an illusion was better than nothing at all.

Running feet thudded over the ground less than a yard from where they lay. Lynn felt Rory jerk spasmodically; she pressed her fingers against her daughter's lips. Against her back she could feel Jess tense. The arm holding the knife went rigid.

If they were going to be discovered it would be now.

Closing her eyes tight, Lynn prayed.

The footsteps ran on by.

It was a few seconds before she remembered to breathe again.

For what seemed like hours they lay there, listening as their pursuers ranged through the forest in search of them. The occasional rattle of gunfire spoke perhaps of deer or other nocturnal creatures disturbed and fired upon by mistake. Once something, or someone, passed so close to their hiding place that Lynn could have reached out and grabbed its leg.

Human or animal she could not be certain, though she suspected the latter. All she knew was it was running. Something that every atom of her being urged her to do.

Except her mind. That warned her to stay still.

Rory trembled in her arms. Lynn discovered that she was shaking too. She hoped her daughter would not feel her tremors or know them for what they were if she did. If Rory knew how frightened her mother was, she would be doubly terrified.

It was a universal truth: Mothers were not supposed to be afraid.

Jess shifted. The knife blade sank into the earth near Lynn's shoulder and the knife was left to stand alone. Jess's arm wrapped around Lynn's waist, holding her tight. His body was warm and strong against her back; his breath tickled her ear.

"We're going to be all right," he whispered, the words scarcely louder than a breath. Lynn realized that he, at least, had felt her tremors and was offering what comfort he could.

Against all reason, Lynn felt comforted. Gradually her tremors ceased.

Beyond their hiding place the forest grew quiet. Lynn could no longer hear their pursuers—or their guns. Maybe they'd gone—or maybe not. Maybe they were waiting, hoping that silence would lure out the prey.

Rory squirmed. Lynn realized that she must be uncomfortable and eased back a degree. Jess shifted too, rolling onto his back. The arm around Lynn's waist slid away.

For a moment she felt almost bereft.

Jess quit moving. For a fraction of a second he lay like a stone. Then he pressed close again, pushing her and Rory down into the loam, reaching for the knife.

"Shh," he said.

Instantly Lynn went as still as a rabbit at the sight of a hound.

A soft footstep, followed by another, then another, broke the silence. Someone was creeping through the undergrowth just beyond where they lay.

Lynn's pulse pounded so loudly that she could hear nothing over the drumming of her own blood in her ears.

The stealth of the movements told its own tale: There would be no reason for such care if the pursuers did not suspect the presence of their prey.

Moments passed, seemingly endless.

Without warning Jess rolled away from her again. His absence left her cold and exposed—and afraid.

Lynn glanced around to see what he was up to. He crouched nearby, bits of moss clinging to his back and head like great hairy spiders. His left hand gripped the knife.

He turned his head, met her gaze.

"It's okay," he said in a near-normal voice. "They're gone."

"How do you know?" Lynn whispered. Not that she didn't trust him, but . . .

"Look." He nodded. When Lynn's gaze followed the direction of that nod, she saw what he was looking at: a trio of mule deer now some distance away, picking their way through the trees, moving as quietly as shadows. "See?"

Lynn realized that if men with guns had been anywhere near, the deer would not have been moving with such quiet grace. They would have been running for their lives.

"Mom." Rory turned her head in Lynn's direction. "Are we safe?"

"Yes, baby." Lynn gave her daughter a quick hug before rolling into a sitting position. "We're safe."

For now, she thought.

The glance Jess sent her brimmed with disagreement, but he said nothing as he folded the knife and tucked it into an outer pocket on his pack.

"I want to go home." Rory sat up, brushing moss out of her hair with both hands. Her voice trembled.

"You and me both." Lynn's answer was heartfelt.

"I guess that makes it unanimous," Jess said dryly. He was grimacing as he felt inside his jacket. A moment later he withdrew his hand; his fingertips looked black.

Blood.

"How bad is it?" she asked. The stain was now as big as a dinner plate.

"I'll live."

"Who *are* those guys?" Rory's question was indignant and despairing at the same time.

"I don't know, and right now I don't think we need to worry about it." Jess gave Rory a quick, crooked smile. "Let's just think of them as the bad guys. We'll work on figuring out who they really are when they're a long way behind us."

"They killed those people." Rory sounded on the verge of hysteria.

"Well, they're not going to kill us," Lynn said firmly, brushing moss off her daughter's back. "They're gone."

"Which is what we should be," Jess said. "Come on, let's get moving."

He stood up, dragging his pack with him, draping it over his uninjured shoulder.

"Your wound . . ." Lynn said, standing, wondering if the hole needed to be bandaged or something. Her knees felt shaky, and for a moment she thought she was going to have to sit down again. With a glance at her companions she willed the weakness away.

It was unsettling to realize that she was the only one who was not injured.

"It's nothing," Jess said impatiently. "Rory, do you think you can make it on your own?"

"I—I think so."

"Then let's go."

Lynn was still struggling into her pack when he started walking.

She gave the pack a final hitch, draped an arm around Rory, and followed.

They walked for a long time, taking a route that seemed to be roughly perpendicular to the one that had brought them to the

clearing. Lynn realized that following the goat trail would probably have been suicidal, but without a path the forest was all but
impassable in places. The undergrowth was waist-high everywhere, and so thick that they had to struggle for each step. Jess
broke trail and Lynn followed with Rory, who grew perceptibly
weaker as minutes turned into an hour and more.

At night the forest had its own silence. The carpet of moss
grew thicker, a foot deep or more in places, and covered everything, even hanging from the lower branches of trees. Footfalls
made no sound. Voices, human or animal, did not carry.

The scent of pine sap hung heavy in the air. The no-see-ums
attacked mercilessly, like tiny sharks in the grip of a feeding
frenzy.

At least, Lynn thought, misery and exhaustion were great anti-
dotes to terror.

"Can't we please stop?" Rory moaned at last. She had been
leaning more and more heavily on Lynn, who realized that the
child was about at the end of her rope.

"Jess!" she called, only a smidgen louder than Rory's muted
whisper. But he heard.

"We're almost there," he said without looking around. "Just a
little farther."

Jess forged onward without so much as breaking stride.
Watching the charcoal gray of his coat become one with the
shifting shadows, Lynn and Rory exchanged despairing glances
and started walking again, arm in arm.

"My head hurts." Rory slumped heavily against Lynn's side.

"I know, baby. Just a little farther, and then we can rest."

Rory said nothing more. Lynn could feel her daughter's
strength dwindling.

Why, oh, why, Lynn asked herself, hadn't she followed her
first instinct and turned thumbs-down on the trip when it was
presented to her? She would be at the station right now, or
maybe on that cruise ship in the Caribbean if she had opted for a
vacation after all, and Rory would be safe at home with her
grandmother, playing video games or watching TV. Or maybe
spending the night at Jenny's.

And if wishes were horses, beggars would ride.

At last Jess stopped. The were within a few feet of a steep, rocky slope that rose past the whispering branches to disappear into the mist. A cliff, in fact, much like the one that had brought them to their current pass.

Leaning against the thick trunk of a mighty ponderosa pine, Jess pointed without speaking to the base of the cliff. Lynn drooped with exhaustion, holding Rory up because she was afraid that if either of them sat they would never get up again. She looked where he had pointed and saw a black semicircular opening in the rock wall, just big enough for a human to crawl through.

"In there," he said. "Then we'll rest."

That was all Lynn needed to hear. Too tired to worry much about bears or bats or anything else that might be inside, she helped Rory over to the cliff.

Lynn entered first. Dropping to her knees, she crawled through the hole. Outside, the moss was spongy and damp beneath her palms. Inside, the ground was hard, cold rock, thick with dust and pebbles. Lynn moved with care, trying vainly to see through the inky blackness. The cave smelled of mold, and the space was small. Trying to stand up, she bumped her head; the ceiling was less than five feet high.

Rory crawled in behind her. Crouching, Lynn reached back to guide and reassure her daughter. With Rory beside her she watched as Jess appeared in the opening, pushing his pack inside before following.

For a moment he was silhouetted by silvery moonlight. His shoulders were broad enough so that he had to turn sideways to fit them through the hole. Maneuvering with a surprising degree of clumsiness, he managed to get inside the cave.

He balanced precariously on three limbs. His head went down, his back heaved, and he made a violent retching sound. Then he collapsed and lay still.

20

"Jess!" It was an urgent whisper. Lynn knelt beside Jess's prone form, with Rory beside her. "Jess!"

She nudged his uninjured shoulder. Still no reply.

"Is he dead?" Rory asked fearfully.

"I think he fainted," Lynn replied. Her hand slid along the back of his jacket. The area around his right shoulder blade was wet, warm, and sticky: blood.

"He threw up." Rory sounded repulsed. "Gross."

Lynn made a sound that was part snort, part laugh. "I guess if you'd been shot, you might throw up too."

Lynn located Jess's ear by touch and laid her fingers below it, against the pulse in his neck. His skin was warm and bristly with five-o'clock shadow. His heart pumped with a strong, steady beat, relieving some of her anxiety. Undoubtedly, that strong pumping was one of the reasons for the amount of blood he still seemed to be losing.

The bleeding needed to be stopped and the wound bandaged. There was a first-aid kit in her pack with gauze and pads and all the necessary materials to do just that—but it was so dark inside the cave that she could not even see Rory, who was right beside her.

How could she bandage a wound she couldn't see? Their flashlight was long gone; she had dropped it when they fled the mining camp.

First things first.

"Let's move him away from the mess," she said.

"Sick," Rory muttered, but she helped Lynn drag Jess deeper into the cave, away from the puddle of vomit. It wasn't an easy task, and when they had finished, both were panting.

"He weighs a *ton*." Rory was sounding less enamored of Jess by the second.

"Wait here with him a minute, will you?"

Lynn scooped dust and gravel over the mess as best she could, then fetched the packs. Unzipping Jess's, she searched out the lighter by feel. Next she located the first-aid kit. Placing the kit at her knee, she lifted the lighter, bent over Jess—and hesitated.

The light might give them away.

Lynn was not sure whether the tiny flame produced by the lighter was of sufficient strength to illuminate the cave opening. Nor was she sure whether the amount of light would be enough to attract attention, or even if there was anyone near enough to see.

But she sure didn't want to take the chance.

Shoving the lighter in her jeans pocket, she decided to do what she could by touch. Anything more elaborate would have to wait for the coming of day.

"Help me turn him over," she said to her daughter.

"Can't we have some light?" Rory sounded very young suddenly. She had always been afraid of the dark.

"No." Lynn didn't spell out why, but Rory didn't argue. Between them they managed to flip Jess onto his back. Lynn felt for his coat zipper, pulled it down.

Jess groaned, stirring.

"It's all right. I'm just going to bandage your wound," Lynn said, in case he could hear.

"In the dark?" His voice was low and ragged, but at least he was conscious.

"You threw up." Rory sounded accusing.

"Sorry."

Lynn wasn't sure if there was a touch of amusement in his answer or if she was imagining it.

"I'm afraid to use any kind of light," she told him.

"Smart thinking."

If Jess thought being bandaged in the dark was smart thinking, Lynn was doubly glad she hadn't flicked on the lighter. He must believe that their pursuers were still on the hunt.

Did she? Lynn wondered. Surely she didn't imagine that they were simply going to give up and go away.

It was a nice thought. Get real, she said to herself.

As Lynn tugged at the sleeve of his goose-down jacket, Jess managed to shrug his arm out of it. Then he made a movement to sit up.

"Stay still." Lynn pressed him back down, her hand firmly in the center of his chest. The front of his T-shirt was sticky and wet with blood. He subsided without protest. "I don't think you ought to move around much until we get this bandaged. You've lost a lot of blood."

"You might throw up again," Rory said.

"I'll try not to." This time there was no mistake: Though his voice was weak, there *was* amusement in it. Clearly he recognized that Rory, with her impossible, girlish notions of what a man should be, was feeling disillusioned.

"Put this under your head." Lynn wadded up the discarded jacket, bloodied side in, and slid it under Jess's head.

"Thanks."

Was it her imagination or was his voice growing weaker? She needed to get his wound bandaged quickly. If he should become incapacitated, from loss of blood or for any other reason, she didn't know what she would do. There was no way she and Rory could move him very far.

"Rory, get him some water, would you?"

"Sure, Mom." Rory rummaged in the packs.

"How'd you know I was thirsty?" It wasn't her imagination. Jess did sound weaker.

"ESP."

To orient herself, Lynn touched his cheek, which, like his neck, felt warm and prickly with stubble. Her hand moved down to his chin, then his throat, and finally reached the soft cotton at the base of his neck.

"Your shirt needs to come off." Her hands moved toward his waist as she spoke, and she began to tug the T-shirt free of his jeans.

"I can manage," he said, his hands there before hers.

"I'll do it. You need to lie still," she said, brushing his hands aside, voice crisp because suddenly she felt self-conscious. Rory's big-eared presence had something to do with that—it was difficult to undress a man, even for such a compelling reason, in the presence of one's teenage daughter—but not everything. Helping Jess take his shirt off simply seemed like too intimate an act.

It was something a woman did for her child—or her lover.

Now who was being ridiculous? she asked herself. The man was hurt, and he needed help. Period.

The tempo of his breathing increased as her hands slid the hem of his T-shirt over his chest. In different circumstances she might have attributed the changes in his rate of respiration to her powers of arousal, but in this case she was pretty sure his rasping could be chalked up to pain.

Nevertheless, she could not help noticing the body she bared. He had a nice abdomen, she discovered as her hands brushed it, all taut skin and hard muscle with a silky trail of hair disappearing into his waistband. And a nice chest too, wide and warm and firm, with its own wedge of silky hair. Or at least the hair would have been silky if it had not been matted with blood.

"Be careful, would you?" he grunted as she reached the critical area. Lynn discovered that some of the blood had started to dry, gluing the cotton T-shirt to his body.

"Here's the water." Rory thrust a cool plastic bottle against Lynn's cheek.

"Thanks," Lynn said, taking the bottle.

"Where?" Jess asked at the same time. Lynn twisted off the lid and pressed the bottle into his good hand.

"Do you need help to drink?"

"No."

She heard him swallowing water. Gently, gently, she tried to disengage the shirt from his person without hurting him more than she had to.

"Ouch!" he said, choking on what must have been a too-greedy gulp.

"It's stuck."

"Well, don't yank! Here!" He poured some of the water over the problematic spot. Lynn wasn't sure that he was doing the right thing, but sure enough, her searching fingers told her that the water seemed to work, liquefying the drying blood.

"Ouch!" He gasped this time as she succeeded in pulling his shirt free of the wound.

"I thought it was unstuck," Lynn said.

"You thought wrong."

"I need you to raise up so I can get your shirt off. Rory, help me lift him."

"I can sit up."

He suited the action to the words before Lynn could stop him.

"Can you lift your arms?"

"Not the right one."

Lynn eased the T-shirt up his left arm and over his head, then pulled it down his right arm.

Before the operation was completed, Jess was leaning heavily against her, his good shoulder pressing into her breasts, breathing harder than ever. She could feel the increasing heat of his body, smell his sudden outbreak of perspiration, and she realized that he was in more pain than he was letting on.

The T-shirt came off at last. He sighed with relief as she let it drop to the ground.

"My head hurts," Rory said, her voice subdued.

"I know, baby. Why don't you lie down for a minute and see if that helps?" Lynn's hands were on Jess's back, feeling their way around. It, too, was warm and wide and hard of muscle—and wet with blood.

A rustling sound told Lynn that Rory was complying with her suggestion. Under the circumstances a headache was only to be expected, Lynn reassured herself. Anyway, there was nothing she could do for Rory at the moment.

Jess, on the other hand, needed her help urgently.

"Can you lie on your side? Your left side," she specified to Jess.

He grunted by way of a reply. Lynn kept her hands on him as he lay back down, on his uninjured side as requested. Once he was settled she reached for the first-aid kit.

During her earlier search for cigarettes she had opened the small plastic box to check out the contents. Now she was profoundly glad that she had. She knew what was in there, basically, and could identify the contents by feel: sterile pads in their paper wrappers, a roll of gauze, a tube of antiseptic ointment. Scissors. Tape. Even Tylenol.

"Maybe you should take a couple of Tylenol," Lynn suggested, rattling the bottle.

Jess snorted. "Honey, I could take the whole bottle and it wouldn't make a dent."

"Do you hurt a lot?" Rory asked.

"Some."

That Jess was admitting to hurting at all told Lynn that her suspicions were correct: He was in a great deal of pain. She wrestled with the lid of the childproof bottle.

"Rory, can you open this?" Lynn gave up and passed the bottle to her daughter. From the age of three onward, Rory had managed to open every childproof container that had come her way. Lynn, on the other hand, was hopeless at it. While Rory worked on the bottle cap, Lynn fished another water bottle from the pack.

"Here, Mom." Rory returned the open bottle, along with the lid. Lynn positioned the lid on her knee and shook two gel caps into her palm.

"You take these, for your head." She passed the gel caps to Rory, along with the water, and shook out two more.

"And you"—she prodded Jess's mouth with an index finger—"open up."

He obeyed, and she popped the pills in. As she twisted the lid back on the bottle and returned it to the first-aid kit, she heard him swallowing water again.

Rory was quiet—resting, probably. Lynn freed a gauze pad from its packaging, smeared antibiotic on it, and gingerly felt Jess's shoulder to locate the wound.

"Ouch!" He flinched. The swelling flesh all around it helped Lynn to find the raised edge of the bullet hole. It was high on his shoulder. Good. Given its location, the bullet had hit nothing vital.

She pressed the gauze pad firmly against it.

"Yeow!"

"Shh!" The sudden yelp made Lynn jump. "Don't be such a baby," she added crossly.

"Baby, my ass," Jess muttered. "That hurt!"

"Hold this for a minute. I need to see if there's a hole in your back." She found his left hand, guiding it to the pad.

"Can't you just bandage it up?"

"You already passed out once," Lynn reminded him, her fingertips feather-light as they moved over his bloody shoulder blade. "From blood loss, I'm sure. If I don't bandage this up right, who knows? You might even bleed to death."

Jess was silent.

"I've got it." She found another raised edge, sticky with gore. The bullet had passed all the way through, which, she thought as she smeared a second pad with antibiotic, was a good thing. She couldn't imagine herself performing emergency surgery on Jess to remove the bullet—especially in the dark.

She had an even harder time imagining him letting her. At the thought of what his reaction to such a suggestion would be, Lynn had to smile.

"Could you hurry up?"

"Sure," Lynn said, and pressed the pad to the wound with a tad more force than was strictly necessary.

"Ow!"

"You can move your hand." She slid her hand under Jess's. Palms flat, she applied direct pressure to both sides of the wound at once.

"Damn, that hurts." He sounded like he was having trouble catching his breath.

"It'll be over in a minute. Stay still."

Blood soaked both pads. Lynn could feel the sticky wetness against her palms. She layered on more pads and applied pressure again. When the bleeding started to let up, Lynn taped the pads in place and wrapped Jess's shoulder and chest in layers of gauze.

"There," she said, finishing at last. "All done."

"Thank God."

Lynn had not realized how tense Jess's muscles were until she felt them relax.

"Is it safe for us to go to sleep, do you think? For a little while?" Rory's voice was small and tired.

"Absolutely." Jess's reassurance sounded too hearty to Lynn, but she hoped her daughter was too young or too tired to pick up on the false note. "We're going to be okay, Rory, I promise. We'll sleep the rest of the night, meet the Jeep tomorrow, and be safe on the ranch this time tomorrow night."

You hope, Lynn added silently, but she didn't say it.

There was no point in scaring Rory any more.

"What if they find us?" Rory's voice was smaller yet.

"They won't," Lynn said, proud of how certain she sounded.

"Your mom's right," Jess said. "The forest is too wild and the entrance to this place is too well hidden. You have to know where it is."

Rory yawned, hugely, the sound so familiar that it made Lynn ache.

"I'll get the sleeping bags," she said. There were two, tied to the bottoms of the packs. Lynn presumed three would have been too cumbersome to carry. Not that it mattered, she thought as she rolled them out side by side. They were plenty big enough for her to share one with Rory.

She unzipped Jess's for him and would have bundled him into it if he had not spurned her offer of help.

"I can manage," he said. "Get some sleep yourself."

Lynn suddenly realized how exhausted she was. Rory was already snug in their bag. As Lynn pulled off her boots and squirmed in beside Rory, she welcomed her daughter's warmth.

She kissed her daughter's cheek, then fell asleep to the sound of Jess's sleeping bag being zipped up.

21

"No! Christ, no!"

Lynn woke to those words. They weren't loud, more of a thick mutter that trailed off into incoherence. But under the circumstances they were enough to blast her from sleep.

For a moment she lay paralyzed, staring wide-eyed into the oppressive blackness and seeing nothing. Sounds assaulted her: anguished mumbling, soft thudding movements, heavy breathing.

Was Jess being attacked?

He was close; his sleeping bag was right beside the one in which she and Rory lay. If he was fighting off an attacker, there was no way she could be unaware of the intruder's presence.

Jess was having a nightmare.

After the day they'd had, she wasn't surprised.

Lynn turned on her side, careful not to disturb Rory, whose even breathing spoke of deep sleep. Unzipping the bag enough to get her hand out, she reached out to Jess.

What she touched was his chin, sandpaper-rough. She lost contact as his head moved. The murmurs grew louder.

She unzipped her sleeping bag, scrambled out, and leaned over him.

Though she could see nothing she could hear his restless movements. His hair was surprisingly soft, she found as she tried to awaken him by touch. When her gentle nudge had no effect she ran her fingers over his face, trying to determine if he was awake, asleep, or unconscious. His forehead was warm and damp with sweat. His brows were thick. The bridge of his nose was hard and finely chiseled. His cheekbones were hard, too, and prominent. His lips were soft, his cheeks and chin whiskery.

His breath fluttered past her hand. His head tossed from side to side. He said something that she could not understand.

"Jess." Whispering, she patted his cheek. "Jess."

Without warning her wrist was seized in a grip like iron. She jumped.

"Jess!"

"Oh, it's you." He didn't sound particularly thrilled about the idea. "What?"

"You were having a nightmare."

"So?" The single-word question was surly.

"So you were talking in your sleep."

"So?"

"So shut up," Lynn said, goaded. "And let go of my wrist."

He let go. "Is Rory awake?"

"No."

"Then go back to sleep. We've got a little while yet before we have to get moving."

"Will they still be looking for us, do you think? In the morning, I mean?"

"Yes."

Lynn shivered. She'd known that, of course, but she hated having him confirm it. The danger had begun to seem like nothing more than a horrible bad dream. Now it was real again.

"Are you in pain?"

"What do you think?"

"Do you want another Tylenol?"

"No."

Lynn was silent for a moment.

"Jess?"

"Hmm?"

"Do you have some kind of plan for getting us out of this alive?"

"What, are you planning to sue Adventure, Inc. if I don't?"

"Yes."

"Posthumously, I guess. Big on plans, aren't you?"

"Do you have one, or not?"

"Yup."

"What?"

"If we come across those guys again, we run like hell."

"I'm serious!"

"So am I."

Lynn glowered, though of course he couldn't see her expression in the dark. He couldn't see her, period. And she couldn't see him, though she was kneeling beside his sleeping bag, her knees nudging his body through the soft padding.

Clearly, if there was to be a plan she was going to have to come up with it herself. If she left it to this big dumb cowboy, she deserved what she got.

"What we have to do is get to where your brother will be waiting with the Jeep. Once we're on the road we'll head straight for a phone and call the police." She was thinking aloud.

"Brilliant." Sarcasm came through loud and clear.

"You're welcome to come up with an alternative." Under the circumstances Lynn didn't appreciate his tone. His life was on the line here too. "If you can."

"You're doing fine."

"Okay." Lynn took a deep breath. "How far do we have to go? To where we meet the Jeep, I mean."

"About eight miles."

"That far?" Lynn chewed her lower lip. "The problem is that they're still out there looking for us."

"Brilliant again."

"You're a big fat lot of help."

"I've got it covered, okay? I've got a *plan*. So relax and go back to sleep."

"You do?"

"Yup."

"What?" Her distrust came through loud and clear.

"Christ, are you anal or what? I bet you make lists. I bet you get up every freaking morning and write down everything you have to do for the day and check it off when it's done. I bet you set aside a certain time to return phone calls. I bet your closet is organized by color. I bet your *bookshelves* are alphabetized."

That was so close to the truth that Lynn flushed.

"What's wrong with that?" she asked defensively.

"Not a thing. Trust me, will you? I can get us to the Jeep without being seen."

"Sure?"

"Guar-an-teed."

Lynn said nothing. She didn't believe him, though she wanted to badly. He couldn't guarantee their safety. No one could. But since he knew the area and she didn't, since he was more at home in the wilderness than she was, since he was part owner of the outfit responsible for her and Rory's safety, she was going to follow his lead.

For the time being anyway. She was quiet for a few minutes, coming to terms with that.

"Jess?"

"What now?"

"The man on the cross—" Lynn shuddered at the memory. "What do you think that means?"

"That there are some real sickos in the world."

Lynn shot him a disgusted glance, which he could not see, of course. "It must have been some kind of ritual killing, don't you think?"

"I don't know. Look, go back to sleep, would you?"

"I can't sleep. I keep seeing that man—and that woman. And the boy."

"*I* can sleep."

"No, you can't. You were having a nightmare. That's not sleeping."

"Works for me."

Lynn didn't answer, but she couldn't bring herself to move.

Having slept off the worst of her exhaustion, she no longer had any inclination to close her eyes. If she did, images of the murders would only rise up to haunt her. They were horrifying; it was too easy to imagine herself and Rory in the victims' places.

She needed distraction to keep her from remembering and then degenerating into a trembling puddle of incoherent fear as she acknowledged that she and Rory—and Jess—were in terrible danger of joining those victims still.

For all their sakes she needed to stay calm. Jess might have the brawn necessary to get them to safety, but she doubted that he had the brain. If, as she had learned on the job, anxiety was crippling to creative thinking, consider how much more crippling abject terror must be.

A cigarette would go a long way toward calming her, but she didn't have a cigarette. Shifting so that she was sitting cross-legged, her hands resting in her lap, Lynn closed her eyes and resorted to the next best thing.

"Om," she chanted softly, concentrating. "Om."

"What the hell is that?" Jess demanded.

Lynn opened one eye. "I'm meditating."

"Jesus Christ."

Lynn opened both eyes. "Do you have a problem with that?"

"Loonies to the left of me, loonies to the right . . ." he sang under his breath, to the tune of "Stuck in the Middle with You."

"Are you implying that meditating makes me a loony?"

"Not just meditating, no."

Lynn absorbed the implications of that. "Oh, yeah? Well, if you ask me it's better to meditate than to spend your life swaggering around doing a bad imitation of Little Joe Cartwright, complete with boots and a big ole cowboy hat. *Like a rhinestone cowboy . . ."* She launched into an abbreviated, barely-above-a-whisper rendition of Glen Campbell's song to retaliate for his earlier stab at musical entertainment.

"Are we talking about truth in advertising here?" he asked when she was finished.

"I'd say that's what we're talking about, yes."

"Then let me say this: At least I don't wear a Wonderbra."

"What?" Lynn's jaw dropped. "Are you implying that I do?"

"I'm not implying anything. I'm saying I know what I saw. It works great, by the way. Makes you look like you have a lot more up top than you really do."

"I have plenty up top!"

"You do?" A hint of amusement in his voice stopped her cold. Lynn realized that she was being led down a path she didn't want to travel.

"Why don't you just shut up and go to sleep?"

"With pleasure." Jess shifted and was obediently silent. Lynn closed her eyes again and tried to meditate—making sure this time that the chant was inaudible—but she couldn't get into the spirit of it.

Loonies to the left of me, loonies to the right . . . The ridiculous paraphrase kept running through her mind, interrupting her concentration.

The state of relaxation she was striving for wasn't going to happen, Lynn realized. Not tonight, not under these conditions. Her eyes opened, to see exactly nothing.

She was all alone in the cold, scary dark, with both her companions asleep.

Maybe.

"Jess?"

"Are you still there?"

"Are you still bleeding? Can you tell?" she asked.

"I'm *sleeping.*" There was a pause. "The bandage is dry."

"Good. We can't get out of here without you, you know. I don't know where we're going."

"Or you would have left me back there when I got shot. I know." There was grim humor in the words.

"Well, no, of course not. But I have to take care of Rory. She comes first."

"Motherly love." He shifted. "You love her, she loves you. So what's this thing you two have going on where you're always fighting?"

Lynn shrugged, then realized again that he could not see in the dark. "She's a teenager. What can I say?"

"So?"

"You don't have kids, do you?" It was a world-weary query from a seen-it-all mother to a nonparent.

"Actually, I do. I have two girls, eight and ten."

"You're kidding."

"Don't sound so surprised. I'm thirty-five years old. How many men get to be thirty-five without having kids?"

"You're thirty-five?"

"Yeah."

"You don't look it. You don't act it either."

"Thanks. You don't look thirty-five yourself. But you sure do act it. Fifty-five, more like."

"Meaning?" Lynn bristled.

"You need to lighten up—especially on Rory. For Christ's sake, you dog every step she takes."

"I do not!"

"You're here, aren't you?" He said that as if it were incontrovertible evidence; Lynn knew he referred to her presence as one of the chaperons.

"That's because—" she began heatedly, then stopped.

"Because . . ." he prompted.

"Because . . . nothing. You're not really interested, and I don't want to talk about it."

"If you're not going to let me go back to sleep, we've got nothing better to do than talk for a while. And I *am* interested. Tell me, why would a woman like you come on a trip like this when you didn't have to?"

"What do you mean, a woman like me?"

"Christ, you have a manicure! You put on lipstick every morning before we head out! You powder your nose before you get in the saddle! And you can't even ride a horse! I bet you've never camped out before in your life."

"So?"

"So why'd you come?"

"I came for Rory, of course."

"Why?"

"Because she's my daughter, and I love her!"

"And?" Jess probed.

"And because we haven't been getting along well lately," Lynn said, finally giving up. It was a relief to admit it. Since she couldn't see him, since he was nothing more than a low, rough-edged voice in the dark, he was surprisingly easy to confide in.

"My guess is you haven't been getting along because you over-protect her." Jess's summation was dry.

"It isn't that so much as it is . . ." Lynn hesitated. "I'm gone a lot. I have to work."

Lynn heard the defensive note in her own voice, and flinched.

"Everybody has to work." Jess's tone was surprisingly under-standing. "So she's mad at you because you're gone a lot. What do you do, leave her alone?"

"No! My mother lives with us—Rory's never left alone."

"So what's the problem then?"

The truth came out in a rush, exquisitely painful. "She blames me because her father's not in her life. Sometimes I think she hates me for it." The total absence of vision was seductive. Never in her life would Lynn have imagined that she would con-fess that to anyone—much less to Jess Feldman, superstud.

"Ah."

"She never knew her father."

"You divorced him when she was a baby?"

Lynn's voice dropped until it was just above a murmur. Rory's breathing was even and untroubled. The sound of it reassured Lynn: Rory had always slept the sleep of the dead.

Lynn didn't want her daughter overhearing this.

"He walked out on me when I told him I was pregnant. He's never even seen her."

"She blames you for that?"

Lynn moved, pulling her legs up to her chest and wrapping her arms around them. Her chin dropped to her knees. She had a sudden, intense craving for a cigarette.

"Yes."

"Is it your fault?"

"No. Well, maybe. Some." Lynn took a deep breath. "I'd only known him six weeks when we got married. I don't know what I was thinking. I was young, you know? And stupid. Just twenty-one, just getting ready to graduate from college. He was a med student, in his first year. He was smart and handsome and he was going to be a doctor—who could ask for anything more? We were really happy too—until I found out I was pregnant. Kids weren't on his agenda right then, he said; his whole focus had to be on getting through medical school, and mine had to be on supporting us financially until he got out and we got on our feet. The bottom line is, he wanted me to get an abortion. When I wouldn't he walked out. I got a divorce, I had Rory, and I went to work. My mother—my father died when I was in college—moved in with us to take care of Rory. And that's the way it's been ever since."

"Does he pay child support?"

Lynn shook her head, then realized again that he could not see. "I never asked for any. Of course, he couldn't have paid any when we got divorced; I was the one with the job. He was in school. But I didn't want to see him—and I didn't want him to see Rory. Not that he ever tried. I never realized how it would affect her—until she was about nine and started really asking about him. Finally I got in touch with him. He was a doctor by then, with a new wife and a new family. He said he didn't want to hear anything about Rory, that I'd chosen to have her without his consent and she was mine, not his. And he hung up. I've called a few times since, and written too. He doesn't want to know."

"So how can Rory blame you for that?"

Lynn shut her eyes. "I couldn't tell her that her father didn't want to see her, didn't even care enough to speak to her on the phone or send her a birthday card. If she knew that it would crush her. She has this fantasy built up—this fantasy that he loves her, that the only reason he hasn't contacted her is because he hates me."

"So you're the bad guy."

Lynn grimaced. "I'm what's standing between her and her fantasy father."

"So she comes on to men old enough to *be* her father, trying to replace him."

Surprised at his perception, she opened her mouth to ask how he could possibly know that—then realized that of course he would know. He wasn't stupid, and the psychology of it was obvious. Besides, Rory had been coming on to him. Lynn had merely filled in the *why*.

"Yes," she said miserably.

"And to punish you, I'd imagine."

"I think that's part of it, yes."

"You need to tell her the truth."

"I can't!" Lynn shuddered at the prospect.

"Suit yourself. But she's carrying around a whole wagonload of anger, and it's not going to just up and vanish one day. You need to tell her the truth and let her deal with it. Accepting the world as it is, instead of as you wish it were, is part of growing up."

"Thank you, Dr. Feldman," Lynn said. "What are you, some kind of lay psychiatrist?"

"Actually, I minored in psychology. I just never got around to hanging up my shingle."

"In college? *You* went to college?" Lynn was glad to be distracted from talking about Rory.

"Why does that surprise you?"

"I just never knew there was a college for turning out fake cowboys."

"Ha, ha. That's very funny."

"Seriously, where did you go?"

"Brigham Young."

"You're joking."

"I am not joking. Why should I be?"

"Somehow I just can't picture you . . . never mind. You went to Brigham Young University, and you minored in psychology. What did you major in?"

"Criminal justice."

"Criminal justice?" Lynn's voice rose with incredulity on the last word. "Did you get a degree?"

"Sure I did."

"And you became a fake-cowboy tour guide?" Incredulity still colored her voice.

"Actually, the first thing I did was go to work for the federal government."

"Doing what?"

His answers were coming slower now, and Lynn got the impression he was in some way reluctant to continue.

"I was an ATF agent."

"A what?"

"An agent for the Bureau of Alcohol, Tobacco, and Firearms."

"For how long?"

"Nine years."

"Then you quit being a federal agent to become a fake cowboy?"

"Would you please stop with the fake-cowboy crap? It's a business, okay? Owen and I make a good living at it. I quit . . . because I didn't like what I was doing anymore."

"Why not?"

"Can we just forget this? I don't feel like talking about it."

"Hey, I told you my life story. It's your turn. Why didn't you like what you were doing anymore?"

Jess took a deep breath. "Because I was at Waco, okay? I was one of the agents at Waco. All those people died—our people, their people, women, little kids—and I was part of that. Was it our fault? Did we make the wrong call? Or did the chief nut case plan to whack his own followers all along? Who the heck knows? All I know is, I just couldn't stand the thought of dealing with the nuts of this world anymore. I had to get out. So I came back here and went into business with Owen."

22

"I SEE."

Lynn did a quick mental review of what she knew about Waco. Cult leader David Koresh and a bunch of his followers had died in an apocalyptic conflagration after a standoff with federal agents in Waco, Texas, in April 1993. The ongoing confrontation and its fiery denouement had been broadcast on worldwide TV. She had anchored parts of the story herself for WMAQ. Some blamed the agents for what happened, calling it a case of government-sanctioned mass murder. Others blamed Koresh and the cultists themselves, saying they set the fire that consumed them. Whatever the truth was, the fact that Lynn remembered the case so well three years and countless other national nightmares afterward was a testimonial to its enduring horror.

"If you want to know, that's what the nightmare was about. I have it sometimes, the same thing every time: I keep seeing that complex go up in flames with all those people inside. I keep thinking about the little kids." The lack of emotion in his voice told its own tale. The scar obviously was deep, and painful. "I keep wondering if they knew what was happening, if they were afraid, if they suffered."

"I remember. I was anchoring for WMAQ when it happened. It was all over TV."

"Hell, we'd been planning that raid for months." Jess made a sound that was part laugh, part snort. "It was called Operation Trojan Horse. We were going to rush in there with no warning, corral the men in one place, the women and children in another, and hustle Koresh out of there. Take out the chief wacko and it was over, we thought. End of raid. No casualties. It was supposed to be a surprise."

"Something went wrong?"

"*Everything* went wrong. We went in in trucks—*cattle* trucks, mind you—covered with canvas, three of them, just went bumping up that long, dusty road in front of the compound overlooked by their watchtower with a three-hundred-sixty-degree view. What was Koresh supposed to think when he saw those trucks coming, that's what I want to know. *Oh, lookee here, somebody's sending me a stockyard's worth of cows*? Right. Then, while we were parked in front of the compound, still playing at being cows, three freaking Blackhawk helicopters carrying federal bigwigs came flying in from the north and started circling the buildings to *observe*. You ever seen a Blackhawk? Nobody's gonna miss one, that's for sure, much less mistake it for a mosquito. So even if the people inside hadn't known we were there—say they were busy throwing up fences to hold all those cows—I'd say they kinda got the picture then. But we kept on truckin', business as usual. What do you do, right? We jumped out of the trucks and started throwing flash-bangs—concussion grenades—while one of our guys was at the door trying to tell 'em we had a *warrant*. They blasted the shit out of us, and all hell broke loose. They had more gunpower than we did. They even had a machine gun with armor-piercing slugs. We lost four agents in the first five minutes. Talk about a freaking comedy of errors."

"It must have been terrible."

"You know what the joke was around the agency afterward? We whacked the Waco wackos. Funny, don't you think?"

"It wasn't your fault," Lynn said quietly. She found his left arm where it rested on the outside of his sleeping bag and touched it comfortingly. His hand rose to clasp hers. Their fingers twined without conscious thought on her part.

"Wasn't it? Like everybody else, I was pretty gung ho. Hell, we thought we were right. We were making the world safe for democracy, or something." He gave another dry, unamused laugh. "We were saving the innocent from the evils of a cult. Only the innocent ended up dead, and if we had kept our noses out of it they might well be alive today."

"You couldn't have foreseen what would happen. Sometimes things go wrong."

His hand, far larger than hers, was warm and strong. Lynn had an unexpected mental image of long brown fingers and a square palm enfolding her own slim, pale hand, and to her surprise she felt her pulse quicken.

"That's what we kept telling each other: When you go out in the world to slay dragons, you gotta accept the fact that sometimes the dragon's gonna win. In this case Koresh was the dragon, and he won."

"You can't dwell on it. There's no point. You did the best you could."

Lynn was mesmerized by her reaction to the feel of his hand on hers. The utter darkness deprived her of her sense of sight. Her hearing seemed heightened as a result. Maybe her sense of touch was too.

She could feel the calluses at the bases of his fingers and on his fingertips. She could feel the rope burns across his palms.

"You think I don't know that? What we saw tonight brought it back. Thus the nightmare."

"You think some kind of cult did that?" The horror of the scene and the condition of the bodies appeared in her mind's eye, momentarily sweeping all other thoughts aside.

"Could be. All the signs were there. Or it could be a drug crime. Hell, maybe some disgruntled employees came back to off the boss in a particularly gruesome way. Who knows? All I can tell you for sure is that there are a lot of dead bodies out there and another madman—or madmen—responsible."

"And they're after us." She shuddered.

Jess must have felt it, because his grip on her hand tightened. His thumb ran over her wrist, back and forth in a gentle, brushing motion that riveted her despite the topic under discussion. Heightened senses or no, the way she felt was ridiculous: For goodness' sake, she told herself, he was only holding her *hand.*

"That's the one thing I'm certain of. Though maybe they'll realize we couldn't identify any of them in the dark and they'll hightail it out of here and leave us alone."

To her relief, his thumb stilled.

"Do you think that's possible?" A tiny note of hope sounded in Lynn's voice.

"Possible? Sure." Unspoken was the rider: Anything's possible.

"But not likely."

"Who knows? Just to be on the safe side we'll assume they're still after us and get the hell out of here as fast as we can."

"If they are, they'll be combing the forest. It'll be daylight soon. They'll see us if we leave this cave. I'm sure we're leaving a trail in the moss. They'll find this cave. They'll find us." The scenario, with all its attendant horror, just occurred to Lynn.

"Not necessarily."

"What do you mean?"

"You're dying to hear that plan, aren't you?" Reluctant humor laced Jess's voice. His thumb began to move again. "Okay. There's a river near here. I fish it sometimes. I've got a kayak pulled up under some bushes. All we have to do is make it to the kayak, and the river will take us to within about a mile of where we want to go. No fuss, no muss."

"They'll be searching the forest."

"We'll be on the river."

"Good plan!" Lynn squeezed his hand with excitement. She was seeing the big dumb cowboy in a whole new light. He'd been a federal agent, he was educated, he had a plan—they might actually get out of this alive. The idea was intoxicating. She felt giddy with relief, and the strength of her euphoria told her just how scared she had been.

"I told you I had one."

His thumb traced circles at the base of hers. A tingle of electricity at the point of contact unnerved her. Lynn stared down at
their joined hands, although the darkness rendered them invisible. What was going on here?

"I thought you might be just saying that to shut me up."

He was turning her on by holding her hand. There was no
point in denying it, especially to herself.

"Now, why would you think that?" Lynn thought she heard a
grin in his voice. "Oh, ye of little faith."

Lynn made a face at him, forgetting that he couldn't see, and
returned her half-fascinated attention to the electricity generated
by their joined hands. The fact was, she had been attracted to
Jess Feldman from the first moment she had laid eyes on him.
She was human, after all; she was as vulnerable to a studly male
as any other woman was. Might as well admit that too, while she
was being honest.

"Hey," she said to cover up, "it's hard to put a lot of confi-
dence in a rhinestone cowboy."

It had been so long since she'd felt the warm, quivery stirring
of sexual desire that she indulged herself. For just a moment, she
simply enjoyed the feeling.

"Rhinestone, my ass. Owen and I grew up out here in Utah.
We're as genuine as cowboys come anymore. That ranch? We
inherited it. Owen had the idea of making it pay, and it does.
Plus it gives us lots of time to do the things we like to do, like
mountain climbing, and fishing, and—"

"All those handy little outdoor skills," Lynn finished for him,
her toes curling as his thumb continued to move. She could lean
over and kiss his mouth. . . .

"Exactly."

"Your parents are dead?" Or crawl inside his sleeping bag
with him. . . .

"Dad is. Mom lives in a condo in Florida."

"Do you see her often?" Could he perform with a bullet
wound in his shoulder?

"In the summer she comes to the ranch for a couple of weeks.
In the winter we're glad for an excuse to head for Florida."

"Do you take your girls with you? And your wife?" Maybe,

was her verdict. Or maybe not. That shoulder had to hurt. Nevertheless, Lynn felt a sudden, burning desire to get naked and put the question to the test.

"The girls sometimes. My wife divorced me years ago."

Enough was enough. Time to call a halt. Lynn tugged her hand free. He let go easily. She pressed her knees together, fighting the lingering heat.

"Why?" She wrapped her arms around her legs again, gripping her wrists tightly with her hands. What had been an admittedly pleasant interlude was now over.

"I was gone a lot, and she got tired of it. She gave me an ultimatum: quit the Bureau or she was leaving. I chose not to quit." He paused, then gave another of those unamused laughs. "There's irony in there somewhere."

"I'm sorry." So he was cute. So what? She was *not* going to make the mistake of sleeping with him.

"I'm over it—and so is she. She's remarried, lives in Houston. I get the girls six weeks out of the summer, every other holiday, and other times when I'm not working and can talk Sandra—my ex—out of them."

"Do you miss them?" And sleeping with him *would* be a mistake. A vacation fling was not her style.

"Yeah. That's the hard thing about divorce—the kids. They're basically growing up without me. Vacations, summers—it's like we're strangers when we get together, and by the time we know each other again they've got to leave."

"What are their names?" How could she even consider such a thing with Rory snoozing not three feet away? To say nothing of the other circumstances, like dead bodies everywhere and mass murderers on the prowl.

"Liz and Kate. Elizabeth and Katherine."

"Do they look like you?" The thought of Rory was sobering. Fourteen-year-old Rory wanted to sleep with him too. So what did that say about the man's powers of attraction?

He snorted. "They look like my ex-wife. Liz—she's the older—is her mother's spitting image. Personality-wise too. Last time we got together all she wanted to do was talk to her friends on the phone and go shopping. I spent three days in a *mall.*" His voice, rueful at first, softened. "But they're good kids. I actually kind of got into looking for the perfect T-shirt to go with a pair of checked shorts Lizzie bought. I didn't know there were that many shades of blue in the world."

"You must be very patient." Despite everything Lynn had to laugh at the picture his words conjured up. The awful thing about it, she thought, was that she was starting to like him. It was bad enough to be sexually attracted to him, but liking him was even worse.

It seemed more personal somehow.

"Or something."

Lynn couldn't be sure, but from the sound of his voice she thought he was smiling.

"Or something," she agreed. She enjoyed the idea that he was smiling, and that alarmed her.

"We ought to check your shoulder," she said, needing to distract herself. Liking a man like Jess Feldman could be dangerous. Caring whether or not she could make him smile could be dangerous. Where would it lead?

Straight to that vacation fling. Which seemed more appealing every time her overactive imagination began filling in the details.

"So check it."

Her fingers touched the warm, smooth expanse of his shoulder, slid along it. It felt hard, and she remembered how broad his shoulders were. Her pulse fluttered anew.

Get over it, Lynn ordered herself, and determinedly turned her attention to the task at hand.

She refused to allow herself to think of him in a sexual way again.

"The bleeding's stopped," she said, voice brisk as she probed the bandage.

"Ouch! That hurts like hell!"

"There's always the Tylenol."

"I think we should save that for Rory. No point in wasting good medicine."

"It might take the edge off."

"I doubt it." He shifted, the movement a soft rustle. "Lynn?"

She liked the way he said her name, in that low, rough-edged voice. Lynn realized that her pulse had quickened again, and she cursed her wayward libido. They were in mortal danger, on the run for their lives; now was definitely not the time to go all goo-goo-eyed over anyone, much less Jess Feldman.

Even if the time had been right, the man definitely wasn't. She'd seen enough heartbreakers to recognize one when he crossed her path.

Though she'd never *liked* one before. That added a troubling dimension to the equation.

"What?" she questioned warily. If he invited her to crawl into his sleeping bag with him, she'd . . . she'd . . . decline. Coolly. Coldly. As if the thought was a not-so-amusing bit of impudence on his part.

The way she would have reacted to such a suggestion twenty-four hours earlier.

A day, she reflected, was a very long time.

She would decline with relief, actually. Because it would confirm everything she knew about his kind.

"Better wake Rory," he said. "It's time to go."

23

THE BABY COUGHED, stirring in her arms.

Theresa stiffened.

"Elijah?" Her voice was soft, wondering. "Elijah!"

He moved again, as if in answer.

She snatched him up by his upper arms, holding him aloft, shaking him.

"Elijah!"

He began to cry.

Though she was deep in the silver mine, the main passage was a straight shot back from the entrance to where she had collapsed with Elijah on her lap. A few rays of moonlight penetrated the gloom, enough to permit her to see the baby's face. His eyes were mere gleaming slits, but they were open; his cheeks were crumpled with indignation. His lips parted in a jack-o'-lantern grimace as he emitted one earsplitting howl after another.

He was crying! He was alive!

"Thank you, God!" Theresa sobbed out loud. Her arms dropped, and she cradled her baby brother close, her body rocking back and forth as if to soothe herself as well as him.

His resurrection was a miracle, a gift from God.

Though He had taken so much, He had given Elijah back to her.

For now. The warning appeared in Theresa's mind out of nowhere, unbidden.

Elijah would live only as long as she could keep him safe. The evil still stalked them.

Casting a fearful glance over her shoulder at the distant starlit arch that framed the killing ground beyond, she thrust her little finger into the baby's mouth to shush him as she got to her feet.

Death was close at hand. He would kill her and Elijah—if he could.

She had to take her little brother and flee.

24

"I FEEL SO DIZZY. I have to rest for a minute." As she spoke Rory sank, panting, to the root-clogged path.

Coming up behind her, Lynn stopped and looked worriedly down at her daughter. They'd been moving fast, trying to get out of the forest and onto the water as quickly as possible. Rory had seemed energetic enough at first, but in the last quarter hour or so she had started to flag.

Now Lynn got a good look at her in the first cold misty light of dawn, and her appearance struck fear into Lynn's soul. Her forehead was much worse than it had been earlier. The skin from just above her right eyebrow to her left temple was purple; the outer edges of the contusion were so dark a shade as to be almost black. In addition, the area over her left eye was swollen to the approximate size and shape of a clenched fist. To make matters worse, Rory was ghostly pale and sweating.

"It's all right, we can take a breather." Jess, who'd been leading the way, had stopped, too, and turned back. He and Lynn exchanged a quick glance over Rory's head. There'd been a change in their relationship during the night: They were friends now, allies. More than that, even, as a subtle electricity charged the air between them. When they got out of this mess—*if* they got out of this mess—maybe she would let herself explore this unexpected chemistry between them, Lynn thought.

Maybe a purely sexual fling would be fun, at that. Kind of like life candy after a long, bare-bones diet of work and child-rearing and doing what it took to get by.

"Drink some water." Lynn pulled a bottle from her pack, unscrewed the lid, and offered it to Rory, who sipped listlessly before passing it back. Taking a drink herself, Lynn then held the bottle out to Jess, who accepted it, tilting his head back to drink.

Lynn watched as he swallowed, then wiped his mouth on the back of his hand. Breathing hard, his pack resting on the ground, Jess looked like an older, black-and-white version of the glorious golden boy she had met days earlier. Beneath his tan his face was pale, and there were shadows under eyes that no longer appeared baby blue but gray. His hair was darkened with mist and looked to be streaked with silver, not gold. Stubble shaded the clean lines of his cheeks and chin. Even his bloodstained goosedown jacket was gray, and his faded jeans, in the dawn light, took on a grayish cast as well.

If anything, Lynn thought, the change rendered him more attractive—at least in her eyes. She doubted that Rory would agree.

The way he looked now, he was candy for grown women, not young girls.

"We're almost there," he said, passing the bottle back to Lynn, who returned it to her pack. "Hear the river?"

"I don't hear anything." Rory slumped dispiritedly, bringing Lynn's attention back to her. "My head hurts."

"You can't take another Tylenol; you've had four in the last hour." Lynn crouched beside Rory, her arm sliding around her daughter's shoulders. Like Jess, they were both zipped up in jackets. Hers was gray, Rory's navy blue. Before setting out that morning they had traded jeans. Lynn wore her own slim Levi's 501s, while Rory's were looser, a trendy, baggy cut. Beneath the jackets were the turtlenecks they had worn the day before, Lynn's white, Rory's butter yellow. Now that Rory no longer needed it Jess had reclaimed his flannel shirt to replace his ruined T-shirt. Its soft red was the only touch of color about him that morning.

It was frightening to realize anew that, besides the blisters on her heels and the slight ache in her shoulder, she was the only whole member of their party.

What would she do if either of the others was unable to go on?

In Jess's case the only viable option was to go for help. In Rory's—she would die before she would abandon Rory.

"The Tylenol isn't helping anyway," Rory said.

Now that she was listening for it Lynn realized she *could* hear the river. Its muted roar was disguised by other sounds closer at hand. The forest echoed with every imaginable bird call, from the croaking of ravens to the fluting cry of a hermit thrush. Branches swished high and low. Insects droned, and small mammals scurried. The air was damp, dense, with a strong scent of pine sap. Mist wafted toward treetops hundreds of feet high, glistening in places as angular shafts of sunlight began to penetrate the canopy. The soft green velvet of the moss cover was intermittent now; huckleberry bushes, denuded of fruit, were conspicuously bare. Earlier, Lynn had almost stepped in a pile of smelly, purple-colored poop. "Grizzly," Jess had explained, not even slackening stride. Lynn assumed that grizzlies were responsible for the moss-free berry bushes and hoped she didn't get to meet any face to face.

Though she would rather come face to face with a dozen grizzlies than their pursuers from the night before.

"If you can make it another five minutes to the riverbank, you can rest there while your mom and I go get the kayak," Jess promised Rory.

"By myself?" Like Lynn, Rory cast an uneasy glance around. Lynn's arm tightened around her daughter. She looked up at Jess in alarm.

"I won't leave her," Lynn said.

"We'll be back in a half hour."

"If I go with you how far do I have to walk?" Rory asked.

"Once we get to the river about twenty minutes more. It's rough going."

Rory's head drooped. "I can't do it."

Lynn glanced up at Jess. "I'll wait with her."

"I'm going to need your help with the kayak." That was the closest Jess had come to admitting that he, too, was at less than full strength. A glance at his body confirmed it: His right arm hung straight down at his side, and he held his upper torso stiffly as if it hurt him to move.

Lynn glanced back at Rory, biting her lip.

"We'll hide her," Jess said. "She'll be all right. I wouldn't suggest leaving her if I wasn't sure of it. We haven't seen hide nor hair of anyone this morning."

That was true.

Rory settled it. "I feel sick to my stomach," she said. "I'd rather wait for the kayak. Honestly, Mom. I don't think I can walk another twenty minutes."

Lynn had no choice but to agree. Rory couldn't walk; Jess, with his injury, couldn't carry her; Lynn hadn't been able to carry her since she was four years old. Fetching transportation to ferry her out of danger was the best available option.

Once they reached the river, a narrow expanse of swiftly moving brown water, it was a simple matter to tuck Rory out of sight under a thick drift of feathery ferns. With both packs at her disposal (there was no point in carrying the packs when they would soon be back, Jess pointed out) they contrived a cozy nest. When the fronds were shaken back into place, not even Lynn's critical eye could find her daughter.

"She'll be all right," Jess assured Lynn, raising his voice to be heard over the rushing water. To Rory he added, "We'll be back in thirty minutes, tops."

"Stay put, baby," Lynn instructed, trying not to sound as anxious as she felt. Armed with beef jerky, a bottle of water, and pepper spray (included in the packs as—and Jess swore this was the truth—grizzly repellent), Rory was as comfortable and secure as it was possible to make her under the circumstances.

Nevertheless, Lynn could not help glancing back more than once as she followed Jess upstream. The riverbank was steep-sided and choked with an almost impenetrable tangle of willow and alder thickets. Lynn stumbled and clawed her way through them. Her hair and clothes caught repeatedly on branches, which jerked out strands of the first and snagged the second. Itchy and dirty to start with, she was soon drenched in sweat and irritable to boot.

"You ever kayaked before?" Jess asked over his shoulder as Lynn battled her way out of the latest thicket.

"No."

"Figures."

They were wading through a tangle of knee-high brambles at that moment, with Jess about an arm's length ahead. Lynn was panting with exertion, dying for a cigarette, and willing to admit that leaving Rory had probably been the smart thing to do. Hurt and exhausted, Rory could have climbed Mount Everest with less effort than it was taking to reach the kayak, Lynn thought. Under the circumstances Jess's air of macho-man superiority hit her the wrong way.

"You ever spent a ten-hour workday in three-inch high heels?" she asked tartly.

"No." Jess glanced around at her in surprise.

"You ever written a news story on a deadline?"

"No."

"You ever given birth?" Lynn produced the clincher.

"No." He was grinning now.

"Figures," Lynn said, the word dripping with all the disdain she could muster.

Jess laughed out loud. "Okay, so we each have our specialties. If I offended you I apologize."

"You did. And I accept."

"The thing is, kayaking's a little tricky, and I've got a bad arm. You may have to paddle."

"How hard can paddling a boat be?"

"A *kayak*," Jess corrected, stopping beneath a spreading pine. "Like I said, it's a little tricky."

"I'm sure I can manage." The claim was pure bravado. In fact, Lynn wasn't sure of any such thing, but she wasn't about to admit it.

"We'll find out. Thar she blows." Jess pointed to a long, cigar-shape craft overturned beneath a drift of bushes just ahead. A froth of intertwined weeds and brambles nearly hid it from view. Jess moved toward it. Lynn followed.

"It's kind of like a canoe, right?" Lynn eyed the kayak askance as Jess dragged it out into full view and flipped it right side up. It was a flimsy-looking contraption of bright yellow plastic, with two padded, blue-rimmed holes for seats. A pair of double-bladed oars were hooked to the sides.

"Kind of. Grab that end, and we'll carry it down to the river."

Lynn did as directed. The kayak was surprisingly lightweight. If Jess had had the use of both arms he would have had no trouble managing alone. As it was she slipped and slid down the steep riverbank holding on to a strap at one end of the craft, ending up ankle-deep in oozing silt through no fault of her own.

She felt lucky that she had landed upright.

"Good job." Jess was at the other end of the kayak, position-ing it and steadying it against the current. Because he was a kayak-length farther out into the river, the water rose above his knees, wetting his jeans. As Lynn watched, he balanced storklike on one leg and pulled off a boot.

She noted that he wore an athlete's thick white cotton tube sock.

"What are you doing?" she asked as he emptied the boot of water.

"What does it look like? Taking off my boots." He tossed the emptied boot into the kayak's rear seat and repeated the opera-tion, appearing to experience no hesitation about plunging his stocking feet into the river.

"Why?"

"Because they're full of water, and they're weighing me down. I suggest you do the same."

"Mine aren't full of water."

"They will be." An evil smile accompanied this. "Trust me."

Judging by how deep the water was on him only about a yard away, it was clear that he was right: Two more steps and her boots would be awash.

Lynn stood first on one foot and then the other to tug off her boots. She wore thin nylon trouser socks on her feet. The icy water was a shock to her toes. The gritty silt immediately sifted inside her socks. Pebbles on the river bottom poked her soles. She dropped her boots into the rear seat beside Jess's.

"Shove 'em as far down into the cockpit as you can."

Lynn did, realizing in the process that the keyhole-shape seat was far smaller than the space actually provided for a human body.

Jess paused in the act of snapping the oars free of their clips to glance at her. "You *can* swim, can't you?"

"Of course I can swim."

His grunt said there was no *of course* about it, but since he was smart enough not to put the sentiment into words, Lynn let it pass.

"Okay, the thing about a kayak is, it requires a little balance, sort of like riding a bike. You *can* ride a bike?"

"Of *course* I can ride a bike."

Jess didn't even grunt this time. He didn't have to. His expression said it for him.

"For your information I'm also very good at softball, tennis, table tennis, and soccer. I can ski. I can water ski. I can do all kinds of things that might surprise you. It just so happens that I have never before had occasion to ride a horse, climb down a mountain, or row a kayak."

"Paddle," Jess said.

"What?" She glared at him. The constant eddy and flow of the silt beneath her feet made it hard to maintain her balance. She was glad for the kayak to hang on to.

"You don't row a kayak, you paddle it. These are paddles, not oars." His tone was semiapologetic. A lurking grin came and went on his face.

"Whatever."

"An athletic woman like you shouldn't have any trouble then. Hop in." He maneuvered the craft so that it was parallel to his body and patted the front seat.

"Hop in?" Lynn cast a quick glance up and down the kayak. It was nothing more than a canoe with a top on it. She could do this. "Fine."

Lynn sloshed through the water—it was *cold*—until it was thigh-deep and she stood beside the front seat. For a moment she looked at the craft consideringly. It sat low in the river. She realized that, once in her seat, the lower half of her body would be below the water line. She glanced up at Jess, who was steadying the nose of the craft, and discovered the fugitive grin playing around his mouth. The muddy brown river swooshed past, moving very fast in the center.

"What about life jackets?"

"Honey, I didn't exactly plan on taking a river excursion when you fell over that cliff and I went down it after you. I didn't bring any life jackets with me. Ditto for helmets. We're just going to have to wing it. So would you please go ahead and get in?"

His patronizing tone irritated Lynn. "We didn't fall over a cliff—the cliff broke. And if you'd warned us that it might, we never would have been standing on it in the first place. That we are here at all is a case of pure negligence on the part of Adventure, Inc. And don't call me honey."

"Not very appropriate, come to think of it. Vinegar is more like it. Will you get in? Please?"

Getting in proved surprisingly easy. Lynn shot a triumphant glance at Jess as she slid her feet down inside the boat shell and wriggled her hips into the seat. Padded areas provided unexpected comfort for her back and legs. The plastic enclosed her to the waist when she was settled. It was kind of like wearing a mermaid tail, she thought.

"Here's your paddle," Jess said.

"Thank you." Lynn reached for it. As she moved, the kayak flipped.

Nothing could have shocked her more. One second she was sitting there smirking at Jess, and the next she was underwater!

Icy water. Completely and totally submerged. Upside down. Trapped in that mermaid tail of a boat.

In the first instant Lynn swallowed about half the river.

Choking, panicking, arms flailing wildly, legs kicking against the rigid polyethylene in which they were trapped, she fought to free herself from the kayak, to get to the surface, to reach air.

25

THROUGH NO EFFORT of her own, Lynn came back up as suddenly as she had gone under.

Gasping for breath, coughing, spluttering, she wiped the streaming water from her face with both hands and opened her eyes.

Jess was standing directly in front of her, not even a foot away, the craft's nose clamped between his body and his good arm. He was laughing so hard he was choking.

"You . . . you!" Lynn sputtered furiously, slinging droplets of muddy brown water at him. "You did that on purpose!"

"I meant to tell you—kayaks—have a tendency to roll," he gasped.

"A tendency to roll!" The paddle she'd been reaching for when it had happened floated in the water next to the kayak. She grabbed it, swung it at him. "A tenden—"

That was as far as she got. The kayak rolled again.

This time her stay underwater couldn't have lasted five seconds. And this time she had enough presence of mind to hold her breath.

"Sit still!" His face was right in front of hers as he leaned over the kayak to steady it. He was laughing so hard he seemed to be having trouble standing upright. "Or you'll roll again. Do you hear me? Sit still!"

"Sit still yourself!" Lynn snarled, and aimed a roundhouse punch at his nose. It never connected. The kayak rolled.

This time when he flipped it upright she sat still, rigid with temper and cold, muddy brown water pouring off her in streams. Her soaking hair was plastered to her skull. Her goose-down jacket had absorbed more water than a Bounty paper towel. She was drenched, drowned, freezing, and furious.

The only movement she dared make was a reflexive one to push the hair out of her eyes.

"Oh, Jesus," he groaned, in apparent pain from having laughed so hard. Lynn eyed him with longing. He was dangerously close—but the thought of another icy submersion dissuaded her. He wasn't worth it.

"Shut up," she said through her teeth.

"That was the funniest thing I ever saw."

"You don't get out much, do you?"

"Just sit still until I can get in." He was beside her, his good hand on the yellow plastic right in front of her, snickering as he pushed the kayak to shore, back end first. Lynn's fists clenched. Just let her get her feet planted on dry land again and she would give him something to laugh about.

"Did anybody ever tell you you're cute when you're mad?"

"No, and nobody better unless he has a death wish." Lynn clutched both sides of the cockpit and wished that looks could kill. If they could, he'd be toast.

"Now, temper, temper."

"Screw you."

He chuckled. She fumed. Had she really, just a little while before, imagined she *liked* him? She must have been nuts. She had never disliked anyone more.

She had never been attracted to anyone less. Handsome or not.

The back of the kayak touched shore, and they stopped moving except for the bobbing of the craft caused by the current. Lynn sat motionless, almost afraid to breathe.

"If you want to take off that wet jacket real quick, I'll hold the kayak steady."

Her jacket was soaked, icy wet, and felt like its stuffing had turned to lead. Pride dictated that she sit in it and sulk. Common sense—and considerations of both health and comfort—told her to take it off.

"You just want to dunk me again."

"I won't let it roll, I swear."

"Like I really trust you."

"Come on, Lynn." He smiled at her, coaxingly, apologetically, the skin around his eyes crinkling. He was so close she could see every individual whisker sprouting on his unshaven cheeks, count every line in his face. His eyes were bloodshot, his hair was unkempt, and she'd be willing to bet he had morning breath.

Even dirty and smelly, he *was* handsome, whether she liked to admit it or not.

"Don't be childish," he said. "I didn't do it on purpose. You moved so fast I couldn't hold on. Only having one working arm takes some getting used to, you know."

Lynn gave him a skeptical look, but she took off the jacket.

"Now what do you suggest I do with it?" Not yet appeased, she held the dripping garment out by its collar like a grimy dog. She was shivering, still awash in muddy water.

"Leave it. There's no chance it'll dry within the next few hours, and we'll be out of here by then."

"So I freeze because of your sick sense of humor." She tossed the sodden jacket toward the bank. It missed, landing half in and half out of the water, one sleeve stretched along the silt. The current caught it, pulling it out until it sank.

"No, I freeze. I deserve it. I shouldn't have let it happen."

She glanced back at him to find that he was shrugging out of his jacket. He had to lift his hand from the kayak to get the jacket all the way off. Lynn stiffened, eyes widening as she clutched the cockpit's padded sides.

It didn't roll.

His jacket dropped in front of her, and his hand returned to the plastic. She breathed again.

"It really was an accident." He sounded semiremorseful. She looked up at him with suspicion. He spoiled it by grinning.

"Bull," Lynn growled. Her turtleneck was soaked too. Putting a dry coat on over a wet shirt was stupid. Too mad—and too cold—to be modest, she yanked the turtleneck over her head and stuffed it down in the cockpit near her feet in case she needed it later.

"Lo-ove that Wonderbra," he said, even as she thrust her arms into his too-big, blood-stiffened jacket and pulled it around herself. Still warm from his body, it felt wonderful. Glaring at him, Lynn hugged it close. Until that moment she had not realized just how bone-cold she had been.

"Listen, Little Joe, I've had about enough of your jokes. If I were you I'd keep my big mouth shut." She zipped the coat.

"Or . . ." He was moving down the craft, his hand sliding over the plastic. Lynn couldn't see him any longer—she was afraid to turn her head to follow his progress—but she could tell he was grinning. She sat very still.

"Or as soon as I get out of this bathtub toy, I'll kick your butt to next Tuesday."

He laughed out loud, pushed the kayak out from the bank, and jumped in. The kayak rocked violently under his weight. Lynn was so mad she didn't even flinch.

She just hung on to the sides as they nosed out into the current and were pulled downstream. The kayak bounced over the bumpy water. Icy droplets blew up from the river to splash her. Sounds behind her told her that Jess was steadying the craft with his paddle.

A porcine porcupine stared at them from the tangle of undergrowth on the bank before waddling up a tree. A squadron of sparrows, flying low, sailed over their heads to vanish upstream. Lynn caught a glimpse of something large and dark—a grizzly?—shuffling away from the bank.

"Here's your paddle." Jess nudged her, then passed the paddle to her over her shoulder. "Dip, raise, dip, raise, from side to side, kind of like a seesaw. Let the paddle grab the water and pull."

Lynn hated to let go of the sides long enough even to grasp the paddle, much less try to follow Jess's instructions, but she did. The thought that sustained her was, Jess was in the kayak with her now. If she drowned, so would he.

It would almost be worth it.

As she rather expected, the kayak didn't roll. Not with Jess in it. He would make sure of that.

Dip, raise, dip, raise. Let the paddle grab the water and pull. First one side, then the other. Lynn quickly got into the rhythm of it. Though no praise was forthcoming from the back, Lynn was proud of herself as the kayak shot smoothly down the center of the river.

"Good thing we've got this current from the spring runoff to pull us along. It doesn't make any difference whether you know what you're doing or not."

This raised-voice observation made Lynn grit her teeth. For a moment she was tempted to turn and bean him with the paddle. The thought of unbalancing the kayak was enough to dissuade her. Vengeance would have to wait for dry land.

She couldn't tell whether he was paddling or not. The craft felt stable, and it was his weight that was holding it so. At the thought a grin tugged at her lips.

"At least you're good for something," she called over her shoulder.

"What's that?"

"Ballast." She snickered, glad to be giving as good as she got.

He said nothing. Lynn resumed her paddling as the thick stands of alder and willow that had taken so much time and effort to wade through flew past. Kayaking, she decided, sure beat walking.

As long as the blasted thing didn't roll.

Along with a bobbing branch and a trio of ducks, they barreled around a bend in the river.

"We need to start pulling toward the side. Rotate your body toward the bank," Jess instructed. "Now let the blade lock into the water and pull."

Lynn tried, feeling clumsy. But it seemed to work. The kayak nosed toward shore.

Rotate your body, she repeated to herself. Lock and pull.

They hit with a bump that was jarring. Lynn almost dropped her paddle, but she managed to hold on to it as the plastic underside of the craft lurched over the rocky river bottom with a gritty screech.

A quick glance up at the riverbank revealed the same wild snarl of undergrowth they had been passing all along.

"Are you sure this is the right place?" Lynn asked over her shoulder. An awful thought had just occurred to her: What if they couldn't find Rory? The tall, straight tree trunks looked the same on all sides, like a crowd risen for a standing ovation. The understory of vines and ragged bushes and deadwood looked the same too.

"See that big boulder up there?"

Lynn nodded.

"I made a mental note of it because I knew we'd be able to see it from the river. About a yard past and two yards to the left of that boulder is where we left Rory."

"I'll go get her."

"Sure you wouldn't rather stay here with the kayak?"

At the thought of sitting in that kayak without Jess, Lynn grimaced.

"No, thanks."

She didn't mean to let the thing roll with her again if she could help it.

"You might need these." Her boots were passed over her shoulder one at a time. It was a struggle, but despite the tight quarters Lynn managed to pull them on.

Given the slippery nature of the craft and her flat-on-her-bottom position, disembarkation wasn't easy, but she managed to get to her feet and step out into the water.

As her weight left it, the kayak rocked dangerously in backlash. For an instant Lynn watched, hopeful that it would roll.

No such luck.

Jess grinned at her as if he had read her mind. He sat in the second seat, his paddle balanced on top of the yellow plastic in front of him and braced to hold the kayak in position. It was clear that he'd been paddling with his good hand, using the kayak as a fulcrum, while the less mobile hand simply held the paddle in position.

The Marlboro Man as kayaker.

"Hurry," Jess said softly, holding her gaze. "Or I just might leave without you."

It was an empty threat. Whatever his faults, and they were many and varied, Lynn knew that he would not leave them. He had proved himself—oh, God, the brochure's wording was popping up in her mind again—*utterly reliable.*

Lynn thought about that as she scrambled up the steep bank and clawed her way through the willow thicket.

Throughout this whole awful ordeal Jess had never failed to come through for her and Rory. When they had fallen down the cliff, who had come after them, saving their lives at no little risk to his own? Jess. Who had carried Rory all that distance from the cliff to the mining camp in the teeth of the child's crush on him and her own suspicions about his motives? Jess. Who in the face of deadly danger had grabbed Rory and run with her, instead of simply taking care of number one? Jess. Who had shown them the way to the cave where they had spent the night, though he was wounded and bleeding badly? Jess. Who had come up with the kayak and the plan that might very well save them all and worked to make it happen despite his injuries? Jess.

He could have left them on the cliff; he could have abandoned them last night. He could still take off without them and have a much easier time saving merely himself—but he wasn't going to.

Lynn was as sure of that as she was of anything in her life.

Whatever his faults, she knew Jess would do his best for her and Rory until they were all safely out of this mess.

The Marlboro Man as hero. In Jess's case, reluctant as she was to admit that maybe she'd been wrong, the reality was living up to the hype after all.

As Jess had said, the wall of ferns was visible immediately once she had made it past the boulder and glanced left. Frothy tendrils poured in a lush green waterfall to the pine-needle carpet. Stately evergreens rose all around like sentinels. A shaft of sunlight sparkled off dust motes in the air.

Rory was as invisible as she had been when they had left her.

"Rory," Lynn called softly, conscious of an eerie feeling that the trees had ears. "We're back. We need to go."

Rory did not answer. Perhaps she had fallen asleep, Lynn thought. Approaching the ferns, she bent and swept them aside with one hand.

Rory was not there.

As she stared at the empty nest where she had expected to find her daughter, Lynn realized what had been wrong with this picture all along: The forest was too quiet.

Except for her own breathing and the hushed rustle of the wind in the trees, there was not a sound.

Not from a bird. Or an insect. Or an animal.

Lynn sensed a presence to her left and whirled. Not three feet away, her daughter stared at her with enormous blue eyes. A man was behind her, portly, black-haired, and balding. Like Rory, he was crouching behind a large pine, partly hidden by the undergrowth. His hand pressed tightly over Rory's mouth, clamping her to him.

A black, businesslike-looking pistol was trained over Rory's shoulder, aimed right at Lynn's head.

26

"WHEN DID YOU TAKE UP with the Judas?" The man was wearing a stained white dress shirt, open at the collar, and a pair of black pants. He had the merest trace of a southern accent. His voice was soft, his tone conversational. He was frowning as he looked Lynn over, but not in a particularly menacing fashion. More as if he found her puzzling.

Not quite understanding what he was talking about, Lynn tried a smile. With her hair wet and her face dirty, clad in a goose-down jacket big enough to be a dress, Lynn realized that she looked far different from her normal self. Usually she could count on racking up a few brownie points for appearance where men were concerned. Not today, as was clear from his lack of response to her smile.

"You aren't one of the Michaelites," he continued. "I don't know you."

He looked, and sounded, disconcertingly normal. The local used-car salesman as homicidal maniac.

Lynn repressed a shiver.

"No, I'm not," Lynn agreed, taking care to speak calmly. Her gaze met Rory's. The pupils of her child's eyes were dilated with fear. As the reality of the situation sank in, Lynn realized that she was pretty frightened herself. Her throat was so dry she couldn't swallow. Her leg muscles felt about as firm as Jell-O.

Obviously, this was one of their pursuers from the night before. It had to be: How many different lunatics with guns could be running around in a few square miles of national forest? They had been caught—by the killers who had massacred that woman, those boys, the man on the cross. And who knew how many others? But perhaps there was hope, after all. He seemed surprised that she was not one of the "Michaelites," whatever that meant.

He had no way of being sure that she and Rory were members of the trio that they'd been chasing. He could not know that they had seen the bodies at the mining camp. Perhaps she could convince him that she and Rory were merely innocent hikers and knew nothing—except that he was holding Rory captive and had a gun pointed at her own head.

That was pretty damning stuff, all by itself.

Lynn felt nauseous as she realized that in all likelihood she was not going to be able to persuade him to just let them go. But she had to try.

"Were you out here hunting?" she said with what she hoped was a disingenuous smile and her best Pat Greer, hearty-camp-fire-girl imitation. "Did we interrupt you? I'm sorry! If you'll let my daughter go, we'll get out of your way and let you get on about your business."

"Is Theresa with you?" He ignored her words completely.

"Theresa?" Lynn was willing to say yes or no, depending on which answer was most likely to please him. Unfortunately, she had no way of telling that.

"Theresa. Michael's daughter."

"Oh." While Lynn did a lightning-fast mental debate as to the possible advantages of telling the truth and disclaiming all knowledge of any Theresa, he shook his head as if dismissing the question.

"Where's the man?" He was watching her intently. Rory was trembling. Lynn could see the pale slim fingers of one hand quivering as they hung down between the child's bent knees. The other grasped the arm that imprisoned her.

"The man?" Lynn took a deep, calming breath as she considered the pros and cons of an ear-shattering scream. It would certainly bring "the man" lickety-split to the spot—but it might also precipitate her own, and Rory's, murder. And Jess's, when he came running.

"The man who was with you last night." He smiled. "Yahweh told me to look for you along the river, you know. You can't hide from Yahweh."

"Yahweh?" Lynn was certain now that she was dealing with a lunatic and was unsure as to what might set him off.

"You call him God, I believe. He speaks to us through the Lamb. He that leadeth us . . . But of course you would think the Judas was the Lamb. That was what he wanted everyone to think." He shook his head sorrowfully. "You Michaelites have been misled, I'm sorry to say. The Judas was but a false prophet. Well, he is answering for his sins now."

"My daughter could go and fetch the man for you—and Theresa too. You and I can talk while she's gone. She would hurry, wouldn't you, Rory?" Lynn was desperate, trying anything she could think of to get the maniac to release Rory. There was a fanatical light in his eyes that told her even more surely than his incomprehensible words that he was irrational. The very reasonableness with which he spewed his nonsense was terrifying.

He would kill without a qualm, certain he was doing the right thing.

Rory nodded fearfully.

"If he's around, gunshots will bring him running." The man smiled, shrugged. "Though that might not work with Theresa. In answer to your suggestion I am reminded of that saying about a bird in the hand. . . . You know it? Yes. So don't worry about the others. They'll join you soon enough, I promise. But here, I mustn't keep you talking all day. I know you're frightened and must long to get it over with. Death is something that is universally feared, I'm quite aware. But it is nothing *to* fear. Just a passing over into a better life."

"Please . . ." Lynn began as his hand shifted from Rory's mouth to her waist. He was getting ready to rise.

"Mom . . ." Rory whispered. The child was visibly terrified. She trembled. Her face was as white as paper; her eyes were huge dark pools as they met Lynn's.

Lynn realized that if she didn't do something Rory was going to die. They both were going to die.

"Don't be worried, young lady. I promise you, death is nothing to fear." The man sounded jovial, like a macabre Santa Claus. Pulling Rory up with him, he started to get to his feet, gathering his body together, his movements ponderous.

The gun wavered as he rose.

Acting out of instinct and pure mother-love, Lynn jumped forward and kicked for all she was worth. The toe of her boot made a solid smack as it connected with his gun hand.

The gun went off even as his hand flew up, and the weapon went flying, spinning top over tail into the undergrowth.

"Run, Rory!" Lynn grabbed her daughter's arm and yanked her away from the man. His momentary shock, plus his bulk, gave them the advantage. Bolting like deer from a hunter, Lynn pulled Rory toward the boulder . . .

. . . And ran headlong into Jess, who was clearly in the process of charging to their rescue. She hit his chest and would have bounced off if he had not caught her by her upper arm, steadying her even as he staggered a pace backward.

"Come on!" Recovering, he gripped her wrist, hauling her and Rory around the boulder in a frantic imitation of the childhood game crack-the-whip.

As his feet skidded on a patch of moss, Lynn realized he was still in his stocking feet.

A lightning glance back told her that the lunatic was frantically searching the bushes for his gun. His ample posterior, clad in shiny polyester slacks that were stretched to the danger point, faced her as he bent to rake the undergrowth with his hands.

"Hurry," Lynn breathed, clinging to Jess's hand now as she went slip-sliding down the steep bank after him with Rory in tow.

Distant male voices and the sound of crashing footsteps told her that their pursuers, summoned by the gunshot, were after them again in full force.

"Get in!"

Jess practically flung her into the river and bent over the back of the kayak. Lynn splashed through the knee-deep water, her boots growing unbelievably heavy as they filled with water, and whipped Rory around her toward the front seat.

"Get in!" she cried to her daughter.

Rory scrambled into the kayak's front cockpit, sloshing water everywhere.

"Get in with her! Hurry!"

Lynn obeyed Jess's instruction, clambering in after Rory as Jess pushed them out into the current. Trapped in mud and weighted down by water, her boots were left behind as her feet slid out of them. She had no time to worry about their loss. Her paddle was thrust past her elbow as soon as her bottom hit plastic. Lynn grabbed the paddle and maneuvered it so that it was in front of Rory. With both arms touching her daughter she could feel Rory trembling. But she had no time to worry about that, either, as she started to paddle for all she was worth.

Grab the water and pull.

A brisk breeze raced up the river, blowing her hair back from her face, smelling of pine. Her feet and legs were numb from the cold water, she was sitting in a puddle, and her freedom of movement was hampered by Jess's oversize coat.

Plus she was scared to death.

Grab the water and pull.

"Hold it steady!"

The kayak was free of the bank now, picking up speed as its nose swung downstream. There was a splash, a grunt, and a violent yawing as a sudden shift in the craft's center of gravity occurred.

Jess was on board.

Instinctively Lynn fought the rolling movement by leaning in the opposite direction. Controlling a kayak was kind of like riding a skateboard, she had discovered earlier. Lean in the direction you want it to go.

"Paddle!" Jess suited action to word. Lynn followed suit. Huddled against Lynn's chest, her body surrounded by Lynn's arms and legs, Rory sat silent and trembling.

"It's okay," Lynn said in her ear. "We're going to make it."

Debris swirled by them, sticks and leaves and larger branches. The banks on both sides of the river were tall, sloping rock walls topped by pines that crowded right to the rocky edge. Sparrows by the thousands had built nests high on the riverbank; an osprey dived from its perch high atop a ponderosa pine to swoop over the river, searching for fish. Roots rose above the water surface near the left bank; the osprey swept its talons through the surface of the water there, emerging with a trout so big it had trouble flying.

"Look!" Rory nudged Lynn, pointing, and at the same time seemed to shrink in her seat. Lynn looked as instructed and immediately wished she hadn't. Almost directly opposite them, standing beside a willow thicket on the bank from which they had shoved off, was a man with a rifle.

He lifted it to his shoulder.

Jess said a word so vulgar that under other circumstances Lynn would have been tempted to cover Rory's ears.

"Keep paddling," he bit out next, as though Lynn needed the reminder. She paddled like a woman possessed as the kayak sought out and rode the swift current at the center of the river.

There was a sharp popping noise, followed by three more in quick succession.

"Duck!" Jess yelled. Rory did, scooting down inside the craft as far as she could. Lynn huddled over Rory's head, protecting it, shielding her own with her arms as best she could. At any moment she expected to feel a bullet ripping into her flesh. The prospect sent an anticipatory shiver racing along her spine. How would it feel to be shot? Would it be an immediate burst of agony, or would the shock numb any pain?

"Mommy!" Rory moaned.

"It's okay, baby." In calming her daughter, Lynn calmed herself. Panic would do neither of them any good.

Pop! Pop! Pop! Pop!

There had to be more than just the one gunman, Lynn thought. Glancing back, she saw that she was right. The lone rifleman had been joined by two others, one the evil Santa Claus. Both newcomers were armed with rifles. Lynn assumed Santa hadn't found his pistol.

A staccato burst of gunfire caused her to duck again. Tiny white spurts in the water all around them marked where bullets hit. A sharp crack signaled that one sharpshooter had gotten the kayak. With Rory hyperventilating in her arms, Lynn battled panic anew.

Thank God for hardened plastic, Lynn thought. At least the thing wouldn't sink.

"Are you all right?" she screamed back at Jess.

"Shut up and stay down," was his reassuring answer.

Obviously he was not killed. Lynn took what comfort she could from that.

Gunshots sounded again, but the absence of white spurts in the water indicated that the bullets were missing their mark. Lynn stayed low, paddled for all she was worth, and prayed that the current would soon sweep them out of range.

They shot around a bend in the river. The kayak heeled dangerously, threatening to roll.

"Lean left!" Jess cried. Lynn and Rory complied.

"You can sit up now. We're safe," Jess said moments later.

He sounded breathless. Lynn sat up, cautiously, and glanced back. Nothing more threatening than pristine forest met her gaze. Sparrows fluttered in great shifting clouds on both sides of the riverbank; a bright colored butterfly floated up from a clump of daisylike flowers to meander deeper into the woods. A pair of mallards, identifiable by their iridescent-green heads, floated past along with branches and other debris.

Santa and his murderous minions were nowhere to be seen. Lynn let out a great sigh of relief.

Closer at hand, Jess rested his paddle across the top of the kayak and let the river do the work of propelling them to safety. Lynn glanced back to find him breathing heavily, and new lines bracketing his mouth spoke of pain. The frantic paddling could not have helped his shoulder. Lynn wondered if his wound was bleeding again. Probably, she decided.

Like herself, he looked much the worse for wear. His hair was a wild, wet tangle blowing in the wind. River water had left muddy streaks on his face. He was pale, sweating, and he badly needed a shave.

But his eyes were bright baby blue again, with a definite gleam.

He met her gaze and grinned. He was, she judged with some surprise, on an adrenaline high. And if she hadn't known better she would have sworn he was enjoying the excitement.

But of course she knew better. She hoped. Who could possibly enjoy this murderous game of cat and mouse?

"We're safe for now," he said. "With them on foot and us on the river, there's no way they can catch up to us."

"Thank God," Lynn said. "Rory, baby, are you okay?"

"He came just before you got there," Rory's voice was high-pitched and shaking. "I had to go to the bathroom, so I crawled out of the bushes. He just grabbed me! I didn't even know he was there! At first he called me Theresa. Then he asked if I knew where she was. Then he was going to kill me. If you hadn't come, Mom, he *would* have killed me!"

"It's over," Lynn said to her comfortingly as Rory slumped against her. "It's all right. We're okay for now."

"Oh, God, I thought he was going to kill you too. Both of us. Right there."

"We got away. Now we've left them far behind."

"I was so scared!"

"I know, baby, I was scared too." Lynn hugged her daughter, a gesture rendered clumsy because of the paddle she held.

"You were awesome, Mom. What you did back there—that was totally awesome." Rory twisted in Lynn's hold to glance back at Jess. "Did you see what she did? She kicked his gun away!"

"Just like Chuck Norris," Jess agreed. "It *was* awesome. What do you do, take karate?"

"Aerobics," Lynn said.

"Aerobics?"

"It helps me stay in shape. Three times a week after work I do the exact same kick."

"You saved our lives," Rory said.

From the rear seat Jess started to sing something under his breath. It took a minute before Lynn was able to make sense of the words.

"Five foot two, eyes of blue, but oh what those five two can do . . ."

"Oh, shut up," she said, feeling better already.

27

*D*EATH IS COMING. Theresa heard the words in her mind as plainly as if someone had spoken them aloud.

They roused her from the steady level of fear she'd existed in for so long to a state of acute terror. She had been about to crawl from the hole that was the rear entrance to the mine. Shrinking back against the cold rock wall, she peered out into the world instead with the near-blind gaze of a mole.

The day was dazzling in its brightness. She had spent so many hours in the dark, the light hurt her eyes. At first it was hard for her to see.

She had to rely on senses other than sight, like the inner voice warning her to beware.

The gravel road that led to the outside world was not more than four yards distant. She knew because she had taken this path to it before.

Death was almost as near.

Shivering, Theresa huddled in the darkness as her eyes became accustomed to the brilliance beyond the hole, waiting for the sunlit road to come into focus through the screen of branches. The hole was hidden behind a bank of forsythia bushes. The yellow flowers were long gone. The branches with their slender green leaves swayed in the wind. A tiny stream, a mere trickle of water really, wet her gown at the knees as it ran past her down into the bowels of the earth, where it no doubt fed the subterranean river that had taken over the mine's lowest level. Fortunately she had recognized the flooding in time to turn back and find a higher passage. From the sound of it the water that had once been no more than ankle-deep was high and fast-moving, swollen with the recent rains.

Elijah slept against her breast, worn out with crying, in a sling she had fashioned for him from cloth torn from her flannel nightgown. Since leaving the root cellar she had had nothing to feed him, though she had let him suck water from a twisted piece of cloth. Still, in the end that had not satisfied him. He had screamed with hunger for what seemed like the last several hours, until he had fallen asleep.

She had not dared to approach the light until he was quiet.

Death had not been in the labyrinthian underground passages with her. He was out here, seeking her in the bright sun.

Theresa felt his presence as strongly as she had felt it outside the cabin door.

Perhaps, she thought, she should stay hidden forever in the dark.

Though if what Death had prophesied came true it would make no difference anyway.

Three people came into view, wading through the knee-high undergrowth, heading toward the road she could now see. Two women, both with bright blond hair, clung together, moving slower than the man, who was tall and whose right arm hung stiffly down at his side, as if it were injured in some way.

Theresa was positive she had never seen the people before in her life.

She had been praying for a miracle, praying nonstop since Death had found her family.

Had He sent the three to act as His instrument in snatching her from the jaws of Death?

Or had Death sent them to lure her out?

28

SOME FOUR HOURS AFTER LEAVING their pursuers behind on the riverbank, Jess, Rory, and Lynn reached their destination: a pitted gravel road that meandered like a twisty thread through this part of the Uintas. After a long and tortuous journey through mountains, streams, and mud bogs, it connected to State Route 150, which in turn led into the town of Kamas.

Once there they would go straight to the authorities.

Lynn thought she wouldn't feel completely safe until she was sitting in police headquarters surrounded by cops, watching through the windows as a squadron of state boys headed out, blue lights flashing, to bring the killers to justice.

The sight of the red Jeep waiting a little distance down the gravel road sure made her feel a whole heck of a lot safer than she had for almost twenty-four hours, however.

"There's the Jeep," she said, squeezing Rory's hand, smiling at Jess because she was just so giddy with relief.

They were going to live!

"Let's go." Jess didn't smile back.

Lynn assumed his shoulder was paining him. Since leaving the kayak behind some two hours before, he had seemed to keep going on pure grit. Though he was not as visibly wilted as Rory, who had required Lynn's arm around her for support nearly every step of the way, he was silent and sweating despite the briskness of the morning.

Silence, coming from Jess, said a great deal.

He and Rory would soon have the medical attention they needed. All they had to do was reach the Jeep and be borne to safety by that wonder of modern technology, the automobile.

After making it so far under her own steam, the thought of riding the rest of the way in comfort was pure bliss to Lynn. To add to her litany of woes, her feet hurt. They were not only blistered but sore from being rubbed every which way but loose by Jess's too-large boots. After they had left the kayak and he had realized that she had only her thin trouser socks to protect her feet, he had pulled off his boots and insisted she put them on. His feet, he said, were tougher than hers.

They had argued briefly. He had won. For his pains he had ended up traipsing through the wilderness in his socks.

At least, Lynn told herself in an attempt to assuage her guilt, they were the thick, white athletic kind.

Or at least they had been white. And thick. A glance told her that they were now grubby gray and full of holes.

But none of that mattered now. They were about to sit down, in a motorized vehicle, and be driven to safety.

Thank God.

It was a beautiful day, Lynn realized, as they walked down the gravel road toward the Jeep, which was pulled partially into the weeds with its back to them. A beautiful, glorious, sunshiny day straight out of the beginning of the world.

In the face of such splendor it was hard to believe that the experience they had just lived through was real. Lynn felt kind of like Alice when she had fallen down the rabbit hole and found herself in Wonderland. What had happened since she and Rory had tumbled off that cliff just kept getting curiouser and curiouser, and now seemed as unreal as the Mad Hatter and the Queen of Hearts.

Maybe it was, she thought, struck by an inspiration. Maybe she had hit her head in the fall and was even now lying in a hospital bed in a coma. Maybe awful dreams—awfully *real* dreams—were where people in comas went.

Unlikely as that sounded, it was no more unlikely than what they had been through.

Maybe she would climb into the Jeep, be conveyed to safety, and wake up.

Maybe that was how it was with people in comas. Maybe they came back from whatever wild journey their subconscious took them on and just woke up. Or not, if they didn't make it back alive.

One way or another it looked as if she and Rory and Jess were going to make it back alive.

The man behind the wheel had his back to them. His head with its ubiquitous cowboy hat rested against the top of the seat. Possibly he was listening to music, or sleeping. Whoever he was, he was not Owen. The shoulders weren't broad enough, and he didn't seem to be as tall.

One of the others, then: Bob or Ernst, or Tim.

With no more than a few dozen anxious glances around to make sure their pursuers were nowhere near, they reached the Jeep.

"Yo, Tim!" Jess said, pounding on the roof with his fist. The man in the front seat started, sat up, and glanced around.

"Jess, man, you made it!" Tim got out of the Jeep and turned to face them. He was grinning broadly, and it was clear from his demeanor that he had no inkling of what they had just been through. "Good to see you, Lynn, Rory! Wow, that's a nasty bump on your head! Owen said you wouldn't have any trouble, buddy. He said you were a mountain man from way back."

"We need to get out of here real fast," Jess said, opening the left rear door as he spoke and indicating with a jerk of his head that Lynn and Rory should get in.

Lynn settled Rory in the seat, pulling her seat belt around her and fastening it, then walked quickly around the Jeep to get in the other side. Jess, she noted, was already heading for the front passenger seat even as he spoke to Tim, who looked confused.

"What? Why?" Tim frowned as Jess used his left hand to open the door. It appeared to occur to him then that Jess was moving oddly, that something was amiss. "Did you hurt your arm, man?"

"I'll tell you all about it on the way. Get in, and let's get the hell out of here, okay?"

"Anything you say, boss." Tim got in and shut the door. Turning on the ignition, he reversed the vehicle in a semicircle until the Jeep was facing the way they had come.

"Hit it," Jess said.

With a quick glance at Jess, Tim nodded and shifted again. They jolted forward, headed toward safety at last, Lynn thought with a relieved sigh.

Though not fast enough to suit her or, she thought, Jess, who drummed the fingertips of his good hand on the dashboard as he stared out the windshield.

Beside his hand, wedged tight in the angle between plastic and glass, was a pack of cigarettes. Pall Mall low-tar, to be precise. Not Lynn's brand, but . . .

"Could you pass me a cigarette?" she asked, light-headed with sudden desire.

Jess glanced back, then followed her avid gaze to the pack beside his hand. With a disapproving quirk of his mouth he picked up the pack and tossed it to her.

"You ought to quit," he said.

"I will, one of these days, when my life is stress-free and I don't care if I gain weight and I get an X ray showing I have lung cancer. Until then I am addicted." Reverently, Lynn turned the pack over in her hand, savoring the feel of the cellophane. The faint smell of tobacco teased her nostrils.

There were only two cigarettes left. But one would be one more than she had had in twenty-four hours.

Oh, bliss.

There was a disposable lighter tucked under the cellophane. She freed it and tapped a cigarette out.

"You're not going to smoke in here, are you?" Rory grimaced with repugnance. "What about the dangers of secondhand smoke?"

Lynn looked from her daughter to the cigarette in her hand.

She wanted to smoke that cigarette more than she had wanted almost anything in her life.

"So tell me—" Tim began, oblivious to the drama in the back seat. He broke off, then spoke again in a very different tone. "Who the hell is that?"

Lynn stiffened and looked up at the road ahead. A young woman emerged from the forest, running toward them, waving her hand for them to stop. Barefoot, clad in a torn, stained, cream-colored flannel nightgown with lace at the neck and wrists, she was tall and bean-pole-thin, with a wild mass of curly brown hair.

The arm that was not waving was clamped around a baby carried in a makeshift sling.

"What's a woman with a baby doing out here?" Tim asked, sounding stupefied.

"Keep going!" Rory cried. "It might be a trick!"

With a single regretful glance Lynn thrust the cigarettes and lighter into her pocket, reached over, and took her daughter's hand. At the same time her brain kicked into gear. The woman had to be in some way connected to the massacre—a survivor, perhaps?

Or a decoy meant to stop them? But whoever heard of a decoy with a baby?

Under the circumstances Lynn could not bring herself to scream "Run her down," though all her instincts urged that they not stop.

"Hell, Tim, stop." At the last minute, as the woman pelted toward them down the road, Jess gave the instruction and Tim stood on the brakes. The Jeep shuddered to a halt. The woman ran around its passenger side.

"Let me in!" she cried, keeping one hand on the Jeep as if she feared it might take off again without her. "Oh, please! Let me in!"

"Do you think we should do this, Mom?" Rory asked fearfully even as Lynn swung open the back door and scooted into the middle, closer to her daughter.

"We can't just leave her here," Lynn answered. "She has a baby."

"Oh, thank you, thank you," said the woman as she scrambled in through the open door and collapsed, panting, in the seat. She was only a teenager, Lynn saw, not much older than Rory. "Please, drive away! Go fast! He's coming!"

"Who's coming?" Tim asked over his shoulder, even as he stepped on the gas. He must have trod down hard, judging from the way the rear tires spun over the gravel. Evidently the new passenger's terror, added to what he had already gleaned from the three of them, was enough to convince him that something very wrong was afoot.

"Death," the girl said tragically, her arms wrapping around the baby she carried, who still slept. "Please, just hurry! Hurry!"

The girl was damp and dirty and distraught. Looking at her, Lynn was seized by a thought.

"Theresa?" she asked.

The girl's eyes were a lovely light hazel, almost gold. "How did you know my name?" she breathed, focusing on Lynn.

"Shit a biscuit! Lookee there!" Tim shouted, lifting one hand from the wheel to point. Lynn jumped, as Theresa whimpered under her breath.

"Oh, my God, it's them!" Lynn cried, recognizing three of the four men who erupted from the trees on either side of the road. "Go, Tim, go!"

Though he still lacked the details needed to put him in the picture, Tim clearly grasped the general idea. He floored it. The Jeep's rear tires slithered back and forth through the gravel as the vehicle fought to outdistance the men who ran first beside and then farther and farther behind it.

The Jeep was winning.

Pop! Pop! Pop!

They were shooting at them! Lynn screamed, Rory screamed, Theresa screamed. The baby awoke, wailing. The men ducked, cursing. The Jeep bumped over the road like a bicycle on a train track.

Another burst of gunfire sounded. The Jeep was hit. The rear windshield shattered, showering the occupants of the backseat with glass.

The women screamed again. Tim cried out. Jess cursed.

The Jeep jolted over a rut and was momentarily airborne, fly-ing off the road to hurtle across about ten feet of weeds before landing with a jarring crash against the trunk of a massive pine.

Lynn was thrown violently forward. Her head crashed into the back of the front seat. For an instant she knew nothing. Rory, who had been restrained by her seat belt, tugged frantically at her mother's arm even as she released the seat belt's catch.

"Mom! Mom! We've got to run! Mom!"

"I'm coming." Lynn was groggy, but Rory's urgency pene-trated her momentary fog. Lynn moved.

"Come on! Come on!" Jess was out of the Jeep, jerking open Rory's door, dragging her out. Lynn rolled out after her. On the other side Theresa scrambled out, clutching the wailing baby, sprinting into the woods.

Steam rose from the front of the Jeep. The smell of radiator fluid was strong.

Slumped over the steering wheel, Tim did not move.

"Follow me!" Theresa screamed over her shoulder.

A glance back told Lynn that their pursuers were closing fast. Bullets sang through the air around them.

"Follow her!" Jess yelled, grabbing Lynn's hand and dragging her with him as he ran after Theresa. Lynn stumbled and nearly fell as she tried to run in his too-big boots. She kicked them off. He pulled her relentlessly on.

"Rory, hurry!"

"Mom, wait!"

Unable to free herself from Jess's grasp, Lynn stretched her hand back to her daughter even as the three of them darted through the trees. Seconds later Rory caught up and grabbed hold.

"What about Tim?" Lynn screamed, glancing back. The front end of the Jeep had been reduced to a smoking heap of scrap metal scrunched against the trunk of the big pine, which was scarred from the impact. Tim's forehead rested against the steer-ing wheel. Had he been knocked unconscious in the crash?

Though they could not possibly have carried him, it seemed monstrous to just leave him behind.

Their pursuers were only a few yards beyond the Jeep.

"He's dead. Shot in the head." Jess, voice emotionless, never glanced around or even slackened his stride.

Shocked, Lynn sucked in great gulps of air, fighting the shivers that raced up and down her spine—and she kept running. Brambles, sticks, and rocks of all sizes stabbed through her socks, but she scarcely noticed the assault to her soles as she ran for her life.

Bullets smacked into trees and ripped through the undergrowth as they leaped fallen logs and dodged tree trunks in pursuit of the elusive cream flannel nightgown.

Lynn was reminded ridiculously of Alice again, in pursuit of the White Rabbit.

They followed the nightgown around a small hillock, losing their pursuers as they rounded it.

All at once the tantalizing flash of cream was nowhere to be seen.

"Where did she go?" Jess stopped, glancing around wildly. Lynn and Rory stopped too, their gazes darting around the forest.

"Here!" The sound came from somewhere close at hand. Lynn glanced around. A needle-carpeted slope rose to their immediate left. Access to it was hampered by a thick clump of leafy shrubs. Ahead and to their right the forest stretched on endlessly.

The sound of a baby crying, centered near her feet, caused Lynn to glance down.

"Here!" the voice said again, urgently. A hand shot through the bushes at the base of the slope to tug at the leg of Lynn's jeans. The baby cried louder.

"There!" Lynn jerked her hands free, pointing. Drawn by the baby's noise, the others were already looking down. The hand withdrew almost as suddenly as it had emerged. The three of them stared for a surprised instant at where it had been.

The clump of shrubs concealed a dark opening about the size of a manhole cover in the base of the slope.

The baby's cry was already growing distant, as if it were being borne away.

"Get in there," Jess said, pointing at the hole. Neither Lynn nor Rory needed any urging. Lynn was on her knees before he finished speaking, squeezing through the bushes, crawling through a trickle of water into the hole. Inside, it was dark and narrow, with more the feel of a passage than a cave. Rory was right behind her. Jess was behind Rory.

Theresa and her nightgown were nowhere to be seen, though Lynn could hear the baby still wailing its little heart out. From the steadily decreasing volume of sound she knew they were some distance away, and moving fast.

Jess's stocking feet had no sooner cleared the opening than their pursuers ran around the hillock.

The sound of the baby crying was faint now.

Too faint for the men chasing them to hear?

29

LYNN WAS NOT WAITING AROUND to find out. With the baby's cries to guide her she crawled along the passage, which sloped downward. Rory and Jess followed. Beneath her the rock was wet and slippery. In the center of the surprisingly smooth stone floor, a stream of water rushed along a well-worn groove.

She kept picturing Tim's blond head slumped over the Jeep's steering wheel. Did he have an instant, as the bullet slammed through his brain, when he had realized what was happening? Had he experienced a flash of blinding pain? Or did he never know what hit him, never even know he was hit? Had he died in a fraction of a second, without ever knowing or feeling anything?

Lynn shuddered. Such thoughts were horrible and did no one, least of all Tim, any good. She forced the disturbing images from her mind. Her focus now had to be on the living—and on staying alive.

As she descended, the damp, musty smell grew stronger. It was so dark now that Lynn could see nothing, not her own hands, not the rock walls on either side of her. Behind her she could hear breathing that told her that Rory and Jess were still with her. Ahead of her the sound of an infant crying beckoned. An insistent squeaky sound from somewhere above caused her to instinctively hunch her shoulders to protect the vulnerable back of her neck. Bats? she wondered with revulsion.

Lynn crawled out of the passage into what she sensed was a larger chamber. There she paused, uncertain of where to go next as she no longer had the walls to direct her path. Rory bumped into her leg and crawled up beside her. Jess joined them.

"They're not behind us, are they?" Rory whispered.

"I don't think so. We would have heard something," Lynn replied.

"Like gunshots." Jess's contribution was dry.

"I hear the baby," Lynn said. "Should we try to find that girl—Theresa?"

"It's going to be kind of hard, considering we can't see a thing," Jess said. "Apparently she knows where she's going. We don't."

"How did you know she was Theresa?" Rory asked.

"Intuition," Lynn said, not bothering to state the obvious: How many stray girls could be running for their lives in this small bit of the Uintas? Santa Claus had been looking for Theresa. Who else could the girl have been?

"You never did smoke that cigarette, did you? What did you do with it—and the lighter?" Jess asked.

"The lighter!" Lynn remembered with sudden excitement. She reached down into the pocket of Jess's goose-down jacket, which she still wore. The lighter was there, along with the cigarettes. Lynn touched them wistfully but left them alone.

At the moment there were more urgent matters to take care of than pampering herself with a nicotine fix.

"I have it!" She produced it triumphantly, started to flick on its flame—and stopped. "Do you think I should?"

"If we're going to find our way out of here, yes."

Lynn flicked the Bic. On the second try a small orange flame sprang to life. Lynn blinked as her eyes adjusted to the flickering light.

"It's a mine!" Rory gasped, glancing around. Her words echoed Lynn's observations. The chamber they were in had been carved out of the mountain by man, not nature. Ancient wooden beams supported the ceiling. More beams shored up the walls. The entrance to another passage, larger than the one they had vacated, was located in the wall opposite where they sat. Unless they retraced their path it was the only way out.

"Theresa must have gone in there," Lynn said, gesturing with the lighter. The movement of the flame cast weird shadows on the stone.

"Then so should we," Jess said.

He and Lynn exchanged glances. The alternative was to go back the way they had come. An unspoken consensus was reached between them: no way.

The ceiling was tall enough to allow all of them, even Jess, to stand without stooping. They did. With a gesture Jess indicated that Lynn should take the lead.

Once again, she reflected sourly, she was the point man because she held the light. One-armed as Jess was, it wouldn't be fair to pass it to him. . . . She guessed.

As Lynn stepped into the passage the faint wailing of the baby told her that they were on the right track. Theresa was in front of them. Theresa, who presumably knew the way out.

Lynn and Rory could stand upright in the passage, but Jess was forced to duck. They had to walk carefully because the floor, besides being wet and slippery, sloped downward at an ever steeper angle. Lynn got the impression that they were descending deep into the bowels of the mountain.

All at once it occurred to her where they were almost bound to end up: the mining camp.

Where all the dead bodies were. The scene of the atrocities. The place where the nightmare had begun.

At the thought of exiting through a field of putrefying corpses, Lynn's stomach churned.

At least the bad guys were no longer there. They were half a day's hike up the mountain, searching for their prey.

Stepping carefully over fallen timber, Lynn glanced back at Rory and Jess. Their destination had occurred to him as well, she felt sure. Only Rory remained in ignorance, and Lynn hoped to keep it that way for as long as possible.

Maybe there was another way out the mine. If there were two entrances, maybe there was a third, or even more. Maybe Theresa was heading for still another opening.

Lynn realized that she could no longer hear the baby crying.

She slipped, threw a hand against the wall to catch her balance, and dropped the lighter. It hit the rocks with a clatter. The flame went out.

A darkness so impenetrable that it was suffocating descended upon them.

"Mom!" Rory's protest was a muted wail.

"I dropped the lighter." Sinking to her knees, Lynn began to feel carefully along the cool, wet stone from one wall to the other. Fortunately the passage was only about three feet wide.

She encountered a large, warm hand groping along the floor and realized that Jess and Rory were on their knees searching too.

"It must have bounced," Lynn said, as she turned up nothing.

"Crawl forward a little bit," Jess directed. "Rory, you stay where you are so we don't lose perspective on where the lighter was dropped."

"It's got to be here—I've got it!" Sweeping through a thin layer of running water, Lynn's fingers touched plastic. She scooped it up, clutching it triumphantly. She got ready to flick the Bic—

"Don't!" Jess warned in a hoarse whisper. "Wait!"

"Why?" Lynn asked, puzzled.

"Look back."

Lynn did as he directed. What she saw made her heart start pumping double-time.

A faint golden glow shone behind them.

A light. Obviously someone was carrying it. Someone else was carrying a light as he traversed the passage—and it didn't require a genius to figure out who the someone must be.

Their pursuers were back on the trail.

"Oh, my God!" Rory whispered, her voice shaking. "They're right behind us!"

"Get going!" Jess ordered. "Move!"

Lynn needed no second urging. Thrusting the lighter into her pocket, she scrambled to her feet. Trailing one hand along the clammy rock wall for guidance, she began to walk as quickly as she dared. Toward where? That was the question. All she knew was that they had to keep going forward.

"Mom, they're going to catch us!" Rory sounded near hysteria.

"Shh!" Lynn whispered fiercely. "They will not! They don't even know for sure we're here."

Somewhere far ahead the baby started crying again. Poor baby, Lynn thought, to be caught up in this. Surely, though, even if Theresa was captured, the baby would be unharmed. What kind of monsters would murder a helpless infant?

The men behind them?

Lynn shivered.

"They know Theresa is here," Rory said. "Maybe they're following her now, not us. But they're going to catch us too. They'll kill us, Mom!"

"Keep going!" Jess said. "And quit talking. They might hear."

Without the lighter it was so dark that Lynn could not see so much as an inch in front of her nose. She felt her way along the passage with her toes and her hands, guided by the faint sounds of the unhappy baby. The passage took a right angle. Footing grew more treacherous as the amount of water running over the stone floor increased.

Glancing over her shoulder, Lynn saw that the light still glowed behind them. It was faint, distant, but unmistakably there.

There was no chance of hiding or turning off and thus eluding their pursuers. The walls were solid rock. There were no crossways or byways. They could go only forward, or back.

Lynn took a deep, steadying breath, fighting the growing panic that threatened to engulf her. All they had to do was reach the exit before the bad guys, then run like hell.

"Hurry!" Jess breathed. He was closer now, right behind Rory. The two of them were practically on her heels.

"You want to lead? It's tricky," she said. "I can't see a thing. I could be on the brink of the Grand Canyon and not know it."

"We're better off if I'm last," Jess replied.

"Oh? Why is that?"

"What do you think they're going to do if they realize we're just ahead of them?"

"Start shooting!" Rory gasped. "Oh, Mom, run!"

"I can't run, and neither can you. We're just going to have to walk out of here very fast." Having said that, Lynn picked up the pace as much as she dared. Despite her fear-dried throat and pounding pulse, a warm, fuzzy feeling lodged in the region of her heart as she absorbed the implications of Jess's words. He was staying in last place to act as a human shield.

It wasn't often that a woman found a man willing to take a bullet for her.

If they survived this, that was a bit of altruism on his part that deserved further exploration.

But first they had to survive.

Lynn was shuffling along at a near jog now, though she truly was afraid of encountering one of the bottomless pits that seemed to be a staple of so many fictional caves (of course, they were in a mine but the principle was the same). On the other hand, she would rather fall down a bottomless pit any day than have a close encounter with the monsters behind them.

Without warning the floor dropped away. Lynn stumbled and fell forward, her heart in her throat. Too late, she took back the preference she had mentally expressed for bottomless pits.

The shock of her four-point landing sent shooting pains through her hands and knees. The drop-off was no deeper than a single stair riser; she was shaken but not injured.

With a little cry Rory tumbled after her. Fortunately for Rory, she fell atop Lynn.

Alerted by Rory's cry, Jess did not fall.

"Lynn? Rory?"

"There's a drop-off. Be careful," Lynn warned him in a sharp whisper. The water running over her hands and wetting the knees of her jeans was ice-cold.

"Mom, are you hurt?" Rory asked, rolling off to crouch beside her.

"No," Lynn said. A hand touched her shoulder, slid down her

arm: Jess. His warm, dry fingers closed around hers, and he pulled her to her feet. Rory stood beside her.

The baby's echoing cry lured them on. Glancing back, Lynn was relieved to see that the passage they had fallen out of remained dark.

A couple of right angles must be blocking their pursuers' light from view. Which meant that the bad guys were still a good distance behind them.

"We've got to risk the lighter," Jess said.

Lynn's throat clenched with fear. But if she could not see the glow from the bad guys' light, perhaps they would not be able to see the glow from hers—unless they had extinguished their light and were moving in the dark, and were much closer at hand than any of them supposed.

Unlikely, Lynn decided. Pulling the lighter out of her pocket, she did a quick flick. The Bic sprang to life.

They were in another chamber, a little larger than the first. The roof was about twenty feet high. A single timber toward the rear supported it. Two others had fallen down at one end, so that they slanted from ceiling to floor. Great piles of rock and other debris almost reached the roof in places. Detritus from years of natural wear and tear, perhaps? Or debris left behind by long-ago miners?

Water rushed across the sloping floor to disappear beneath a pile of rubble that filled most of one corner. More water fell in a steady drip, drip, drip from the roof.

The chamber had no exit.

Lynn's eyes grew wide and her breath stopped as that single most crucial fact registered. Glancing at Jess and Rory, she realized that they were just coming to the same conclusion themselves.

"We're trapped!" Rory breathed. Her eyes were dark with fear. Lynn's heart contracted in response.

"There's got to be a way out. Listen, can't you hear the baby crying? Theresa got out of here. So can we," Lynn said with determination.

"Your mom's right." Jess took the lighter from Lynn and held it high, scanning the chiseled stone walls, the rubble-strewn floor, the dripping ceiling.

Lynn put her arms around Rory. The teen clung to her, her head dropping onto her mother's shoulder. My baby, Lynn thought fiercely, and vowed that whatever it took, Rory would live.

"There it is," Jess said with satisfaction. Lynn looked where he indicated and saw a hole about the size of a car tire in one wall near the ceiling. A pyramid of loose rock served as a kind of natural staircase to the hole.

A glance around the chamber confirmed that it was the only means of egress.

If there had ever been another entrance—and there must have been once—it was now blocked by debris.

"Up you go. Hurry."

Jess let the flame shine for a moment longer as the three of them crossed to the pile of stones they would have to climb to reach the hole. Then he doused the light. Lynn scrambled up the rock with Rory behind her.

The only sound besides the distant rush of water and their own labored breathing was the clatter of dislodged pebbles, which echoed as they hit. Behind them, the entrance to the passage they had exited remained blessedly dark. Ahead of them, the baby did not cry.

A hideous thought occurred to Lynn: Was it possible that only one or two of the killers were behind them? Could the others be ahead, waiting, with Theresa as their prisoner?

After crying from the moment they had entered the mine, the baby was now silent. Why?

Lynn's throat grew dry as she considered the myriad possibilities.

All of which she kept to herself for the moment, so as not to scare Rory. They had no choice but to go forward. What awaited them in that direction was pure speculation; what was behind them was not in doubt.

Lynn reached what felt like a firm rock shelf and pulled herself up on it. She could hear Rory's scrambling movements, then feel the brush of her body as her daughter joined her. Jess, behind them, clambered up on the shelf as well.

A quick flick of the Bic revealed that they were crowded on what seemed to be a natural rock ledge about four feet below the roof. The ledge, in the far corner of the chamber, was approximately seven feet long by three and a half feet wide. It provided access to the hole, which opened off its left end.

"Go," Jess said, dousing the light. Not that anyone needed any urging. It would just be a matter of a few minutes, Lynn knew, until their pursuers appeared.

Rory was closest to the hole. She entered first.

"This is really small," Rory whispered, pulling back to shed her jacket. Lynn took it and laid it aside as Rory wriggled into the hole once more.

"I'm going to have to crawl through on my stomach," Rory reported back.

"Be careful, baby."

As her daughter slithered away, Lynn closed her eyes and said a quick, fervent prayer, the first she'd had time for since rolling out of the Jeep.

"Please let this be the way out," she prayed. "Please help us. Please save us. Rory, and me, and Jess."

Funny how natural it now seemed to include Jess.

Suddenly the baby started to wail again. Though the sound was just audible, it was clear that it came from somewhere beyond the hole. Relief made Lynn weak.

The baby was crying. Lynn considered the angry wail an answer to her prayer and felt heartened to know that the Big Guy was on the job, if maybe a little late.

Divine intervention might turn out to be the only thing that kept them alive.

Lynn kept a hand first on Rory's leg and then on her foot to monitor her progress. As Rory pulled away from her touch a light, faint but unmistakable, showed in the opening of the passage they had so recently vacated.

"They're coming," Jess whispered. "We're out of time. Get in there."

Galvanized by that yellowish glow, Lynn scrunched down and

slid into the passage after Rory. Circumference-wise, it was more akin to a large prairie-dog tunnel than a passage intended for human use, and the fit was tight. The goose-down jacket! That was at least part of the problem. Just as Rory had, she would have to take it off.

Rory was wearing a shirt under her jacket. Because the soaked turtleneck had never dried and had been left behind with the kayak, Lynn had nothing beneath but her bra.

"What are you doing?" Jess whispered as she squirmed back out onto the ledge. A glance confirmed that the yellowish glow in the passage had not gone away.

"Stripping," she whispered back without taking time to explain. Thrusting the jacket into his arms, Lynn once again tackled the hole.

To progress she had to lie on her stomach and pull herself forward with her elbows. The rock was cold, and it scraped her bare skin everywhere it touched. She scarcely had room to lift her head. The tunnel was so small, in fact, that it scratched her shoulders and back as well as her stomach as she wormed herself along.

After no more than a minute or so of this, Lynn found herself doing battle with an almost overwhelming attack of claustrophobia.

Only the sound of the baby crying gave her the courage to wriggle on.

The passage seemed to grow narrower. Lynn was about ten feet in now, fighting for every inch, reminding herself equally to breathe and not to panic.

She had never liked enclosed spaces.

To get past a rocky projection she had to scrunch her shoulders as small as they would go. Pushing with her poor abused toes, pulling with her once well-tended nails, she managed to inch through.

Until her hips caught.

Lynn twisted, and wriggled, and pushed, and pulled. She squirmed. She fought.

Nothing worked. She didn't fit!

She was stuck.

30

"MOVE IT!" Jess's voice was muffled as he flicked on the lighter briefly to check on her progress, but the urgency of the message was clear. Lynn knew he must be still on the ledge waiting for her to clear out of his way. But she couldn't move, at least not forward. Try as she would, her hips were not going to make it past that projection.

Not without major liposuction, anyway, which at the moment was not an option.

Rory was two sizes smaller in the hips. From the look of her, so was Theresa.

Death by pear shape!

"I can't!" Lynn whispered back frantically.

"What? Why not?" Jess demanded. From the sound of his voice, his head was inside the hole.

"Mom! Mom, come on! There's a way out—a way to the outside! Theresa's here; she's going to show us! But she's scared. She's afraid to wait! Hurry!" Rory's voice, floating to Lynn from the other end of the tunnel, at once filled her with relief—there were no bad guys waiting to grab them as they exited—and thrust like a stake through her heart.

Lynn wasn't going to be able to make it out. Rory would have to go on alone.

At least, Lynn thought, the most crucial part of her prayer had been answered.

If only one of them could survive she would rather by far that it be Rory. If she survived and Rory did not, the pain would be never-ending. Lynn didn't think she could endure it.

Such was a mother's love.

"Rory, baby, listen!" Lynn's voice was suffused with intensity because she knew time was running out. "I can't get through this way—Jess and I are too big. We're going to have to find another way out. But you go on! Do you hear me? You go on!"

"Come on, Mom!" Rory either didn't hear or didn't comprehend what she was saying.

"You're going to have to go on without me, Rory! I can't fit through this tunnel! It's too narrow! You go on!"

"Mom . . ." The sudden fear in Rory's voice told Lynn that this time her words had been understood. "Mom, what do you mean you can't fit through? You have to!"

"Baby, I can't!"

"Damn it, Lynn! Move it!" Jess's exhortation was savage. It barely distracted Lynn. If she and Jess were done for, so be it. Rory had to save herself.

"Mom, Theresa's leaving! Hurry! Please, hurry!"

"Rory Elizabeth, you go with Theresa. Do you hear me? *You go with Theresa!*"

"I'm not going without you!"

"You go!" Lynn took a deep, steadying breath and lied as she had never lied in her life. It would be too hard on Rory to leave her mother to a near-certain death. She had to give Rory hope to cling to, at least. "Jess and I are going to have to find another way around. We'll be fine. You go with Theresa! Go for help!"

"Mommy, she's leaving!"

"Go, Rory! Go on! The best thing you can do for me is go for help!"

"I don't want to leave you!"

"Go on! I mean it! Go on!" Lynn made her voice sound as harsh and authoritative as she could. To speak to her daughter in that tone when she might never get a chance to talk to her again was one of the hardest things she had ever done. Inside, her heart was breaking. Rory . . .

"Mommy . . ." Rory was crying, Lynn could tell from her voice. Lynn felt hot moisture well into her own eyes. Her throat ached with the force of unshed tears. Rory . . .

Images of her daughter as a smiling infant, a roly-poly toddler, a ponytailed six-year-old, flashed unbidden through her mind. Oh, Rory . . .

"Go with Theresa!"

"I'm going. I'll bring help if I can." Rory gave a great gulping sob, which Lynn had to fight not to answer in kind. "I love you, Mommy!"

"I love you too, Rory Elizabeth," Lynn said fiercely. "Now, get! Hear me? Go!"

"I'm going. I love you!" Rory's sobbing faded, as if she were obediently moving away. Then, fainter still: "Theresa, wait!"

"Oh, Rory," Lynn whispered aloud, and closed her eyes. Her heart seemed to swell with pain.

Would she ever see her daughter again?

Please, God. Please.

"What the hell are you doing? They're almost here!" Jess sounded both angry and frantic. She felt his hand prod her ankle as if to speed her along. If he was able to reach her he must have head and shoulders in the passage.

Lynn wiped the tears from her eyes with both hands. Go with God, she said inwardly to her daughter, then forced herself to concentrate on the second-most pressing matter at hand: saving her own life.

"Back out of the way!" She kicked at Jess in case her order needed translating.

"What?"

"Back up!" She kicked again. Seconds later the change in the quality of the air reaching her feet told her that Jess had obediently pulled out.

Now all she had to do was get out herself.

Pushing with her palms and pulling with her knees, Lynn

found that she could move in reverse, and much faster than she had crawled forward.

"What the hell do you think you're doing?" Jess growled as she emerged feetfirst. "We've got to get out of here!"

"I couldn't get through," she said, maneuvering carefully so she wouldn't fall off the ledge. On her hands and knees she glanced up at him and took a deep, steadying breath. Whatever happened, Rory was now in God's hands and she had to focus all her energies on herself. "I don't fit."

"You don't *fit*?" The exclamation was explosive. A glance showed Lynn that the light from the passage was much brighter now. Their pursuers had almost reached the chamber.

The glow allowed her to see Jess—and Jess to see her. He was looking her over in patent disbelief.

"You won't fit either," she said, giving his body a quick once-over in turn. His hips were slim for a man of his size, but they were wider than hers. As for his shoulders—forget it. "The passage is too narrow. We've got to hide."

"There's no damn place *to* hide," Jess said. "Rory?"

"She made it through. She said there was a way to the outside. Theresa was there with her and was going to show her." Lynn kept her voice steady. If pain showed in her eyes Jess knew better than to acknowledge it.

"She should be all right then." He was bracing, not sympathetic, for which Lynn was thankful. "One good thing about it: If you can't fit through that tunnel you can bet your sweet life that none of these guys will be able to. They won't be able to follow her."

When we're dead, he meant. The sentiment was unspoken, but Lynn heard it loud and clear. Their gazes met.

So be it, she thought. Her life for Rory's. It was a trade she was willing to make.

A man's silhouette darkened the entrance to the passage. Lynn glanced down and saw that he was carrying a flaming torch.

Despite all her avowals her mouth went dry with terror. This was it then.

A sneaking question entered her mind: Did it hurt to die?

Three men followed the torchbearer. One was Santa Claus.

All four—Lynn counted them—were armed with rifles. At least all of them were here. That meant Rory had a real shot at escape.

Once they stepped out of the passage, though, the light from the torch would illuminate the entire chamber. There was no chance that she and Jess could escape detection.

Their present position was horribly, hideously exposed. All the men had to do was look up. Which, sooner or later, they would.

For a brief, desperate instant Lynn thought about squirming back into the passage. At least in there she would be out of sight.

But they would find her. There was no possibility that they would not. That passage provided the only other egress.

At the thought of being trapped and then shot in that coffin-like space, Lynn felt a cold chill run down her spine. She would rather by far meet her end in the open, where at least she could put up a fight.

"Get down!" Jess lay prone. Lynn quickly dropped down beside him. The hard warmth of his body pressed close against hers. Absurdly, given the circumstances, she took comfort from it.

The torchbearer stepped into the chamber. The flame seemed to grow. Warm orange rays stretched into every nook and cranny.

"There's no way out," one of the men said in surprise as the other three entered.

"There has to be a way out," Santa Claus replied, frowning heavily as his gaze probed the corners. "You saw the footprints. They came this way. They can't just have vanished. Ergo, there has to be a way out."

"What difference does it make if we lose them anyway? What harm can they do? There's so little time left! Can't we spend it some other way?" The speaker was a thin, balding man with stooped shoulders and rimless spectacles. He looked like Lynn's idea of Bob Cratchit in *A Christmas Carol*.

"You sound like you're beginning to have doubts, Louis," Santa Claus said. Suddenly all eyes—including Lynn's and

Jess's—were on Louis. "Are you questioning the words of the Lamb?"

"No! No!" Louis sounded afraid. "Of course not! It's just . . . I never bargained on having to kill people."

"Everything we do is at Yahweh's direction! Even this! It is for the greater good. We are only performing the mission we were put here on earth to carry out. We act not out of hatred, but out of love."

"Love heals!" The other two spoke in unison and exchanged knowing nods.

"We don't know what the Judas may have told them," the torchbearer said reasonably. "Like the others, they could well be his agents. They might try to interfere."

"I know, I know, but even if Michael told them everything there's nothing they can do now to stop it. It's too late. I—"

"You're an old woman, Louis, and you always have been," the torchbearer said impatiently. "Can we get on with this, please? If possible I'd like to be at the compound with the Lamb when the time comes."

"So would we all," Santa Claus said, and Louis's qualms appeared to be dismissed.

For a moment there Lynn had almost begun to hope again. Though of course there had never been any real chance that they would just turn around and go away.

"Look for an exit. There has to be one," Santa Claus said.

The torch was raised high. The four men began a visual probe of every nook and cranny, starting at the entrance to the passage and turning slowly toward the far wall.

It was just a matter of seconds now, Lynn knew. Hugging the surface of the ledge, making herself as small and flat as possible while continuing to watch the quartet's every move, Lynn experienced a whole gamut of emotions, from helpless terror to rage to despair.

Rory! Her thoughts flew to her daughter. *Please, God, keep her safe.*

Beside her, Jess seemed to vibrate with as much tension as a just-plucked guitar string.

I don't want to die! Lynn screamed inwardly. Then, *don't let it hurt.*

"There they are!" The torchbearer saw them, pointed. The other three swung around to look.

For an instant, lying flat on that ledge next to Jess with her head cocked up like a baby's in a crib, Lynn stared death in the face and knew it. Her blood ran cold.

Santa Claus laughed, an eerily cheerful chuckle that made the hair rise on the back of Lynn's neck. He lifted his rifle to his shoulder and looked down the sight.

He was going to kill them without a word.

Her fight-or-flight response kicked into high gear. But there was nowhere to run—and no way to fight.

Jess's muscles bunched. Lynn could feel him getting ready to—do what? What could he possibly do? She wasn't waiting to find out.

Acting instinctively, grabbing for the only weapon near at hand, she snatched up a large rock, reared back, and threw it with all her strength at Santa Claus's head.

It connected with a satisfying smack!

Santa Claus cried out, staggering backward. The rifle arced upward. His finger depressed the trigger reflexively. A staccato burst of gunfire roared from the weapon, exploding through the chamber with white streaks of light like dozens of tiny lightning bolts. Bullets ricocheted off the ceiling and floor and walls. A man screamed in agony. All four dropped to the ground as Lynn cowered and covered her head. The torch fell, its flame flickering wildly as it rolled down the wet, sloped floor.

Jess threw himself on top of Lynn, flattening her, driving the breath from her body.

The ceiling came down.

Just dropped straight down with an eardrum-shattering crash, obliterating the bad guys, extinguishing the torch, and producing a huge, choking cloud of dust.

A split second later came another roar, more terrible than the first, followed by an enormous splash.

What felt like the earthquake to end all earthquakes shook the chamber. Sprawled flat on the unforgiving ledge with Jess's far from inconsiderable weight atop her, Lynn clung to the rock with every muscle in her body.

The shaking ended quickly. The echoes lasted longer. When at last all was still, the chamber was as black as pitch. The air was thick with dust. Lynn heard what she thought was rushing water not too far below.

Other than her own and Jess's breathing, there were no human sounds.

Just an ominous, gurgling roar.

31

"ARE YOU OKAY?" Jess asked in her ear.

Lynn couldn't draw enough breath to answer.

"Lynn?" He sounded anxious. Gently he brushed the hair back from the side of her face. His hand felt for and found the pulse at the side of her neck. His fingers rested there, warm and callused. Sprawled on top of her, he made a very effective shield, Lynn reflected. Of course, she might just die of suffocation in the process of being protected.

"Could you . . . get off me?" she managed.

"Oh. Sorry." His hand moved, and he rolled to one side. Lynn lay where she was for a moment, enjoying the luxury of drawing air into near-flattened lungs.

Even if the air was full of dust.

"Lynn? Are you okay? You weren't hit?" He lay on his side with his back against the wall. Lynn wriggled around to face him. She felt limp with the aftermath of danger and emotion. For the moment she just wanted to lie there and savor having looked death in the face and survived.

His good arm, which was bent at the elbow—she assumed his hand cushioned his head—formed a convenient pillow. She allowed her cheek to rest on it, luxuriating in the solid strength of his body, which she could feel along the whole length of hers. It felt wonderful to be alive, unhurt, and—at least temporarily—safe.

"No. I'm okay." She was cold, shivering in fact, and he radiated heat. She scooted closer. The stone on which she lay was hard and bumpy. The chest she snuggled against was hard too, but in a different kind of way: resilient-hard. And warm. So warm. "You?"

"I'm fine."

His arm moved, wrapping around her shoulder and pulling her more firmly against him. As he spoke, his breath feathered her cheek. His large hand curled around her bare upper arm. She got the impression that his mouth was tantalizingly close, and her pulse quickened in response.

"I didn't think we'd get out of that one," she said, ignoring the quickening.

"I kind of had doubts myself."

Her head still rested on his biceps. As his arm flexed she was treated to a firsthand demonstration of the hardness of the muscle there. Lying right up next to him as she was, her hands flattened against the soft flannel covering his chest, her thighs pressed against his, Lynn realized just how strong and muscular his body really was. She realized something else too: that in Jess's arms was just exactly where she wanted to be.

In different circumstances, maybe, but definitely in his arms.

Common sense pulled her back from the brink. Get a grip, she scolded herself. This was neither the right time nor the right place for a romantic interlude.

Even if he just might be the right man.

Lynn pulled free and rolled to a sitting position, not without a twinge or two of regret.

"Careful." His hand rested on her hip. Lynn, to her combined amusement and annoyance, liked it there. It was kind of casually possessive, she thought.

She liked the idea of Jess being casually possessive of her.

"The dust is dying down," she said.

"That's good."

He sat up beside her, his movements seeming more ponderous than usual. Lynn wondered if his shoulder was bleeding again. It almost had to be, considering the abuse he had subjected it to. He had to be in considerable pain as well.

It occurred to her that he was surprisingly tough, physically.

"Is your shoulder bleeding?" she asked.

There was a moment's silence, as if he were checking.

"No. It's just sore as the devil."

"That's good."

"I'm glad you think so."

Lynn smiled at the dryness of his tone. "It's better than bleeding to death."

"I suppose."

"I don't hear anything, do you? Down there?" She cocked her head, listening.

"Nothing alarming."

"Do you think they're dead?" she asked.

Now that he was no longer behind her, she eased back until her shoulder blades touched the wall. The rock felt clammy against her bare skin. She was shivering again, with either cold or fear or some combination of the two. Drawing her knees up to her chest, she wrapped her arms around them.

Snuggling with Jess again even for so basic a necessity as warmth would be a mistake. Right now what they had to concentrate on was survival.

"If not, I'd say they're definitely out of commission." A hint of humor colored Jess's words. "Were you *aiming* for that guy?"

"Of course I was aiming for that guy," Lynn responded, shooting him an indignant glance that was wasted since he could not see it through the darkness. "I'll have you know that I'm a dead shot when it comes to hurled objects. I was the star pitcher on my high school softball team. I struck 'em out every time."

"Oh, what those five two can do," Jess quoted, his shoulder brushing hers companionably as he rested against the rock wall beside her. "I think you just saved our lives."

"It wasn't on purpose, I have to confess. I only threw the rock because it was there. I didn't expect it to really help. At best I

204 • Karen Robards

guess I thought it would give our killer a headache to remember us by."

"Honey, I doubt he would have any trouble remembering you." Jess's voice was warm, caressing, and amused.

"If he were alive," Lynn clarified, ignoring the *honey,* which actually sounded kind of sweet, coming as it did from Jess. She suddenly felt anxious. As pitch black as their surroundings were, it wasn't hard to imagine Santa Claus and his henchmen emerging Terminator-like from the destruction. "Do you think you could flick the Bic for a minute? I'm getting the creeps sitting here in the dark. What *is* that sound?"

It was the same mysterious rushing gurgle that had been present since the roof fell, only it seemed to be growing louder.

A moment later, after a little rooting around that Lynn could hear and feel rather than see, Jess obligingly flicked the Bic.

What Lynn saw as she looked down made her eyes widen with shock.

The good news was, the bad guys were gone. The bad news was, the floor was gone. Everything except the ledge on which they perched was gone.

The entire chamber had fallen into a swirling black river.

Which was now climbing the walls.

Toward them.

Fast.

"Oh, my God!" Lynn breathed. "What happened?"

"At a glance I'd say that an underground river runs beneath this mine. Like all the other rivers in these parts, it's up because of the rain and the spring runoff. I'm guessing here, but I think the water rushing beneath it must have weakened the floor. When you hit the kook in the forehead with the rock, and he sprayed everything in sight with automatic-rifle fire—except, by some miracle, us—the ceiling, also weakened by water, couldn't take it. A huge slab of stone dropped onto the floor and, not incidentally, the bad guys. The floor collapsed under the added weight, falling into the river. Voilà."

"So why is the river climbing the walls?" Lynn asked, staring down in dismay at the roiling object of their discussion. The water gleamed as black as oil, throwing the reflection of the tiny pinpoint of light that was the Bic back at them.

"I think the word is rising," Jess said, lifting the lighter high as he scanned the ceiling. Despite having lost a good chunk of its substance, it still appeared solid. "At a guess I'd say having about two tons of rock dumped in it dammed the thing up."

"Oh, my God! If it keeps rising we could drown!"

"Never a dull moment," Jess said, and turned his head to smile at her. For a moment those baby-blue eyes were bright and intent on her face. "Doesn't it say that about our vacations somewhere in our brochure?"

"If it doesn't," Lynn replied with heartfelt sincerity, "it should."

His smile widened. "Still thinking about suing Adventure, Inc.?"

"I'll make a decision once I've survived."

His smile coaxed an unwilling curve to her lips. He was close, she realized, so close that she could see the reflection of the lighter as dancing twin flames in his eyes. So close that she could smell the distinctive aroma of masculine sweat. So close that she could see every whisker and scratch and grimy smear on his face.

So close that she could shift sideways just a few inches, lift up her face, and kiss him.

She was tempted. *So* tempted.

"Honey, I've got news for you. I think we *have* survived."

"What?"

"The bad guys seem to be dead."

"They do, don't they?" As the ramifications of that rising river finally sank in, a tremendous wave of relief swept over Lynn. They were dead, and she no longer had to fear being murdered. Not for herself, or Rory, or Jess.

The thought of Jess being murdered was almost as painful as picturing herself or Rory as victims.

"I think I've figured out who they were. Remember when they were talking, and they said *love heals*? They're Healers."

"What are Healers?" Her forehead wrinkled.

"A religious cult. Officially, the World Assembly of the True

Disciples of Our Lord God. That's the name they're incorporated under. Known informally as Healers because when they go around preaching their half-baked philosophy, they always end by saying, *love heals.*"

"They're incorporated?"

Jess shrugged. "The Most Reverend Robert Talmadge, otherwise known to Healers as the Lamb—as in Lamb of God, you know—was a corporate lawyer in his former life. Then he got hit on the head by a bolt of lightning or something, found religion in his own peculiar way, and started this cult. When I was checking into him—I told you we did a lot of preparation for Waco, and scoping out other cult leaders who might have been able to persuade Koresh to surrender was part of it—he had control of about a billion dollars' worth of other people's assets and fifty thousand True Disciples spread out all over the world who would cut off their hands if he told them to. They sign everything over to him: houses, cars, trust funds, retirement savings. But there's no law against people doing that of their own free will, just as there is no law against people joining cults. Everything Reverend Bob does is legal and aboveboard. They keep tabs on him, but the authorities can't touch him."

"As far as I know, murder isn't legal."

"Yeah, well." He grinned at her. "You have a point. He's crossed the line. They can touch him now. I figure what happened last night must have been the result of some sort of intracult dispute, and we got in the way. Whatever, the cops will descend on Reverend Bob like a flock of ducks on a kernel of corn when we tell them there are upward of a dozen corpses out there on the mountain, courtesy of his group."

"How can people do such horrible things in the name of religion?"

Jess shook his head. "The world's an insane place."

"I keep thinking about Tim," Lynn said softly. "He had nothing to do with it. He was killed because they were after us."

"Yeah, Tim." Jess's eyes clouded, and his jaw hardened. Watching him, Lynn realized that he fought the pain and guilt of Tim's death by pushing the murder out of his mind and carrying on as if it had never happened. Such denial, she decided, was perhaps the best way to deal with a tragedy for which there was no cure.

Lynn could tell by looking at him that he didn't want to talk about Tim anymore, and she respected that. In fact, she understood how he felt. She didn't want to talk or think about Tim, or the other victims either. What they had to concentrate on for the present was saving themselves.

"We're still not out of the woods, you know," she reminded him, glancing down at the rising water.

"You mean the water?" He looked over the edge. "It's got about eleven feet to go before it reaches us. I'm betting it won't get this high."

"Oh, really? What makes you say that?" His lack of panic, groundless as it might be, was heartening.

"It's not rising as fast as it was. Look for yourself. And most of the debris that fell was loose rock. The floor and ceiling slabs probably broke when they hit. More loose rock. Which means that sooner or later, with nothing solid in its way, the water will shift the blockage or seep through it so that it can return to its natural path."

"Oh, great. I hope we're still alive when it happens."

"We will be. It should start going down in a couple of hours."

"Assuming we haven't drowned by then."

"We won't drown," he said positively.

"What are you, psychic?"

He laughed. "Okay, listen. We won't drown because if the water should get up this high—which it won't because it's just about stopped rising—it's going to go down the tunnel behind us. Picture it like this: this room as a giant bathtub, and the tunnel as the overflow valve. The water can get only so high before it's drained off. If that should happen we'll still have about three feet of air above us to play with. Worst case scenario is we'll get a little wet."

"So what else is new?" Lynn said, absorbing his words and deciding they made sense. "I haven't been dry in two days. And I'm freezing. What did you do with the jackets?"

Jess grimaced. "I'm afraid they got jettisoned in all the excitement."

"Down there?" She pointed.

He nodded in confirmation.

"Great."

His eyes moved over her. Lynn met his gaze, read his mind, and gave him a look that dared him to say anything about her Wonderbra.

"You're all scratched up," Jess said instead.

"The tunnel was a tight fit." Lynn realized that she was no longer one bit cold. If anything, under his gaze she was starting to feel warm. All over.

"This one's bleeding." He rather gingerly shifted the lighter to his right hand and touched a scratch on her shoulder with a forefinger. About the size of a dollar bill, it was more scrape than scratch. Though tiny drops of blood beaded on its surface, it bothered her not at all.

"It doesn't hurt," Lynn replied, her gaze moving from his finger to his face.

"So's this one." His finger trailed along her collarbone, leaving a path of heat in its wake.

"I'll live."

"You've got dirt on your nose." He touched that next, swiping the rough pad of his thumb down the slender bridge as if to wipe the grime away.

"So do you." Lynn managed a laugh, though her heart was beating a mile a minute at what she saw in his eyes.

"You're beautiful," he said. "Even dirty."

"So are you," she responded, then bit the tip of her tongue in chagrin for what she had revealed. Telling him she found him physically attractive was probably a big mistake.

"Think so?" His eyes gleamed at her. The Bic went out. His good arm moved, sliding around her shoulders. She could feel him shifting so that he was lying down again even as he drew her with him.

Just as she'd thought, *big* mistake.

She went without resistance.

"We need to be thinking of a plan to get out of here," she said severely, even as she battled the urge to give it up and wrap her arms around his neck.

"Anal," he chided.

"I am not anal." Lynn pressed her palms flat against his chest. The idea was to hold him off. Or, she thought as her hands registered the masculine allure of the chest she was touching, maybe not.

"Go ahead, lie to yourself." He pulled her closer, and she went without even a token protest. She lay facing him, her head on his biceps again, his arm around her shoulders. His face was so near that all she had to do was lift her chin a fraction more and their mouths would meet. She knew, because her nose made tingly contact with the scratchy underside of his chin when she lifted her head that first little bit.

"So I make lists," Lynn said. "That doesn't make me anal."

"If you say so," he murmured with patent disbelief, his head tilting so that his forehead rested against hers. "Know what?"

"What?"

"Plan or no plan, until the water goes down we're stuck." The warmth of his breath feathered across her lips.

"We are?" She wanted to bridge the fraction of an inch that separated their mouths more than she had ever wanted to do anything in her life.

"Unless you were joking about us not being able to fit through that passage." His voice was husky. The arm beneath her head was as taut as a stretched-to-the-max bungee cord.

"No."

"I didn't think so." His nose touched hers. It was a nothing touch, really, quick and elusive, probably accidental. It sent fire shooting clear down to Lynn's toes.

"Jess," she said, and stopped because she had forgotten what she was going to say. One thought filled her mind to the exclusion of all else: She wanted to kiss him. She wanted to make love to him. Badly.

"Lynn." His turnabout mimicry was both humorous and tender. She could feel the warmth of his breath against her mouth. "Lynn."

The second time he said her name, he sounded serious.

"What?" Her heart was beating faster. Her hands curled into his shirtfront, clung.

"Remember that first day at the airport, the way you scowled at me when you caught me looking at your legs?"

"Yes." Lynn had no trouble at all conjuring up a vision of the tall, handsome, tawny-maned stranger in skintight jeans, boots, and a cowboy hat, whom she'd caught eyeing her legs before they even said hello. She had frozen him with a look at the time, and deservedly so.

Now the memory made her hot.

"Know what I was thinking?"

"I'm afraid to ask."

"If I have anything to say about it, that lady's going to have one hell of a vacation fling."

"Is that so?"

"Yes, ma'am."

Lynn couldn't be certain, but from the sound of his voice she thought he was smiling.

"I was planning on including myself as part of your package deal," he added.

"For one all-inclusive price?" As she said it, Lynn found herself smiling too. That had been the wording in the brochure, after the specific listing of what the outfitters would provide. Included in the quoted price were housing, all meals, and such amenities as showers. Not included was Jess.

"Heck, you might even have been able to talk me into a discount."

"What made you think I'd be interested in a fake cowboy?"

"Aren't you?"

"Not then."

"Now?"

"Maybe."

"Maybe?"

"Maybe."

Whether she tilted her chin the requisite fraction of an inch or he moved his head, Lynn couldn't have said. All she knew was that after that last *maybe* his mouth was on hers.

It was firm and warm and almost unbearably tender. Irresistible, in fact.

With a sound that was part moan, part sigh, she slid her arms around his neck and gave herself up to Jess.

32

LYNN HAD NOT REALIZED how hungry she was for him until she felt his tongue slide into her mouth. It had been a long time since she had felt real sexual pleasure, many months, even years, in fact. The boyfriends she'd had since her divorce had been few and far between, and none of them—not one—had affected her like Jess.

All he had to do was touch his mouth to hers and heat exploded inside her like a bomb filled with fiery shrapnel.

She returned his kiss wildly, burning for him, feeling as if her nerve endings had been doused with napalm and set aflame. Her arms wrapped around his neck. She clung to him, her fingers tangling in the hair at his nape. She pressed her breasts against his chest, loving the way the muscles there refused to yield to her softness. A rhythmic throbbing sprang to life inside her, and she rubbed its source against the bulge in the front of his jeans.

The drugging heat of his mouth and the hard masculinity of his body were what she had craved for what seemed like forever.

He shifted onto his back, taking her with him without breaking the kiss. The upper part of her body lay across his chest. His hand was on her breast, caressing her through the thin nylon and lace. It was large enough to cover her completely and warm enough to feel shocking against her chilled flesh. Her nipples, already hard, ached as his fingers spread and his palm flattened. Gasping, Lynn wriggled closer to encourage him. He broke off the kiss to press his open mouth to her neck.

"Oh, God." She closed her eyes, abandoning herself to sensation. He moved so that she was once more lying beside him. The wet heat of his mouth moved down her neck to her collarbone, to the upper slope of her breast, only to be thwarted by the lacy edge of her bra.

His mouth burned there against the softness of her skin.

Lynn could scarcely draw breath.

"Do you know how many times I've imagined doing this to you?" His voice was a husky whisper as his hand slid under the bra band to find her bare breast. His skin was slightly rough, his fingertips callused. His hand curved over her breast, caressing it, possessing it. His thumb found her nipple.

The throbbing inside her heated and grew more urgent, threatening to spiral out of control.

He pushed her bra up out of his way, and suddenly her breasts were free. His head descended.

Knowing what was coming, Lynn tensed in almost unbearable anticipation. Her nails dug into the nape of his neck.

"Every hour, on the hour, since you gave me that first go-to-hell look."

His mouth found her nipple. He touched it with the tip of his tongue, withdrew, did it again. Unable to bear such teasing, Lynn grasped his head and pulled his lips down to her breast.

As the scalding warmth of his mouth enveloped her, Lynn gasped. Her hands moved to cradle the back of his head. He suckled her, nibbled her, teased the sensitive nubs with his tongue.

Lynn was reduced to making mewling sounds of pleasure. She heard them, knew they came from her own mouth, but didn't care. Her head was thrown back, her fingers buried in his hair as she pressed herself against him, demanding and beseeching at the same time.

"Ah, Lynn. I knew you'd be hot." His voice was thick. His

thigh slid between hers. Lynn felt the hardness of his leg pressed against the part of her that burned and throbbed with need, and she thought she was going to explode.

"Jess. Jess." Beyond coherence now, she could only manage his name. She couldn't wait, not so much as another second. She reached for him, blind in the pitch darkness, one hand sliding beneath the flannel shirt to stroke his flat, washboard-hard belly, briefly distracted by the sheer sensuality of touching him at will as she sought the waistband of his jeans. She meant to free him, but she found to her surprise that she couldn't manage the snap. Her passion-drugged fingers were too clumsy. Thwarted, she slid her hand inside his pants. He was there, swollen almost to the waistband, waiting for her. She touched him, her fingers crawling over him, closing around him. He was huge and hot and damp, and hard as a granite monolith in her hand.

As she squeezed him he groaned, then groaned again, rolling over with her until her back was pressed against the rock and he was on top of her, yanking at her jeans and his own. She helped him, on fire for him, wanting him inside her *right that second* more than she had ever wanted anything in her life.

"Oh, God. Lynn."

His breath came in hard, fast bursts. He was heavy, covering her, urgent now as he freed himself from his jeans. As he got her pants down he thrust his hand between her legs. Lynn squeezed her thighs around his hand, holding him tight, quaking, feeling like she was going to come right there and then and wanting him inside her when she did.

She pushed his hand away, kicked free of her jeans, and pulled him between her legs. Her hands were shaking as she guided him to the place where she needed him to be, lifting her hips off the rocky bed to meet him as he touched her. His body was on fire, burning her.

She whimpered.

With slow control he pushed inside her, forcing her hips back down against the ledge, filling her with a hot, damp, velvet-over-steel instrument that felt better to her than anything in her life ever had. Moaning with pleasure, Lynn arched her back, squirming beneath him, feeling as if she would die from the pure bliss of having his body joined to hers.

He withdrew, then thrust again, deep and slow. She cried out. So did he.

They kissed with greedy passion. Lynn's lips, like her body, opened to him endlessly. Their tongues mated in the same drugging rhythm as their bodies, hot and fierce, nakedly hungry.

He pressed her down into the cold unyielding stone, his movements slow and controlled and yet relentless, rendering her mindless with desire. Her legs twined around his waist, her fingers clutched his hair. She panted and squirmed and lifted her breasts for his delectation and her hips for his taking and called out his name.

His hand slid between them, seeking the place where their bodies joined, finding the quivering flashpoint that was already stimulated almost beyond bearing.

When he touched her, she went utterly still for an instant. Then her hips arched off the stone, begging him to plunge even deeper inside her. In answer he thrust so hard that in a rational state Lynn might have feared being injured. But she wasn't rational. She was mindless, out of her head with passion, with pleasure, with need. He thrust again, and she could stand no more. Sensations she had denied for years burst scaldingly inside her.

Lynn cried out, clung tight, shivered and shook.

As she came, so did he.

How long it was before she surfaced Lynn couldn't have said. Except for her socks and her bra, which was twisted from armpit to armpit, she was naked. She lay sprawled on top of Jess, who had obligingly maneuvered himself so that he lay on his back on the stone. Her arms looped loosely around his neck, and her head rested on his chest.

He wore his socks and his shirt, which, from the feel of him beneath her, was wildly askew.

From mid-chest to ankles, he was naked. Wonderfully naked. Gloriously naked. Seductively naked.

Lynn wriggled a little, experimentally. She felt that most-essential part of him stir in response.

"Hi," he said into the darkness above her head.

Lynn smiled, remembered he could not see, and wormed up his body the few inches that were necessary to allow her to kiss his mouth.

"Hi yourself," she said. Her bra was cutting into her skin. She reached behind, unfastened it, and pulled it off, all without changing position any more than she had to.

"I don't know about you, but I'm up for seconds," he said with an unmistakable verbal leer.

"Greedy," she chided, and kissed him again, lingering over it this time as she felt him stiffen to complete attention beneath her.

His hand found her breast.

"We should check the water level first," she said into his mouth, even as she enjoyed the ministrations of that hand.

"To hell with the water level."

His hand, the one on his injured side, curled around the nape of her neck, pulling her closer as he kissed her. The hand that had been fondling her breast slid down to close over a bare buttock, squeezing intimately.

"We really should check . . ." Lynn lost her train of thought as the hand on her bottom moved lower still, sliding in between her legs, caressing her.

"Jess . . ." she whispered his name against his lips as he put two fingers inside her, pulled them out, and pushed them in again. "Oh, Jess!"

Her mouth left his to move down his body, kissing his neck, his chest, his navel, while his fingers delved and played. She meant to kiss other places as well, meant to take him into her mouth and drive him as crazy as he was driving her, but she wanted him inside her too badly to wait and ended up astride him instead, her legs straddling his hips, her head thrown back, and his hands on her breasts as this time she set the pace.

She came as thoroughly, as wonderfully, as unbelievably as before, crying out his name.

"Jess! Jess! Jess, oh, *Jess*!"

"Yeow! Watch the shoulder," he cautioned seconds later,

snatched from the afterglow by pain as she collapsed atop his chest, sated.

"Sorry. Did I hurt you?" She smiled and snuggled closer as she said it. His arm slid around her waist.

"Just my shoulder. The rest of me feels . . . pretty damned good."

"Is that so?" She kissed the bristly side of his neck.

"Yes, ma'am. Want to go for thirds?"

"We really should check the water level. And your shoulder." Reluctant but determined, Lynn rolled off him. Being careful not to get too close to the edge, she kept a hand on the wall to keep perspective on her location.

"Jess, where's the lighter?"

"Tell the truth: You're not interested in checking the water level at all. This is just a ruse to see me naked." He sat up, and she could feel him groping around the ledge in the dark just as she was. "The lighter's in the front pocket of my jeans. They should be down here somewhere—got 'em."

"Thank goodness." Lynn had been assailed by a vision of his jeans, lighter and all, being kicked over the edge during their recent endeavors. She sat with her legs curled beneath her, her back against the wall.

The Bic flicked. Lynn found herself eyeball to eyeball with the man with whom she had just been locked in the steamy throes of unbridled passion.

He looked like a wild man, was her first thought. His hair hung in a tawny tangle around his shoulders, his face was dirty and scratched in places, and the normally clean lines of his cheeks and chin were obscured by a thick growth of dark stubble.

Naked except for his flannel shirt and mangled socks, he was on his knees, the lighter held high in one hand. His baby-blue eyes gleamed brightly as they met hers.

Lynn's second thought was that sex appeal definitely did not depend upon immaculate personal hygiene. Or upon dignity either.

Because even half-naked, grungy, and in a ridiculous position, Jess was the sexiest thing she had ever seen in her life.

"Hi," he said softly, and leaned forward to plant a kiss on her mouth.

"Hi," she replied when he lifted his head. Every nerve ending in her body radiated warmth. Her mouth tingled. She knew her eyes must be glowing. She smiled at him, feeling all marshmallowy inside.

"I didn't *think* you needed that Wonderbra," he said, openly appraising her body.

Lynn promptly covered her breasts with her hands and scowled at him.

"Hey," he said, letting the Bic go out as he pulled one of her hands away and kissed the soft tip of her breast. "I think they're the perfect size. You didn't imagine that I was the kind of Neanderthal who goes for women with really big chests, did you?"

"Yes, as a matter of fact I did."

He kissed her other breast, put the lighter down somewhere—Lynn heard the faint chink of plastic on rock—and loomed over her. His breath was warm on her face.

"Okay, I admit, I might have been—once," he said, one hand coming up to cup and fondle the body parts under discussion. Lynn's pulse quickened as he whisked his thumb back and forth over a nipple. "Not anymore though. I go for brains now."

"Brains?" Her voice radiated skepticism.

"Yeah." Lynn thought he was smiling. "And butts and boobs and—"

She hit him on his sound arm. He yelped anyway. Then he kissed her again.

It was a while before they got around to checking the water level.

When they did, Lynn was wearing his flannel shirt over her jeans. Her bra listed to the left; a strap had broken under the force of Jess's tender ministrations. Jess was reduced to wearing nothing more than his jeans, socks, and the gauze bandage around his shoulder.

"We can't lose any more clothes. We'll be naked," Lynn observed, eyeing him as the Bic flicked to life again.

"Fine by me." He grinned at her. Lynn realized that, although by now there was hardly a millimeter of his body she had not explored by touch, she had never actually seen him without a shirt. Nice, she thought, admiring the breadth of his shoulders and the wedge of dark hair in the center of his chest that tapered down to disappear beneath the waistband of his jeans. Very nice.

She'd take a dozen just like him, wrapped up in a big bow.

"Look, there's my jacket." Jess was peering over the edge now, and Lynn followed suit. His goose-down floated just below the surface of the water. The sight of it triggered another fierce craving for nicotine, which she had been more or less successfully fighting off since untwining herself from Jess.

There was something about a cigarette after sex . . .

"There were two cigarettes in the pocket," she said mournfully.

"You need to quit anyway." He looked and sounded unsympathetic.

"Do you suppose Rory is all right?" Jess had temporarily wiped everything else from her thoughts, but now that her mind was functioning properly again Rory was the first thing that popped into it.

"She should be. We know where the bad guys are, and they aren't chasing her. You said she was going to follow Theresa out of the mine. If she did she's up there walking around in the sunshine, in a lot better shape than we are."

"I bet she's scared."

"Being scared won't hurt her."

"Jess."

"Hmm?" He was on his knees near the edge, holding the lighter high as he examined the opposite wall.

"Did Rory ever tell you that she wanted to have your baby?"

He looked around at her. "Told you that, did she?"

"She really did?"

" 'Fraid so."

"Oh, my God. What did you say?"

"That I'd rather put one in her mama."

Lynn's jaw dropped. "You didn't!"

He grinned at her. "No, I didn't. But I thought it."

"So what did you say?"

"I just laughed. The key with kids is not to take everything they say seriously."

"Thank you, Doctor."

"You're welcome." He went back to inspecting the opposite wall.

"Jess?"

"Hmm?"

"I'm sorry I suspected you of being a pervert lusting after my daughter."

He glanced around at her with a quirking smile.

"And so you should be."

"I was wrong."

"Yes, you were. About as wrong as you can get. But I forgive you."

"Thank you."

"Anybody else would have seen the truth right away."

"What truth?"

"That it was you I was interested in from the time you got off that plane. At first I was just being nice to your kid to get on your good side." He shook his head at her reproachfully. "Then I did it to make you mad. You're cute when you're mad."

"And you," she said, narrowing her eyes at him, "have a death wish."

He laughed. "See? Real cute."

"Did anybody ever bean you with a rock?"

"Not when they were busy apologizing."

"I already apologized."

"Not good enough. You're going to have to make it up to me."

"With pleasure." A slow smile curved Lynn's lips as she considered ways and means.

"Yeah?" He looked interested.

"Yeah." Her smile widened, and she scooted over to kiss him.

Glancing down, Lynn's heart nearly stopped. A pale oval face stared up at them from the shiny black water some eight feet below.

33

Jess's eyes were closing in anticipation of the touch of Lynn's lips on his mouth when she let loose with what must have been the mother of all screams right in his face. Shocked, he leaped back, his eyes popping open, so startled that he nearly tumbled off the ledge into the water.

"What? What's wrong? What is it?"

Recovering his balance, he looked where she pointed wordlessly, saw the white, sodden face staring up at them, and felt his stomach clench. Maybe it wasn't manly to be scared. If so then he was about as manly as a drag queen, because for just a moment after seeing that face in the water, he felt scared to death.

And it wasn't the first time in the last twenty-four hours either.

Of all the things he had not needed to be confronted with, it was another wacko cult preaching God and wreaking death. One Waco was more than enough for any lifetime. Ever since they had stumbled across the bodies he'd been waging a mental battle with phantom killers alongside the physical battle with real live ones. Once or twice he'd caught himself wondering if maybe he was simply imagining the whole thing, as if somehow he'd failed to wake up from one of his own nightmares.

That way, he feared, lay insanity.

Common sense reasserted itself with comforting firmness. The face in the water belonged to a corpse, of course. And the corpse belonged to one of the men who'd been trying to kill them and instead had died himself when the stone collapsed. Creepy, yes. Scary, no. Not anymore.

The eyes of the creepy-not-scary corpse were wide open, and they seemed to be staring into his own eyes. Unable to help himself, Jess stared back.

"H-help!" the blue lips said.

Beside him Lynn gasped. Jess felt like gasping himself.

Then he saw the man's arms moving and realized that he was treading water; he was, in fact, alive, not dead.

Jess couldn't decide which was scarier: a live bad guy or a dead one.

"Help!" the man said again.

Jess leaned over, letting the meager light of the Bic shine full upon the man in the water.

It was the doubting Thomas—er, Louis.

"Oh, my God," Lynn said. "He's alive!"

She looked wildly around the ledge as if searching for a weapon. Fortunately for the dude in the drink, they were down to nothing more than the clothes on their backs.

"Please," Louis said. He sounded as if he were tiring fast. Jess remembered the temperature of the water. All they had to do was exactly nothing, and the problem would take care of itself in less than fifteen minutes. The guy couldn't save himself. There was nowhere to go but the ledge, and eight feet of slick, vertical, unclimbable rock loomed between the surface of the water and their perch.

"Should I try to sink him?" Lynn nudged him. Jess glanced at her and had to smile. She was armed with a handful of rocks, the largest about the size of a golf ball, with which she obviously proposed to bean the guy.

It was weird to look at this blond-haired, blue-eyed, outrageously sexy female—who wasn't much bigger than a minute and wouldn't from the looks of her put fear into the heart of a gnat—and find himself thinking, That's one formidable woman.

"I don't think we need to stone him to death. If we leave him alone he'll sink in about ten to fifteen minutes. From the looks of him the water temperature is already starting to induce hypothermia."

"Please, help me!" Louis sounded and looked pitiful. Jess watched him bob up and down, his arm movements growing less and less coordinated, then scanned the surface of the water and the walls of the chamber warily. It had just occurred to him to wonder: Where had this guy been for the last hour or so?

Unless he had gills, not underwater.

Jess blinked at a hideous thought: If Louis could survive, so could his cohorts. The question was, had they?

"Where've you been?" Jess called down to him. "You haven't been underwater all this time."

"When everything fell I got sucked into an underground tunnel. There was an air pocket. I crawled into it, but I started running out of air. So I tried to swim out. I came up here."

"What about the others?"

"Can you help me, please?"

"What about the others?" Jess insisted.

"Dead. All dead."

"You sure?"

"How could they have survived?"

"You did."

"By a miracle," Louis said, his voice sounding weaker. "A miracle. Please, will you help me?"

"I don't think God would waste a miracle on you." Jess sank back on his heels and looked at Lynn. "What do you want to do?"

"Oh, God," Lynn groaned under her breath. "I don't think I can just sit here and watch him drown."

"He would have watched us get shot," Jess pointed out. "Or shot us himself. In fact, he might have been the one who shot me, or Tim. They were all firing pretty good out there today. And last night."

"Still . . ." Lynn's voice trailed off as she glanced over the side. Louis's white, pinched face floated just inches above the surface of the water.

It was a sad sight. Jess felt a stirring of compassion himself.

But just a small one.

"Please, lady. Please," Louis begged, obviously having pegged Lynn as the soft touch of the pair staring down at him. "Help me!"

Lynn looked back at Jess. "If we've got to do this, maybe you should put out the lighter. That way at least we wouldn't have to look at him."

"No way," Jess answered positively, though he neglected to add that the idea of waiting in the dark while one creep died and the others might or might not be alive and trying to sneak up on them gave him the willies.

Real men didn't get the willies. Or at least they didn't admit to getting them, if they did.

"You want to watch?" Lynn sounded appalled.

"I want to make sure that this time he's dead." Jess kept his thumb firmly on the little wheel that kept the flame alive.

"You have to help me! I have a mission. I must tell . . ." The rest of Louis's plea trailed off into an unintelligible mutter as he sank a couple of inches and swallowed water.

Jess glanced at Lynn, who appeared both scared and heartsick, then looked back over the edge.

"The end of the world," Louis gasped, bobbing up.

"What a bunch of crap," Jess muttered.

"It's coming . . . the end of the world!" Louis was more agitated now, as if he sensed that his time was growing short.

"I don't want to hear any more of that religious bull, you hear? Or I'll let you drown for sure."

Just the thought of how brainwashed the guy was made Jess angry. He knew it was ridiculous, knew it had nothing to do with him how many stupid sheep allowed themselves to be gulled by a cleverly disguised wolf, but he couldn't help it: The unmitigated idiocy of it made him mad.

He guessed it had something to do with the memory of those children at Waco.

Which he promptly banished from his mind.

"It's the truth!" Louis cried. "It's the end of the world! It's coming! Monday at nine A.M.! I swear!"

All at once Jess remembered the sign carried by the Healers at the airport on the day he and Owen had picked up Lynn and her group. They, too, had prophesied that the world would end, on a specific date he couldn't quite remember, at nine in the morning.

Bunch of kooks.

Jess frowned, pursed his lips, and fought his anger by glancing at Lynn again. She was looking at him, wide-eyed. Kneeling, her fingers closed around a handful of dirty rocks, her delectable body shrouded in his favorite red plaid shirt, her face dirty and scratched, and her hair tousled into a yellow halo around her head, she looked fuckable, not formidable. Jess imagined fucking her, felt his tense muscles relax at the images thus conjured up, and gave her a slight smile.

"He really believes it," she whispered.

"They all do," Jess replied, and shook his head at the man in the water.

"Wrong answer, dude," he told him. "You've been brainwashed. I know all about your Reverend Bob, and he is a first-class lunatic as well as a first-class con artist. I bet you signed your life savings over to him, didn't you? I bet you sold your house and gave him the money. He says jump, and you ask how high, isn't that right? Man, you have been taken for a ride. The world is not going to end on Monday at nine A.M. Trust me. He's wrong."

"No, you're wrong!" Louis argued. "It's true! On my mother's grave, it's true! The Lamb is going to make it happen!"

Going to make it happen? That caught Jess's attention.

"What?" he asked slowly.

"The Lamb is going to make it happen! Two years ago after a session of prayer and fasting, Yahweh—God—appeared before the Lamb and told him the sacred time: June twenty-third, nineteen ninety-six, at nine A.M. And He also told him this: The Lamb is to be the blessed instrument that brings about the end of the world!"

"He's nuts," Lynn whispered.

Jess nodded, but something in Louis's tone bothered him. He

sounded both desperate—and truthful. Of course, as Lynn said, he was nuts. Probably the fact that he believed what he was saying accounted for the authenticity Jess thought he detected in the man's demeanor.

"And just how is Reverend Bob intending to be the instrument that ends the world?" Jess asked.

"Pull me out and I'll tell you," Louis bargained with frantic cunning.

While Jess engaged in inner debate Louis went under once and came back up, gasping. His face was turning purple around his mouth and at his temples. The rest of his skin was so white it appeared waxen. Jess figured he only had about five minutes left until the hypothermia rendered him unconscious and he sank.

Five minutes to determine whether or not Reverend Bob really had hatched some half-baked plan to destroy the world. Even as Jess put the thought into words in his mind, it sounded ludicrous.

There had to be a limit to what one maniac could accomplish.

"Please," Louis said again.

Jess made up his mind abruptly. He passed the lighter to Lynn and started taking off his jeans.

"We can always throw him back in," he said to Lynn as he pushed the denim down his legs. Clad only in his briefs, he lay flat on the ledge and dangled one leg of his jeans at arm's length, over the edge.

"Grab hold," he told Louis. "If you can climb up you're in business. If you can't you're out of luck, because I can't lift you. Blame yourself: You and your pals shot me."

"Thank you! Oh, thank you!" Louis shook his head, as if to fight off lethargy induced by the cold. Then he dog-paddled the few feet necessary to reach the denim lifeline and latched on.

The first try was unsuccessful. Louis fell back into the pool with a splash before his body was out of the water as far as his waist.

The second time was the charm. Louis locked on to those jeans like a pit bull grabbing a poodle and refused to let go, dragging himself up hand over hand, his feet slipping against the stone. Jess felt his unaccustomed lack of strength more with every inch the man rose above the water, but one-handed or not he managed to hang on until Louis was within reach. Then he grabbed one arm, Lynn grabbed the other, and they dragged Louis up onto the ledge.

Good thing Louis was a scrawny man.

"Now," Jess said, patting Louis down as the man sprawled gasping on the rock, "tell me your fairy tale. How is Reverend Bob planning to end the world?"

"With nuclear bombs."

Louis was clean. Jess sank back on his heels, eyeing him. Clad in the seen-better-days white dress shirt and dark polyester slacks that Jess was starting to think of as the cult-nut uniform, Louis lay shivering in the puddle he created, his eyes closed. His teeth were chattering so hard that Jess wasn't sure he had heard correctly what the man said.

"With nuclear bombs?" he repeated in disbelief, pulling on his jeans. "Where the hell is Reverend Bob going to get nuclear bombs?"

"We made them." Louis opened an eye, sounding proud. "At Yahweh's behest, the Lamb liquidated all our assets and bought enriched uranium from the Russian mafia. We smuggled it into this country. A hundred pounds of it in a suitcase with a detonator is enough to blow a three-square-mile area to smithereens, you know."

Jess felt a tingle at the base of his spine that warned of the seriousness of what he was hearing. Still, "A three-square-mile area is not the world."

His gaze never leaving Louis, Jess zipped and fastened his jeans. Louis's lips twitched in what could have been a would-be smug smile. If it was he was too cold to pull it off. Lucky for him, Jess reflected. If Louis had smiled he would have been hard-pressed not to punch the man's face in.

"We have six of them. Six bombs in suitcases, already in the hands of our True Disciples. Early Monday morning they will stroll like tourists into the hearts of what Yahweh says are the most strategically important cities in this country: Washington, D.C., New York, Chicago, Los Angeles, Denver, and Seattle. At nine A.M. the Lamb is to detonate them by computer from the compound. *Whoosh!* The centers of those cities gone in a blink; hundreds of thousands of citizens dead."

There was a pause as Jess considered.

"That won't end the world." Jess's voice was harsh. He was still hoping this was no more than a sick fantasy, but the feeling he was getting in his gut was not good. "There would be many survivors."

"There is a second wave of destruction scheduled to be launched at the same time. Did you know that there are six sites in the middle of the country where huge stockpiles of chemical and biological weapons are stored? Sarin—you've heard of it, perhaps, from the Tokyo subway attack? Ricin, which is so powerful a Baggie full of it can kill three thousand people. Lots more. All these man-made instruments of death are slated to be destroyed, but the U.S. government can't seem to come up with a way to do it that won't contaminate everyone for miles around. But the Lamb has said that there is a divine purpose for the government's hesitation. The weapons are meant to further Yahweh's plan. The Lamb has simpler bombs slated for the weapon-storage sites, but they'll do the job. Some of the harmful agents will be burned off in the blast, no doubt, but enough should escape to wipe out a great many who survive the nuclear blasts."

Jess was shaken by what he heard. The Healers were fanatical in their devotion to Reverend Bob, he knew. They would sacrifice their children if he ordered them to—or blow themselves and any intended targets to hell with a smile.

The question was, were these just the ravings of a zealot or part of a plan that was being put into motion even as they spoke?

"Even if Reverend Bob was able to pull off all this, that still wouldn't end the world. It would devastate this country perhaps, but it wouldn't end the world." Jess was calculating the odds of such a tale being true.

"Obviously, you are not a student of the Holy Bible." Louis turned on his side, pushing a soaked strand of hair out of his face as he looked at Jess with narrowed eyes. "Or you would know that once America the Superpower is destroyed, the Red

Hordes will pour out of the East to take over the world, which will bring about the Armageddon, which in turn will lead to the Second Coming and the joyous reunion of the Faithful with Yahweh, who will rule over an earth of peace and harmony forever."

"With Reverend Bob at his right hand," Jess said dryly.

"Exactly," Louis answered, and closed his eyes.

34

LYNN LOOKED AT LOUIS, who lay in his puddle like a landed fish. She then glanced at Jess, who had positioned himself between her and Louis as though he would protect her from him.

Atavistic or not, came the fleeting thought, Lynn found that she quite liked protectiveness in a man. At least, in this man.

Jess was staring down at Louis. His expression was hard to decipher. He looked, she decided, both alarmed and increasingly angry.

The implications of that were scary.

"You don't think that nonsense he's spewing is true, do you?" she asked, aghast.

Jess glanced at her. "Maybe."

"Of course I am telling the truth." Louis opened his eyes and sat up, shivering, water pouring off him in streams. Jess shifted backward to avoid the growing puddle. "But while I was underwater, when I thought I must surely drown, I prayed to Yahweh for help and He led me to the air pocket. Then He spoke to me: He said, 'Louis, you must stop it. The Lamb has made a mistake. You must go to the Lamb and tell him he is wrong, that now is not the time.' "

"Yahweh said that?" Jess asked carefully. Glancing from Louis to Jess, Lynn felt a stirring of fear. Jess believed him. Lynn could tell.

"I must find some way to reach the Lamb, to tell him what Yahweh has revealed to me."

"What time is it?" Lynn asked, as realization started to hit.

Louis glanced at the watch on his wrist. "I have two forty-seven."

If Louis was telling the truth and horrific bombs really were dispersed about the country and scheduled to go off on Monday, June 23, at nine A.M., they were running low on time. This was Sunday, June 22. They had just a little more than eighteen hours until half the country was blown into the stratosphere, and the other half was afflicted with a plague of deadly toxins.

Eighteen hours until the population of the United States was all but wiped off the map.

And the Red Hordes descended.

The thought was so ridiculous that Lynn had trouble taking it seriously.

Until she looked at Louis's face. And Jess's. *They* were taking it seriously. Both of them.

If Jess believed Louis there was a very strong possibility that Louis was telling the truth.

Unbelievable as it seemed, a fanatical religious cult might really have come up with the means to end the world.

At least, the world as they knew it.

I have to get to Rory! It was Lynn's first panicked thought as the terrible implications sank in.

But how? She and Jess were trapped—trapped in a flooded, abandoned mine with this apocalyptic knowledge that no other sane person shared—and they couldn't do a thing to alert anyone, much less the authorities, to the dreadful danger.

They were as helpless as bees in a jar.

In eighteen hours she and Jess were going to die. Rory was going to die. Her mother was going to die, and Jess's daughters, and all the girls on the camping trip. Owen would die. Pat Greer would die. Her house would become so much cosmic dust. Chicago would become so much cosmic dust. Half the freaking United States would become so much cosmic dust.

And Lynn couldn't think of any way to stop it from happening.

Except prayer. She tried that, feverishly.

"Where is the Lamb now?" Jess asked Louis. Focusing on him to quell her rising panic, Lynn was impressed with his calm. He was grim but in control. There was not a trace of panic about the man.

"At the compound. Near Castle Rock, South Dakota, in the headquarters we built in the geographical center of the country. The Lamb chose the location for just that reason. The True Disciples should be gathering there with him to await the end."

"Very loyal of them." Jess's voice was dry. Lynn marveled at his coolness. She didn't feel cool. She felt sick. And very, very scared.

"They want to sit with the Lamb at Yahweh's right hand. They will go to Yahweh with joy, singing hymns of praise. But the time is not right. Yahweh does not want us yet. He told me so, and I must tell the Lamb. But how?" Louis glanced around fretfully. He looked as convinced of their captivity as Lynn was.

"Good question." Jess turned to Lynn. Over Jess's shoulder, Lynn kept a careful watch on Louis. Who knew what the lunatic might try? The whole cockeyed story might be nothing more than a trick to get them off guard.

Lynn wished she could make herself believe that. But instead of attacking Jess as soon as his back was turned, Louis's eyes closed once more, and he folded his hands as though he were praying.

How could a man capable of helping to kill hundreds of thousands of innocent people pray?

"Lynn, listen."

Jess's murmur focused Lynn's attention on him. Well, most of it. Out of the corner of her eye she still kept tabs on Louis. She trusted him about as much as she would have a coiled rattlesnake.

"If Louis is telling the truth—and I have a real bad feeling that says he might be—we can't just wait here and let it happen. We've got to try to stop it."

"I agree." Lynn was all for stopping mass murder whenever possible. Especially when she, Jess, and her daughter were slated to be three of the victims. But the scope of the undertaking required to even begin to halt this was mind-boggling. "Unfortunately, I think we have a little problem: Until the water goes down we're trapped in here."

"I'm going to try to swim out. See how the water ends about eight feet below us? I'm betting that it's at that same level everywhere in the mine. If I can find the passage we came in through, I should be able to swim along it until I reach the surface of the water, then walk on out."

Lynn considered that for a moment. "What if the passage is blocked?"

She remembered the barrage of falling rock when the ceiling and floor had collapsed. The passage could have collapsed, too, in the violent shaking that followed. In fact, it probably had.

"Then I swim back, and we think of something else. Like trying to widen this tunnel behind us."

"It's solid rock," Lynn objected. It would take a jackhammer at the very least to widen that passage.

"That's why I want to try to swim out first."

"It's dangerous." Lynn glanced down at the shiny black lake below them, realizing as she did so just how true her words were. The man-carved walls rising on all sides to the cavern roof were smooth, slippery with moisture, and vertical. Once he was off the ledge it would be nearly impossible for Jess to get back up. Neither she nor Louis, or even the two of them together, would have the strength to pull him up or to anchor any kind of lifeline while Jess climbed it. Besides, with his injury she doubted that Jess could climb anything. Certainly he would not be able to scale the sheer rock wall the way he had the face of the cliff.

Once he was in the water the die would be cast. There could be no turning back. He either made it out or drowned.

She pointed this out.

"Lynn, sweetheart, there's no choice. I can't just sit here twiddling my thumbs while Reverend Bob does his best to blast us and the whole country with us to kingdom come."

Sweetheart. Jess used the endearment as if it were the most natural thing in the world for him to call her. If any other man had said it Lynn would have taken offense. But coming from Jess—Lynn was surprised by how very much she liked having him call her that.

She wanted to be his sweetheart.

Meeting his gaze, Lynn felt a warm glow of pure happiness start in the center of her chest and spread tingling along her nerve endings. It was then that the realization hit: If he was life candy, then she was going to want some every day.

The future suddenly teemed with wonderful, exciting possibilities to be explored.

All because, she thought misty-eyed, she had found Jess.

Just in time to be blown into sub-atomic particles with him in the next day's nuclear holocaust.

"No *way*," Lynn said aloud.

"What?" Jess frowned at her apropos-of-nothing vehemence.

"We've got to get out of here," she said with determination, glancing at the surface of the water below. Maybe they could swim out. Before—once the bad guys were dead—they had no immediate incentive to try to escape. In fact, she had secretly welcomed the time alone with Jess.

But now all that she held dear was on the line. And life was suddenly too precious to lose.

"We?" He looked at her with lifted brows.

"You don't think you're leaving me behind, do you? If you're swimming out I'm swimming out."

"It's dangerous," he objected, just as she had.

"I'm going," Lynn said, her gaze meeting his. For a moment they measured strength of wills.

Then Jess shook his head.

"You *did* say you could swim, right?" It was capitulation, and they both knew it.

"Just get in the water, Romeo. I'll be right behind you."

"Romeo, huh?" Jess grinned, leaned over, and kissed her, hard and quick. Lynn's toes curled at the contact. "I'll take that as a compliment."

"Take it any way you like. But get in the water."

Jess glanced at Louis, his face hardening. "Okay, let's go."

"Me?" Louis looked over the side and shuddered. "I can't get back in that water. I can't!"

"I thought you wanted to carry a message to the Lamb." On his knees, Jess moved inexorably toward Louis.

"There must be some other way—" Louis's objection ended in a shriek as Jess shoved him off the ledge. Arms flailing, he hit with a loud splash. Jess glanced at Lynn.

"Saves arguing," he said with a lopsided grin.

"We could have just left him here."

"We may need him. He may know something we need to know. And I don't want to leave you alone on the ledge with him." Sinking back on his haunches, he glanced down at the floundering Louis and then focused a suddenly serious look on Lynn. "That water's *cold*. And the passage may be blocked. The smart thing for you to do would be to wait here and see if I make it through. If I do, I'll come back for you."

Lynn shook her head. "I'd go out of my mind worrying, wondering if you got through or if you got trapped under there and drowned. If you didn't come back within a reasonable time, I'd end up coming after you anyway. Besides, think how much time we'd waste if you made it and then had to come back for me. Time *is* kind of a consideration here, remember?"

Jess's lips tightened. He looked at her with a frown. "I think you ought to stay here."

"Haven't we already had this argument?"

"Lynn, listen. I—"

Before he could finish his objection she doused the Bic and tucked it deep inside her bra for safekeeping. Holding her nose, she swung her legs over the side and pushed off.

"Lynn!" Jess's voice echoed in her ears as she fell feetfirst into the water.

It was like plunging into an ice-water-filled sensory-deprivation chamber. The intense cold was shocking. The blackness was impenetrable. Lynn could neither see nor hear nor breathe. It was so dark that for a moment she could not be certain which way was up. Feet kicking, arms beating the water, she fought for the surface.

She came up, gasping. Never in her life had she felt water so cold. Hypothermia suddenly went from being an abstract concept to a real possibility.

At least, she thought with black humor, if the passage was blocked they would die fast.

Just another of the thousand and one ways she had found to possibly meet her Maker on this happy camping trip!

Was she having fun yet? Lynn gave a mental snort at the question. Next time around—if there ever was a next time—she was opting for that cruise.

"Lynn, swim away from the side. I'm coming in," Jess called. Lynn obeyed, wondering without much real concern if Louis would follow suit. Splashing sounds told her that he had. A much louder splash announced when Jess hit the water.

She waited, treading water, feeling like a cork bobbing on the surface of a dark, deep, arctic sea. Her movements were rendered clumsy by the cold and the weight of her soaked clothes. Shedding them was an option, she knew—it would certainly make swimming easier—but when and if they ever reached daylight again, she would be down to her underwear.

Saving the world in a Wonderbra and matching panties was not an option she cared to consider.

Jess surfaced with a splutter and called to her.

"Okay," he said when she reached him, touching him to signify her presence. "We're going to swim over to the far wall. Stay close."

It was hard in the pitch darkness to determine where the far wall was, but since Jess had just come off the ledge they turned their backs on that and swam. When Lynn's fingers brushed solid rock she stopped swimming, treading water instead. Jess floated beside her.

"Louis?" Jess called.

"I'm here," Louis answered in a thin voice. He sounded as if he was just a little farther along the wall. "You shouldn't have pushed me in. Yahweh would have provided a way."

"This *is* the way, so shut up and stay put until I tell you otherwise," Jess said to him. Then he spoke in a much gentler tone to Lynn. "I want you to hold on to one end of this"—he

pushed something that felt like icy wet string into her hand—
"while I hold the other end, so I don't get disoriented in the dark
and lose track of where the surface is. I'll swim down, find the
entrance to the passage, and come back to get you."

"Where did you get the string?" Lynn asked, mystified. All
they had were the clothes on their backs, and not many of them.
She had seen no string anywhere.

"It's the gauze you wrapped around my shoulder," he answered. "You must have used a good fifteen feet of it. Hang on
to your end."

Before she could say anything more, he plunged underwater
and was gone. Lynn stared into the darkness, treading water,
clutching her end of the gauze for all she was worth.

Not too far away she could hear Louis breathing, but she
spared him scarcely a thought.

Her whole being was focused on Jess. Please God, she prayed,
please help him. Help us all.

Though her hands, like the rest of her body, had grown numb
with cold, she could feel Jess at the other end of the line through
the tension on the string. If anything went wrong she would
know it.

The gauze went slack. Before she could panic Jess popped up
beside her, drawing in air with a loud gasp.

"Are you all right?" Lynn reached out, encountered a bare
shoulder, and moved closer until she could feel the movements
of his feet and hands with hers. Treading water, she faced him,
careful to keep close enough to the wall so that she occasionally
brushed against it. Without the wall, and Jess, she feared she
might grow disoriented enough to panic, lose her bearings—and
drown.

"Fine," he said. "One good thing about the water being so icy,
it works to numb the pain. When I move my arm I can't feel a
thing."

"Great," Lynn said.

"It is under the circumstances."

"Did you find the entrance?" Just having him so near made
her feel warmer, Lynn discovered, though the effect had to be
purely psychological as he had no body heat to share.

"Yeah. You ready?"

"Yes."

"I'm going to need both arms free, so I'm going to tie the gauze to one of the belt loops on my jeans. Then I'm going to tie it to you. That way we won't lose each other in the dark."

"Okay."

Lynn got the sense that he disappeared beneath the surface, and she guessed he was suiting action to words. She felt a tug at her waist and realized that he was tying the gauze around one of her belt loops too.

"There."

He surfaced beside her again and must have shaken his wet head like a soggy dog, because she felt a sudden barrage of droplets. Her arm brushed his as their limbs moved back and forth through the water. It was reassuring to know he was so near.

The utter blackness combined with the icy-cold water lapping around her shoulders was starting to unnerve her. It was like being in a cold, wet grave.

"Louis, get over here."

Splashing sounds and then breathing close at hand announced that Louis had complied with Jess's order.

"You hang on to the end of this piece of gauze. That'll keep you with us. Drop it, and you're on your own. Hear?"

"We're going to drown," Louis moaned.

"You will for sure if you don't hang on to that gauze," Jess told him. "We're going to have to swim through the passage single file. I go first. Lynn, you're behind me. Louis, you bring up the rear. And Louis"—Jess's voice hardened—"if you screw us up, or cause any problem at all, I'll drown you myself. And that's a promise."

Lynn was still absorbing that when she felt Jess's mouth against her cheek and turned her head to find it. He kissed her, quick and hard. His lips were as wet and as cold as a corpse's. But the inside of his mouth was warm.

"See you on the other side," he whispered in her ear. Then, louder, "Ready?"

"Ready," Lynn answered.

"Ready, Louis?" Once again his tone was very different.

"I think attempting to swim out of here is a mistake. We should focus our efforts on regaining the safety of that shelf while we still have the strength to try. I'm already growing weak, and—"

"You're welcome to stay behind and try to get back up on the ledge if you want." Jess sounded as if he shrugged. "You're not gonna make it, but there's nothing stopping you from giving it your best shot. We're outta here."

"If we wait, and pray, Yahweh will provide a better way. He has already made it clear that He does not wish me to drown. Doing this is not His will."

"Yeah, well, if it makes you feel better just look at it this way: God—or in this case Yahweh—helps those who help themselves," Jess said. "As my grandmother used to say."

"Even the devil can quote scripture," Louis replied bitterly.

"Truer words were never spoken," Jess answered. "Lynn, when I say three we go. Got it?"

"Got it," Lynn said.

"You coming, Louis?"

"You must join me in asking Yahweh—"

"I wouldn't ask your Yahweh the way to the mall. One . . . two . . . *three!*"

A splash and a tug at her waist told Lynn that Jess was gone. Taking a deep, lung-filling gulp of air, Lynn sent her own prayer winging skyward and went under too, swimming down into the icy dark water, one hand on the gauze that linked her to Jess.

35

ELIJAH WAS CRYING AGAIN. Walking along the gravel road that was really not much more than two parallel trails, Theresa tried soothing him by putting her little finger in his mouth so he could suck. He latched on greedily but spit her pinky out almost at once and resumed wailing. She had used that trick too many times in the last few days for him to be fooled by it for long.

His screaming grated on her nerves. Theresa's fists clenched then relaxed as she looked down at the golden-haired baby in the makeshift sling. His noise would give them away to anyone within earshot, she knew, but there was nothing she could do about it. Even to save herself, she would not offer him harm again. He was her one precious link with everything and everyone she loved.

But his hiccuping cries were upsetting. Having no relief to offer him, she just joggled him some, which satisfied him not at all. His wailing grew shriller, more demanding. He squirmed, kicking, his tiny fists beating the air, his face redder than a fire engine.

He *sounded* like a fire engine.

"What's wrong with the baby?" the girl behind her asked.

"He's hungry." Theresa kept walking, not even bothering to glance around. She had done her part to help the girl, who'd been crying intermittently ever since she'd emerged from the crawlway, by leading her out of the mine. Since then the girl had stuck to her like a leech, as if she expected Theresa to save her.

She didn't need anyone else depending on her, Theresa thought. Her efforts had to focus on Elijah—and herself. With her whole family gone now, as she was pretty certain they were, there were only the two of them left.

Whatever the future brought, she had to look after Elijah. When he had awakened in the mine, after she had been so sure he was dead by her hand, she had heard her mother's voice as clearly as if Sally had been standing next to her.

Take care of your brother, she had said.

Those were the terms of the miracle, Theresa knew. You can keep him only if you take care of him.

For her mother, her brother, and herself, Theresa meant to do her best.

"Why don't you stop and feed him?" the girl asked.

"Do I look like I have anything to feed him with?"

This time Theresa did glance back. With her ponytailed blond hair, yellow turtleneck, and slouchy jeans, the girl didn't look that much different from herself. It was her attitude that was different. She was clearly of the world. She had been to school, to movies and malls and restaurants. She had friends, maybe even a boyfriend.

A twinge of envy, which she almost immediately dismissed as ungodly, narrowed Theresa's eyes.

"Can't you, uh, nurse it or something?"

"He's not my son, he's my brother."

"Oh." The girl was quiet for a minute. Then, "Would he eat this?"

Theresa glanced over her shoulder again, then stopped walking and turned to face the girl, who was holding out a flat, ruler-size rectangle wrapped in yellow and white cellophane.

"What is it?" she asked, ignoring the rumble in her own stomach. How long since she had eaten? she wondered, then decided she was better off not knowing the answer.

"Beef jerky. I had some in my pocket."

"Thank you." Theresa took the package and placed it between her teeth. As she ripped the package open, the smell, spicy and tantalizing, made her salivate. Glancing down at howling Elijah, whose face was redder than ever and wet and crumpled with distress, she removed the opened package from her own mouth and extracted the strip of brown meat.

Getting it into his mouth was not a problem. He was crying with such intensity that she could see clear back to his tonsils. Touching his cheek with a finger, murmuring to him, she placed one end of the strip on his tongue and kept hold of the other end so he wouldn't take too much and choke.

He sputtered, gulped, and closed his mouth around the jerky like a fish taking bait. His face was still red, his blue eyes still teary as he met her gaze, but he gummed the meat. And frowned. Theresa supposed that he didn't like the taste, but he didn't let up, sucking and chewing for all he was worth.

Theresa watched him use the new tooth that had been such a source of pride for their mother. She felt a sharp pang of loss.

"He likes it," the girl said.

Theresa glanced up at her. "What's your name?"

"Rory."

"I'm Theresa."

"I know."

Theresa nodded, then looked back at the baby. "This is Elijah," she said.

"Hello, Elijah." The girl met Theresa's gaze. "Why are you and he all alone? Where's the rest of your family?"

Theresa felt a surge of emotion, which she immediately forced back. As Daddy had said more than once, you do what you have to do when you have to do it. She would mourn later.

"They're all dead. Those men who attacked us in your car— they killed them. I saw my cousin—his throat was slit. The others—my mom and brothers and sisters—were lying there in the grass, too. They were so still. . . ." Still holding the end of the jerky while Elijah chewed ravenously at it, she turned her back and started walking again.

"Was that your family down at the mining camp?" Rory

asked, sounding both awed at the prospect and sympathetic, too, as she fell into step beside Theresa. "We—my mom and Jess, who's kind of our guide, and me—found the bodies, but the killers saw us. They started shooting at us—only they looked like ghosts because they were all white and floating when we first saw them. But they have to be the same men. Don't they?"

"They are the Elders, and they wear white robes when they do their Work. They didn't have them on back there at your car," Theresa said. "Let's not talk about it, please."

She could not think about her family and their fate anymore. If she did she would surely die of grief.

"Okay."

They trudged on for a few minutes without speaking. Then Rory said, "Look, my mom's back there."

Theresa had already been witness to Rory's near-hysteria at leaving her mother behind.

"So's mine," Theresa said quietly.

"But mine's alive," Rory insisted. "I have to bring help back to her. Does this road *go* anywhere?"

There would be no help for her own mother, Theresa knew. But maybe—the idea was born reluctantly—she could help Rory save hers.

Rory had provided food for Elijah.

"Into town, eventually," Theresa said. "But it's a long way."

"How far?" Rory asked.

"It usually takes about two hours."

"To walk? That's not so far."

"To drive."

"Oh." Rory absorbed this, then looked at Theresa with despair. Theresa realized that Rory was fighting back tears again. "Do you know anywhere around here where I can go for help?"

Theresa thought about it, then shook her head.

"Then I've got to go back and help my mom." Rory stopped walking.

"Wait," Theresa said as Rory turned to head back toward the mine. "Can you drive?"

36

Without the taut gauze to guide her Lynn would have been lost. Deprived of sight and hearing and the ability to speak, her skin aching from the frigid temperature of the water, she followed Jess down and then forward. Her breaststrokes were rusty but adequate. Her fingers brushing rock walls on two sides told her when they entered the passage.

Her lungs began to hurt. How long had they been underwater? Thirty seconds? A minute? More? It seemed like an hour. It seemed like an eternity.

The gauze slackened. Lynn caught up to Jess, touched his leg, his back. He had stopped and seemed to be in trouble. His movements were not the rhythmic strokes of a swimmer, but the struggles of a man . . . doing what? In the violent throes of drowning? Battling another survivor, like Louis?

Her lungs felt as if they would burst. Lynn pushed beside Jess, meaning to pass him if need be, desperate to survive, to reach air. Her outstretched hands encountered rock. She realized that the passage was, as she had feared, blocked.

They had to turn back.

But Jess was working to clear the blockage. Those were the

frenzied movements she had felt. Fighting panic, Lynn stayed put, clawing at the barrier, dislodging stones of various sizes. She could feel them shift under her hands, feel the disturbance of water around her as they fell. How many were there? How long would clearing an opening take—if it could even be done?

If they did not turn back soon, it would be too late. There would be no time to make it to the oxygen that she knew was behind them in the chamber they had just left. There would be no time for anything at all.

They would die, their bodies floating lifelessly in the passage they had drowned in. In time when the water went down, the corpses, hopelessly bloated by then, would be recovered.

Rory and her mother would cry at her funeral. . . . But of course there would be no funeral. In eighteen hours there would be nothing at all.

Tearing frantically at the barrier, Lynn fought back terror. The urge to breathe, to exhale and then inhale even though she knew she was surrounded by water rather than oxygen, was overpowering. It took every bit of mental strength she possessed to fight it.

If she surrendered to the foolish demands of her body, she would not survive.

If she even allowed herself the luxury of releasing the stale oxygen inside her, which her burning lungs screamed at her to do, she feared she would not be able to keep herself from inhaling again.

She had always heard that drowning was an easy way to die. Whoever thought that had never experienced the searing pressure in the lungs, the sense of suffocation, of panic, that came with not being able to breathe. Not being able to try to breathe.

Her body was undergoing excruciating torture. *She had to breathe.*

A hand grabbed hers, pulling her forward. Woozy, disoriented, she knew that she was being propelled through a tiny opening in the rocks, but every bit of her consciousness that remained was focused on battling the urge to fill her lungs with whatever substance was available.

She had to breathe.

Her kicking toes smashed hard into stone. The bottom! She could feel the bottom of the passage! Had she sunk, or . . . Pushing off with her feet, Lynn launched herself upward.

Crack! The top of her head hit the roof. The pain was sudden, sharp. She totally disregarded it, because her mouth and nose were above the waterline. Opening her mouth, she emptied her lungs and filled them again with air.

Sweet air.

Treading water, she breathed in and out, in and out, in and out. With the restoration of respiration her senses sharpened, and she realized that the wheezing sounds beside her were Jess and Louis doing the same thing.

Breathing. How precious was the ability to breathe!

"We made it," Jess said, his voice hoarse and rasping. "We're in the passage, above the waterline."

He moved, his hand on her arm drawing her forward. Lynn's toes hit rock again, then her knees. Weak, shaken, soaked to the skin, and nearly frozen, she half swam and half crawled from the water, then fell forward, eyes closing as she lay prone on the hard stone floor.

Jess sprawled beside her, breathing as greedily as she. Crawling up behind them, Louis gasped and gurgled as he, too, made it to dry land.

They lay there for what seemed like a long time, though when Jess got to his feet and said it was time to go, it wasn't long enough to suit Lynn.

Physically and mentally, she was exhausted. Her body felt like it had been run over by a Mack truck. Her mind reeled when she tried to form a coherent thought. She simply could not go on. She had to rest.

"Get up, Louis," Jess said. Louis muttered a protest. From the ensuing sounds Lynn got the impression that he was being dragged to his feet.

Then Jess knelt beside her, touching her arm with a gentle hand.

"Lynn, listen. We've got to go. There's only so much time."

Jess's words cracked her torpor. The memory of what they were up against broke it wide open.

"I'm coming," she said through her teeth. Summoning every scrap of willpower she possessed, she got unsteadily to her feet. For a moment she had to stand with her hand braced against the wall.

"Do you still have the lighter?" Jess asked out of the pitch darkness.

"Wait." Lynn felt inside her bra. The lighter was there. She pulled it out and tried to flick it to life. No such luck. The lighter, soaked through like the rest of her, was out of commission. "It won't work. It's too wet."

"Okay. I think I know where we are anyway. Stay close."

The gauze still tied to her belt loop left her little choice. With one hand pressed to the clammy rock wall for guidance, she followed in Jess's wake, shivering as she felt her way along, stumbling at the rear of their little trio. Jess kept Louis in front of him, presumably so that he could keep tabs on the man in case he should try anything.

Which suited Lynn fine. Total blindness enhanced all her other senses, including her sense of fear. Whether he was temporarily on their side or not, Lynn was afraid of Louis. He was a full-fledged nut case, and a murderer as well.

What if Louis changed his mind about the Lamb being mistaken and decided to turn on them, right there in the dark? She didn't fancy getting clobbered over the head with a rock.

They were in the twisty passage that led to the chamber they had first entered, walking uphill where before they had traveled down. Lynn thought they must have surfaced about a third of the way along it, because as they progressed she recognized various landmarks by touch: a splintery timber here, a rocky outcropping there, as well as several slick spots hollowed out of the stone floor by years of wear.

"Careful," Jess's voice warned. From the sound of it—it no longer seemed to be coming from the bottom of a well—she thought he had reached the chamber. Remembering the difference in heights from one floor to the other, Lynn moved cautiously, feeling for the drop-off with an inquisitive set of toes. Her care was rewarded as she found the edge and stepped down.

"Lynn?"

Jess was waiting for her. His strong hand closed around her badly chilled arm, steadying her as she descended the eight inches or so that separated the cavern floor from that of the passage. For a moment after she was on level ground again she permitted herself the luxury of letting her body rest against his.

His arm wrapped around her waist. She was *so* tired, she thought, leaning. Nothing less than a life-or-death emergency could compel her to take another step.

Unfortunately, a life-or-death emergency was exactly what they faced.

Jess had to be tired too, and probably weak from loss of blood as well, but he showed no sign of it.

"Come on," he said, about five centuries before she was ready. His arm left her waist. Setting off across the chamber, he pulled her with him, his hand gripping hers.

"Keep going, Louis," he prodded, and Lynn realized that Louis was stumbling through the dark just ahead of them.

"I'm tired. And I can't see anything," Louis complained.

"The entrance should be on the left. We had to crawl through the passage, remember, so it must be really low," Lynn said, mostly to Jess, as her outstretched hand touched the opposite wall. By dint of sheer willpower she was regaining her strength. She had to go on, and she would.

Without light the only way to find the opening was by feeling along the vertical rock, which consumed precious minutes. Finally Jess made a triumphant sound.

"Got it!" he said. "Louis, you go first. Don't forget to duck."

"Ow!" Seconds later a dull thud and Louis's cry underlined the wisdom of Jess's advice.

"I'll go next. You come after me," Jess said, having no apparent sympathy to spare for Louis. From the sound of his voice his head was no higher than waist level.

"Okay," Lynn answered, crouching. A tug on the gauze that still connected them told her that he was moving.

"Watch your head."

Lynn followed him into the passage on hands and knees, her head carefully lowered. The example of Louis's close encounter was strong.

The floor was as wet and slippery as she remembered. Crawling uphill was less treacherous than crawling down, however, if more tiring. Minutes later Lynn saw the first glimmer of daylight. With a quirk of her lips she realized that she was looking at the proverbial light at the end of the tunnel.

"We made it!" Jess said exultantly as Louis reached the opening. For an instant Lynn pondered the wisdom of letting Louis exit first into a world of rocks and sticks and who knew what other potential weapons. Jess apparently had the same thought at the same time, because he grabbed Louis by the ankle when the man would have crawled out.

"Wait just a minute, buddy," he said, and the two left the passage in tandem, pushing through the leafy forsythia branches that masked the entrance. Lynn brought up the rear.

Even beneath the thick forest canopy the brightness of the day was so intense that it hurt Lynn's eyes. Squinting as she emerged, she could see practically nothing. A gentle breeze caressed her face. Redolent of pine and fresh summer growth, it was doubly welcome after the musky dankness of the mine. Despite the warmth of the afternoon she was freezing. Soaked, chilled to the bone, she shivered uncontrollably under the touch of that soft wind.

Jess's hand on her arm helped her to her feet. She leaned against him again, and his arm went around her waist in a gesture so natural that it warmed her heart. Her body, however, remained dog-tired. And she was still so *cold.*

Jess had to be as cold as she. She was wearing his shirt, which left him bare above the waist. Despite his recent submersion, though, his skin felt warm against her hand and cheek.

"I see now that it was Yahweh's will that I join forces with you," Louis said. Lynn's adjusting eyes found him sitting on the ground not far away, knees up, his back against a fallen log. Seen by clear daylight in such a prosaic position, he did not look like a maniacal killer. He looked . . . ordinary. And rather pitiful. His thinning black hair was plastered against his skull; without his spectacles his eyes had the rheumy, lashless look of a rabbit's. His skin was pasty white, his torn clothes showed glimpses of the even paler flesh they imperfectly hid, and like themselves he had lost his shoes. He was cadaver-thin. "You have been sent by Yahweh as His instrument to take me to the Lamb."

His gaze was on Jess, who was also soaked, pale, and bedraggled but presented a far different picture than Louis. Shirtless, his sodden, ripped jeans clinging to his legs, scratched and scraped and dirty, Jess was handsome still. With his broad shoulders, muscular chest, and arms, and lean, fit build, he could have been a poster boy for virile masculine health. Except, of course, for the wound in his shoulder. The two dime-size holes that pierced him front and back were surrounded now by twin mounds of swollen purple and black flesh. Just looking at them made Lynn wince.

He needed a doctor. He had to be in pain, and what if infection set in?

"Yeah, well," Jess said dryly. "Yahweh works in mysterious ways."

"He does, doesn't He," Louis replied with perfect seriousness. Jess rolled his eyes at Lynn. Lynn would have smiled if she hadn't been so tired—and so scared.

"What time is it?" she asked, pulling away from Jess's side to stand upright. She discovered that her head hurt and she felt slightly nauseous, but she could function, because she had to.

"Three-thirty—*one*, to be precise," Louis answered, glancing at his wrist.

They—and most of the rest of the country—had approximately seventeen and a half hours left to live.

Lynn and Jess exchanged wordless glances. They both were thinking the same thing.

"Let's get going," Jess said, his arm dropping away from her waist as he took a couple of restless steps forward.

"First I've got to find Rory," Lynn demurred. "Anyway, before we do anything I think we need a plan."

Realizing what she had said, Lynn glanced up to find Jess looking at her.

"Don't say it," Lynn warned as their gazes met.

She knew the situation was dire when he didn't reply.

"Want a plan?" he said instead, sounding impatient. "Okay,

here's a plan: We go as fast as we can to the nearest phone and call the cops and the ATF and the FBI and the freaking White House, if necessary, and tell them that a lunatic has hatched a plan to blow up the country at nine in the morning. Then we let them figure out how to stop it."

Lynn thought for a second. "How far are we from anyplace where we might be able to find a phone?"

Jess grimaced. "At a guess I'd say about fifty miles."

"We can't possibly walk that far in time! Wouldn't we be better off trying to hook up with your brother and the rest of the group? At least they have horses!"

"Owen will come looking for us sooner or later, but it may be later and it certainly won't be before morning, because when we don't turn up he'll figure that Tim drove us straight into town to see a doctor, or back to the ranch, or somewhere like that. We could try to find them, but I'd guess they're about twenty miles away and halfway up the next mountain by now. It would probably take us the whole seventeen hours or more to get there on foot. And we might miss them on the mountain."

"I don't suppose there'd be a cellular phone or a CB or anything like that in the Jeep?" Just the thought of what else was in the Jeep caused Lynn to repress a shudder.

"Nope."

"Then what do we do?" Anger at Adventure, Inc.'s absolutely inexcusable failure to have any means of communicating with the outside world in an emergency sharpened her voice. She glared at Jess.

"We walk," Jess said, tight-lipped. "That is the plan. The whole plan. The entire plan. The only possible plan. You can stay here and think about it some more if you want, but I'm walking out of here. Maybe we'll get lucky and somebody will give us a lift once we get closer in."

"I have to find Rory," Lynn said. "I can't leave here without Rory."

"Rory is going to be toast, as we all are, if we don't get this thing stopped," Jess said. "Anyway, you sent her for help. If she has a brain the size of a flea's, she'll be walking along the road. We'll catch up to her. So let's go. Louis, get up."

"Don't upset yourselves. Yahweh will help us," Louis said serenely, getting to his feet. Jess started off, discovered that he was still tied to Lynn, stopped, and tried to break the gauze.

"Hold still," Lynn said when it became obvious that wet, twisted gauze was difficult to break. Moving close to Jess, she picked delicately at the knot encircling his left front belt loop with the ruins of her nails.

"To hell with that," Jess snorted, hooking his fingers in the belt loop and ripping it loose. He passed the torn-off belt loop, gauze rope attached, to Lynn.

"That works," Lynn said, accepting the offering. Gathering up the trailing ends, she didn't bother to try to free herself—there wasn't time—but instead wrapped the gauze around her waist in a makeshift sash and knotted it.

"Let's go," Jess said. "Louis, what are you doing?"

Louis, head bowed, had his eyes closed and his hands clasped under his chin. Lynn would have thought that what he was doing was pretty obvious, but she didn't say so.

"Praying to Yahweh to help us if it is His will," Louis said, opening his eyes. "Specifically, I asked Him for transportation."

"Come on, both of you," Jess said impatiently. "Yahweh can work his miracle on the road."

They started off, reached the road, and had been walking downhill for a good while when a sound—a *strange* sound—stopped all three of them in their tracks.

37

"WHAT *IS* THAT?" Lynn asked, glancing at Jess. From his expression she decided that the wheezing bellow was not, at least, the mating call of a grizzly, which she assumed he would recognize.

"Got me." Like Lynn and Louis, Jess stared at the vine-shrouded forest wall from behind which the bellow emanated. The cry sounded again, long and mournful, and ear-piercingly loud.

Whatever it was waited about twenty feet in front of them, hidden by a veil of foliage.

"A moose?" Lynn wondered aloud.

"We don't have time for this," Jess warned. He prodded Louis in the back, and the three of them started walking again. Louis was slightly in front so they could keep an eye on him. Jess and Lynn walked more or less side by side. They moved cautiously, all eyes on the spot. If Lynn had been in a mood to notice, she would have been amused at how they all suddenly hugged the side of the gravel track farthest from the sound.

"Whatever it is is answering *you*," Jess said. "I told you you were yelling loud enough to be heard clear to Salt Lake City."

"I want Rory," Lynn said. "And I'm going to yell loud enough so that she can hear me. I can't leave here without her."

"We'll run across her—" Jess began, only to be interrupted by another hiccuping bellow.

The leaves hiding the creature from view swayed. Lynn realized with horror that whatever it was was coming through the barrier onto the road about five feet in front of them.

Clutching Jess's arm, she stopped, staring. So did he. Louis stopped too, sucking in his breath.

A head—large, furry, and tan—thrust through the leaves. Big brown eyes blinked at them. Rabbit ears twitched. A huge mouth opened to reveal square yellow teeth and a thick pink tongue.

"Haw-hee! Haw-hee! Haw-hee!"

"It's a donkey!" Lynn exclaimed in relief. It was only then that she noticed the halter it wore. "A *tame* donkey."

"Thank God it isn't a wild one," Jess said dryly.

Lynn silenced him with a look. "What's a donkey doing out here, do you suppose?" Struck by the possibility that it might belong to a camper with a cellular phone, she said, "Is somebody with it? *Hello, is anybody here?*"

"Would you please quit yelling in my ear?" Jess freed himself from Lynn's grasp on his arm and crossed the road to check the creature out. Lynn followed him. It wasn't even a large donkey, and she certainly wasn't afraid of it.

"She's hooked to a cart." Jess had parted the leaves and was looking the donkey over. "She's stuck. And I'd say she's on her own."

"Poor thing." Lynn gave the animal a pat as Jess pushed through the foliage to the donkey's side. It brayed at her. She stepped back, wincing at the noise.

"Somebody must have been using her to fetch supplies when she got loose," Jess said from beyond the barrier. "There are groceries in the cart. Apple, anyone?"

A hand holding an apple pushed through the leaves. Lynn salivated. Before she could grab it the donkey beat her to the punch. Those big yellow teeth latched on to the apple with a hungry crunch.

"No!" Lynn yelled despairingly. Half the apple dropped from the greedy beast's mouth to fall into the dirt. Lynn's eyes followed it down.

"Ow!" Jess exclaimed at the same time, snatching his hand back through the leaves. From behind the barrier he let loose with a string of curses. Lynn realized that the donkey had crunched flesh as well as fruit.

"Stupid animal," she muttered, going after what was left of the apple. Under most circumstances she wouldn't even have considered making a meal out of a donkey's leftovers. These, however, were not most circumstances. Kneeling in the dirt, she picked up the half-eaten remains.

The apple's smell made her close her eyes. She realized that, along with being exhausted and cold and scared and minus one daughter, she was starving.

"Don't eat that." Jess frowned at her through an opening in the screen of leaves. Reaching through the tangle, he took the apple from her and offered it flat-palmed to the donkey, who grabbed it with relish.

"What about me?" Lynn asked indignantly, standing up.

"There's a whole sackful."

Jess passed her another apple, red and shiny, which Lynn bit into with relish. The crispness of the skin, the sweet-tart flavor of the flesh, the lushness of the juice were all sensations to be savored—at least when she wasn't starving, she decided as she gobbled it down.

"Bottled water too," Jess continued, passing a green plastic bottle through the leaves. "Potatoes. Powdered milk. Flour and lard. And sugar, and cocoa."

"I'm hungry too," Louis said, sounding plaintive.

Jess passed him an apple and a bottle of water. The donkey brayed close to Lynn's ear, making her jump.

"Shut up, you," she said, scowling at the beast. It brayed again. Lynn had little doubt that it was demanding another apple.

"Here, girl, let me get you out of this." Jess was talking to the donkey. His hand appeared through the foliage to close over the halter, and he pulled the donkey's head back through the leaves. Moments later he led it onto the track.

Its back wasn't any higher than Lynn's elbow. A lead fastened to a brown leather halter was wrapped around Jess's hand. A three-wheeled cart, obviously homemade, was attached by wooden poles to a makeshift harness that fit over the animal's shoulders. The cart, like the poles, was made of wood, well-weathered, with a hinged lid. The lid was open, revealing an interior stuffed with provisions.

"I told you Yahweh would provide," Louis said with satisfaction.

Lynn and Jess both glanced at him to find that he was looking at the donkey.

"Transportation," Louis explained smugly, catching those glances.

"You've got to be kidding." Jess swigged water, polished off his own apple, and fed the core to the appreciative animal. "We can probably travel faster than she can. And there's no way she can carry all three of us."

"Maybe we can take turns," Lynn suggested, feeling the full weight of her exhaustion now that there was a prospect of moving and sitting at the same time. "At least that way we won't have to stop to rest."

"Why not?" Jess shrugged, looking resigned. Opening the cart's lid, he snagged another apple. "Lynn?"

"Thanks."

He passed it to her. Following his example, Lynn offered her core to the donkey. It accepted with surprising daintiness.

"All right, we're out of here. Lynn, do you want to ride first?"

She eyed the donkey. Riding a horse had been an unpleasant experience, but this small creature looked both cute and harmless. Anyway, she would be sitting atop the cart, not the beast, and Jess would be holding the lead. Still . . .

Exhaustion battled trepidation, and exhaustion won.

"You know, I could be on a cruise ship right now. I had that choice." Lynn suppressed any lingering nervousness, tossed her empty water bottle inside the cart (even in the face of imminent mass destruction, littering did not feel right), and hitched herself

aboard. The prospect of sitting for a while was simply too entic-
ing to resist. Of course, for her to ride while Jess—and Louis—
walked was sexist, no doubt about it.

At the moment, Lynn discovered, she didn't particularly care.
She was too tired.

It felt good to sit. Even cross-legged on a hard and precarious
perch.

Jess gave her a sudden, slashing grin. "Just think what you
would have missed."

You. The word shot through Lynn's mind as she looked into
those dancing baby-blue eyes. And she realized that, whatever
happened, she wouldn't have skipped this vacation for the
world.

Now if she could only manage to survive it.

"By the way," Jess said, starting off, "she's a burro."

Lynn clutched the sides of the cart as it lurched into motion.
Gravel crunched beneath the tires. The cart rocked back and
forth. Triangular in shape, it had one small wheel in front and
two large wheels attached to either side that looked as if they
had been taken from a child's bicycle. It was just large enough
for Lynn to sit on. Cross-legged, she perched atop the wooden
lid, holding on for dear life.

Comfortable, Lynn thought, didn't even begin to apply.

Of course, since her hands were occupied, a small swarm of
no see ums appeared out of thin air to buzz around her head.
She risked her life to swat at them, missed, barely kept her seat,
and gave up. When the buzzing stopped at last, Lynn assumed
the little fiends had finally drunk their fill and lurched off.

She made a mental note to add itching to her list of miseries.

"Rory!" she yelled, in case her daughter should be within
earshot.

The donkey—burro—started nervously. Only Jess's hold on
the lead kept it in check. Patting the creature's neck, Jess threw
her a killer look.

"Are you yelling again? You're lucky you're not riding a run-
away right now. You don't make sudden noises behind an animal like this. Like horses, they're very sensitive creatures."

"Jess, I told you, I have to find Rory."

"And I told you she's probably ahead of us. She had a good two-hour start, remember? We'll catch her. Whether we do or not we have to keep going. Our first priority has to be to get to a phone. If we don't do that and Reverend Bob goes through with his plan, finding Rory won't matter."

"I know."

Lynn *did* know. But she couldn't stand the thought of leaving her daughter behind in the wilderness.

Jess grimaced. "Look, I know how you feel. If we should miss her we'll send a search party back for her. It's the best we can do under the circumstances."

"I know." Lynn knew that what he was saying was true. She knew that with the exception of Louis the local bad guys were—with ninety-nine percent probability—dead, so the only immediate risk to Rory was a close encounter with a grizzly. She knew that climbing off the cart and beginning her own search of the forest would be almost certainly futile. There was simply too much area involved.

And, as Jess said, Rory was in all likelihood on the road ahead.

Still, with an instinct too strong for mere logic, she wanted her daughter.

Though if she faced the truth she could do nothing to protect Rory when nine tomorrow morning rolled around. If the bombs exploded, Rory would be better off up here in the High Wilderness area of the Uintas than almost anyplace she could think of.

On the other hand, being a survivor might in the end be a worse fate than going instantly at ground zero.

"What time is it?" she asked. Their pace was maddeningly slow. Lynn doubted they had covered three miles since finding the burro.

"Four forty-five," Louis answered.

A little more than sixteen hours to go. And they still had to cover approximately forty-five miles.

"We're not going to make it," Lynn said.

"We will if it is the will of Yahweh," Louis said. "You must have faith."

Jess flicked a glance at Lynn.

"Hang on," he said, and started to jog.

The cart lurched forward. The burro, pulled into a trot, pro-tested by flicking her ears back and forth and swishing her tail. It smacked Lynn in the face once, twice, three times. Being jounced to death, afraid to let go to defend herself from that rhythmic lash, Lynn endured for as long as she could, then yelled for Jess to stop.

"What now?" He did as she asked but didn't look happy about it.

"Your turn," she said, climbing off the cart. "I'll lead her."

"You can't lead her," Jess protested. "You don't know the first thing about burros. Anyway, in case you haven't noticed, we're running now."

"Listen, you sexist pig," Lynn said. "I can run as well as you. I've had a nice rest sitting back there, and *I* don't have a bullet wound. As for leading the stupid burro, how hard can it be? If we have any hope of getting out of these mountains in time, we're going to have to take turns running and riding. And it's *your* turn to ride."

"I'll ride," Louis offered hopefully.

"Hang on to the damned lead then. And for God's sake don't yell." After staring at her for a moment, Jess passed over the leather strap and straddled the cart. Both he and Lynn ignored Louis. If someone had to be left behind, he would be the one. They both recognized that fact without even having to discuss it.

From his lack of argument, so did Louis.

Lynn closed her fingers around the lead.

"Hang on," she echoed Jess's warning as she glanced back. Despite the direness of the circumstances she had to smile. Jess looked ridiculous perched cross-legged on the small cart, bare-chested, tawny hair hanging to his shoulders, his good hand curled around its front corner. His other hand, she saw, rested in his lap.

Her smile faded.

If Jess was favoring his wounded side he had to be in pain. The effects of the cold water, which had allowed him more mobility than he probably should have used, had clearly worn off. They were lucky the wound hadn't started bleeding again.

"Giddy-up!" Resolving to be as careful as possible to avoid

subjecting Jess to any unnecessary discomfort, Lynn tugged hard on the lead and started off.

Running was something she did occasionally, but not in tattered socks over a surface of unfriendly gravel. She stuck to the thin strip of grass at the side of the track, keeping an eagle eye out for sharp objects, and tried to hit a steady pace.

Tugging an obstinate burro behind her did not make that easy. Lynn felt as if she were towing a small barge. In minutes she was panting. Louis, obviously no jogger himself, huffed and puffed beside her. A glance back showed Jess clinging doggedly to the jolting cart.

With every shadow that shifted across the road Lynn felt the weight of time passing.

"Come on, you!"

Wheezing now, Lynn pulled harder, trying to keep the burro from following its unmistakable intention to slow into a walk. What she was doing wasn't running, she decided. It was the kind of hard labor appropriate for convicted felons.

"*Ah-ooo-gah!*" A horn blasted deafeningly behind them. Lynn started, then went wide-eyed with delight as she glanced back to see an ancient truck skidding to halt in the gravel.

Motorized transportation was the thought that ran through her mind.

The burro, unfortunately, was not so delighted by the truck's advent. Galvanized by the sound of the horn, it leaped forward, knocking Lynn to the ground even as she glanced back at the truck. The lead whipped from her hand as the animal took off.

Sprawled on her stomach in the grass, Lynn could only watch with horror as burro, cart, and Jess rocketed past her, heading at a mad gallop down the road.

"Whoa!" screamed Jess, clinging to the bucking cart like a rodeo rider to a crazed bronc as they careened over ruts and rocks and ridges. "Whoa!"

"Yahweh save him," Louis muttered piously.

"Jess!" Lynn scrambled to her feet and gave chase. Running, she watched open-mouthed as the cart, with Jess still grimly hanging on, hit a rock and was suddenly airborne, flying forward in what looked like an insane attempt to leapfrog the burro!

38

When Lynn caught up with Jess he was lying flat on his back on top of a crushed snowball bush, cursing a blue streak. Broken harness still attached, the overturned cart rested on the roadbed nearby, its wheels still turning sluggishly. Of the burro there was not a sign.

A steady string of well-enunciated profanities had reached her ears before she actually caught sight of him, assuring her that he wasn't dead.

"Are you hurt?" she asked as she approached him, trying hard to control a wayward twitch of her lips.

"It's a damned miracle I didn't break every bone in my body," he said, from which she deduced he wasn't. "I *told* you to hang on to that lead."

"Ride 'em, cowboy," she said, unable to hold back any longer, and giggled.

The look he gave her was withering. Groaning, he got to his feet, removing a mesh bag of potatoes from his chest in the process and dropping it to the ground. Lynn noticed that the area around the bush was littered with groceries, and giggled again.

"Was that a truck?" He felt his shoulder, grimacing.

In all the excitement Lynn had almost forgotten the truck.

"Yes!" She turned back to look up the road. A bend hid the truck from sight. But she was just in time to see Louis run into view, arms and legs pumping as he pounded toward them. He was yelling something, though Lynn couldn't understand the words.

Right behind him came a slender young woman in a cream-colored nightgown, hair flying behind her, a stout stick raised above her head.

"Theresa!" Lynn exclaimed as Theresa took a swing at Louis. The stick missed him by what looked like mere inches, and Louis spurted ahead. Lynn was amazed at how fast the man could run when he had to.

"What now?" Jess groaned, and stepped into the roadbed to intercept Louis. "Hold it!"

"Don't stop me!" Louis screeched as Jess grabbed him when he would have run past.

"Murderer! Murderer!" Theresa was upon them within seconds, beating Louis about the head and shoulders with her stick as Jess yelled at her to stop. Louis, cowering, tried to fend her off with an upraised arm.

"Help! Help!" Louis cried, darting behind Jess, who with only one good arm was unable to both hold on to him and grab for the weapon. He lost his grip on Louis.

"Ow! Dammit!" Jess wrested the stick from Theresa with a quick twist of his wrist, in the process apparently catching a blow intended for Louis.

"He killed my family! Murderer!" Disarmed, Theresa pummeled Louis with her fists, kicking him, tearing at his hair as both Louis and Jess tried to hold her off. She looked like an avenging fury, with tears pouring down her face all the while. "He killed my family!"

"Theresa, don't!" Heart aching for the girl, Lynn caught her arm, trying to get her attention, to distract her from the attack. Theresa turned on her, a wild look in her eyes, her lifted fist threatening. Lynn braced herself for the blow. The girl, though slender, was several inches taller than she and beside herself with anger and grief. But the lifted fist never fell.

"He was one of the men who killed my mother," Theresa said pitifully, looking into Lynn's eyes. The fight drained out of her and she fell to her knees, her head dropping onto her hands as she dissolved into paroxysms of sobs.

"It's all right," Lynn murmured, bending over Theresa, putting an arm around the girl's heaving shoulders. Theresa's distress made her own eyes fill. Poor child, what had she been through? "Shh, now. It's all right."

"Why?" Theresa lifted her face to hiss at Louis, ignoring Lynn's attempts at comforting her. "Why did you do it? My mother never hurt you or anyone! Neither did my little sisters, or my brothers, or any of my family! We just wanted to be left in peace! Why did you have to chase us down and kill them?"

Held now by Jess's grip on his arm, Louis seemed to shrink under Theresa's impassioned gaze.

"Michael Stewart always sat in the most honored position at the right hand of the Lamb, yet he turned traitor. He ran away in the dead of night, taking his family and followers with him! He was going to betray us! The Lamb sent us on a holy mission to find and destroy the Michaelites before they could reveal Yahweh's divine plan." Louis's voice was almost pleading.

"The Lamb! The Lamb!" Theresa practically spat the words. "Robert Talmadge is no more the Lamb than you are! Do you know what he did? He tried to rape me! I was only fifteen years old! That's what opened my father's eyes; that's why he took us away! My father meant no harm to anyone! Why couldn't you just leave us alone? That's all we wanted, to be left alone! Murderer!"

The fire returned to Theresa's eyes, and she surged to her feet, fists clenched and teeth gnashing.

The wail of a baby behind them made her, and everyone else, look around.

"He started to cry," Rory said, approaching with the screaming, squirming child held awkwardly in her arms. "I didn't know what to do."

"Rory!" Lynn looked at her daughter as Theresa took the squalling infant from her. She felt a great weight fall away from her heart. "Rory!"

"Hi, Mom," Rory said, surrendering to Lynn's hug and even returning it. "Are you okay?"

"Oh, Rory" was all Lynn could say as she buried her face in her daughter's shoulder and held her tight. "I'm fine. What about you?"

"I was really scared, but I'm okay now," Rory confessed. "I was afraid you might not be able to escape from those men. Is he really one of them?"

Her daughter had to mean Louis.

"Yes," she said.

"They killed Theresa's whole family. Except for Elijah. That's the baby's name."

"I know. I'm so sorry."

"Folks, we can sort all this out in the truck. We need to make tracks into town." Jess, keeping one hand on Louis's arm and a wary eye on Theresa, who was cradling the bawling baby, herded them all back down the road.

Rory, walking arm-in-arm with Lynn, broke away from her mother to snatch up an object from the side of the road.

"Look, Theresa, it's powdered milk!" she said, holding up the red-and-white box so the other girl could see it. A glance around sent her flying after something else. "And bottled water to mix it with! Elijah can have some milk!"

"Where did that come from?" Theresa asked, looking at the items Rory held. Her voice sounded dull. Her eyes were still awash with tears, but they no longer ran down her face. It was, Lynn thought, as if she had deliberately damped down her emotions.

"We found them in a cart attached to a lost burro," Lynn said. "Someone must have been using it to haul groceries, but it got away."

"Was the burro tan or gray?" Theresa said, as if there were only the two choices.

"Tan."

"Esther." Theresa almost whispered the name. "The gray one is Ruth. My father was bringing back supplies. The burros must have run away when—" Her lip quivered and she broke off, her chest heaving as she obviously fought to regain control.

"Yahweh forgive me, I never thought of the pain we might cause," Louis whispered, staring at Theresa.

Her head swung around, her long hair whipping through the air. She fixed him with fierce eyes. "God—not Yahweh, *God*—will never forgive you, and neither will I! You will burn in hell for what you did, you murderer!"

"Here's the truck," Jess interrupted.

Lynn glanced up to find that they were, indeed, at the truck. It was a blue Ford pickup with *Supercab* stenciled on the left front. Below that in flaking chrome was the designation *F-250.*

Opening the passenger-side door and pulling the front seat down, Jess said to Louis, "You ride in the back."

Louis clambered into the spartan rear seat without argument and scooted over as far as possible. He was still the same scrawny, stooped, pitiful-looking little man he had been fifteen minutes before, but he had been forever transformed in Lynn's eyes. Theresa's raging grief had given an all-too-real face to the victims of the slaughter in the mining camp. From being a crank who had tried but ultimately failed to do significant harm to her and Rory and Jess, Louis metamorphosed into a monster who had participated in the murders of Theresa's family.

"I mixed some milk for Elijah," Rory said, offering a green plastic water bottle to Theresa. "I don't know what we can do for a nipple though."

"Thanks." Theresa accepted the bottle, tilted the baby so that he was upright, and pressed the bottle's open lip to his cheek. The baby's sobs subsided as he eagerly turned his head in search of the promised sustenance. Theresa put the bottle to his mouth and carefully tilted it. "My mother already taught him to drink from a cup."

There was both pride and heartbreak in her face as she watched the baby swallow.

"All right, everybody in." Jess walked around to the driver's side. "Louis, pass me your watch. I'm tired of asking you what time it is."

"Almost six," Louis said in a subdued tone, unfastening the watch and handing it over. When Rory tried to scramble into the backseat with Louis, Lynn stopped her with a hand on her arm.

"Wait a minute," she said to Rory. Then, following Jess, "I'm driving. You're wounded, remember? Get in the back with Louis."

"*You're* driving?" With his left hand on the open driver-side door, he turned to look at her. Both his tone and his expression left no doubt about his feelings. Lynn narrowed her eyes at him.

"You have only one working arm, and you need to stay close to Louis, just in case. Believe me, I can drive as well as you."

"This is a *truck*," Jess objected. Though he didn't say it his meaning was quite clear: Men drove trucks.

"Get in back," Lynn said through her teeth. Jess hesitated, shrugged, then walked around the truck to join Louis in the back. The three women plus Elijah, who was hungrily gulping milk, crowded into the front.

As she started the truck Lynn remembered Louis saying it was six o'clock. They had fifteen hours to go.

She trod down hard on the accelerator. The rear tires spun, the truck jumped forward, and they were off.

"Jesus," Jess muttered in apparent reference to her driving as the truck bumped at breakneck speed over the pitted road. His hand gripped the seat back between Lynn and Rory. A glance in the rearview mirror told Lynn his eyes were glued to the road.

"Where did you find the truck?" Lynn asked the girls, ignoring Jess.

"It's my father's. I knew where it was, but I can't drive." Theresa was busy wiping milk from Elijah's quivering chin as she spoke.

"You can't drive?" Lynn glanced at her in surprise. Theresa shook her head. "Then who . . ."

Her gaze shot to her daughter, who was sitting beside her. Rory grinned at her sheepishly.

"I've driven go-carts," she said.

"Oh, my *God*." Lynn closed her mouth and shook her head as

she focused on the road again. Obviously, Rory had reserves of resourcefulness and courage that her mother had never suspected. Lynn felt a surge of pride in her daughter.

And a surge of fear as well.

Would Rory live long enough to grow into the woman Lynn had just been afforded a tantalizing glimpse of?

39

NEARLY AN HOUR LATER the truck lurched from the gravel road onto State Route 150 and, at Jess's direction, headed west.

Though they were still high in the national forest, surrounded by towering trees with nary a soul in sight, at least the two-lane road was paved. Lynn stepped on the gas and watched the accelerator climb from 35 to 50 to 70 to 90 in a matter of about two minutes.

"Aren't you driving a little too fast, Mom?" Rory asked, clutching the edge of the bench seat with both hands as the truck took a curve on what felt like two wheels. Lynn knew that her daughter's opinion of her driving, often expressed, was not high.

"We're in kind of a hurry," Jess said, leaning forward. Lynn glanced in the rearview mirror and saw that he was watching the road intently.

By mutual—though unspoken—agreement, neither Lynn nor Jess had said anything about the nine A.M. deadline since they'd all piled into the truck. It was obvious from Rory's demeanor that she thought any danger was well past.

Lynn hated to frighten her daughter anew, but there was no

help for it. Briefly, she told her and Theresa the newest wrinkle in the saga.

"Can they do that?" Rory, white-faced, asked after a moment's appalled silence.

"I didn't know the date had been set," Theresa said, her mouth twisting into an odd grimace, before Lynn could reply. Theresa's arms cradled the baby, who now slept facedown across her chest.

"You knew about the bombs?" Jess asked her.

"Yes."

"Michael Stewart designed them," Louis burst out bitterly from the backseat. "No one was supposed to know outside of the Inner Circle. It was a sacred trust that he was not supposed to reveal even to his family. Yet *she* knows! You see now that he *was* a traitor! He betrayed the trust of the Lamb!"

"He told us nothing until we had left the congregation. He was no traitor! He woke up and saw the truth!" Theresa turned her head to glare at Louis. "Everything Robert Talmadge says is nothing but lies! Robert Talmadge is *evil!*"

"Hush your mouth, girl, before Yahweh punishes you for your blasphemy!" Louis's voice quivered with outrage.

"All right, hold it right there, both of you!" Jess intervened. "Your father designed the bombs, Theresa? Do you know anything about them? Did he ever tell you anything about how they worked or anything like that?"

"No." Theresa took a deep breath, then burst out passionately, "My father was wrong to do what he did, but he was deceived! We all were! We all truly believed Robert Talmadge was the Lamb of God, that God came to him and spoke to him and told him His name was Yahweh and made divine revelations to him! When Robert Talmadge told my father that Yahweh had chosen him to help fulfill the prophecies in the Holy Bible about the end of the world, my father *believed* Yahweh spoke through him! My father was wrong, but he wasn't evil!"

"Anybody can make a mistake," Jess said, his tone soothing, while Louis muttered under his breath and Rory patted Theresa's arm with clumsy commiseration. Lynn's eyes met Jess's through the mirror, and she realized that they were thinking the same thing: Being trapped in the cab of a pickup with warring cult members was like being swung in a sack with a pair of angry cats.

"If your dad knew they were planning to blow us all up, why didn't he go to the police?" Rory asked.

It was such a reasonable question that Lynn was proud of her daughter anew.

"He was afraid that if he did, the True Disciples would be after us forever. He said they would never forgive a public betrayal, and they would hunt us down." Theresa caught her breath. "He thought that if he just went away quietly, they might leave us alone. He didn't know they would hunt us down even if he didn't betray them."

"But he did betray us! He did! Yahweh Himself proclaimed Michael a Judas when he left!" Louis leaned forward, practically yelling in Lynn's ear.

"Liar!" Theresa jumped at him, one arm locking the baby to her chest, the other grabbing for Louis's face. Her face was contorted, her fingers curled into claws.

"Enough!" Jess roared, catching Theresa's wrist, making Lynn jump, and waking Elijah, who immediately began to cry.

Releasing the girl's wrist, Jess added more mildly, "You'll get justice for your family, Theresa, don't think you won't. But for now Louis is on the side of the good guys. He had a visit from Yahweh, who told him that Talmadge has got the timing of the end of the world all wrong, and Louis means to help us find him so he can tell him so. Isn't that right, Louis?"

"The Lamb is only mistaken about the date," Louis muttered.

"The Lamb *is* a mistake," Theresa said, joggling Elijah in her arms to quiet him.

"You—" Louis began heatedly, only to be silenced by Jess's upraised hand.

"No more," Jess said. "The new rule in the truck is, we just don't talk. Quiet, everybody."

For some time after that no more was said.

The road sloped downward. Lynn realized they were descending out of the mountains. The shadows across the pavement had lengthened, and the sky was no longer as bright as it had been.

In one place a small furry animal stood on its hind legs at the side of the road to sniff the air for the coming of night. The day was slowly drawing to a close.

The last day of their lives?

Lynn shuddered at the thought. A surreptitious glance at Jess's wrist revealed the time in digital numbers: 7:32 P.M.

A little less than thirteen and a half hours left.

Lynn felt herself begin to sweat.

A small green roadside sign flashed by. The truck was already flying past before Lynn registered what it said: KAMAS, 12 MILES.

Eight minutes later they were in the heart of town. It wasn't much: a church, a used-car lot, a gas station, a Stop-and-Go market. A lot of green yards and neat, ranch-style homes. Everything, even the houses, looked deserted. Of course. It was Sunday night. In rural Utah. Everybody in this quiet town would be in church, Lynn realized.

Glancing at the small white clapboard church with its classic steeple and crowded parking lot, Lynn hesitated.

Even under these, the direst of circumstances, she discovered that she was squeamish about darting into a church full of people and breaking up the service by screaming her news.

"What we need is a phone," Jess said.

A phone. Of course. Lynn looked around and pulled into the Stop-and-Go. A pay phone on the brick wall outside promised salvation.

"Anybody have a quarter?" Jess asked.

"You don't need a quarter to dial nine-one-one." Lynn slid out of the truck. Everybody else, even Louis, spilled out behind her.

"Lynn, honey, it's about time you got this through your head: You're not in Chicago anymore." Jess came around the front of the truck toward her. "Out here in the wide open spaces you can't just pick up any old pay phone and dial nine-one-one and get help. You have to have a quarter, and you have to actually punch in a number to get the police."

Not prepared to just take his word for it, Lynn marched to the phone, picked up the receiver, and tried it. Jess was right. Without a quarter the phone wouldn't work.

"Told ya," Jess said. He was already heading inside the store. Lynn followed him.

It was only when she saw the plump, gray-haired woman behind the cash register eyeing Jess with growing alarm that she realized how disreputable he looked. Clad in jeans that by this time had been ripped almost to tatters, toes poking through holey, filthy socks, Jess was bare-chested, long-haired, and dirty, with that awful-looking wound in his shoulder.

If she'd been the clerk and he had walked up to her, she would have been scared of him herself.

"Ma'am, can I trouble you to use your phone?" he asked with his best ingratiating smile.

"Pay phone on the wall outside," she replied, her manner abrupt as she returned his smile with a forbidding frown.

"There's been an accident," Lynn intervened, joining Jess at the counter so the woman would be reassured by her presence. "And we need to call the police. Please, may we use the phone?"

"What kind of accident?" the woman asked suspiciously. She looked Lynn over without softening. Her expression hardened into concrete as her gaze slid beyond Lynn to the rest of the party.

A quick glance back revealed Rory with her discolored forehead, Theresa in her tattered nightgown clutching a wailing baby, and cadaverous Louis.

Taken all together, Lynn realized, they were as grungy-looking a group as she personally had ever seen.

"A murder," Jess said, reaching for the phone behind the counter as he fixed the clerk with an inimical stare. The clerk took a step backward, her face tightening, then reached downward and fumbled beneath the counter.

She came up with a nasty-looking pistol, which she pointed straight at Jess.

"Now you just hold it right there," she said, one hand reaching beneath the counter again. Neither the gun nor her eyes ever wavered as she picked up the phone herself.

A quarter of an hour later the Stop-and-Go was aswarm with police.

Jess and Louis, hands cuffed behind them, sat in the back of one patrol car, while Lynn, Rory, and Theresa with Elijah were confined in the back of another. Lynn and Rory had their hands cuffed in front. Only Theresa was allowed to remain without handcuffs so that she could hold Elijah, who was howling in earnest now and whom the troopers clearly did not care to deal with.

The officers had been perfect gentlemen when they patted the women down. They were a little rougher on Louis and especially Jess. At one point Lynn thought a burly cop was going to clout Jess over the head with his nightstick. She had to admit, though, that Jess brought it on himself: He struggled when they cuffed him and cursed with furious vehemence between bouts of trying to explain to first one cop and then another about the coming end of the world. It didn't help when Louis chimed in to second his claims.

If she didn't know better, Lynn thought, she, too, would have marked them down as a pair of possibly dangerous mental cases.

Unfortunately, in this instance the dire warnings they spewed were all too true.

They wouldn't listen to Lynn either. Or Rory. Or Theresa.

The troopers weren't buying any part of so wild a tale. With their prisoners secured they took a few minutes to relax. Lynn stared at them through the window as they sipped cups of coffee and exchanged pleasantries with the clerk. As they were getting ready to get back in their cars, she hustled into the store and came back with a bottle of milk for Elijah.

One trooper opened the back door of the patrol car and handed the bottle to Theresa. The whole squad piled into their cars. Then, ignoring every single thing their irate captives said, they hauled them all off to jail.

40

I T WAS ELEVEN P.M. Lynn, Jess, Rory, Theresa with Elijah, and Louis were locked together in the single large holding cell in State Police Outpost Number 27. Jess had given up cursing and was now pacing. He paused from time to time to grip the bars at the front of the cell and glare at the indifferent officer on duty, who by now had heard their story at least a hundred times and ignored Jess's demands to exercise his right to make a phone call at least a hundred more.

Lynn sat on one of the two mattressless bunks, her back against the concrete-block wall. Rory lay with her head in her mother's lap, almost asleep. On the other bunk Theresa was curled up with a thankfully sleeping Elijah. Louis sat in a corner, his head in his hands.

In ten hours a dozen bombs would explode, killing millions and plunging the country into devastation.

They had managed the impossible, she and Jess, Lynn thought tiredly, escaping from a band of murderers and a flooded mine and making it across more than fifty miles of wilderness to sound the warning before it was too late.

And nobody believed them.

Under less dire circumstances it would have been downright comical.

The phone blared on the officer's desk. He let it ring four times—he was sitting right beside it but must have held off answering to give the impression of being busy—before finally picking it up.

As he spoke into the receiver, then listened, his expression changed. He glanced at Jess, who was once again gripping the bars at the forefront of the cell with renewed interest.

"What? What is it?" Jess demanded.

Without answering, the officer replaced the receiver, stood up, and hurried to open the door that separated the holding area from the rest of the police station.

A brisk tap sounded on the door just as he reached it. The officer opened the door, and another man in police uniform—a higher-ranking officer from the way the first deferred to him—entered.

The door closed behind him.

"Listen, this is life or death—" Jess began desperately.

"We found the bodies," the man said, interrupting. He looked Jess up and down. His gaze then slid over the other occupants of the cell as if weighing them. Feeling it on herself, Lynn had to fight the urge to flip him the bird.

Talk about your Keystone Kops. They almost deserved to be blown up.

"Then you realize that this is serious, and what I'm telling you is God's honest truth," Jess said. He gripped the bars with renewed urgency, his bare feet (he'd lost the remnants of his socks in the strip search that they had all endured) planted just slightly apart. Every muscle in his body seemed taut.

"Before you say anything else I want to caution you." The man held up his hand to stop Jess's words. He was about fifty, Lynn estimated, still reasonably lean but with a slight paunch that hung over his belt. His face was lined, and his salt-and-pepper hair was cut military-short. From the way he looked at Jess, he didn't think much of long-haired, bare-chested men in torn jeans and bare feet.

"You have the right to remain silent. Anything you say can and will be used against you in a court of law. You—"

"What?" Jess exploded, cutting him off. "*I* didn't kill those people! Haven't you idiots been listening to a single fucking thing I've said?"

Face hardening, the officer continued inexorably, while Jess pounded the flat of his hand against the bars in frustration. The other occupants of the cell, with the exception of Theresa and Elijah, both of whom were asleep, watched this exchange with only tepid interest. If Rory and Louis felt the way she did, Lynn thought, they were too exhausted at the moment to care about anything but sleep. Fighting city hall was too much work.

If the world was destined to blow up in the morning, then so be it.

"Look, I told you the bodies were there, I told you the condition they were in, and I was right on the money, wasn't I? Everything else I've told you is just as true. You don't have to believe me. Just let me make one phone call. Just one, okay? Can you just at least do that?"

Both policemen looked at him with identical frowns. The younger officer stood a pace behind the older, mirroring him down to the hands clasped behind his back.

In other circumstances Lynn might have found that funny too.

"I'm not letting you out of that cell until we get your identity confirmed, and the phone won't reach."

"Then could you make the call for me? I'll stand right here and tell you the number and everything to say. Please. Dammit, man, if you keep us in here much longer we're all going to die. Do you have a family? They're going to die. Do you hear what I'm saying? Half the freaking country is going to be blown to hell at nine in the morning!"

The older officer's eyes narrowed. "Is that a threat?"

"*No!*" Jess rested his forehead against the bars in obvious despair. He looked up. "No, it's not a threat. I told you I'm a former ATF agent. The man I want to call was my superior officer. What harm can it do to talk to him? If he tells you I'm a fucking nut, then I guess I am."

"Jess," Lynn said, her eyes flicking from Jess to the older man, whose face had tightened more with each profanity, "I think you'd do better if you didn't swear at them."

"I'll say fucking pretty please if he'll let me use the fucking phone," Jess growled, flicking Lynn a fulminating glance over his shoulder.

He was too angry to contain himself, Lynn recognized. She didn't much blame him. She had told them her name and that she was an anchorwoman for WMAQ in Chicago until she was blue in the face. They patently disbelieved her even while telling her they'd check it out.

In the morning.

There was no penetrating denseness like that.

"Is the call you want to place long-distance?" The officer was reaching for the phone, but he still looked undecided.

"Yes. Yes, it is. But I'll pay for the call. You can put it on my credit card—hell, I don't have it with me, and I don't know the number. You can charge it to my home phone."

"There's no one there to verify the charges," the officer said, his hand withdrawing just as it had been about to touch the receiver. "We already tried calling to see if we could get somebody down here to confirm your identity."

Jess groaned. "Owen is still out with the damned tourists! I know—call collect. Ben will accept a collect call from me. Just try. Please."

"What's the number?" The officer picked up the receiver.

Gripping the bars so tightly his knuckles showed white, Jess told him.

The officer punched in the numbers, listened a moment, then spoke into the mouthpiece, presumably to the operator.

"I want to make this call collect." He listened again, then glanced at Jess. "What name do you want to give?"

"My name, Jess Feldman."

This information was repeated into the mouthpiece.

A minute passed, then another. The phone at the other end of the line was obviously not being picked up.

Despite having learned better by this time, Lynn felt herself getting tense all over again.

The officer's face changed expression. Lynn realized that someone had answered.

"No, this is Commander Avery Wheeler of the Utah State Police. A man who claims he is Jess Feldman is in jail with us here and asked me to place this call for him. Who am I speaking to, please?"

He listened a moment. "Ben Terrell." He glanced sideways at Jess. "And what is your job, please?"

A pause. Then Wheeler continued in a very different tone, "ATF Deputy Director. I see. Well, sir, I'm sorry I had to question you like that, but this fellow here's involved in a mass murder and—"

"Ben," Jess yelled. "Ben, tell him to let you talk to me. It's urgent! Ben!"

Wheeler glared at Jess, then appeared to listen. With a sour expression he placed the receiver on the desk and picked up a set of keys.

"I'm going to let you out of there, and I'm going to let you talk to the man. But we're going to be watching you real close," he warned.

Jess was so eager to get to the phone that he didn't even answer as Wheeler walked to the cell and unlocked the door.

Freed, Jess snatched up the phone and began to relate the whole convoluted story into the mouthpiece. Even with occasional interruptions and backtracking, presumably to answer questions, Jess was finished in under ten minutes.

"Louis, get over here," Jess ordered, beckoning. Louis looked alarmed, but he got to his feet and shuffled over to the phone. He moved like a very old man. Lynn realized that, like all of them, he had endured a hard couple of days.

"Tell him about the bombs," Jess instructed. "How many there are, and where they are. And how they're going to be detonated."

He handed Louis the receiver.

Lynn listened as Louis related the story one more time. Six nuclear bombs in six vital cities. Six lesser but still deadly bombs at six chemical and biological weapon–storage facilities around the country, one in Utah, another in Kentucky. . . .

Lynn glanced at the clock as Louis rattled off the list of places that would be blown off the map when the Lamb typed instructions into a computer at the appropriate time.

It was now 11:32 P.M.

A little less than nine and a half hours to go. Lynn's pulse rate increased at the thought. Deliberately, she calmed herself down, chanting under her breath until her pulse was steady again.

Om . . .

There was no point in getting excited. Whatever happened from this point on was out of her hands.

Louis gave the phone back to Jess, who reiterated his belief in everything Louis had said.

"He wants to talk to you again." Jess held the receiver out to Wheeler, a smug expression on his face.

Jess was entitled to look like that, Lynn thought. The police had treated him like a cross between a lunatic and a criminal since they had first laid eyes on him.

Here he was trying to save the world, and no one was interested.

"You mean you think that whole cockamamy story is *true?*" Wheeler exclaimed into the receiver as Jess, grinning widely, gave Lynn a thumbs-up.

Lynn smiled at him. Sitting beside Lynn now, Rory glanced from Jess to her mother and back again with a frown. Lynn smiled at her too.

"Well, now," Wheeler said, hanging up the phone. "That changes things a little, I guess. Deputy Director Terrell said you were one of the best agents he ever had working for him. He said he'd vouch for you all the way. That being the case I'm going to move you to more comfortable surroundings. I'm not letting you go, mind you, until I get more information and some verification, but I'm willing to transfer you to the county jail for the night. They have mattresses on their bunks, and they can get you a meal. We'll get this all sorted out in the morning."

"What?" Jess exploded, turning to stare at Wheeler.

"If we don't get this taken care of tonight, there won't be a morning," Lynn said tiredly. She'd said it a thousand times before, and it never seemed to penetrate. She had no real expectation of it penetrating now.

Wheeler smiled at her, then at Jess. He seemed much friendlier now that he had spoken to Ben Terrell, if just as obdurate.

"Well, see, there's a bunch of bodies up there on that mountain. I can't just let you go. Even if you didn't kill them you could be classified as material witnesses."

"Okay." Jess took a deep breath and looked around at Lynn. "It doesn't matter anyway. Ben's taking care of it. I guarantee you he's on the horn right now, rounding up everybody short of the U.S. Marines and getting them up to Castle Rock, South Dakota, to stage a raid on that compound. They'll yank Reverend Bob out of there before he knows what's hit him."

"Crisis averted," Lynn said, suddenly feeling limp. Until it ebbed she didn't realize just how tense she had been.

"Crisis averted," Jess agreed, smiling at her.

Lynn took a deep breath. If they weren't going to die in a few hours there were practical considerations that needed to be attended to.

"That being the case I think we could use some medical attention here." Addressing Wheeler, Lynn got up from the bunk, moving stiffly as every muscle she possessed seemed to protest in unison. "My daughter needs to see a doctor; she may very well have a concussion. Jess, as you can see, has a bullet wound. Theresa"—Lynn pointed to the sleeping girl—"has been through a terrible trauma. The baby is probably dehydrated and no telling what else. As for Louis, I'm sure he needs checking over too. Instead of taking us to the county jail you need to take us to the nearest hospital."

"Well, now . . ." Wheeler hesitated.

"Think lawsuit," Lynn said sweetly, and smiled at him. Being given a reprieve was invigorating, she found.

"We could have a man go along with them to the hospital to make sure they don't run off anywhere," the younger officer said to Wheeler in a whispered but still audible aside.

"We don't have anybody to spare."

"I'll go. If they're not in here, then I don't need to be in here watching them."

"That's true."

Wheeler nodded and directed his attention to his prisoners. "We'll get you to the hospital, then. Marty, why don't you go tell Katz to crank up that helicopter? And call the Hospital of Latter Day Saints in Salt Lake City and tell them we're coming."

"Yes, sir, Commander," Marty said, and left the room.

"While we wait is there anything I can get for you folks? A cup of coffee, maybe? A soda?"

"Could I get a Coke, please?" Rory asked.

"Sure you can, young lady."

Wheeler was growing positively affable, Lynn thought as Jess requested a cup of coffee. Lynn opened her mouth to order coffee too, when all of a sudden it occurred to her that she could at last have her heart's desire.

"Could I possibly get a cigarette?" Lynn asked. Her voice was little more than a croak. Her nerve endings palpitated at the thought. Her taste buds quivered. Her toes curled in delicious anticipation.

Jess and Rory scowled at her in near-identical expressions of disapproval.

"Sorry, no smoking allowed in the police station," Wheeler said cheerfully. "Anyway, I doubt we have any cigarettes around. None of my officers smokes, at least not on the job. It's against department policy. The Coke's easy though. And the coffee."

He picked up the phone.

Having gone so long without a cigarette, Lynn told herself she could survive a little while longer. *Maybe.*

"You really ought to quit smoking," Jess said.

Rory nodded agreement.

"Just order me a cup of coffee then," Lynn said to Wheeler, and scowled at both her daughter and Jess.

41

"So, Mom, what's going on with you and Jess?"

The hospital room in which Rory was ensconced was a nice one as hospital rooms went, Lynn thought. The walls were the inevitable concrete block, of course, but they were painted a cheerful shade of yellow rather than the standard institutional green. Enlarged photographs of what Lynn assumed was the Utah countryside livened up the walls.

She noticed these things to give her a moment's respite before answering her daughter, whose perception took her by surprise.

"What do you mean?" she asked carefully. As far as she knew, she and Jess had done nothing to prompt such a question. They had never even touched each other in Rory's presence, and barely spoken.

"*Mother.* I'm not blind. It's obvious you guys have something going on."

Rory, having been X-rayed, bathed, swabbed with disinfectant, and fed, should have been exhausted. Instead, she wriggled higher on her pillows and fixed her mother with a chiding gaze.

"All right. Maybe during the course of our, um, adventure, I did come to appreciate his good qualities," Lynn conceded, pouring herself a glass of water from her daughter's carafe and taking a sip.

"Is he your boyfriend now?"

"Rory!" Trust her to cut right to the heart of the matter.

"Mom, I'm not a little kid anymore. You always want me to tell you things. It's not a one-way street, you know. And this affects me too."

Her daughter had a point. Lynn hesitated, taking another swallow of water.

"I don't know if I'd describe him as my boyfriend, exactly. But . . . okay, I like him. A lot."

"And he likes you back."

"I guess so." Lynn made a face. "Do you mind?" she asked gently.

Rory shook her head. "Nah. He really is kind of too old for me, isn't he? But he's still a babe. I'm glad we're keeping him in the family."

Lynn stared at her daughter, then had to laugh. "I'm glad you're glad. Now do you think you could go to sleep? I'm going to pop into your bathroom and take a shower."

Rory obligingly scooted down in the bed, pulling the covers up to her armpits, her head snuggling into the pillow. Lynn smiled at her, ruffled her hair, kissed her cheek, and headed for the bathroom, thankful to have gotten through that so easily. She would have expected Rory to pitch a fit, or at the very least sulk for days. Maybe Rory was starting to grow up. Or maybe Rory had learned the same thing from their ordeal that she had: When the chips were down, the little differences they'd had with each other ceased to matter. The bond between them was unbreakable, superglued by love.

"Mom?"

Lynn had her hand on the bathroom doorknob when Rory spoke again.

"What, baby?"

"You should have told me the truth about my father. I wouldn't have been so nasty to you if I'd known."

"What are you talking about?" Lynn's hand fell away from the knob, suddenly nerveless. She turned to look at her daughter.

Rory's blue eyes regarded her without blinking. "Come off it, Mom. I heard you and Jess that night in the cave. I wasn't asleep."

"You were faking!" Lynn said, remembering the rhythmic breathing she had been so careful to check for. She walked swiftly to her daughter's bedside. "Oh, Rory, I didn't want you to hear that!"

"I'm glad I did. I needed to know. Like I said, I'm not a little kid anymore." She touched Lynn's arm. "I love you, Mom."

"I love you too, Rory Elizabeth," Lynn said fiercely, and swooped down on her daughter, hugging her close.

It was quite some time later before she managed to take that shower. When she emerged, dressed in the same filthy clothes she'd been wearing for days but feeling a whole lot fresher nonetheless, Rory was asleep.

Lynn walked over to the bed and stood looking down at her sleeping daughter for a moment. The bruise on her head looked terrible. As Lynn had suspected she did have a concussion, but, the doctor assured her, not a serious one. A night or two in the hospital, a little rest at home, and she should be right as rain within two weeks.

Lynn pulled the white thermal blanket a little higher around Rory's shoulders, touched her cheek, and left the room. Her heart was lighter than it had been in months. Her world sparkled suddenly, because things were right again between her and Rory, and because she had found Jess.

With Rory taken care of, she thought, it was time to see what had become of Jess. When last seen he was being wheeled off on a stretcher by a no-nonsense nurse, his protests unheeded, Marty the cop trailing behind.

It was three A.M., Lynn saw as she emerged from her daughter's darkened room into the brightly lit hospital corridor. Six hours until the bombs were scheduled to explode. Except that was over now. She didn't have to count the hours and feel afraid.

She only had to check on Jess, then she could fall into the cot that had been made up for her at the end of Rory's bed and go to sleep.

Tomorrow would be a bright, beautiful day—and she still had almost a whole week of vacation left.

Lynn felt a spurt of surprise as she realized that. It seemed as if she'd been swallowed up by the mountains forever. In reality, it had only been four days since she'd flown out of Chicago.

Four days since she had first set eyes on Jess.

A woman on duty at the nurses' station at the end of the hall glanced at her as she passed. Lynn stopped to ask Jess's whereabouts, which the woman obligingly called up on her computer. Jess was on the fifth floor. Rory was on the third. The elevators were down the hall and to the left.

A row of pay phones was recessed into the wall beside the elevators. Lynn hesitated. She was on vacation, for goodness' sake. And it was the middle of the night. But if she could get hold of her station manager, WMAQ would have an exclusive.

So call her a workaholic. She made the call. Fifteen minutes later she was free to visit Jess.

The only difference between Jess's room and Rory's, she saw as she opened his door a crack and peeped in, was that the walls were painted soft blue.

Jess lay in the hospital bed, his head turned away from the door. His shoulders almost spanned the width of the mattress, and his skin looked bronzed and healthy against the white sheets, which were pulled just higher than his waist. A professional-looking bandage adorned his shoulder.

At first Lynn thought he was asleep. Then he glanced around, saw her, and smiled. That smile did strange things to Lynn's insides.

"Hi." Lynn stepped inside the room. "Where's your bodyguard?"

"With me tethered to the bed he decided Louis was a better bet as an escape risk. How's Rory?" he asked. He was still unshaven, but Lynn decided she liked him that way. The thick black bristles gave him a piratical look that went well with the shoulder-length tumble of his hair.

"She's got a concussion, and they want to keep her at least overnight, but the doctor said she'll be fine," Lynn answered, closing the door gently behind her and moving to stand beside the bed. Not having needed any treatment herself except a steroid cream for her insect bites and an antibiotic ointment for her scratches, she felt a pang of guilt as she took in the IV needle taped to Jess's arm. It didn't seem right, somehow, that out of the three of them she was the only one to suffer no significant injuries.

"What did they say about your shoulder?"

"That it could've been a lot worse." He reached for her hand. Her fingers entwined with his.

"What's that for?" She indicated the IV with a nod.

"They're pumping me full of antibiotics. They didn't think the wound was a big deal, but the nurses who cleaned it out went on and on about how much dirt had gotten into the hole. They made me take a shower before they'd work on me."

"Oh, yeah?" Lynn looked him over. "You *were* pretty dirty. They probably burned those jeans. By the way, what do you have on under that sheet?"

"You're welcome to find out for yourself." He moved their clasped hands toward the edge of the sheet suggestively.

She pulled her hand free of his, shaking her head at him. "Uh-uh. You need rest. Where's your hospital gown, anyway?"

"I hate the damned things. They don't have any backs. I told the nurses not to bother."

"Did they say how long they're keeping you in here?"

"Why? You're not planning to sneak off back to Chicago while I'm stuck in here, are you?" He caught her hand again and carried it to his mouth. The touch of his mouth on her skin sent a tingle snaking up her arm.

"I've got to go home sometime," she said lightly, surprised to discover how much the thought of leaving him hurt.

That was the problem with vacation flings, she told herself. When the vacation was over, the fling was too.

He kissed the back of her hand again, then turned it over and pressed his lips to her palm. The tingle shot down her spine.

"What's Chicago got that Utah doesn't?" he asked, kissing the tips of her fingers one by one as he watched her over their clasped hands. Her toes curled as she gazed into those baby-blue eyes. They were watching her intently, and something about their expression reminded her of how really, really much she liked having sex with Jess.

"My job," Lynn said. "And my mother. And my house."

"No boyfriend?"

Lynn made a face at him. "I thought Rory filled you in on that."

"She could have been mistaken."

"She wasn't. No boyfriend worthy of the name."

"Good." He tugged on her hand. "Come here."

"Wait a minute." She resisted. "What about you? I can't believe you don't have a girlfriend tucked away somewhere."

"None worthy of the name. Are you going to kiss me or not?"

"Not," Lynn said, drawing back. This time he kept his grip on her hand.

"Why not?"

"Because you need sleep, and I need sleep, and tomorrow's a brand new day. And there's no need to rush this, because I have six whole days of vacation left."

Jess's eyes gleamed at her. "Oh, a lifetime," he said.

"Close enough." Bowing to his pressure, Lynn sat on the edge of the bed, careful not to disturb his tubing. "If you'll just hurry up and get out of here, that is."

"We don't have to wait."

"Oh, yes, we do." She leaned forward, pressing a quick kiss to his mouth. He wrapped his arm, IV and all, around her waist to keep her where she was even as she lifted her lips from his. "Call me kinky, but I don't do it with wounded men in hospital rooms."

"I'd love to call you kinky. Just give me the chance."

Lynn laughed. His mouth was just inches from hers. His arm was hard around her waist. His chest was warm and bare and well-muscled and just furry enough to be interesting.

Wrong time, wrong place, right man.

"All right, enough. Let me up. We both need to go to sleep."

"Sleep with me."

"In here? No way."

"Talk to me, then. I don't know about you, but I kinda got a second wind going. Must be adrenaline or something."

"What do you want to talk about?" Lynn was sleepy, but not quite sleepy enough to really want to pull free of Jess and walk away. What was between them was too new, too magical, to let a little thing like exhaustion get in the way.

"Tell me about you. Start with your childhood. I want to hear all about it."

Lynn told him. By the time she was finished, her head was pillowed on the firm muscles just above his breastbone and one hand was splayed across his bare chest, playing idly with a curl of dark brown chest hair. His arm was around her waist. She wasn't quite lying in bed with him though. One foot still touched the floor.

"Your turn," she said at last. "Did you and Owen really grow up on that ranch?"

"Would I lie about a thing like that?" He grinned and stroked her hair. "My, you are suspicious. Yes, we really did."

"Tell me all about it," she ordered, entranced.

He did. Somewhere in the middle of his recital she must have fallen asleep, because when the phone shrilled beside the bed it awakened her with a start. She lifted her head, shook it, and glanced up at Jess, who was blinking groggily as he groped for the phone.

He must have fallen asleep too, she decided, and smiled at him as she sat up, rubbing her eyes.

Locating the phone on its fourth or fifth ring, he silenced it by the simple expedient of bringing the receiver to his ear without ever lifting his head from the pillows.

"Hello," he said, and listened a minute.

Lynn smoothed her hair back from her face and checked the buttons on her flannel shirt.

"What?" Jess exploded, sitting bolt upright, every last trace of sleep vanishing from his face in an instant.

All Lynn's body systems instantly went on red alert.

"What time is it?" he asked into the phone next. Then, "Jesus Christ, we've got *three hours!*"

No, Lynn thought, oh, no.

"Where can I reach you?" Jess fumbled on the bedside table for a pen. Lynn tried to pass him a pad of paper, but he shook his head at her and wrote the number he was given on the back of his hand.

"This way I can't lose it," he said to her, covering the mouthpiece with his hand.

"I'll be in touch," Jess said into the phone again, and put the receiver back into its cradle.

For a moment after he hung up he simply stared into space. Then he looked at Lynn.

From his expression Lynn knew it was bad before he even opened his mouth.

"They got to the compound, and all the Healers were there as advertised, singing hymns and praying and waiting for the glorious end. They staged a raid, got everybody out, searched the place from top to bottom. Reverend Bob wasn't there."

"What time is it?" Lynn asked, as her mind came to grips with the ramifications.

"Six A.M.," Jess said.

42

Jess reached down and, with a grimace, carefully untaped the IV line and pulled the needle from his arm.

"What are you doing?" Lynn demanded, appalled.

"What does it look like? Getting out of this damned bed."

"You should call a nurse!"

"Honey, we're out of time. Didn't you hear what I said? Reverend Bob wasn't in the compound with the rest of them. He could be anywhere in the country, anywhere in the world as a matter of fact. All he needs is a computer and a modem to detonate those bombs."

"Oh, my God!" Having Jess put it into words made the horror real.

"Exactly," Jess said, dropping the needle so that it dangled at the end of its tubing. He pressed the tape back down over the blood that trickled out of his arm and swung his legs over the side of the bed, clutching the sheet to his waist as he glanced around in irritation.

"Can you believe this? I don't have any clothes," he said.

"Where are you going anyway? *You* can't find Reverend Bob." Lynn's mind was beginning to recover from the shock. "What about the FBI? What about your friend Ben and the ATF? What about the national guard, or the police, or the CIA, or whoever? Don't they have some way of tracking people?"

Jess got to his feet, wrapped the sheet around his waist, and headed for the door. "Believe me, somebody in that list you mentioned will find him, sure enough. Given enough time."

Time was what they didn't have. Lynn acknowledged that as she ran after Jess.

"I'm not even going to try to find Reverend Bob," Jess said over his shoulder as he strode past a surprised nurse. Just as the woman realized that the half-naked man was an escaping patient and spun around, he disappeared from her view by turning down the hallway that held the elevator bank, where he punched the UP button.

All too aware of the pursuing nurse, Lynn scooted in after him.

"If you're not going to find Reverend Bob, then what are you going to do?" she asked, breathless.

"If the bombs can be detonated by computer it stands to reason that they can be foiled by computer. We just have to figure out how. I'm going to see if Louis or Theresa can tell us anything that might help."

"You don't even know what room they're in," Lynn wailed. As the doors shut she got a glimpse of the nurse hurrying around the corner toward them.

"I know where Louis is. And I'll find Theresa, believe me."

The elevator rose two floors. The bell pinged, announcing their arrival. Jess was out the door and halfway down the corridor while the doors were still opening. Lynn, running, was right behind him.

Lynn saw Marty the cop lounging at the nurses' station, sipping coffee and chatting with the nurse on duty, as Jess raced past. Marty's eyes widened, but it was clear to Lynn that he didn't quite absorb the full import of what he was seeing until she, too, ran past him.

"What the hell?" he stuttered, putting down his coffee so fast it sloshed over the rim of the foam cup. Lynn glanced over her shoulder and saw him sucking on the flesh just below his thumb as he ran after them. The coffee must have been hot.

He was also fumbling to free the pistol from his belt.

Unmindful of coming trouble, Jess charged into Room 709, where Louis slept curled in a hospital bed.

"Get up, Louis!" Catching hold of Louis's green hospital gown, Jess dragged the man from his bed.

"Wh-what? What?" Snatched from sleep, Louis batted ineffectually at the hand twisted in the front of his gown, which was all he wore. Lynn tried not to look down at the expanse of spindly flesh revealed by Jess's grip.

"Hold on there!" Marty charged into the room, his pistol drawn. Before the door swung shut behind him Lynn saw two hospital security guards running down the corridor toward them.

The nurse had obviously summoned backup for Marty.

"You! Release that man!" Marty stopped just beyond the door, feet spread and planted, both hands clutching his pistol at chest level as he pointed it straight at Jess.

"That's right, put me down," Louis bleated, pawing at Jess's hand. Jess didn't release him, but he did at least turn with him and then lower him so that his feet were flat on the floor. That maneuver, Lynn noted, put Louis between Jess and Marty's gun.

Good thinking, was Lynn's verdict.

"Listen, you imbecile, this is a matter of national security. I am a federal agent," Jess barked at Marty over Louis's head. "And I don't have time for this! Now put that gun away!"

"You are not. . . . I mean, you are?" Marty looked uncertain.

"Just reactivated over the phone," Jess said. "You can check it if you want, but we have only three hours until we're going to be the victims of an act of domestic terrorism so huge it'll blow your socks off. Literally."

That last word almost made Lynn smile.

"Did something go wrong?" Louis gaped at Jess. Jess released his stranglehold on Louis's hospital gown.

"I'd say so. We need to get together and brainstorm, you and Theresa and I. Put your pants on, Louis. Marty, you wouldn't happen to know where Theresa is, would you? The girl with the baby?"

"She's, uh, she's, uh . . ." Marty was clearly wavering between shooting Jess and cooperating. Louis was stepping into and then yanking up his pants.

The door burst open and the security guards rushed into the room. Like Marty, they had drawn their guns.

Three weapons pointed at Jess.

It's all over, Lynn thought, cringing. She took care to shrink back out of the way.

"It's all right, it's all right, he's a federal agent," Marty said, holstering his gun. Then to Jess, "That girl's in the pediatric ward with the baby. Second floor."

"Good job, Marty. Your country is going to be proud of you." With those words of praise Jess had a convert, Lynn saw. Marty's chest swelled visibly.

"Louis, you ready? Let's go get Theresa." Hitching up his sheet again, holding it in place with his injured arm, Jess wrapped a hand around Louis's elbow and hauled him toward the door. The security guards and Marty stood aside to let them pass. All of them, including Lynn, fell in for the race to the second floor.

Theresa was awake, sitting beside Elijah's crib, watching the baby as he slept. Elijah was sprawled on his back, one arm flung over his head, his lips busy nursing even in sleep. Though he was hooked to an IV line he looked content.

Careful not to disturb the baby, Jess beckoned Theresa out into the hallway.

"We need to talk," he said to her. Theresa glanced around, her eyes widening at the size of Jess's entourage. Lynn smiled at her reassuringly.

"There's nobody in this waiting room," one of the guards said, having glanced inside and now holding open the door.

"Come on." Jess ushered Louis and Theresa inside as the two exchanged hostile glances. The others crowded in behind them.

Theresa turned to Jess. "What is it?" Her eyes betrayed her apprehension.

"Just sit down for a minute, and I'll be right with you. Louis, come over here."

Theresa obediently sat in one of the waiting room's green vinyl upholstered armchairs. Jess hauled Louis over to a corner and loomed above him, hemming him in. Trailing in Jess's wake, Lynn saw Louis's shoulders hunch from the effects of severe intimidation as he looked up into Jess's face.

"There's something that's been bothering me, Louis, and I want you to give me the answer," Jess said, low enough to prevent Theresa from overhearing. *"Why* was the Lamb so determined to destroy the Michaelites? Why not just let them go?"

"I—I only followed orders. I don't know. Because Michael was a Judas, I guess." Louis crossed his arms over his chest as though he were cold. Clad in the open-backed hospital gown over his own imperfectly fastened black pants, Louis looked uncomfortable. His gaze shifted sideways.

"Why'd you torture him, then?" Jess's voice was sharp but still low. Standing behind him, having carefully positioned herself to block Theresa's view of Louis as she caught the tenor of Jess's questioning, Lynn had to strain to catch his words.

"We . . . we . . ." Louis looked guilty and scared. "I don't know what you're talking about."

"The other victims were all neatly laid out. Except for having their throats slit there was no other visible trauma to the bodies. *They were fully dressed, down to their shoes.* Michael, on the other hand, was naked. He'd been roughed up, hadn't he? You didn't just string him up on that cross for fun, now, did you? You and your buddies did it for a reason. What was it, Louis? What did Michael know, or have, that the Lamb wanted?"

"Nothing! I—I don't know."

"Louis, listen carefully here: Federal agents raided the compound in South Dakota. The Lamb was not there. He's somewhere out there, Louis, getting ready to push the button that will blow us all to kingdom come. Women and children, Louis. Little babies. You said Yahweh came to you in that air pocket in the mine and told you that the Lamb had the time wrong. We can't find him to tell him that, Louis. So all we can do now is try to stop the bombs from detonating. *It's Yahweh's will that you help us, Louis, don't you see?"*

Louis was breathing fast now, his eyes darting to and fro. His feet shifted, and he grimaced more than once.

"What were you trying to get from Michael, Louis?" Jess asked.

"The plans," Louis said, seeming to shrink. "When he ran away Michael took all the plans. They told how to build the bombs and how everything was to happen."

"Written plans?"

"Records, is what we were told. Some kind of records. The Judas had been trained as a scientist, you know. He was meticulous. He kept excellent records."

"Thank you, Louis," Jess said, very gently.

As Jess turned away, Lynn saw his face. It was grim and strained. She had never—throughout all the crises they'd endured—seen Jess look like that.

A glance at the clock on the opposite wall told her why. It was 6:25.

Two hours and thirty-five minutes left.

As Louis slumped into his chair, Jess crossed the room to Theresa and sat down beside her. She looked at him without speaking.

"Louis just told me that your dad took some records with him when he left the Healers," Jess said, his tone to Theresa far different than the one he had used to Louis. "Do you know anything about that? Did your dad keep papers around, maybe some kind of journal or a notebook? Or a file of some kind?"

Theresa shook her head. "Not as far as I know. I never saw him with anything like that. If he did, he didn't keep it in the cabin with us. It was so small, I would have known it. Since I was the oldest girl I had to do most of the housekeeping."

This was such a typical teenage complaint that Lynn almost smiled.

"Did you?" Jess seemed in no hurry. Lynn, watching, wanted to jump out of her skin. Time was running out, seeming to speed by faster and faster with every second that passed. If she had been asking the questions, Lynn thought, she wouldn't have been able to stay quite so low-key about it.

"Where did he keep important papers, Theresa? Like his children's birth certificates, and his and your mom's marriage certificate, and things like that? Were those things in the cabin?"

Theresa shook her head. "He was always afraid we'd have to leave fast and lots of things would get left behind. All that stuff was in a safe-deposit box."

"A safe-deposit box." Jess drew a deep breath. Lynn's pulse raced. The tension in the air was so thick that she was surprised she could still catch her breath.

"Do you know what bank it was in by any chance?"

Theresa nodded. "Daddy took me with him the last time he went. The Second National Bank branch on State Street in Provo."

"That's where we look first then." Jess smiled at Theresa and stood, hitching up his sheet as he moved across the room. His gaze touched Lynn's, then slid past her to find Marty.

"Where's that helicopter? And can somebody please find me a pair of pants?"

43

Seen from the air, the streets and homes and businesses of Salt Lake City twinkled through the darkness like thousands of tiny white Christmas-tree lights. By the time they reached Provo, though, there were no city lights anywhere to be seen. Dawn had broken on a new day, obliterating them.

The helicopter landed in the street right in front of the bank. Two state-police cars were waiting for them in the parking lot. More police cars blocked either end of the street. A stocky, white-haired man dressed impeccably in a dark business suit stood by the steps leading up to the main entrance, flanked by a pair of uniformed police officers. Lynn assumed he was a bank official, summoned to open the bank and the vault where the safe-deposit boxes were kept. Jess had called the number on his hand before leaving the hospital. On the other end, Ben Terrell, speaking from somewhere in the air between South Dakota and Utah, was apparently powerful enough to get results in a hurry. And the result Jess had wanted was to be met at the bank by an official with access to the safe-deposit boxes and a list of the people who rented them.

As the helicopter rocked down onto its runners, Jess—clad

now in green surgical scrubs scrounged from a hospital supply closet—jumped to the ground, ducking his head as he ran under the still-whirring blades. Lynn, Theresa, and Louis followed. Marty brought up the rear. All had been brought along on Jess's orders in case he might find them useful.

Jess converged with the troopers and bank official at the curb, shaking hands with the latter as they all rushed across the sidewalk and up the steps. A key was produced, the bank door was opened, and they entered. To Lynn the lobby smelled like bank lobbies always did: of other people's money. The air-conditioning had been left on overnight. The coolness was amplified by marble floors, and without any customers the deserted bank felt as frigid as the inside of a refrigerator. Even in Jess's flannel shirt, Lynn was chilled.

As they were leaving the hospital someone had handed her and Theresa pairs of terry slippers. Lynn was thankful not to have to stand on the cold marble in bare feet.

"Do you have the list?" Jess demanded as soon as they were inside.

"The names are in alphabetical order." The bank official—Lynn hadn't caught his name, though he had introduced himself to Jess—handed over a loosely folded computer printout with no more than a single I-hope-I'm-doing-the-right-thing glance at the trooper nearest him. He had already cast a jaundiced eye over Jess's motley retinue. Lynn found it a new experience to be dismissed with a verbal sniff.

Standing, Jess flipped pages and scanned through the list of names. A frown darkened his face when he glanced up.

"Theresa, are you *sure* this is the branch you and your father visited?"

Theresa nodded. She was still wearing her torn nightgown, though her face and hands were clean and she had taken the time at some point to brush her hair and twist it into a knot at her nape.

"I remember the roses." She gave Jess a sad little half-smile. "Only last time I thought they were real. I guess they're not, or they wouldn't still be here."

Lynn followed her gaze to a crystal bowl of roses on a

credenza opposite the entrance. The roses were a mix of yellows and reds. While some blooms were lush and full, at the peak of their beauty, others were faintly brown at the edges and over- ripe, as if they were on the verge of losing their petals. Theresa was right, Lynn thought. They made a memorable arrangement.

"There is no Michael Stewart on this list." Jess's voice was sharp. He would speak to Theresa like that only if he were under tremendous stress, Lynn knew. She watched as his gaze dropped back to the computer printout, which he flipped back to the beginning. As he read through the list of names from beginning to end, his face was a study in growing tension.

"There is no Michael Stewart listed," he said again. He looked at Theresa once more. "The three Stewarts listed are William T., Bruce H., and Virginia R. Do those names mean anything to you?"

Theresa shook her head.

"We may have to look in those boxes anyway," Jess said to the bank official, whose eyes widened with alarm. "Hell, we may have to look in them *all*."

The bank official took a step backward and shook his head. "It's against policy. I was told to open only one box. I—"

"It's seven twenty-eight, Mr. Thompkins," Jess said after a quick glance at his wrist, which still sported Louis's watch. "You do know what happens at nine A.M.?"

The bank official nodded unhappily. "I'll open anything you want," he said. "But we have over eight hundred boxes here. Do you know how long that's going to take?"

Jess groaned and glanced at Theresa again. "Did he ever use an alias, Theresa? Another name?" This time his voice was pa- tient. Lynn realized the control he was exercising to make it so.

Theresa shook her head. "I never heard him use one."

"Okay." Jess passed his hand over his face. "Theresa, you sit down at one of those desks over there and read through this list of names and see if any of them strikes you as something your father would be likely to use. Lynn, kind of keep her on track, would you? Time's growing short here. Mr. Thompkins, you and I better start opening boxes."

Lynn accepted the printout from Jess, led Theresa over to a

desk, and sat down beside her. Jess and Mr. Thompkins, accompanied by a state trooper, disappeared into the interior of the bank. Marty hovered behind Theresa and Lynn. Louis, clad in borrowed surgical scrubs like Jess, found a comfortable-looking couch and slumped down on it.

A list of eight hundred names, Lynn discovered after just a few minutes, made for dull reading. Having no idea what she was looking for, she scanned page after page nonetheless, her gaze following Theresa's finger as it slid from name to name.

Theresa was a slow reader. Lynn was glad there was no clock anywhere in sight. If she had been able to watch the minutes tick past while they performed this interminable chore, she would sooner or later have had to jump up from her chair and scream.

Marty abandoned his vigil to join Louis on the couch. Unlike Louis, though, who was as motionless as a rag doll, Marty chewed a thumbnail, jiggled his leg, and tapped his toe.

More than once Lynn felt like yelling at him to sit still.

They were near the bottom of the last page when Theresa's moving finger stopped.

"Here," she said, glancing at Lynn. "This is something he might have used."

Lynn read the name just above Theresa's finger. "Wormwood, Star. Star Wormwood?"

"It's from the Book of Revelations, I think. Wormwood is the name of the star that is going to fall on the earth and wreak great destruction when the world ends."

Lynn stared at Theresa for no more than a millisecond before grabbing a pencil and a Post-it note from the top of the desk, scribbling down the number corresponding to the name, jumping up, and screaming "Jess!"

When there was no response she ran to the door of the vault.

Jess, Mr. Thompkins, and the trooper were perhaps a tenth of the way down the long wall of bronze-fronted safe-deposit boxes. They were rifling through the contents of a metal box that was pulled drawerlike from its nest when Lynn appeared.

"She's found one! Star Wormwood sounds right, she says." Lynn flew down the steps to hand the Post-it note to Jess.

"Six seventy-three," Mr. Thompkins read the number aloud,

then moved down the wall with a shake of his head. "We would have been here a long time."

The box was on the far side of the wall, in the third row up from the bottom. Everyone rushed to join them in the vault as the box was pulled out.

Lynn held her breath.

Mr. Thompkins inserted a key into the small lock in the front and opened the lid. Jess picked up the topmost item, a thick sheaf of papers that had been ripped from a spiral notebook. The pages were held together with a paper clip and folded lengthwise so that the uppermost side was blank. Spreading the papers open, Jess glanced down at them, then up. His gaze met Lynn's, though the others all crowded around.

"We got it," he said.

Lynn breathed again.

"That's it? That's Michael Stewart's box?" she asked as Mr. Thompkins bore the box out of the vault. Jess stayed right behind him, leafing through the sheaf of papers as he walked. Lynn stayed beside Jess. The rest of the crew followed. Lynn barely heard the comments, exclamations, and explanations that flowed back and forth around her. Her attention was all on Jess —and the papers he held in his hand.

"These are the plans," Jess said to Lynn as Mr. Thompkins sat the box down on a table. He leaned against the table's edge and turned back to the first page, moving through them more slowly as he scanned the cramped handwriting and tiny drawings the pages were filled with.

"Oh, my God." Lynn covered her mouth with her hand. "Thank God."

She sat down abruptly in a chair. Jess, still reading, started to frown.

His expression made Lynn's stomach tighten.

"What's wrong?" she asked.

"There's something missing," he said. Putting the sheaf of papers down on the table, he searched through the box. Digging through the clutter of folded papers and ignoring such detritus as a pair of diamond ear studs and a small tennis trophy, of all things, Jess came up with a computer disk in a gray paper jacket that had been placed at the very bottom of the box.

On the front of the jacket was scribbled *Wormwood.*

"Here we go," Jess said. Glancing at Mr. Thompkins, he added, "I need to use a computer."

"Every one of our loan officers has one," Mr. Thompkins said proudly, leading the way back to the main part of the bank. "I hope that disk is IBM-compatible."

Jess glanced down. "It is."

He walked around the first desk they came to—computer-equipped, just as Mr. Thompkins had claimed—and turned the machine on. Hitting a few keys, he waited a moment, then inserted the disk into the drive.

Immediately an icon blinked onto the screen, asking for the user's password.

With everyone leaning wide-eyed over his shoulder, Jess hesitated only a second before typing in *Wormwood.*

The screen blinked and went blank. A whirling circle appeared in the middle of the darkness. It was, Lynn realized, a revolving image of a globe. The globe disappeared, to be replaced by a pinpoint of brightness in the middle of the dark screen. The pinpoint enlarged until it filled the monitor with light. There was the sound of a phone number being dialed as the program sought Internet access. The monitor blinked once, twice.

Welcome, Michael read the words on the screen.

Beside her, Lynn heard Theresa catch her breath. She reached over, gripping the girl's hand. Theresa's fingers felt icy in her grasp.

For Theresa, watching Jess pull up the information her father had left behind must be almost like encountering his ghost, Lynn thought.

There was another desk next to the one Jess was using. He crossed to it, snatched up the phone, glanced down at his hand, and punched in the number.

"Ben?" he said into the mouthpiece seconds later, bringing the receiver with him as he returned to stand in front of the computer. "We found what we were looking for. The detonators for the nuclear devices—and the other bombs too—are wired to alphanumeric pagers. Yes, you heard me, alphanumeric pagers. You know, those things the drug dealers carry so they can receive messages like 'Where's my heroin?' "

Jess paused for a minute to listen, then nodded. "Yeah, and phone numbers. Those things. I've got a list of twelve numbers on my screen—I'm on a computer here at the bank—that I think correspond with the pagers. From what I can tell the thing is set up so that one code can be sent over the Internet to all twelve pagers at once, and that detonates the bombs. All Reverend Bob needs is a computer and a modem and that code, and he can blow us all to hell from anywhere in the world."

Jess paused for a moment, a faint grin flickering over his mouth before disappearing as suddenly as it came.

"I'd call him that too. Stewart also apparently put a fail-safe on the system, so that he—or someone—could override the *go* code and keep the bombs from going off. Yeah, sort of like a *stop* code. You type in this code, punch the transmit button, and the detonators are deactivated."

Jess listened a minute. "Well, now, that's our problem: The *go* code is here, plain as day: *love heals.* No, I am not kidding. Reverend Bob types in *love heals,* and the whole country goes kapooey. But there's only a series of asterisks where the *stop* code should be. Yeah, asterisks: eight of them. No, I don't think that can be the code. I'm no computer expert though, and we need one here, pronto, to see if he can do more with this than I can. How fast can you get somebody to me?"

Jess paused, his face tightening. "There's got to be someone nearer than that. Jesus, that's cutting it close." He let out his breath with a whoosh. "Okay, tell him to hit it. I'll keep working on it at this end. Yeah, I'll let you know."

Jess hung up the phone and ran the tip of his tongue over his lips. Lynn had never seen him employ that particular gesture before, and she knew it boded no good.

But when he glanced at his audience he seemed to have himself in hand again.

"Listen, folks, we have everything we need to disarm the bombs except the right code. There's a *stop* code built into the system, but the word or phrase Stewart chose is not on this disk. Just asterisks. Let's put our heads together. Theresa, can you think of anything your father might have used as a code to stop a bomb from going off? Did he have any phrases he used a lot?"

Theresa thought for a minute. "The early bird catches the worm?" she suggested. "He said that to us kids nearly every morning."

From Jess's expression Lynn could tell he didn't think that was a likely code.

"Why not?" he said, shrugging. "Let's try it."

He typed the phrase into the computer in the appropriate space and pressed *enter*. Seconds later a message blinked back at him: *code not allowed.*

"Any other phrases?" Jess asked Theresa.

She shook her head. "I can't think of any."

"Let's try family names. What was your mother's name?"

"Sally." Theresa's voice broke, but she did not cry.

Jess typed in *Sally*. The computer came back with *code not allowed.*

Far more patiently than Lynn knew she would have been under such circumstances, Jess worked through the Stewart family names.

Somewhere a clock chimed eight.

Lynn's blood ran cold.

They had only an hour left to live.

44

"ALL RIGHT, LOUIS, let's give it a shot. Are there any words or phrases you can think of that Stewart might have used? Do Healers ever say anything real catchy besides *love heals*?"

"We consider the name Healers insulting," Louis said. He was standing in front of the desk that the computer rested on, while Theresa sat in a chair that had been pulled up for her. Jess still stood behind the desk.

"Come on, Louis, think," Jess said impatiently. "Something biblical maybe, like Wormwood."

Wormwood. Something about that teased at the corners of Lynn's mind. All at once she realized what was bothering her.

She stood up, crossed to where the list of safe-deposit-box renters still rested on a desk near the entrance, and turned to the last page.

Her pulse speeded up as she found what she was looking for.

The name Star Wormwood was printed not once, but twice. Of course, it could just be a computer error, but . . .

Running her finger across the line to the corresponding box number, she sucked in her breath: 289.

"Jess!" she cried. "Jess, I think I know where the *stop* code might be: box two eighty-nine!"

"What?" He looked up from his typing to stare at her. With the lobby between them, their gazes met.

"There are two boxes rented to Star Wormwood!" Lynn said urgently. "Number six seventy-three. And number two eighty-nine!"

"Let's check it out." Jess abandoned the computer to head for the vault again, Mr. Thompkins in tow. The rest of them followed.

Box 289, when pulled, contained only a single sheet of spiral-notebook paper rolled into a neat scroll and bound with a rubber band.

Lynn's heart pounded as Jess pulled off the rubber band and smoothed out the paper.

Michael Stewart's inelegant scrawl was unmistakable. But from where she stood she could not quite make out the words he had scribbled in black ink.

Jess read them aloud: "No man knoweth the day or the hour." He looked up. "That's it," he said. "That's got to be it."

"What time is it?" Marty asked.

"Eight twenty-seven," Mr. Thompkins answered. Jess was already on his way back to the computer with Lynn at his heels.

Half an hour left.

With Lynn beside him and everyone else jockeying for a good view, Jess typed in the words.

No man knoweth the day or the hour.

The computer screen blinked once, twice. A message appeared.

Code accepted, it said. Seconds later they all watched as twelve winged postcards were dispatched over the Internet, one right after the other.

The computer screen blinked again, then offered another message.

Pager contact completed. Bombs deactivated.

For a moment a silence so thick it was tangible hung over the room. All of them, from Jess to the state troopers, stared at the screen.

Then, "Yes!" Jess said, pumping his fist skyward and sweeping Lynn up in a one-armed bear hug. Cheers erupted all around them. Marty jumped up and down like an excited chihuahua, while the troopers whooped and exchanged high-fives.

"It's over, isn't it? Just like that!" Lynn clung to Jess, her arms wrapped around his neck, laughing and crying at the same time.

"It's over," he confirmed, kissing her mouth and then setting her back on her feet. "Give me a minute, I've got to tell Ben."

Stepping to the adjacent desk, he glanced at his wrist and made the call.

"Found the code," he said laconically into the receiver. "A verse from the Bible: No man knoweth the day or the hour. Crisis over. All that's left for you guys to do is clean up."

Listening, his eyes narrowed. "No, I hadn't thought of that. Thanks for sharing."

He was silent for a moment. "He could be anywhere in the world. What are the chances we're going to find him in a half hour?" Pause. "Okay, I know, I know. I'll do my best. Yeah, I'll call you back."

Jess put the receiver down and looked glumly at Lynn. Around the computer the celebration continued unabated. No one else had paid any attention to the conversation.

"What now?" Lynn asked quietly.

"Ben just mentioned the interesting possibility that the Healers might have been smart enough to get the bombs rewired after Stewart ran out on them. Now, I don't think they did, because if so they would have had no reason to come after the guy like they did, but they might have. It is still theoretically possible that we might have bombs going off at nine A.M."

"Oh, no!" Lynn groaned. Then she started to get angry. After all they had been through this was too much! "So what are they doing about it? Somebody is working on this besides you and Ben, aren't they? Like the FBI, and the CIA, and the Pentagon . . ."

A half-smile crooked Jess's mouth. "Honey, they're all working on it. Ninety percent of the security forces of this country are on it, most of whom are en route from South Dakota at this moment. It just so happens that we're at ground zero. Ben wants me to see if Louis or Theresa knows anything that might help us locate Reverend Bob."

"Just in case," Lynn said.

"Just in case," Jess agreed, glancing around. "Theresa, would you come here a minute, please?"

Like Lynn, he seemed loath to share the bad news with the others just yet. The atmosphere in the room was so buoyant with relief that Lynn, for one, dreaded having to watch it dissipate.

Theresa joined them beside the desk, looking up at Jess inquiringly.

"Do you have any idea where Robert Talmadge might go to await the end of the world? Did your father ever mention some kind of hideaway?"

Theresa shook her head. "I would expect him to be in the compound with everybody else."

"He wasn't there. Federal agents raided the compound."

"Maybe he just hadn't made it back to South Dakota from Utah yet when the agents came."

Jess frowned. "What do you mean, maybe he hadn't made it back from Utah? When was he in Utah?"

"He came to our cabin when they . . . attacked. He was there."

"You saw him?" Jess stared at her.

Theresa shook her head. "I never saw him. I hid in the root cellar with Elijah when they came. But I heard his voice." She shivered. "I would know his voice anywhere. After we left the congregation we all—us kids—started calling him Death instead of the Lamb. You know, from the Bible: Death is his name, and Hell follows with him. Because our lives became like hell to us because of him, because we had to do without so much and be afraid all the time and hide."

"Are you *sure* it was Robert Talmadge's voice you heard?"

Theresa nodded.

Jess pursed his lips thoughtfully and glanced around. "Louis?"

His voice sharpened. "Where's Louis?"

Louis was gone.

After a quick but thorough search of the bank, Jess ran outside, down the steps, and into the street. The helicopter waited, blades idle now. Its pilot watched incuriously from behind the controls. Patrol cars still blocked either end of the street. More patrol cars waited in the bank's parking lot.

Louis was nowhere to be seen.

A trooper got out of one of the cars in the parking lot and headed toward them. Watching him come, Jess motioned to him to hurry. The man picked up his pace.

"Did you see a man come out of the bank? A black-haired man in a green hospital gown and black pants?"

"Sure did. He walked down to the end of the street and hopped a cab." The cop frowned as he looked at Jess. "We didn't have any instructions about keeping people from leaving. Should we have stopped him?"

"Too late now," Jess said grimly. "Not your fault, anyway. See if you can find out where that cab went, would you, please? And fast."

The trooper ran back to his car. Jess looked at Lynn.

"I have a feeling Reverend Bob's been under our nose the whole time. I think I've started to get a feel for Michael Stewart, and I don't think he chose Utah to hide out in at random. He wanted to be close to something, and my bet is that something is the place where Talmadge planned to go to detonate the bombs. Stewart's been keeping an eye on things all along, staying out of sight until it was time to use the *stop* code he secretly programmed into the system. Only somehow Talmadge found out about the code and came after Stewart. Now that Stewart's gone, Talmadge thinks he's home free." Jess smiled grimly at Lynn. "But he's wrong."

The trooper came running back, clutching a piece of paper, which Jess took. "The cab went to 22079 Orkdale Road. It's a farm out toward Springville," the trooper said.

"Okay, get together all the backup you can and meet me there. Tell everybody, no sirens. I'm going to take the helicopter." That grim smile flickered again, and his gaze slid to Lynn. "I might even beat Louis."

The trooper ran for his car, while Lynn darted after Jess as he headed toward the helicopter. The pilot, seeing something was afoot, already had the rotors in motion.

Jess glanced back, saw Lynn, and stopped just as he was getting ready to duck beneath the blades.

He turned and caught her arm. "You stay here," he yelled over the sound of the rotors.

"I'm coming!" Lynn screamed back.

"Oh, no, you're not! You're a civilian, and a woman, and this is the big leagues!"

"Listen, you male chauvinist pig—" Lynn began furiously, only to find herself shoved back out of the way as Jess sprinted toward the open doorway and leaped aboard. Before she could recover, the chopper lifted off.

Jess waved jauntily at her from the passenger seat as the chopper banked sharply left and headed aloft.

The state boys burned rubber getting out of the parking lot. Lynn had to jump out of the middle of the street.

One car stopped as it passed, brakes squealing. The trooper who had spoken to Jess leaned out the passenger window.

"By the way, you had a message: You're to call this number," the cop yelled, waving a piece of paper. Lynn barely had her hand on it before the car shot off again.

She glanced down, read the message, and ran back inside the bank past Theresa, Marty, and Mr. Thompkins, who had come out onto the steps when the commotion outside penetrated the euphoria within.

Snatching up the phone, she dialed.

"Lenny, I'm in Provo, at the Second National Bank on State Street," she said before the man who answered had even finished saying hello. "Where are you?"

"Knockin' at your back door, baby," he answered. "When I showed up at the hospital as requested, a nurse tipped me off to where you'd gone. What's up, girl?"

"You're on cellular, aren't you? Then I'll wait and fill you in when you get here. Hurry, Lenny! This is the big one!"

"Hurryin', baby," Lenny promised, and rang off.

45

Jess WENT IN ALONE because he was afraid of what could happen if he didn't. The memory of the botched raid at Waco was too fresh in his mind. And this time his backups were not federal agents, but a bunch of state troopers he didn't know. In Jess's mind that made for a pack of wild cards in a game nobody could afford for him to lose.

At his direction the chopper and the squad of cop cars converged just out of sight of the farmhouse, using as cover a fence, a herd of cows, and a thick copse of trees.

There was no way of knowing if the stop code had worked until after nine A.M. To be absolutely one hundred percent safe, he had to stop Talmadge from trying to detonate the bombs at all.

Just another day in the life of a federal agent. Jess was reminded all over again of why he had quit the Bureau. Laying his life on the line made him nervous.

So here he was already, doing it again. Only this time without health benefits or a pension plan.

Jess waited as long as he dared to see if Ben and his crew might make it in time, but they didn't. By 8:51 he would have welcomed even the ATF's arch-rivals, the FBI. Advised of Jess's destination en route, those guys were on their way.

On their way did Jess no good at all. At 8:52 he could wait no longer. As he ran across the long field that separated the farm where Talmadge was possibly holed up from its neighbor, Jess tried to think of a plausible reason to come knocking on the door. After all, his suspicion was still unverified; Louis could have been paying a visit to a maiden aunt.

Subtlety wasn't going to work, Jess realized. Even if he could convince everybody else that he was Goldilocks, Louis would recognize him at once.

Having already hit upon the brilliant notion of having the farmhouse's electricity shut off—no electricity, no accessing the Internet—Jess had learned that the place had its own generator.

His mission, and he'd had no choice but to accept it, was to knock out that generator.

How hard could that be?

Courtesy of the state boys he was armed with a pistol, a two-way radio, a pair of insulated gloves, and an industrial-strength wire cutter.

All he had to do was find the generator, cut the wire running from it to the house, and summon his posse to mop up.

Easy.

The generator was simple to locate. He heard it chugging away before he saw it. Rounding a corner of the house—a two-story white clapboard with a picturesque front porch—he spotted his target instantly. It was out in the open, its unadorned metal casing gleaming in the morning sunshine.

Nobody was around. Taking a deep breath, Jess pulled the gloves on, grabbed hold of the wire cutters, and went for it.

A glance at Louis's watch told him that it was 8:57 A.M.

Seconds later something slammed with blinding force into the back of his head.

46

W<small>HEN</small> J<small>ESS OPENED HIS EYES</small> he was watching CNN. This was so surreal that for a moment he blinked at the TV screen as if blinking would make it disappear.

He was, he discovered when he tried to move, tied to a ladder-back kitchen chair. His hands were bound behind it, and loops of rope wrapped tightly around his waist secured him to it. A strip of cloth was wound around his lower face, gagging him.

His mission had obviously not been a success. Maybe he should have tried playing Goldilocks after all.

Jess glanced around. From all appearances he was in a bed-room of the farmhouse. A nearby window was curtained, but the filmy panels didn't quite meet in the middle. From the glimpse he got outside he could tell he was on the second floor. The walls were white, the floor covered with a mauve area rug, and there were no furnishings as such. Except for the TV and his kitchen chair, which he was willing to bet was an extremely recent addition to the decor.

And a long, utilitarian, conference-style table.

A glowing computer served as the table's centerpiece.

As he spotted it Jess thought, uh-oh.

A group of men in flowing white robes entered the room. The man in the lead was fifty-two, six foot four, 220 pounds, with regular features and a leonine head of silver hair.

Robert Talmadge. Though he had seen only a picture to go with the statistics he had researched in connection with Waco, Jess would have recognized him anywhere.

Without sparing so much as a glance for Jess, Talmadge moved to stand in front of the computer.

Somewhere in the house a clock began to chime the hour. Jess mentally counted along: six, seven, eight, *nine.*

"It's time, my children," Talmadge said.

"But Yahweh said—" An unhappy voice protested, and Jess recognized Louis under one of those white robes. Talmadge silenced him with a stern look and an upraised hand.

"It's time," he said again and began to type.

Though Jess knew it was ridiculous—either the country was going to blow up or the stop code had worked and it wasn't—he braced himself.

"Love heals," the group chanted. On the screen Jess caught just a glimpse of e-mail postcards, one after the other, winging away into the infinite universe of the Internet.

"Yahweh's name we praise," Robert Talmadge said. The group echoed him, then turned as one to stare at CNN.

They wanted to watch, Jess realized. They wanted to watch the the effects of their handiwork. Here in Utah they would probably survive the nuclear blasts and perish later by poison gas or chemicals or pestilence or whatever was released in the second wave.

Jess wouldn't have chosen that fate for himself. Being decimated instantly by a cataclysmic explosion seemed kind in comparison.

On CNN an unidentified reporter was standing in front of the Washington Monument babbling about Whitewater.

And the Washington Monument was still standing.

Jess felt a wave of relief so intense his muscles sagged. The *stop* code had worked!

The realization that something had gone wrong appeared to occur to Talmadge at about that time.

He turned to stare at Jess. The group turned too. Even Louis, Jess discovered, could look positively diabolical in a white robe with religion in his eye.

"I hope you've been a good boy, Mr. Feldman," Talmadge said quite gently and turned back to the computer. The others turned with him. The tension in the way they stood gave Jess an inkling of what was afoot.

Talmadge began to type.

Jess's adrenaline kicked in. He got his feet beneath him, stood up, took a running leap, and threw himself out the second-floor window, chair and all, just as the farmhouse blew up.

He hit the ground hard and blacked out.

When he came to, lying on his side, still tied to the chair, fire trucks and police cars surrounded the house, sirens wailing. Firemen wielded a gigantic hose off to his left. Policemen ran around yelling into walkie-talkies. An ambulance jolted into the yard. Smoke and the acrid odor of something burning made his eyes water.

Lynn stood over him, a microphone in her hand, talking into a camera as a man focused it on her. She gestured first at Jess as the paramedics bent over him, then at the burning house behind him.

Only when the camera was shut off did she crouch down beside him. He was just being loaded onto a stretcher.

"Well, hi there, hero," she said, squeezing his hand.

"What the hell are you *doing*?"

"Reporting," she said. "It's what I do. And, believe me, the end of the world makes a heck of a story."

47

LATER THAT DAY in the hospital in Salt Lake City, Theresa was rocking Elijah, who sat in her lap. His IV had been removed only an hour before. Except for a bad case of diaper rash, which was healing, Elijah had been pronounced well on the road to recovery.

The doctor said he could go home the next day.

The thought made Theresa's lower lip quiver. They had no home to go to.

A family of nine had been reduced to two: herself and Elijah.

She knew she would never let him go. But she didn't know how she was going to take care of him.

Babies needed things. Like food. And shelter. And diapers.

Things she could not provide. All she had to give him was love.

She was scared, so scared.

Elijah let out a piercing baby squeal and wrapped a hand in her hair. Theresa smiled down at him even as tears welled in her eyes.

"Theresa Stewart?" A uniformed policeman stood in the doorway looking at her.

Theresa nodded warily, her hold on Elijah tightening. A terrible fear crystallized into words in her mind: Had they come to take Elijah away?

If she could not provide for him, would they give him to someone who could?

"Could you come with me, please?"

She had been raised all her life to obey authority; she didn't want to now. But the way the policeman looked at her seemed to give her little choice. She stood up, clutching Elijah to her breast, and followed the policeman down the hall.

The nurses at the nursing station, who had been so kind to her, looked at her strangely as she passed them.

Her throat tightened, and she held Elijah closer still. The baby kicked and bobbed his head against her neck.

At the elevators she almost balked.

"Where are you taking us?" she asked the cop before she would get in.

"Just down to the second floor," he said, and smiled. It was a kindly smile, and it reassured her a little. "It's okay."

Theresa got in.

Once on the second floor he ushered her down a hallway and stopped outside a room. Opening the door for her, he gestured for her to go inside.

A young man in a long white coat was leaning over a patient, who was lying in bed.

The man looked up as she entered.

"I'm Dr. Silva," he said. "I think you may know this woman."

Only then did Theresa look down at the patient.

"Mother!" she gasped, almost dropping Elijah. The room seemed to spin. Her heart pounded. Her knees shook.

"Mother?" she whispered again, walking to the bedside on unsteady legs. Eyes closed, face turned away, Sally Stewart did not respond. But there was no doubt it was she.

"Is she alive?" Theresa could scarcely bear to hope, even now. It seemed impossible. It was impossible.

"Very much so." The doctor, who'd been writing something on the chart he held, smiled at her. "She ingested a large amount

of a very strong sedative. And she's suffering a little from expo-
sure. But she'll be fine."

"But I thought she was dead!" Theresa burst out, looking
from the doctor to the policeman, who had entered the room
behind her. She had never actually *seen* her mother dead. She
had just assumed. . . . "I thought . . . I thought they had
murdered her!"

The policeman glanced at the doctor, then cleared his throat.
His eyes were compassionate as they met hers. "When we
reached the mining-camp site we found numerous people laid
out on the ground. The majority of the victims were arranged
around a single central victim, who I understand was your father
and who was—ahem!—in a different position. All the victims on
the ground had been heavily sedated. Five had had their throats
slit, and were dead. We suspect the plan was to murder the
others too, but something interrupted the perpetrators before
they could finish the job. However it happened, this lady and five
of her children survived. Two more were listed as missing. I
believe you and the baby here may be those two."

Theresa simply stared at him for a long moment without
speaking. His words percolated slowly through the shock that
had insulated her from her emotions since the nightmare began.
When at last she realized the truth of what he said, she broke
down and cried bitterly, sinking into a chair they pushed out for
her.

She clutched Elijah and cried, her tears soaking the baby's
golden head.

"Theresa?" It was a weak whisper, so weak Theresa could
scarcely hear it. Something touched her head.

Theresa looked up. Her mother's eyes were open and she was
looking at her. The touch she had felt on her head was her
mother's hand.

"Mother." Theresa almost choked on her tears. "Oh, Mother,
I thought you were dead!"

Her mother smiled. "I see you took care of Elijah for me," she
said, her hand moving to caress the baby's cheek.

"Yes, Mother, I did."

"Don't cry. Everything's going to be all right." With that Sally closed her eyes.

Theresa looked up at the doctor in alarm.

"She's going to be all right," he said. "It'll just take a little time."

Theresa closed her eyes and thanked God, who she was now sure existed by whatever name.

Because He had given her a miracle. Though He had taken her father, He had given the rest of her family back.

48

Lynn was just finishing the last story of the day when she saw him. She continued to smile and talk into the camera, even though her heart was racing.

She was seated at the anchor desk at WMAQ in Chicago. Behind the lights and camera, Jess watched her.

When they'd parted after their vacation fling—those five days they'd had together after he was released from the hospital—she had told herself it was over.

That was the trouble with vacation flings, she kept reminding herself. They ended with the vacation.

Only her longing for him hadn't. If anything it had increased. Lynn hadn't realized quite how much she wanted to see him again until now.

And she realized something else too, as she smiled through the closing credits while trying not to shoot little sideways glances at Jess: Somewhere, in the course of their vacation fling, she had fallen in love with her rhinestone cowboy.

When the cameras stopped rolling she stood up, unhooking her mike from her elegant navy blue blazer. Her coanchor, Mike

Knox, said something to her, to which she must have replied with a modicum of sense, because he nodded.

Then she walked over to Jess.

He was leaning against the wall, wearing jeans, a denim shirt, and cowboy boots. His tawny hair was a little shorter than it had been when she'd last seen it, but it still brushed his shoulders. His eyes gleamed at her as she approached, sliding down her body and over her legs before moving back up.

When those to-die-for baby blues met hers, he grinned. Lynn knew he was remembering the first time he had stared at her legs like that, when she had done her best to slay him with a look.

This time she smiled at him.

"Hi, hero," she said as he straightened away from the wall.

"I could have done without that." He grimaced wryly.

Thanks to Lynn's reporting, Jess had found his fifteen minutes of fame in the aftermath of the farmhouse explosion. He hadn't enjoyed the experience, she knew.

Since in the end only a few people had died and only one house was blown up by a very small bomb, the story hadn't stayed in the news for long—though it had been long enough to win Lynn a very lucrative job offer from CNN. She had even been approached with an offer to write a book about her experience, though the amount of money mentioned had been minuscule.

"What are you doing here?" she asked, curling her hand around Jess's arm and leading him away from the interested eyes of her colleagues.

"I came to take you out to dinner," he said. "If you're free."

"You came all the way from Utah just to take me out to dinner?" She wrinkled her nose at him.

"Among other things."

" 'Night, Lynn!"

"See you tomorrow, Lynn!"

Two of her coworkers walked past, heading out the door. Lynn answered them absently, not even registering who they were. She had eyes for no one but Jess.

"Like what kind of other things?"

He shrugged. "Oh, this and that. You coming to dinner with me or not?"

"All right. Let me wash my hands."

At Lynn's suggestion they headed for da Vinci's, a little out-of-the-way Italian place with the best fettuccine Lynn had ever eaten. They never made it.

They ended up in Jess's hotel room instead.

Later, Jess flipped on the lamp and looked down at Lynn. She lay with her head on his chest, threading her fingers through the crisp brown curls that grew there. The wound in his shoulder, she saw, was mending nicely. It had healed until it was no more than a puckered red scar.

"I missed you," he said.

"I missed you too." She slanted a quick smile up at him and tweaked a curl on his chest. They were stretched out side by side, naked, with her leg thrown over his and his arm around her shoulders as he idly stroked the skin of her throat. The bed-clothes had been kicked to the floor, and Lynn, at least, was too lazy to retrieve them.

Besides, with Jess's arms around her she certainly wasn't cold.

"Did you? How much?"

There was something about his tone that made her look up again. She was trying to avoid meeting his eyes, because she was afraid of what he might read in hers.

"More than I miss cigarettes." Having managed not to smoke for the duration of their adventure, Lynn had vowed to quit. It was one of the hardest things she had ever done. If she ever took those publishers up on their offer, maybe she'd turn her experience into kind of a self-help tome. She could just picutre the title: How to Stop Smoking and Save the World.

"Is that a lot or a little?"

Lynn laughed. "Only a lifelong nonsmoker would ask that."

"A lot, huh?"

"Don't get cocky."

"In that case, how do you feel about commuter relationships?"

"Sometimes they work, sometimes they don't."

Jess sighed. "You're not going to make this easy, are you? Open that drawer by the bed."

He indicated the nightstand. Wriggling onto her stomach, Lynn did as he said.

In the drawer, on top of the room-service menu and various advertising circulars, was a small square box wrapped up in silver paper with a big white bow.

Looking at it, Lynn felt her heart start to pound.

"What is it?" she said, glancing up at him.

"Open it." He wasn't smiling now, and the look in his eyes was both wary and, she thought, eager.

Lynn picked up the package and slowly removed the wrappings. As she had part hoped, part feared, a red jeweler's box was revealed.

She stared at it for a long moment before flipping back the lid.

A diamond solitaire twinkled up at her. It wasn't large, but it was perfect.

"I think we could make it work," he said. "Think of the great vacations we could take with all our frequent-flyer miles."

Lynn looked up at him, at the baby-blue eyes, the handsome face, the long, faintly smiling mouth.

"Do you think you could say something? The suspense is killing me." He hitched himself higher on the pillows, pulling her up with him.

Lynn decided to throw her cap, her heart, and everything else over the windmill.

"I'm in love with you," she said.

"Well, that's nice to hear." A slow smile stretched his mouth, warmed his eyes. "Because I'm in love with you too."

Then he kissed her.

A long time later, when they were wrapped in each other's arms and so sated that Lynn for one thought she would never move again, he spoke out of the darkness: "I take it that means yes?"

"Yes," Lynn said.

EPILOGUE

December 15, 1996

THE NIGHTMARE WOKE JESS with a start. He lay in the darkness, his heart gradually regaining its normal rhythm. In his arms, Lynn stirred, muttering. She didn't wake.

They were in a hotel room in Bermuda. On their honeymoon. He'd just enjoyed three days of the hottest sex he had ever experienced in his life. With a woman he admired, desired—and loved.

Life doesn't get much better than this, he thought.

Except for the nightmare. He hadn't had it for a long time now. He had thought it was a thing of the past.

Lying in the dark, staring up at a ceiling he couldn't see, Jess realized something: It was the same nightmare he always had.

Only this time there was something different about it. Pondering, Jess finally figured out what it was.

In this nightmare the raid still went awry, agents who were his friends still died, the complex still burned.

But he hadn't felt to blame.

Because in some weird way what he had done in Provo had been an act of atonement.

It had allowed him to accept a bitter fact: In life, when a man does battle with a dragon, sometimes the dragon is going to win.

But not in Provo.

The dragon had been slain.

Chalk one up for the good guys, Jess thought. Wrapping his arms around Lynn, he rolled over and went back to sleep.